D1569197

DEVOTED FRIENDS

JOE POYER

DEVOTED
FRIENDS

ATHENEUM   *1982*   NEW YORK

Library of Congress Cataloging in Publication Data

Poyer, Joe.
    Devoted friends.

        I. Title.
PS3566.098D4   1982   813'.54   81–69139
ISBN 0–689–11251–3   AACR2

For

S U S A N

in some small return for years of love and support

"What experience and history teach is this—
that people and governments never have learned
anything from history, or acted on the principles
deduced from it."

Philosophy of History,
GEORG WILHELM FRIEDRICH HEGEL

PRINCIPAL CHARACTERS

TATIANA NIKOLAEVNA ROMANOVA, grand duchess and daughter of Tsar Nicholas II

WILLIAM HUGHES EVANS, member of the American diplomatic service

NIKOLAI KHRISTOFOROVICH SHEREMETIEV, former captain, Imperial Russian Army, Cheka commissar

SECONDARY CHARACTERS

ROYAL FAMILY

Nicholas Alexandrovich Romanov II, tsar of Russia
Alexandra Fedorovna Romanova, tsarina of Russia

Olga Nikolaevna
Marie Nikolaevna   } Daughters of Nicholas II,
Anastasia Nikolaevna   and grand duchesses

Alexei Nikolaevich Romanov, son of Nicholas II

Peter Boyd, American military attaché at Petrograd
Dr. Eugene Botkin, royal family physician
Lili Dehn, close friend of the royal family, and confidante of the grand duchesses
Natalia Vasolova Florinskaya, Evans's mistress
David R. Francis, American ambassador to Russia
Fedor Mikhailovich Orbelesky, former general of the Imperial Russian Army, leading member of the Constitutional Democrats (Kadets), head of the Crimean National Front
Mathilda Eugenovna Orbeleskaya, wife of General Orbelesky and Evans's mistress
DeWitt Clinton Poole, American counselor official at Archangel
Maxime Rovolovich Obrechev, colonel, Crimean National Front army

O T H E R S

Mikhail Borisovich Chizov, Cheka commissar

Felix Edmundovich Dzerzhinsky, first director of the All-Russian Extraordinary Committee for Combating Counterrevolution and Sabotage (Cheka)

Maria Antipova Galitina, Sheremetiev's mistress

Pierre Gilliard, Alexei's tutor

Isiah Goloschekin, commissar, Ekaterinburg

Alexander Kerensky, prime minister in the provisional government

Eugene Kobylinsky, commander of guard detachment at Tsarskoye Selo and Tobolsk, loyal to the provisional government

Veronica Maximievna Lodoskaya, resident of Ekaterinburg

Otto Mazachesky, general, Czech Legion

Nagorny, sailor-bodyguard to Alexei

Gregory Rasputin, "eminence grise" and confidant of the tsarina; priest and holy man

Jacob Sverdlov, president, Central Executive, Committee of All-Russian Congress of Soviets

Vasily Vasilevich Yakovlev, commander of grand detachment assigned to escort Nicholas to Moscow

Jacob Yurovsky, commander of guard detachment, Ekaterinburg

Russian names are often confusing to westerners, but should not be. The first name alone is normally used between close friends and family members. The middle name is composed of the father's given name and the ending of "vich" meaning "son of" or "evna" meaning "daughter of", i.e., Tatiana Nikolaevna—Tatiana, daughter of Nicholas. The majority of feminine names will end in "a." Certain foreign first names will not, i.e., Marie.

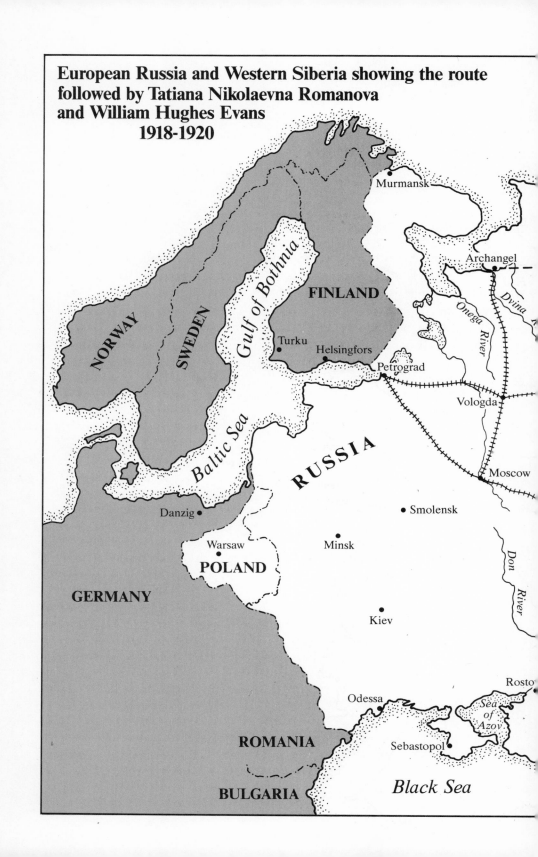

European Russia and Western Siberia showing the route followed by Tatiana Nikolaevna Romanova and William Hughes Evans 1918-1920

NORWAY

SWEDEN

FINLAND

Murmansk

Archangel

Gulf of Bothnia

Onega River

Dvina R.

Turku

Helsingfors

Petrograd

Vologda

Baltic Sea

RUSSIA

Moscow

Danzig

Smolensk

Don River

Warsaw

Minsk

POLAND

GERMANY

Kiev

Rosto

Odessa

Sea of Azov

ROMANIA

Sebastopol

BULGARIA

Black Sea

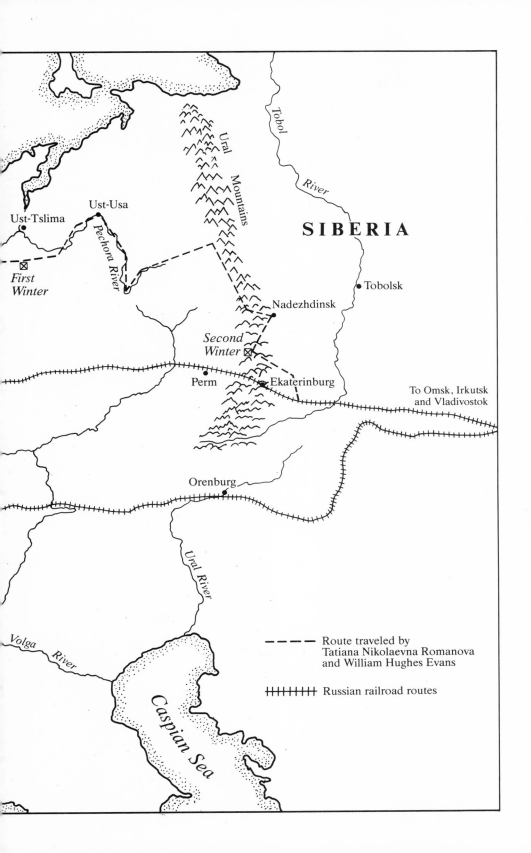

Ust-Tslima

Ust-Usa

First Winter

Pechora River

Ural Mountains

Tobol River

SIBERIA

Tobolsk

Nadezhdinsk

Second Winter

Perm

Ekaterinburg

To Omsk, Irkutsk and Vladivostok

Orenburg

Ural River

Volga River

Caspian Sea

– – – – Route traveled by
Tatiana Nikolaevna Romanova
and William Hughes Evans

++++++++ Russian railroad routes

DEVOTED FRIENDS

I

In defiance of his orders William Hughes Evans chose to travel across the Gulf of Bothnia by ferry from Stockholm to Åbo, in Russian Finland, then via Helsingfors along the southern coast of the province. His already poor opinion of Russia did not improve and the interior of the Finland Station in Petrograd only intensified his dislike. He had been told that Russia was a land of contrasts. It was that, he thought.

Ragged workers or peasants or both shuffled among fashionable women in summer frocks and were in turn surrounded by herds of dun-colored conscripts, who exhibited the patience of cattle waiting for the knacker's hammer. None of the soldiers had rifles, and Evans wondered if the stories about Russian troops' arming themselves with weapons from fallen comrades might not be true after all.

He supposed it could have been worse. Without his father's influence, he could be disembarking somewhere in Arabia or Africa, although Petrograd seemed hardly any better. God only knew how long he would be forced to serve his exile behind a minor functionary's desk in this benighted backwater while his peers climbed through the ranks of the Diplomatic Service in France, Germany, Great Britain, Italy.

He had been told to look for railroad porters in white aprons; but there were none to be seen, and angrily he grabbed his own suitcase. The bag was heavy, and Evans paused to rest halfway down the platform. The sun blazed through the crust of grime and coal smoke

3

covering the glass roof and turned the interior of the station into a greenhouse. A heavy, unpleasant smell, compounded of coal smoke, hot oil, unwashed humanity and stifling heat, irritated him. Opposite, a contingent of soldiers were drawn up at parade rest. Their lines were ragged, and baggage was strewn about the platform. An officer stood at sufficient distance to make it clear that while he commanded this rabble, he was not of them.

As Evans started again toward the main concourse, the crowd parted abruptly and a huge soldier advanced on him like the wrath of God. The man was clad in a tall fur cap, a sky blue jacket, to which a dozen cartridge loops had been sewn, and scarlet trousers. A curved sword clattered at his side, and he brandished a whip.

The man, followed by three women and more Cossacks, marched along the platform as Moses must have done, never doubting that the Red Sea would part for the elect of God. The oldest woman was tall, rather horse-faced and determined. The two younger women were quite striking. One, the prettier Evans thought, glanced at him and smiled a demure smile that brought an answering grin to his lips. She was dressed in the latest fashion, a form-fitting skirt without the previous season's hobbles, and her hair was a thick mass of chestnut that glowed in the sunlight. Her smile widened, and Evans found himself staring into a pair of large, blue-gray, almost violet eyes. Her younger companion said something, at the same time throwing Evans a disapproving look.

Maybe Petrograd wasn't going to be so bad after all, he thought, watching the two neat figures sway along. Only then did he realize that people were bowing as they passed. The conscripts stiffened to attention, and without warning a Cossack at the end of the procession swung his rifle butt at a young soldier who had leaned forward for a better look. The boy clutched his face and collapsed without a sound. The three women disappeared into a train car, unaware of the incident. The crowd muttered, and two of the soldiers cursed and shook their fists. Evans understood then why they were not armed.

The spaciousness and scale on which the city of Saint Petersburg— renamed as the more Russian-sounding Petrograd in August 1914—had been conceived were impressive, Evans thought. The skyline, as the train had approached, mounted the ruler-straight horizon like an immense fleet of galleons. Flat northern light shimmered on marshes and lakes, accenting the horizontal and providing a feeling of vast, uncluttered space. Petrograd was a city of islands and canals, even more than Stockholm. Impressive buildings with classical façades copied after Italian and Austrian designs lined the Parisian-wide boulevards, giving the city a decidedly Western flavor.

The river Neva glittered in the afternoon sun as the old-fashioned horse cab crossed the Alexandrovsky Bridge. In either direction as far as Evans could see, bridge after bridge spanned the broad reach, and traffic and pedestrians filled the streets. The city gave an impression of immense vitality strictly at odds with the rumors of a disintegrating Russia that were rife at the Stockholm Legation. It seemed to Evans that Petrograd at least was as vital and busy as New York—an impression heightened by the number of American automobiles on the Nevsky Prospekt.

The American Embassy was a gray, imposing building on the Furstatskaya Olitiza, a narrow, closed street four blocks south of the Neva. Evans's immediate superior was an elderly man with parchment skin and trembling hands who made it clear that nothing was to jeopardize his pension in his final year of service. The one-sided interview lasted just three minutes, and Evans was dismissed.

Ambassador David R. Francis was in Moscow. Half the offices were empty, but the embassy tennis courts were full. In the canteen Evans found the duty officer, Howell Fulbright, a weedy young man who made it plain he had nothing but contempt for Russia, its government and its people.

"Don't get me wrong, old man," Fulbright whined in familiar prep school accents, "country's a bit like the old U.S. But the people! My God! Little better than ignorant savages. From the imperial family on down, the whole government is corrupt, but totally corrupt. That insane priest Rasputin has more influence over the tsar than all his ministers together. Or should I say the tsarina?" He sniggered, and a typist sitting with him rolled her eyes and giggled.

Evans began his official duties the following Monday. The janitor showed him to a tiny third-floor office smelling of damp mops. It contained a beaten-up wooden desk, a single side chair and a bad print of George Washington that had been ancient by the time of the American Civil War. His exile had begun.

The day following the ambassador's return, he was summoned for the "new boy" interview. The ambassador waved him to a chair and folded his hands across his ample middle.

"Well, young man, you seem to have gotten yourself into quite a scrape in Stockholm." The opening statement hung in the air between them, and the ambassador smiled. "My boy, when you reach my age, you are allowed certain liberties, so don't take offense."

Ambassador Francis hitched himself forward in the chair. "Look here. You might not think so from the exalted height of your thirty-one years, but I regard you as wet behind the ears, knowing nothing and a fool besides. I daresay your father does as well.

"Whether you follow my advice or not is up to you, but you *have* disgraced yourself, your family and your government. Normally, after an incident like that in Sweden, you would have been dismissed from the Diplomatic Service, but the secretary has been persuaded to give you

5

another chance, if only for the sake of your father. So it now becomes not just a matter of disgracing not yourself further, but others in the State Department who have gambled for your father's sake. I think you take my meaning?"

Evans did not know what to answer, nor did he dare say what he would have liked. He recognized the implications of the old man's words and resented the burden they imposed.

"Well, young man?"

"Uh, yes, sir." Evans nodded. "I understand."

The old man watched him skeptically. "All right, we'll say no more about it. Now, as to your duties here, I am certain they have been explained in sufficient detail. You will know, of course, that ever since the trade embargo of 1911 over persecution of the Jews, relations between the United States and Russia have been strained. But Russia is now engaged in a war in which I am certain we too will soon be caught up. When that happens, Russia unfortunately will become our ally—a fact with which President Wilson is not at all happy. Until then as representatives of a neutral country we will act as such. Our position, in short, is delicate. Do you understand what I am telling you?"

"I am to behave myself."

The ambassador gave him a sharp look. "I hope I do not detect petulance in your tone, young man. More than that, you are to do your job as best you can, at all times. You must avoid becoming embroiled with certain Americans who are determined to milk the Russian war effort for their own benefit. Turn a deaf ear to their complaints, sir. Refer them directly to the Commercial Section, which will deal with them as they deserve. Above all, avoid this young rabble-rousing newspaper reporter John Reed."

"I understand, sir," Evans responded in a more even tone. The ambassador grunted, and he was dismissed.

"You're the new boy, aren't you?"

Evans looked up from the paper he was translating to see a thin-faced man in an officer's uniform grinning at him. At six feet three inches, Evans had always been proud of his height, but the figure before him, filling the doorway with only an inch or two to spare, gave him a twinge of insignificance.

"Name's Boyd, Peter Boyd. I'm the military attaché." He flicked the shoulder bars on his jacket. "You get to be a captain if you master the trick of drinking hot tea from a glass."

Evans grasped the muscular hand that shot across the desk and winced. "William Hughes Evans," he responded through gritted teeth, and retrieved his hand.

"I hope to God you like duck hunting. Old Fulbright's a perfect milk and water, far too prissy for my liking. Wouldn't know which end of a shotgun is which."

6

"Well, I've done a little, but not in some—"

"Good. That's settled then. Place down near Bogorodskoye, southeast of Moscow, where the duck hunting is excellent. Makes for a longish weekend, but worth it. We can take the train down on Thursday afternoon and back on Sunday. Knew you'd be keen."

Boyd plopped down in the rickety side chair, produced an apple and bit half away. He examined Evans carefully as he chewed.

"I understand you were almost thrown out of the Diplomatic Service," he said tentatively.

Evans stared back with a bland expression. "Old Francis didn't put you up to this, did he?"

Boyd grinned. "Nothing more than pure curiosity."

Evans thought about it for a moment, then decided he liked Boyd's openness. "There was this lady. A very pretty lady. And a country inn. Swedes are a sanctimonious lot until you get them to a country inn. Unfortunately the lady's husband caught us *in flagrante delicto,* so to speak."

He narrated the entire story in some detail, and Boyd's grin stretched from ear to ear by the time he finished. "What happened then?"

"The constable arrived, arrested the lady for indecent exposure, the gentleman for assault and me for brawling in public."

"I assume your sentence to Coventry has to do with the public nature of the scandal?"

"No." Evans chuckled. "It stems from the fact that she was the wife of the Swedish foreign minister."

Boyd laughed so hard that the chair gave up the struggle and collapsed.

In later years Evans would look back on that weekend as the watershed of his life, the realization waiting, of course, upon the leisure to examine the events that ensued from a peculiar meeting with the top and bottom of Russian society. Then the conclusion that his life's course had been determined by that shooting trip would become inescapable. But for a long time to come, it would remain only a distant and painful memory.

The crowded train ran out of the Nicholas Station, and as the last suburb was left behind, the two men began to exchange confidences as people will when circumstances leave them little else to do. The talk was desultory at best, but Boyd discovered that Evans, who had a natural aptitude for languages, had learned Russian as a child, from a nurse who, with her husband, had served the Evans family for years.

The train ran on ruler-straight tracks across the immense, incredibly flat land baking under the early-autumn sun. Mile after mile of shimmering gold slipped past, interrupted now and again by a crossing gate beyond which a peasant cart might be waiting or an occasional village with nothing more remarkable to be seen than a church dome or a panting dog in the road.

The train slipped into Bogorodskoye in late evening, and Boyd hired a surly boy to trundle their baggage in a barrow to the village's only hotel. The landlord woke them early with steaming glasses of tea, and they washed, dressed and went down to a huge breakfast of pancakes and clotted cream and platters of fried eggs.

The sky was red with dawn as they trudged across the fields toward a darkish line of trees edging the marsh. The air was crisp, but already they could detect the coming heat as the sun climbed higher. An elderly peasant waited in a wooden boat. Boyd greeted him affectionately, calling him Daddy Shulga, and the man doffed his cap to Evans. They rowed to an island fringed with reeds, where Evans and Boyd lugged ashore a wicker basket the landlord had prepared, along with their shotguns and equipment.

"We ought to do well this morning." Boyd's voice boomed in the silence, and Evans started. They laughed at that, and the restraint imposed by unfamiliar surroundings broken, they set about clearing debris from the blind. Boyd placed the decoys, and they took their places.

Evans's shotgun was a Winchester Model 97 takedown in twelve gauge, while Boyd preferred a British-made Churchill double. He chuckled at the Winchester's pump action. "Five shots? Aren't two enough for the mighty hunter?"

Instead of replying, Evans held up a warning hand.

The sun slipped behind a bank of clouds, and the day was suddenly gray and silent. It came again: the faraway honking of migrating ducks already fleeing south ahead of the Siberian winter.

The cool morning, the muted colors of the marsh, freedom from the restraint of the embassy all came together as the first flight of ducks appeared beyond the treetops, perfectly silhouetted against the pink-gray sky. The wary birds circled to examine the water, the island and the near shore for predators.

They both fired when the first ducks were even with the treetops and brought two down. Evans shot again and missed; the bird flew on unharmed before it realized the full extent of its danger. When it did so, it sculled twice with its wings; Evans saw the tail feathers slant, then watched its wing edges curl slightly as the bird lifted and turned away.

A black dog slashed from the weeds on the far bank and swam for the wounded duck, ignoring the dead bird floating nearby. Daddy Shulga waded after it, whistled once, and the dog veered toward the man, the wounded duck in its mouth.

Boyd sat back on his haunches, broke the Churchill to eject the empties and dug out a curved pipe. "Christ in heaven!" He laughed. "This is the life! Why couldn't I have been born rich?"

*   *   *

At noon the old peasant lit a tiny cookfire to grill the ducks, which, with huge pork sandwiches liberally spread with hot mustard, made their lunch.

"Damn," Evans mumbled around a mouthful of food. "This is the best campfire meal since I hunted last in Wyoming."

Boyd sat up eagerly. "You've hunted there? God, I've always wanted to see the West!"

"My father is a partner in a cattle ranch on the Wind River," Evans explained. "After Harvard I was sent west to make a man of me. I hated it at first, but by the end of the summer I had to be ordered home. I went back the following summer and stayed two years."

Evans sank back on the autumn leaves, laced his fingers behind his head and stared at the sky. "That first winter was unbelievable. Boston winters are tropical in comparison. My God, the cold, the snow. Unbelievable amounts of snow. Like nowhere else in the world."

"Wait until you experience a Siberian winter before you make that judgment," Boyd said with a snort.

"Ha! Not a chance. That one was bad enough. The ranch lost eight hundred head of cattle, and two hands froze to death in a line shack up on the Little Wind River. Got snowed in, and we couldn't get to them." Evans fell silent, recalling with regret his abandoned half-formed plans to ranch in Wyoming.

"Why did you leave?" Boyd asked, as if sensing the direction of his thoughts.

"My father didn't think ranching a suitable occupation for a gentleman. He preferred that I waste my time in the Diplomatic Service. Follow in his footsteps, so to speak."

They whiled away the afternoon hours with target practice. Boyd, Evans discovered, was an inveterate gun collector. His proudest possession was a Colt automatic pistol in .45 caliber, the new army model, which he had purchased two years before in London.

"I couldn't get the army to issue me one. They were sending all they had to the cavalry at the time, so I bought my own." Evans was forced to admire the gleaming blue finish while Boyd discoursed at length on the advantages of the semiautomatic pistol versus the revolver. He pointed out the British proof marks and the fact that the caliber was the American .45 and not the British .455. "Damned rare gun. I don't think they sent more than a few hundred of these to England before the war began."

By Sunday their toll of ducks had risen to a dozen each. The companionable hours had tapped a responsive chord in both men. They had much in common. Both had been dominated by and rebelled against their overbearing fathers, both preferred hunting and camping to organized sports, although Evans had captained the Harvard eleven

9

and Boyd had played baseball at West Point, and they were separated in age by only four years.

Their train back to Petrograd was due at five, and they started for the station a few minutes early. The sun shone with a golden tint of autumn, touching and burnishing the weather-beaten wooden houses, and they collected a mixed parade of children as they walked along the dusty, unpaved road.

At the crossroads that formed the village square an angry crowd was gathering. The women stood to one side, clutching their shawls with the helpless air of women everywhere when their men are about to do something dangerously foolish. Boyd and Evans exchanged puzzled glances. On one side was the Orthodox church; on the other, a run-down two-story stone building with an overhanging porch and a broken fence. Wooden houses with gingerbread fretwork occupied the two remaining corners, and their windows, Evans noted uneasily, had been shuttered.

A youngish man with heavy shouders and long, powerful arms swaggered through the fence and into their path. Boyd stopped and tipped his hat.

"Why is a foreigner in our village?" the Russian demanded, a bit nettled at Boyd's good humor. "Are you looking for more cannon fodder to fight your damned capitalist war?"

"No"—Boyd grinned—"but if I were looking for a village of ill-mannered oafs, I'd certainly be in the right place."

The Russian's eyes widened, and he swung a ponderous fist. Boyd stepped inside the punch, and the man screamed and collapsed, writhing on the ground, clutching his genitals.

Evans just had time to recall that the shotguns were cased and straped to the valises and the pistol was inside—and out of ammunition besides—before the crowd began to move toward them. At a shout he half turned, and a rock crashed against his head. The crowd surged from both directions, and a shotgun exploded. Bodies swirled through the golden dust with curious slowness, and Evans slipped into a black pit.

The clattering of wheels woke him. A baleful light gleamed, and the world swayed in time to the noise. The light brightened, and he realized that it was a cigarette. When he tried to sit up, an agonizing pain made him gasp.

"Awake, are you?" Boyd asked. "I'd lie still. Move your head as little as possible until a doctor sees to it."

"What happened?" he managed to ask as a wave of nausea swept him.

"A local revolutionary decided that we'd make an excellent *cause célèbre* and stirred up the happy peasantry. He convinced them we were

French and personally responsible for the war. Old Daddy Shulga saved our necks with his shotgun."

"I'll be damned," Evans muttered.

"Very nearly were, old son. Doesn't take much to fire up the Russian peasant. He's an antisocial beast at best. Has a strain of xenophobia traceable to the Tatar invasions."

Evans stifled a groan and tried to find a comfortable position on the hard couch; but his head ached abominably, and the swaying coach made it worse.

"The Russian peasant," Boyd went on, "is one of the most abused people on earth, running a close second to our own Negro sharecropper."

Evans realized that Boyd was talking to distract him, but the train's jolting caused pain to scream through his head. The car banged hard, and Boyd was at his side in an instant. The train slowed. Boyd turned on the electric light and examined the spreading stain around the bandage.

"Damn, it's opened again," he muttered. "This is no good. That wound needs attention. I'm going out to see why we're stopping. If there's a doctor nearby, I'll find him." Without waiting for a reply, he opened the door and was gone.

Evans must have dozed in spite of the pain, for he woke to see a rotund bearded man leaning over him. The man clucked at the laceration, then lifted and turned his head gently. He issued a stream of orders, and two soldiers crowded in to lift Evans onto a stretcher.

The night air was sharp against his face. Illuminated windows appeared, and the stretcher tilted as he was lifted onto a platform. Evans glimpsed female faces which seemed vaguely familiar and a bearded figure of medium height in bathrobe and slippers who drew the doctor aside.

The stretcher jolted hard, and he fainted.

Sunlight flooded the windows when Evans woke again. Telegraph poles slid past with deliberate speed. His head and neck were swathed in thick bandages, and he found he was naked beneath the blanket. His mind seemed mired in molasses, and he was content to drowse until the compartment door opened and he saw the fat man from the night before.

"So, the young gentleman is awake? Good, good! An excellent sign! My name is Eugene Botkin, Dr. Eugene Botkin." He sat his bag down, unwrapped the bandages and bent to sniff the wound. Evans, startled by the strange action, tried to back away, but the doctor stayed him with a muscular hand and sniffed again. He bounced up and said to the bearded man, who had appeared in the doorway, "No sign of putrefaction. He will recover completely."

The man gave him an encouraging smile and drew the door closed.

"You will experience stiffness and pain, but that will pass," the doctor murmured. "You had a very severe concussion and could easily have died. It is possible that the skull may have been fractured, and certainly the flesh has been subjected to severe laceration. Fibers of clothing were taken into the wound to cause infection. But even so, I predict that with care and rest you will recover completely."

"Where is Pete . . . Peter Boyd?" he croaked.

"Peter Boyd? Ah, you must mean the tall American. He remained on the other train. There simply was not room for him here. But don't worry. He'll arrive in Petrograd a few hours behind us. All trains have been delayed because of troop movements. So—"

"What train am I on?" Evans interrupted. "Is it going to Petrograd?"

"Of course. Now, you mustn't worry, and sleep. Quite beneficial to the healing process. When you are a bit stronger, all your questions will be answered."

"I am very grateful . . ."

Botkin waved a hand. "No, no, not necessary at all. That such violence should befall a foreigner on Russian soil is unthinkable. And a diplomat . . ." The doctor pressed a hand to his cheek and shook his head. "His Majesty was most distressed."

"I'd like . . . His Majesty . . . the Tsar?"

"This is the train of Tsar Nicholas the Second. He is returning to Petrograd from a short family holiday in the Crimea before going on to the front. Your train was stopped nearby, most fortunately for you. Your friend inquired if there was a doctor. . . . It was quite simple, really."

"The tsar's train . . ." Evans was astounded. "But then . . ."

"Yes. Quite so. Now, you must please lie back. I will send the orderly in to bathe you."

"But . . ."

Botkin was replaced by the impassive orderly, bearing a basin and cloth. It was an embarrassing ordeal, but once the orderly had helped him into a crisp white night shirt and he lay back on clean sheets, he felt immeasurably better.

Toward evening he awakened to a knock, and the figure he had seen in the doorway, a man a little above middle height, well set up and with a soldier's ruddy complexion, stepped in. He motioned for Evans to lie still and smiled.

"I understand you are feeling better. I must apologize on behalf of my people for the injury you suffered. Such actions are inexcusable." His voice was high-pitched for his build, and he fixed a blue-eyed stare on Evans as if assessing his value to some royal cause.

This time Evans recognized the tsar immediately. He tried to sit up against the pillows, unsuccessfully concealing the pain. "Your Excellency, please, I must thank you for—"

"Now, no more about it." The tsar sat down. "I understand you are attached to the American Embassy in Petrograd. As we have not met, you must have arrived recently."

Evans smiled at the tsar's diplomacy. His rank was hardly sufficient to rate a presentation at court. Strange, he thought, the tsar, though certainly handsome, was not an impressive man. He stared, rather defensively, Evans thought, from beneath thick brown eyebrows. He wore a pair of old army trousers tucked into red leather boots and, because of the heat, an army blouse without tunic. Other than a single gold wedding band, he wore no jewelry and no medals or ribbons to indicate that he was the most powerful autocrat on the face of the planet.

They sipped the tea a servant brought in a moment later and talked about inconsequential things: duck hunting, automobiles, yachting and the American West, which the tsar admitted he longed to visit. He thought it might compare with the Siberian provinces, and they discussed geography until an aide knocked and the tsar, with obvious regret, excused himself. "We must continue this fascinating discussion another time, my dear Mr. Evans. Perhaps your Mr. Francis could spare you for tea some afternoon when you are fully recovered?"

"I would be honored, your Excellency."

The tsar bowed and left, and Evans settled wearily against the pillows, not quite believing his luck. Of all things to happen, he thought, to drink tea privately with the tsar.

It was raining quite hard when the train stopped again two hours later in an immense railyard. Other trains stood nearby. The cinders glistened under the glare of arc lights, and three figures hurried across the tracks to another passenger train; sentries snapped to attention as the figures disappeared inside, and the train began to move immediately.

As darkness was beginning to settle, Evans heard a tentative knock on his door and saw the handle turn. A young girl peeked in, and when he grinned encouragement, she pushed the door wider to reveal two attractive older girls and a middle-aged woman.

The youngest, a bit on the chubby side and with long braids and clear blue eyes, came to stand by his bunk.

"Papa told us you had been badly hurt," she said, and leaned down to kiss his cheek. The oldest girl laughed while the younger frowned. "Do you feel better now?"

Evans flexed an arm. "Why, after that I could get up from this bunk and slay a thousand Germans, that's how good you made me feel. If you give me another kiss, I'll make it two thousand." Laughing, she kissed him again. Evans recognized the two older girls as the young women on the railroad platform the day he had arrived in Petrograd.

Amused at his own audacity in flirting with a grand duchess while lying in his nightshirt beneath a single thin blanket, he smiled. "I know who you are. You must be Verushka," he said, referring to an imaginary princess in a Russian folk tale.

She giggled. "Of course not. I'm Anastasia Nikolaevna Romanova."

Evans snapped his fingers. "That must be why I mistook you for Verushka then. Grand duchesses are said to have magical powers."

"I am afraid not, Mr. Evans." The oldest smiled. "May I introduce two of my sisters, Anastasia and Tatiana, and I am Olga. This is our chaperone, the Countess Hendrikova."

Evans grunted with feigned pain when he tried to sit up, and Olga hurried to press him back on the pillows.

"No, please don't try to sit up. We came only to tell you how sorry we are that such a shameful thing has happened."

Evans sank back, conscious of her fingers on his shoulder. Olga smoothed the blanket, and he bravely returned her smile. He had been pleasantly surprised to see how attractive all three daughters were. Their features were striking, beautiful in fact. Olga and Tatiana both wore their chestnut hair piled high in the current mode. Olga's eyes were a pale violet, and in his opinion she was quite the most beautiful woman he had seen in months. Both Olga and Tatiana were slender, but Tatiana had a firm chin that, according to his old nurse, was a certain sign of stubbornness in Russian women.

He felt he could lie for hours merely looking at Olga, but a gong sounded somewhere in the car, and she frowned. "The dinner summons! I am afraid we must go, Mr. Evans. Father told us he has invited you to tea, so we will meet again." She smiled once more and ushered her sisters out. The countess, who had remained silent, studied him with skepticism as she closed the door.

Captain Nikolai Khristoforovich Sheremetiev watched the train roll out of the yard until the rain hid the red light on the last car. The tsar and his family were said to be aboard, and the patients and staff had been all aflutter. It was well known that Nicholas visited wounded troops at every opportunity. It was said he had once sat on the bed of a dirty Georgian muzhik to question him about where and how he had received his wound. And the German woman, the Tsarina Alexandra, and her daughters were Red Cross nursing volunteers. When the tsar's train left, a collective groan sounded through the car, and only Sheremetiev was not surprised.

He shifted uncomfortably on the vermin-ridden straw. It was cold in the carriage in spite of the packed bodies. Carriage, he thought with a

14

snort. It was a freight wagon, an old freight wagon with gaping seams. The wounded were too numerous these days to be transported in ambulance carriages. In fact, enlisted wounded were rarely transported more than a few miles from the front. If they could not be treated where they were, they died. Carriages were reserved for generals.

Sheremetiev's indifference to the tsar would have enraged his father, a peasant farmer with sense enough to become a merchant. A bourgeois but still a peasant at heart. His father's relative wealth had afforded Sheremetiev an education—high school and a year at the university. The army was his choice, one far preferable to clerking in his father's dry-goods store or mucking cow shit on the family farm.

A nursing sister made her way along the aisle between the packed cots. Nothing there, he thought for the tenth time. Fat and dumpy. A cow. He hadn't seen a decent woman in six months, but even so, this one didn't stir the slightest interest. He turned back to the crack in the boards that served as his window, grimacing at the pain in his leg.

Rain slanted onto the cinder yard. Dun-colored buildings shouldered out of the mist like the prehistoric monsters in those damned stories by that Frenchman—what the devil was his name? Jules Verne? An occasional slicker-shrouded sentry stamped to keep warm, and the signal lamps glowed yellow, red and green, the only colors visible in the gathering dusk. Would they never move on to Petrograd? he wondered. His leg ached badly in the damp, and he knew he was feverish again. He held his breath for a moment, then exhaled slowly and breathed in through his nose, struggling to detect the faintest indication of putrefaction. Gangrene was the terror of his life. That and mustard gas. Here, only a few hundred miles at best from Petrograd, there was no danger of gas shells, only gangrene. Satisfied that his wound remained uninfected, he closed his eyes.

When Sheremetiev awoke, the train was moving ponderously through the night. There was nothing to see through the split boards, and he could feel exhaustion as a peculiar fluttering in his chest. Sleep eluded him now, and he listened to the sounds around him. One man groaned in a thin, monotonous whine. Someone else breathed noisily; the chest wound, he decided. The man had been brought aboard after him, still wearing the remnants of his uniform jacket, so hasty had the field surgery been. One torn shoulder board proclaimed him a staff colonel. So even a cushy, behind-the-lines job couldn't save you from the slaughterhouse of the Carpathian front! The man's chest wound was so bad that the dumpy nurse had gasped aloud the first time she changed his bandages.

But a staff colonel, someone's pet, had influence. If the train ran straight through to Petrograd, he might live. Sheremetiev smirked. Straight through, indeed. Before the war the train had made the journey from Odessa, on the Romanian border, to Petersburg—Petrograd, he corrected himself—in eighteen hours. Now it took four days. Four days of that unvarying gasping, bubbling sound as more air percolated through his chest wall than went in and out of his nose and mouth. The colonel was some sort of ghastly tribute to the inherent strength of the human organism. If hospital trains were given priority, he might live. But priorities were reserved for troop trains rushing more live fodder up to the front so they could be turned into steaming masses of dead meat. Even the tsar gave way to the troop trains.

The tsar. He remembered a day in November 1914, when he had been decorated by Nicholas Alexandrovich himself. He remembered how the tears had come to his eyes at the honor. How naïve he had been. But of course, that was before the killing acquired a momentum of its own, when the war still made sense, when the enemy had to be killed before the Teutonic folk could overrun Mother Russia as they had threatened for a thousand years. He would have given his life for the tsar then. But too much had happened since: too many needless deaths, too many useless wounds, too much insane pain. He had learned, however, one extremely valuable lesson, Sheremetiev reminded himself. First and foremost, insure your own survival.

The train reached Petrograd in midafternoon, and by some miracle the staff colonel was still alive. The stretchers were placed on the greasy cobbled platform to await the ambulances so that the train could leave immediately. The day was cold, and a damp wind roamed the hollow structure of the Nicholas Station. It was long after dark when the ambulances finally arrived. The staff colonel had died an hour before.

An overworked surgeon operated on Sheremetiev's leg the following day. There was no ether, and he was injected with a weak solution of morphine to dull the pain. The surgeon cut and trimmed damaged flesh as Sheremetiev clenched his teeth on a folded rag and stared at the overhead lamp, enduring. That night he couldn't sleep for the pain and asked an orderly for more morphine. The man laughed and told him it was reserved for surgical cases.

"Be brave," he said, and Sheremetiev cursed him for never having been closer to the front than the roadhouses in the islands west of the city.

He slept toward morning and dreamed the dream once more. Two German soldiers walked toward him out of the morning mist, unaware that he was sheltered by the bulk of the tree. He took careful aim and shot each one with his Nagant revolver. Both men stared at him in open-mouthed surprise, and he woke as usual when the first man's face dissolved in blood.

For a long time he lay staring at the dirty tin ceiling. The dream was quite real. The Germans were not supposed to have penetrated so far. If they had seen him first, they would have killed him just as quickly. His first shot had smashed one man's cheekbone. The second

16

man had panicked and turned to run and so was struck in the back. He had taken a long time to die, and Sheremetiev had crouched behind the tree, listening to him gasp and mumble, then scream in short, sharp jerks that continued for hours.

He woke again as pale morning light suffused the crowded ward and saw a nurse and an official reading the tag attached to his stretcher.

"This one," the official said. The nurse made a note on her pad, and they passed on. At noon he was taken in a horse-drawn ambulance across the city to an infirmary in the Peter and Paul Fortress.

Nikolai Khristoforovich Sheremetiev had enlisted in 1907 and learned quickly that work in the army was done by enlisted men directed by noncommissioned officers. Commissioned officers made an appearance, signed orders, countersigned passes and spent the day drinking, gambling, whoring or playing polo. Sheremetiev achieved promotion to sergeant within two years, then studied hard to pass the entrance examinations for the officers' training academy. In 1911 he passed out of the Frunze Military Academy a newly commissioned coronet.

War in August 1914 sent his company of the Fourth Battalion, Second Regiment of the Guard Rifles to the East Prussian front and an isolated spot in the forest near the village of Tannenberg. This initial test of the new Russian army began well enough. Coronet Sheremetiev's regiment was being held in reserve some five miles behind the front. East Prussia was a pleasant country, and at first there seemed to be a minimum of confusion, even though vast numbers of men and machines on both sides stalked one another through the wooded farmlands and between the jewellike lakes.

All during their first night the heavy guns on both sides had never stopped, and Sheremetiev was nearly sick with fear and excitement. An hour before dawn they were ordered to stand to and shortly afterward were marched up to the line to support a grenadier regiment. They stepped out briskly in the fragrant dawn, and staff officers came out of their tents to smile and applaud as they marched past. A mile short of the position they left the road and wheeled right very neatly, into a dark wood of pine and birch. German guns could be heard in the distance, but otherwise, only the songbirds broke the early-morning stillness.

They kept their lines parade-ground neat and so were mowed down in ranks when they came on the German machine guns where they should not have been. In one terrible instant Sheremetiev had seen the front of his tunic blossom red. He sat down very suddenly, and it was some time before he realized that the blood belonged to the man ahead.

Sheremetiev was never certain how long he sat on the moldering remains of that tree trunk while men died around him. But eventually he remembered who and where he was and saw what had to be done if any of them, including himself, was to survive. He would never forget the preternatural clarity of the forest and the gray-green Germans streaming across the meadow to support the machine gunners. He had crawled back several hundred yards to the rear, rallied a company of terror-stricken soldiers and circled to the right. Their avalanche of rifle fire and hand grenades had silenced the guns, and the German flanking attack was stopped for that day.

Two months later the tsar pinned Russia's highest decoration on his tunic, the Cross of Saint George, the first of three he would win. In December he killed the two German soldiers, and in January Sheremetiev was wounded for the first time. By March 1915 he had been promoted to the rank of captain.

In late October Evans was pronounced healed by the British Embassy physician who provided medical services to the Western diplomatic community and returned to his two-room suite at the Hotel Europe, where he was quickly caught up in the madhouse atmosphere that prevailed among the neutral businessmen who made it their headquarters.

"I heard you've been invited to tea at the Alexander Palace."

Evans looked up from the report on wheat production he had propped beside his plate in the hotel restaurant while he struggled to understand the flowery prose and intentionally obscure tables. Peter Boyd grinned down at him, an aloof beauty on each arm. So much for the report, he thought.

"By God, you don't look at all well, Bill." Boyd signaled the waiter for chairs. "I go to Moscow for a week, and when I get back, what do I find?" He appealed to the two women. "Can you imagine? Reading government reports and eating alone? Now, what's this about tea at the Alexander Palace? Is it true?" Without waiting for an answer, he explained the reason to his two companions.

Evans shrugged. "The tsar invited me, but I didn't expect him to remember after two months."

"Nicholas is an extremely polite man," the redhead said.

Evans glanced at her. "You are acquainted with the tsar?" he asked mockingly.

"Of course. We are distant cousins." Her voice was somewhat deep for a woman, he thought, but pleasant nevertheless. He noticed that she did not have a Petrograd accent.

"It is his courtesy as well as his ineptness that is destroying Russia. It is not uncommon for a minister to be summoned for praise one day, yet receive a letter the following day asking for his resignation." She looked at Evans with huge, luminous eyes.

"William Evans, may I introduce Natalia Vasolova Florinskaya?" Boyd made the introductions with a flourish and sat down again. "After

18

dinner, perhaps we could all go up to your suite and get to know one another better. Discuss the imminent downfall of the Russian Empire or something like that."

Evans looked both women over carefully and decided he liked the idea and the redhead with the interesting eyes. He saw but paid no attention to Boyd's amiable shrug.

Near midnight Evans lay on his stomach while Natalia knelt astride his waist and massaged his shoulders and neck. She was from Moscow, old nobility, she had told him with a flash of humor that disappeared when she went on to say that all her family had died some years before. She had been reared by an aunt and attended the Imperial University in Moscow for a year in 1914, then left to become a Red Cross nurse. Besides being a very beautiful woman, Natalia was excessively amiable and very inventive, as he had already discovered.

When and where Boyd and the other lady, a Cossack from the Don region, had disappeared, he didn't know or care. Right now he was content to have Natalia soothe away the interminable headache that had tormented him since the incident at Bogorodskoye. Evans realized that for the first time in weeks, the pain was almost gone. He rolled over and pulled her down. "You know, you just might be worth keeping for a while."

Evans presented his credentials to the resplendent guard at the Alexander Palace, and a servant conducted him across a spacious courtyard that reminded him of the palaces built by the Hohenzollerns during the eighteenth century. Inside he was led up two flights of magnificent stairs to an ornate set of carved walnut doors guarded by a huge Negro in red turban, vest and pantaloons. The servant knocked and opened the doors to reveal the family seated around a large table.

The tsar crossed the Oriental carpet to welcome and formally introduce Evans to his family. The tsarina, Alexandra, a tall, prematurely aged woman in her early forties, inclined her head to his bow. Olga smiled and dimpled, Tatiana stared appraisingly, Anastasia bobbed up to curtsy and Marie inclined her head in imitation of her mother's aloofness.

The tsarina poured tea, and Evans discovered that he was perched on the edge of his chair. He shifted back, only to bob forward again as the cups were passed. For the first time in his life he was ill at ease in a social situation, felt, in fact, as if he possessed ten thumbs or had left his pants unbuttoned. The tsar asked about his injury, and the tsarina asked one or two polite questions about his family and thereafter left her husband and daughters to conduct the interview. From time to time she stole glances at the gold watch suspended from her ample bosom.

Everyone deferred to Evans, and it was clear that the Romanovs were a very close family and enjoyed one another's company. Evans liked being the center of attention, and by the time they finished tea he was again at his charming best, bestowing small compliments on the ladies, remarking on certain actions of the Russian army and eliciting modest but proud responses from the tsar. When Nicholas recalled their previous discussion of the American West, Evans moved smoothly into a series of personal stories about his time in Wyoming.

As he talked, he noted that Olga was fashionably dressed in a blue frock a great deal gayer than those her mother and sisters wore. From time to time he caught her eye and smiled, and her faint blush only added luster to her complexion.

A pale young boy of about thirteen limped into the parlor. Evans happened to be looking at the tsarina at that moment and saw her expression bloom. Of a sudden, she seemed twenty years younger. The boy moved awkwardly across the room as his mother stood to enfold him in her arms.

"Your manners, Alexei," the tsar murmured, and the boy turned, bringing both heels together with a click and bowing slightly. Evans rose and held out his hand. Alexei hesitated for an instant, grinned and took it. Evans was surprised at the boy's weak grasp.

"Father told me you were an American," the tsarevich piped in a thin voice. "And I have heard that Americans do not believe in royalty."

"Now, Alexei," his mother remonstrated, but Evans chuckled.

"On the contrary, every American secretly believes that his ancestry includes royal blood and that one day a telegram will arrive notifying him that he is the long-lost heir to the ducal fortune."

As the family laughed, Evans was startled by an odor of pine tar soap so out of place that he turned in bewilderment to see a heavily bearded face glistening with oil. The man wore garish clothes over his broad-shouldered frame and peered out at the world with black, hard eyes. For a moment Evans had the irrational idea that those eyes were boring through his skull to examine his very soul.

The Tsarevich Alexei retreated to the man and took his hand. Smiling, the tsar introduced Gregory Efimovich Rasputin as the *starets,* a man of God. No one seemed to find anything incongruous in the strange creature who rested a proprietary hand on the young Tsarevich. Evans had heard the rumors about this Rasputin even in Stockholm, but he never thought to come face-to-face with him. Until that moment he had not really believed such a person existed.

"Our friend"—Nicholas smiled—"comes to visit us so infrequently. You are fortunate that he was able to come today." The tsar indicated a chair near Evans, and the monk sat down. Evans tried breathing through his mouth.

"Batiushka"—Father—"has told me of you," Rasputin said. Evans

was taken aback by his pleasant, modulated voice and distinct Siberian accent.

"You have recovered from your wound." It was not a question but a statement, and Evans nodded. "You will be troubled by headaches, but they will pass in time."

Rasputin's hold on the imperial family was said to be total, and the reason remained a mystery. Ministers had, according to rumor, been dismissed at a word from him, and countless others jailed. There were tales of wild orgies, involving even the tsarina and her daughters. All this was nonsense, of course, but even so, Evans wondered what Nicholas could be thinking of to allow such a creature in the same city—let alone the same room—as his wife and daughters. The four girls were obviously entranced with the monk.

It seemed an eternity before the Vienna regulator on the mantel-shelf chimed five and a servant entered carrying a silver salver with a note summoning Nicholas to an appointment. Evans, only too glad now of an excuse to go, thanked them all for their hospitality. His ego swelled at Olga's crestfallen expression, and he indulged in a courtly farewell speech that made them all laugh. Rasputin regarded him thoughtfully.

In the courtyard Evans inhaled vast gulps of cold air to rid his nose of the starets's odor. He recalled a recent weekly briefing at which the first secretary had discussed Rasputin and his apparent influence on the government. "The man has not been reported at the palace for more than a year now, and our information is that relations between Rasputin and Nicholas are strained, although he remains on excellent terms with the rest of the immediate family. He continues, at the tsarina's request, to vet all appointees to the higher offices."

Evans's watch showed 5:20. Plenty of time to return to Petrograd for his supper date with Natalia. The electric streetlamps caused the fresh snow to sparkle, and the houses lining both sides of the street were alight and inviting. A sleigh passed, bells jangling pleasantly and its three young passengers called out to him in fun. As he strolled through the crisp winter evening to the railroad station, he decided that after dinner they might drive out to one of the roadhouses along the gulf. Fortunately he didn't have to be in the office until 10:30, leaving him ample time for another exploration of Natalia's charms. He had to be careful there, he cautioned himself, or Natalia might begin to show all the unpleasant signs of taking their relationship too seriously.

It wasn't until he and Natalia returned to his suite that it occurred to him that this was an evening he could never hope to have with Olga, and he laughed at himself for his foolishness. But later that night, as he made love to Natalia, he imagined it was Olga in her place.

II

Shivering and nearly blue with cold, Captain Nikolai Khristoforovich Sheremetiev coughed as the doctor demanded. The stone-flagged ward was icy, its doors and windows so ill-fitting that the wind whistled off the Neva and through the room as if they did not exist.

"Dress." The slovenly doctor turned away and scratched something on the chart before he moved to the next man. Sheremetiev tugged on his underwear and uniform trousers, then sat down to pull on his socks and boots. All were new issue, of poor-quality cloth and worse tailoring; but they were warm, and he was grateful for that.

He took his chart down three floors to the administration office and joined one of the endless lines stretching across another stone-flagged room to a counter behind which listless clerks sipped tea, warmed their fingers and noses over cast-iron containers of charcoal— those who could afford them—and initialed documents.

The clerk read his papers without glancing up, scratched his name at the designated place and rummaged through a cardboard box of envelopes containing orders for those officers considered fit to return to duty. In theory, the clerk was supposed to review the officer's file, then select a set of orders appropriate to his qualifications. Instead, an envelope was selected at random and pushed across the desk. Sheremetiev hesitated, on the verge of protesting, but the clerk's stare changed his mind.

He limped out of the frigid cavern and down several more flights to the junior officers' mess, where, because each man subscribed five rubles a week, the room was at least warm and the food edible. Shereme-tiev took a seat near the stove and signaled to the attendant for a cup of tea. He rubbed his hands together until the numbness receded, then slit the envelope.

Six weeks in that hellhole called an infirmary had come close to killing him, and he would have accepted any assignment to get out. The granite Peter and Paul Fortress was built in 1703 by Peter the Great, and rumors persisted that the cells reserved for political prison-ers on the levels below the river were more comfortable than the in-firmary or any part of the fortress above the third floor. Sheremetiev never doubted it.

The heavy parchment was full of exquisite printing and flowery phrases dedicating the officer named herein to the defense of God, the tsar and Mother Russia. Sheremetiev skipped the verbiage, found the important line at the bottom and sighed with relief. No front-line duty, thank God! He was instructed to report the following morning to the barracks of the Vologda Regiment, where he would assume command of a company of infantry to be used for police duties in and around the capital.

The barracks was a long, single-story, unpainted wooden affair paralleling the Neva and overlooking a frozen waste of marsh. Clearly nothing had been spared, he thought cynically, in making certain the army did not occupy property with the slightest commercial value. In summer, the combination of river and marsh would breed mosquitoes as large as pigeons and malaria would be so rife as to make the land useless for anyone but soldiers.

Inside he found a slovenly sergeant major sitting in his underwear before a small stove. The man tried to stand to attention, but he was too drunk. The room stank of unwashed clothing and alcohol. A vodka bottle was sitting on a shelf above the stove, and Sheremetiev slipped it into his pocket.

"Sergeant Major," he intoned, "my name is Captain Nikolai Khris-toforovich Sheremetiev. I am assigned to command this company. You will present yourself in full-dress uniform, at the head of this company, in ten minutes on the parade or face immediate transfer to the front. Do I make myself clear?"

Sheremetiev did not bother to acknowledge the fumbled salute and stepped outside to wait. A cold wind whistled off the Neva, and he shivered in spite of his ankle-length greatcoat. The door to the barracks opened, and a crowd of sullen men filed out, still buttoning portions of their uniforms. They lined up in slovenly fashion, and it was obvious the majority were drunk. The sergeant major, sobered by Sheremetiev's threat, executed an acceptable salute and reported the company present for duty with the exception of twelve men in the infirmary.

"What are they in for, Sergeant Major?"

The sergeant major's already-red face had gone the color of a new brick in the icy wind. "Influenza, and one bellyache. Sir," he added in the nick of time.

Sheremetiev nodded. "You and I will visit the infirmary this afternoon, Sergeant Major. Chances are good that eleven of them will sleep in the barracks tonight."

The men were beginning to stamp their feet against the snow and mutter among themselves.

"Silence in the ranks!" Sheremetiev shouted. "Sergeant Major, take the name of the next man who speaks." Sheremetiev suspected that the majority were the dregs of front-line units clever enough to avoid prison or the punishment battalions. They had probably been transferred at the first opportunity by officers anxious to avoid a bullet in the back. A subordinate officer would have made all the difference, but the shortage was so acute that he could not expect to have a lieutenant assigned to him. He would have to make do with the sergeant major.

"Company, remove overcoats and tunics!" he barked. The men stared at him blankly. Only two began to do as ordered—new recruits, he thought, sent directly from an enlistment station.

Smiling, Sheremetiev unholstered his pistol and aimed it directly at the largest man in the front rank. He cocked the hammer, and the man tore off his coat and tunic. The others moved to follow suit. When he had them standing coatless and shivering before him, he walked along the double rank, pistol dangling by his side, examining each man in turn. They were, he thought, sufficiently good material that given enough time, he could have made them into excellent soldiers. In his three years at the front he had developed a high respect for Russian soldiers. Individually they were brave, utterly fearless and loyal to a degree he would never have believed. And because they were, the officer corps as a whole had squandered an entire generation of Russian men to the guns.

He resumed his place before the front rank. "Company, right face!" he shouted. The men looked at him in amazement. A Russian officer leading drill was unheard of, but the pistol insured compliance. "Company, double time around the parade ground!"

He kept them at it for an hour, until a third had fallen in exhaustion and his own barely healed leg threatened to give way to the cold and exertion. Afterward they cleaned the barracks and washed their clothes.

Sheremetiev's first assignment came three days after he assumed command of the company. A messenger delivered hastily written orders to report in full strength to the Kirlov Works in the southern suburbs, where it was reported that a workers' strike was in the making, in spite of wartime laws to the contrary.

As Sheremetiev loaded his men aboard the lorries, he watched them closely. He had placed all the ammunition in the charge of the sergeant major. The man was a pathological drunkard who could no longer function without alcohol, but his request to have him replaced had been turned down. Only transfers to the front were being considered. Sheremetiev dismissed the reply; he might as well shoot the man himself.

The lorries rolled through snow-covered streets thronged with people who gave them hardly a glance; military columns had long since lost their novelty. The temperature, which for the past week had hovered a few degrees below the frost mark, was expected to take a sharp drop when the cold front edging Finland moved across the gulf during the day. The streetlamps had gone on early, and the sky seemed to press directly onto the rooftops. Christmas holiday decorations did little to lighten the gloom, and the only color was provided by the red kettles of the Salvation Army lasses, the first he had ever seen.

They disembarked half a mile from the Kirlov Works, and Sheremetiev spoke to his men, emphasizing that they were present only to maintain peace and prevent violence, nothing more.

"The police are responsible. We take orders from them. Do not show by any sign, action or word that you are in sympathy with one side or the other," he told them, emphasizing the *one side or the other*. "Ammunition will be issued if and when, in my judgment, it becomes necessary. Remember, you are soldiers of the Imperial Russian Army. Act accordingly."

At the intersection, where a mass of ugly electric transmission wires came together in a forest of ice-slick poles, the blue-coated police were drawn up in ranks three deep facing the factory buildings. Hundreds of workers milled about and shouted occasional taunts. Sheremetiev halted his company as a harried police inspector ran up.

"Thank God you've come." He drew Sheremetiev aside. "I don't know how much longer their leaders can or will hold them back."

Sheremetiev peered past him. The workers were unruly, but they certainly did not seem out of hand. Several men were trying to harangue the crowd from the steps of the main building, but the strikers shouted them down with a great deal of laughter. Certainly there was nothing in their taunts to indicate that the police were in danger of being overrun.

"What are you talking about?" he snapped. "The whole thing looks more like a lark to me. What are the workers' grievances?"

"Grievances?" The inspector was brought up short. "How the hell would I know? Listen to me." He peered at Sheremetiev's shoulder boards. "I know what I'm talking about. I've seen and dealt with a hundred of these affairs since 1905, and I know the symptoms. All it will take is one agitator to raise the call, and they'll bolt like cattle!"

"I fail to see the problem," Sheremetiev told him, as patiently as he could. "If they go home, then the threat to the police is over, isn't—"

The police inspector stared at him. "Captain, you forget yourself. The law is very specific. There can be no strikes of any kind. Even to express sympathy for such actions is against the law. Of course, they will try to go home. It is our duty to see that they don't."

While Sheremetiev wondered if he had lost his sanity, the man turned and shouted at his own sergeant, then gave brusque orders for the soldiers to be drawn up across the entrance to the main avenue, on the left flank of the police.

"If you fire, Captain, instruct your men to take care not to strike my police."

The vigil began. To make it easier on the men, Sheremetiev shortened the line as much as possible and divided the company into three ranks. Two stood at parade rest, while the third retired around the corner, where, with the ingenuity of soldiers everywhere, they built fires to warm themselves and brew tea. Every ten minutes the ranks were rotated forward so that in contrast with the police, who remained in line continuously, no one had to stand freezing in the snow and wind for more than twenty minutes at a time.

At noon the orators had put down the hecklers long enough to get their messages across. Sheremetiev could hear snatches whenever the wind quartered, but the words were indistinguishable. The workers crowded the steps to the main building, huddled together for warmth while they listened to one speaker after another. The cheering, it seemed to him, was perfunctory at best. The building, constructed of the usual red brick, now a dirty gray under the combined onslaughts of industrial smoke and weather, was several stories high, and on the top floor, behind tall windows, he saw a number of well-dressed men watching.

At one o'clock the speeches were finished, and he sent the sergeant major to bring up the third rank; if there was to be trouble, now was the time. The workers milled about in uncertainty, and a deputation of four men started forward. When they were well isolated from their fellow workers, the police inspector walked to meet them. An elderly, bearded man and a priest in a threadbare coat each offered a piece of paper. The inspector tore them up without a glance. The wind flung the pieces away, and Sheremetiev saw the priest's shoulders slump. He turned to the workers, arms held up, and the inspector shouted and dropped flat. Before Sheremetiev realized what was happening, a volley of shots tore across the intersection. Men collapsed, and others ran to the building, only to find the doors locked. The police fired a second volley. Sheremetiev stared in horror, then ran toward the police lines, screaming at them to cease fire. The inspector had scrambled to safety on hands and knees, and Sheremetiev plucked him up and jammed his pistol into the man's teeth.

"Order them to stop firing," he screamed, "or I'll kill you."

It took five minutes to stop the firing and disarm the police at rifle point. His own men stood it surprisingly well, standing rock-steady, pointing their empty rifles at the police. He wanted to send a runner to call for ambulances, but the priest refused to allow it. Clutching an arm streaming with blood, he thanked Sheremetiev for preventing a worse massacre. "We will take care of our own, Captain." He glared at the angry police inspector. "God will curse you to eternal damnation for this day's work," he roared, then, as if unable to trust himself, dashed back to the wounded and dying strikers.

Madame Gaborva was an aging *grande dame* with dreadful hennaed hair who had once been a reigning beauty of Petrograd. William Hughes Evans endured her effusive greeting and allowed himself to be introduced as an important personage from the American Embassy. The reactions were all of a kind: The men—all elderly—stared dully, and the women—for the most part young and beautiful—appraisingly.

He fell into conversation with a ravishing beauty escorted by an elderly staff colonel. It didn't take long for her to send the colonel after refreshments and trap Evans against a bookcase to question him about his position at the embassy and his impressions of Petrograd.

"I am really Princess Mathilda Eugenovna Orbeleskaya," she confided. "Tonight I am incognito." Glancing about the room, she whispered, "Almost everyone is using a false name," and giggled. Princess Orbeleskaya wore a mauve hobble gown cut indecently low, and she had a way of leaning forward that invited the eye into the cool depths of her décolletage. She and her husband had come to Petrograd from their home in the Crimea for the winter season, she told him, and shivered entrancingly when he commented on the differences in climate.

"Ah, the climate in the Crimea. The sun is so warm, and the air always soft. You must visit me in the spring, when it is best. By then, we shall be, I hope, the best of friends." She touched his chin with a fingertip.

"And what about the colonel?" he asked in a conspiratorial fashion.

The princess smiled. "What about him?"

"Wouldn't he object if I just popped in one day?"

The princess pressed against his arm and shrugged. "He is my husband and nearing eighty. He has been quite good to me, but as a father, not a husband. He is, I am afraid, too old for that sort of thing, although he does sometimes like to watch me with men. He is very, very rich." She laughed, as if that explained everything.

Evans grunted. This was getting to be much too advanced. Struggling for something to say, he blurted, "Then why is he only a colonel?"

Mathilda stood on tiptoe and whispered in his ear, "But he is really a general, and a prince as well. His real name is Fedor Mikhailovich Orbelesky. It does not pay to be foolhardy. He is a very important man." She ended by flicking his earlobe with her tongue.

While he was still shivering, the doors swung open and conversation ceased. The princess abandoned him instantly to join the crush about the door. Cries of "Grigor, Grigor . . ." welled up as Rasputin entered. Again, as at Tsarskoye Selo, he dominated the room with his imposing presence. His hair had been washed; but it hung in damp strings across his shoulders, and he still exuded the familiar scent of pine tar soap. One hand was pressed against his breast, and with the other he traced the cross, Orthodox fashion. All the while he stared about the room as if calculating the strengths and weaknesses of everyone present. Satisfied, he moved to Evans, ignoring whispered pleas and hands outstretched to touch him.

"I am so happy you could come," Rasputin intoned. He held out his hand to be kissed, but Evans, restraining a look of disgust, chose to misinterpret the gesture and shook it without bowing.

"I am honored that Madame Gaborva invited me. Minor functionaries are seldom—"

Rasputin motioned with his free hand, and his voice seemed to deepen an octave. "No one who is admired by *Batiushka* and *Matiushka* is insignificant. You have it in your power to affect affairs of state. You must take care that you exercise that power to good advantage."

Meaning to your advantage, Evans thought. His hand was still caught in Rasputin's strong, dry grip, and he shifted his weight, thinking the monk would release him and pass on; but then Rasputin's eyes rolled up so that he was presented with blank whites. The effect was so alarming that he would have drawn back had the monk's grip not held him fast. A murmur of awe ran through the room.

"You will be of immense value to the royal family," Rasputin intoned in a voice that, in spite of his cynical understanding of the man's theatrical technique, caused Evans to shiver. "Their enemies are legion. You will be their savior. Guard them well!"

Rasputin released Evans's hand and, as if nothing untoward had happened, turned and led the way from the library to the dining room, chatting easily with his awestruck hostess. As he followed, the other guests examined Evans with new curiosity. In the case of the princess, Evans could tell that more than curiosity was involved.

When Evans stumbled into his suite at the Hotel Europe in the early hours of the morning, he found Boyd sleeping on the sofa. He came awake instantly and swung his feet to the floor.

28

"So what happened?" he demanded.

"How the hell did you get in here?"

Boyd grinned and rubbed his thumb and first finger together. "Never trust a hall porter. Now talk to me." He followed Evans into the bathroom.

Since it was plain he would get no sleep until Boyd's curiosity was satisfied, he went back into the sitting room and poured two tumblers of bootleg vodka.

"I tell you, it was something to see. *He* eats with his hands, literally snuffles food into his mouth. Even soup."

"Aren't you exaggerating a bit?"

"Exaggerating, hell! He cupped his hands and scooped! And do you know where he wiped his hands? On his hair! Jesus Christ, the man's an animal."

"I'm not particularly interested in his table manners. What happened after dinner?" Boyd demanded.

Evans rolled his eyes. "Remember that religious sect you told me about that practices sex to find God? Rasputin must have invented the game. Coffee and brandy were served in the library. Rasputin discussed sex and fornication, not the evils, mind you, but the pleasures and what he called the human need. Damn, but the women were excited. Hung on every word. After half an hour of this Rasputin pointed to one of them. She squealed, popped up like a cork and practically dragged him from the room. That was the signal to choose up partners apparently because the room emptied in a flash, leaving me and the Princess Orbeleskaya. I never did find out what happened to her husband."

Boyd groaned. "Mathilda Eugenovna Orbeleskaya? You lucky bastard!"

"Think so?" Evans rolled his eyes. "I never worked so hard in my life."

"And?" Boyd prompted.

"And what? If you think you're going to get a blow-by-blow—no pun intended—account, you're sadly mistaken, buster."

The last weeks of 1916 in Petrograd were full of contradictions. Disaster followed disaster on the German and Austrian fronts. Romanian intervention against Austria, announced with such fanfare and high expectations in August, had by autumn turned into a complete rout as the Central Powers orchestrated their vast reserves into a formidable army that quickly defeated the Romanians in a series of textbook battles.

Boyd commented at a weekly staff meeting, "What can you expect of an army composed of illiterates, whose high command has to restrict the wearing of facial make-up to those above the rank of major?"

In late November a combined German-Bulgarian army under

General August von Mackensen crossed the Danube at Ruschuk, and by December 7 it had captured Bucharest. Romania ceased to be anything but a liability.

Unrest throughout Russia grew with astonishing swiftness and not without reason. Real wages had risen 113 percent since the start of the war, but inflation had increased several hundred times. In fact, it had become so bad that the banks no longer bothered to cut apart printed sheets of currency. And as more and more of the national railroad rolling stock was pressed into war service, shortages of food and clothing began and prices shot even higher.

Even so, life in Petrograd and, according to newspaper accounts, in Moscow and the other large cities as well was the gayest anyone could remember. It became impossible to obtain a reservation for dinner, and theaters and ballets were forced to add extra performances to meet the demand. In spite of a national prohibition on the sale of vodka, the roadhouses strung along the Gulf of Finland, less than an hour's drive from the city, were jammed to capacity twenty-four hours a day. The tango had come to Russia, and Latin American motifs were everywhere.

Evans's work at the embassy made few demands on his time, and he was quickly caught up in the whirl. Within a week of the supper for Rasputin he had become a sought-after guest for dinner parties among the closest court circles friendly to the *starets*. He also found himself enmeshed in two demanding love affairs, one with Natalia Vasolova Florinskaya and the other with the Princess Mathilda Eugenovna Orbeleskaya. Two or three afternoons a week were spent in the princess's bed; evenings were reserved as much as possible for Natalia. The routine would have destroyed most men, but Evans thrived on it.

A second invitation to tea at Tsarskoye Selo arrived in mid-December. When Evans presented himself at the appointed hour, it was apparent that his status had risen. A chamberlain escorted him from the gate. "I am sorry to inform you that His Majesty is still at the front, Mr. Evans. He was expected to return for the Feast of the Epiphany, but developments require that he remain."

Evans found himself making the mental adjustment he was compelled to from time to time when the Russian calendar entered the picture. The central Christmas holidays were celebrated in Russia in early January, centering on the Feast of the Epiphany, rather than on December 25. But the Russian calendar was thirteen days behind the Gregorian calendar, and as a result, the Russian Christmas came three days before the Western Christmas, even though it fell on a later date.

With mounting disgust, Tatiana watched her older sister simper over the American. How foolish, she thought. Olga was treating him as if he were a great hero or a candidate for marriage, like those silly German and Austrian princes who used to parade through the court. Tatiana looked the American over carefully; what did Olga see in him? As far as she was concerned, he was just like all other Americans who were always trying to imitate the English.

She decided he did qualify as good-looking, if not exactly handsome. He had a high forehead and clear blue eyes and sandy blond hair that refused to stay parted. His mustache was well trimmed and full and would probably tickle, Olga had said, and even Marie had laughed. And he was certainly tall enough.

Tatiana concealed a small sigh. She had little patience for such nonsense. Olga and Marie were natural-born flirts, even though her younger sister was becoming awfully prissy of late.

"What do you think, Tatiana, dear?"

Olga's question startled her, and she turned from the window to see the American watching her with a sardonic expression. She flushed, and that made her angry. What had the question been, something about Austrian successes?

"I do not believe we can judge the situation at this remove," she answered frostily. "Many things are concealed for security reasons."

Evans chuckled at her manner rather than at her answer, and before she could retort, her mother intervened.

"I am sure Tatiana is right, Olga. And you must not place our guest in such a delicate position. He is a diplomatic representative of a neutral government after all."

Evans gave a half bow, and Olga smiled demurely and reached across to pat his hand as she apologized. All very natural, Tatiana thought, but my God, how the man glowed when she touched him.

When Alexei, who had been quite subdued all afternoon, yawned, the tsarina whisked him out of the room with a polite apology. Evans noticed that he walked stiffly, as if his knees pained him, and thought to himself that the boy was far too pampered by his overbearing mother and four sisters. No wonder he seemed like such a sissy. More than once he had heard rumors that the boy was afflicted with the "royal disease"—hemophilia, or bleeder's disease, but Evans had only a hazy idea that it entailed uncontrollable bleeding at times.

A woman only a few years older than Olga came in to take the tsarina's place as chaperone. Olga introduced Lili Dehn as a family friend. She had a gay, infectious quality about her, and within minutes they all were shouting with laughter over the smallest jokes. Evans felt like a schoolboy again, attending his first mixed party.

As the shadows lengthened, and the gloom deepened in spite of the electric lamp on the table, the jokes became fewer, and the talk more serious. Evans found the four girls quite intelligent but so limited in experience that it was difficult to realize they were growing up in the

31

twentieth century. They knew little of life beyond the artificial walls imposed by the court. Certainly they had little conception of the war except as a great adventure. Olga spoke of the wounded—probably carefully selected, he thought—men they had assisted in their volunteer nursing as if each were a shining hero and not a common, ordinary soldier, a human being to whom in different circumstances they would not have given a second glance. He remembered the Cossack's rifle butt smashing the young soldier's face because he tried to get a better look at a grand duchess. They were, he thought, prisoners of their own naïveté.

Olga, taking advantage of a lull in the conversation, began to monopolize him once more. Tatiana excused herself.

The tsarina returned an hour later and resumed her seat at the table. Evans was surprised to see the deep shadows in her cheeks and the hollows beneath her eyes. In the pale light cast by the lamp, Alexandra appeared to be on the verge of exhaustion. Lili noticed his expression, glanced at the tsarina and jumped up, exclaiming at the time.

"My dears, I had no idea it was so late. I must really run and change for dinner."

Reluctantly Evans took the hint and rose too. He made his goodbyes, and Pierre Gilliard, Alexei's tutor, who had joined them a few minutes before the tsarina returned, volunteered to see him out. The girls gathered at the parlor door, and he left in a hail of Merry Christmases and a last lingering smile from Olga. For an instant she was framed in the rococo doorway, a breathtaking vision in mauve as she accepted his bow.

Gilliard noted Evans's expression. "She is the loveliest of the four," he said in cultured French as they walked through the echoing hallways.

Evans absently agreed, and as they reached the main entrance, Gilliard stopped. "You should be aware, Mr. Evans, that the Grand Duchess Olga is a young woman in the process of discovering that she is exceptionally beautiful. She is, of course, constantly surrounded by men of all ages and ranks, and they have one thing in common, the one thing you lack."

He had Evans's attention now. "Deference, Mr. Evans. Deference for her position. They react to her as servant to mistress, and therefore, she thinks of them only as servants. But you are an American, and any deference you might exhibit is mere politeness and quite refreshing to her, coinciding as it does with her awakening as a young woman. It allows her to see you as the handsome, personable man you are. Add to that the rather romantic circumstances by which you came to her notice, and infatuation is a most logical result. You must consider this: Such infatuation cannot be allowed. You may never hope to see her socially, and a more permanent liaison is out of the question. She *is* a grand duchess."

Gilliard looked keenly at an astonished Evans. "If you persist in responding to her smiles and invitations, you will only cause difficulty for her, for yourself and for your—"

"Wait a moment." Evans found his voice at last. "What invitations?"

"Why, the invitation to tea this afternoon. From whom else did you think it came? The grand duchess invited you without consulting her mother. The excuse was the progress of your recovery. The grand duchess Olga is well aware that Rasputin has given you a favorable report. The grand duchess Tatiana informed me of the situation and asked that I speak to you before trouble resulted. Good day, Mr. Evans."

Gilliard's words astounded him, but he had no chance to object before the tutor pushed the door open and Evans found himself outside in the freezing courtyard.

"I'd say you were getting in over your head," Boyd commented when Evans told him of Gilliard's remarks. "I should have said something myself, but I had no idea you were that serious."

"Serious! What the hell are you talking about? Serious about a grand duchess? That's asinine!"

Boyd stared down his long nose. "Bill, it's written all over you. One more invitation from the grand duchess, and you can guess how the Russian Foreign Office will react. They'll have you out of the country in twenty-four hours."

"God damn it, have you lost your mind?" Evans shouted. He stamped around the apartment. "I've seen her three times. And besides, it was your own goddamned idea in the first place. 'Here's your chance to be a hero, Billy boy,' " he mimicked in a parody of Boyd's accent.

Boyd laughed. "When I said, 'Get to know the royal family,' I meant the tsar. I had no idea you were going to try to get one of the grand duchesses into bed." He laughed at Evans's expression of outrage. "It would seem that the grand duchess Tatiana is a very perceptive young lady."

"And a royal pain in the ass. She reminds me of my kid sister."

Evans picked up his glass and sniffed suspiciously at the contents. "This stuff is really rotten. Fulbright told me how to make gin in a bathtub. I think I'll try it. It would have to be better than this."

Boyd shook his head. "That bottle of vodka is symbolic of the whole Russian problem. Full of ideals that never quite translate into practice. The prohibition on vodka at the start of the war was probably a damned good idea from a theoretical standpoint. Stop widespread drunkenness, and you'll decrease absenteeism, reduce the police forces, cut crime and so on. Except, of course, that what it's actually done is to create a whole new illegal industry. Liquor consumption isn't any lower than before prohibition, but crime is higher, public drunkenness is worse, production has dropped and the government has lost millions in taxes."

Evans remained on tenterhooks as the holidays dragged by, expecting a third invitation to Tsarskoye Selo now that the tsar had returned. While intellectually he accepted what Gilliard and Boyd told him, emotionally he could not. He remembered the way Olga had looked at him from beneath lowered eyelashes, the way her smile had dazzled. And, too, there was Gilliard's own admission that she had done the unthinkable for a grand duchess and taken it upon herself to invite him to tea. He even entertained the suspicion that Gilliard, himself in love with Olga, was attempting to reduce competition. But in saner moments he realized that whatever his own shortcomings as a suitor, they applied even more to the Swiss tutor. Even so, he refused to entertain the idea that Olga was merely toying with him to relieve the boredom of the royal seraglio in its Victorian extreme.

Mathilda Eugenovna Orbeleskaya and her husband departed for their estate in the Crimea, and he concentrated his attention on Natalia. So much so that Boyd began to kid him about a wedding date.

The news of Rasputin's assassination swept Petrograd.

The American Embassy, which, since the departure of John Reed, had lapsed into its usual somnambulant state, was jerked awake as cable after cable poured in from the War, State, Treasury and Commerce departments, demanding to know what effect the death of the starets would have on the war effort, Russian-American relations, trade and loans. People rushed about with mad gleams of excitement, predicting the long-awaited revolution. Within days it was known that five conspirators, two of them close relatives of the tsar, had murdered the monk and thrown his body into the Neva.

The monarchist newspapers were restrained in their comments, stopping far short of condemning the murderers, and the liberal press rejoiced. The revolutionary underground press was jubilant and, in spite of the fact that the assassins were of the highest nobility, referred to them as national heroes. The mood at all levels of society was the same, united once more, as it must have been in September 1914, Evans thought. But the optimism proved ill-founded. By the end of the first week it was clear that no significant changes in the government were pending. In mourning the tsarina might have been, but she continued to meddle openly in governmental affairs even while Nicholas, said to be on the verge of a nervous breakdown, remained at Tsarskoye Selo instead of returning to the front. With the royal family in mourning for

34

Rasputin, any chance of a third invitation to Tsarskoye Selo for Evans glimmered away.

The winter of 1916–1917 was the hardest on record. In January the temperature fell to thirty-five below zero. Railway engine boilers cracked, throwing the transportation system into total disarray. Food shortages worsened, and fuel for heating and cooking—if there had been food to cook—disappeared, even from the black market. Lines formed outside food shops and bakeries. In spite of harsh fines, parks and riverbanks were raided in broad daylight for firewood. Faces grew sullen, strikes became frequent and the war news from all fronts was so bad that one no longer listened.

The government stumbled on under the totally corrupt and insensible Alexander Protopopov, who, rumors suggested, was trying to step into Rasputin's Russian leather boots. He was reputed to hold séances at night during which he received instructions from the murdered starets, which he then telephoned to the tsarina the following morning.

Rumors of coups d'état circulated constantly and involved everyone from Rodzianko, the president of the Duma, to one of the tsar's own uncles. In the midst of the uproar—as if to suggest the court discounted all such rumors—it was announced that Nicholas was returning to the front on March 8 to prepare for a spring offensive.

All during January Evans spent long afternoons and evenings with Natalia, neglecting his meager duties at the embassy. They divided their time between the roadhouses and parties which often grew so boisterous that the police were required to break them up. When a Russian officer accompanying their group one night ran his motorcar off a bridge and drowned, it took all of Boyd's diplomacy to keep the ambassador from sending Evans home in disgrace.

Boyd came down hard on him, appealing shamelessly to their friendship. Evans still tended to treat it all as a huge joke, but evidently Francis had written to his father because he received a blistering letter. "You can damned well work here at headquarters"—the ancient block of musty brick and masonry that housed the family's Boston publishing firm—"where I can keep an eye on you." Judging that his father meant it this time, Evans made a diligent effort to pay attention to the job Boyd had given him: preparing reports on the interminable sessions of the squabbling Duma, the Russian Parliament.

III

The day the tsar left Petrograd for the front, the revolution began. At the time no one recognized it as such, but it was the beginning, nevertheless. Evans's first inkling came the following day, when he stumbled over a body lying in the snow.

He had just left the Admiralty and was hurrying along the Dvortsovaya Naberezhnaya, chin tucked into the fur collar of his coat, when he saw a crowd gathering at the near end of the Troitsky Bridge. As he approached, he could hear shouting. A knot of policemen in dark ankle-length overcoats and heavy fur caps watched from the center of the bridge.

The man lay on his back, arms and legs thrown wide in the nerveless sprawl of death. There was a spot of blood at the corner of his mouth, dullish brown against the lifeless skin. His eyes were open and sightless.

Shock carried Evans into the crowd. The shouting was barely intelligible, but he made out the words, "Death to the tsar!" repeated over and over. Perplexed, he tried to get some sense of what was happening from the people around him, but they all seemed caught up in a kind of frenzy. It occurred to him that he had stumbled into the midst of a mob in the purest sense, a mob driven mad by the death of one of their own. He discovered with horror that they were advancing on the armed policemen in purposeful order.

36

Over bobbing heads he could see the officer in charge, a middle-aged man standing rock-steady to one side of the police line, sword in one hand, pistol in the other. Behind, on Troitskaya Plaza, Evans saw a company of soldiers drawn up, and in that instant the scene burned itself into his mind—the Cathedral of Saint Peter and Saint Paul frowning on the Neva, the trees in the Alexander Park wreathed in frozen mist, the great clock in the slender tower striking noon and the bells beginning to chime the national anthem.

They were on the bridge proper now, and their howling had grown in volume. Evans shrank back as the police officer raised his sword. He could see his lips move as he gave a quiet order to steady his men. Hands worked rifle bolts in ragged sequence. The mob began to run, dragging Evans with them, and still, the officer stood, sword raised, judging the psychological moment.

Evans heard the order given firmly above the cries of the mob, and one or two rifles were actually fired before the blue line wavered. The police officer turned in astonishment as his men broke rank, throwing their rifles away, and ran for the protection of the soldiers. The mob submerged him just as Evans broke free.

Captain Nikolai Khristoforovich Sheremetiev cursed the police troops and most particularly their officer. The man was a fool. He peered across the river at the crowd. The shouts, even at this distance, were clear enough. Lately he had had sufficient experience with mobs to know exactly what to expect.

It was beginning to snow again. If it snowed hard enough, he thought, the mob would disperse. The wind blowing off the gulf was channeled around the bulk of the cathedral to whistle past his own troops drawn up in two shivering ranks. Since assuming command, he had drilled them relentlessly into something approaching first-class soldiers, but he still was not certain he could depend on them. These days a Russian officer's greatest fear was a bullet in the back.

The mob had advanced well onto the Troitsky Bridge. Once more Sheremetiev cursed the fool in charge of the police. It should have been so simple. Raise the damned drawbridge, and the mob would have nowhere to go. But his orders were very specific: He was to act only if the mob appeared about to cross the bridge.

The clock on the church steeple finished tolling noon and began to chime the national anthem. Midway through the first bar the officer's sword flashed and a few rifles went off. The mob surged forward, and the police broke and ran, with the mob howling in pursuit. Sheremetiev waved to his sergeant major, who wheeled the two ranks to the right to block the bridge approach. The police had almost reached them now;

he could see faces distended with fear, eyes wild, and, directly behind, the leading elements of the mob.

"Ready!" he made his voice crack. Twenty-five men knelt in one smooth motion, and twenty-five men stepped back one pace, fifty rifles coming to fifty shoulders. "Aim!" The police, realizing that they were also in the line of fire, threw themselves down. One man panicked and vaulted the bridge railing thirty feet to the ice below. Those in the front of the mob tried to stop as they saw the steady line of rifles, but pressure from behind drove them on.

Sheremetiev cursed aloud and shouted, "Fire!"

A single volley crashed out, and people fell all along the length of the bridge, thrashing and screaming. The mob hesitated, but the madness had also infected Sheremetiev and his troops. The sound of rifle bolts being worked took him back to the Carpathians, and he shouted, "Fire!" a second time.

The mob turned and ran, streaming back across the Troitsky Bridge, screaming in fear. Sheremetiev held himself stiffly upright, fearful that if he relaxed for an instant, he would collapse, vomiting. Never again, dear God, he thought. Never again.

The following Friday evening Boyd stood in the doorway watching Evans dress. He flicked his patent-leather shoes with a cloth and slipped into his jacket.

"Hell of a time to attend a party."

Evans shrugged irritably. "Why not? If things are as bad as you say, there might not be many more. So I guess I'd better take advantage, hadn't I?"

Boyd shook his head and grinned. "Bill, I wish to God I had your outlook on life. Doesn't anything ever bother you?"

Evans adjusted his tie and tugged on white gloves. "Nope."

The cab stopped at the Red Cross nurses' barracks, where Natalia waited for him. It had begun to snow, and the temperature had risen somewhat. Even so, the interior of the cab was icy in spite of the charcoal brazier. As they drove through the snow-covered streets to the Radziwill mansion, the city seemed empty of everyone but soldiers. Troops were to be seen here and there along the quays or stamping their feet on street corners to keep warm.

Natalia moved her feet closer to the brazier and leaned against him. Annoyed, Evans shifted position. "They are saying," she murmured, "that more than two hundred people were killed by the police today."

"So I heard."

"The tsar has announced he will return to Petrograd. Do you think that will do any good?"

"How the devil would I know?"

The sleigh stopped, then jerked toward the brilliantly illuminated mansion. A line of motor cars, carriages and sleighs was ahead of them, and it was several minutes before they were close enough for Natalia to be handed down by a footman. They hurried up a walk heated by hot-water pipes to keep it clear of ice and snow. Inside, it was excessively warm, and Evans was dizzy for a moment with the drastic change in temperature.

A footman handed them both stirrup cups of heated brandy and milk, and they followed another servant, clad in an eighteenth-century uniform of sky blue coat and white breeches over silk stockings, into the main ballroom. The uniform blended perfectly with the opulent décor, but between the servant's powdered wig and his collar, Evans noticed several angry flea bites. The analogy, he thought, was perfect. Beneath the expensive façade, shoddiness and human suffering.

They were announced in stentorian tones by a chamberlain, then left to their own devices. Natalia, of course, as a cousin of the royal family seemed to know and be known by everyone. Evans was introduced to so many heel-clicking, monocled middle-aged men that he soon lost track of names and titles. Younger men were in short supply, and fluttering women of all ages stared at him over their fans.

"The Grand Duchess Olga was to have been here tonight," he heard his hostess telling Natalia as she tapped her on the arm to emphasize her point. "But with the upset in the city apparently it was decided that she must not leave Tsarskoye Selo. Oh, my dear, I hope this won't be another 1905. And what do you think, Mr. Evans? You Americans know all about revolutions. Didn't you invent them?"

Evans dragged his mind away from the surprise of hearing that Olga was to have attended the ball. "Uh, no, Princess. I believe your ancestors did. Wasn't there a man named Stenka Razin?"

Natalia drew him toward the long buffet table. "How very clever of you," she murmured. "Do you wish never to be invited again?" Evans shrugged and picked up a plate. "My, but you are in a foul mood tonight." Natalia tightened her grip on his arm. "Please do not spoil it for me."

Evans glared at her and turned away. Although the lights gleamed and the orchestra played smoothly and the prima ballerina of the Petrograd ballet was in attendance, the talk was of strikes and mobs in the city and the action the tsar might take. No one, no matter his position in the government, seemed to have a clear idea of what might be done. All admitted that unrest was growing, but because troops from the front were expected in the next few days, no one seemed worried that the rioting would last beyond Friday. Evans wasn't so certain. He remembered the faces of the soldiers staring after the grand duchesses and their Cossack escort in the Finland Station the day he had arrived.

Finding himself alone near the buffet and feeling a light touch on his arm, he looked around to see the Princess Orbeleskaya smiling up at him.

"And how are you this evening?" she murmured. "Have you recovered?"

Her sudden appearance flustered Evans. "From what? I haven't been sick."

The princess was wearing an exceedingly daring gown in the latest Paris fashion that emphasized her opulent figure. The bodice was cut loose and fringed with lace. As she leaned forward to kiss him, it fell away, revealing a glimpse of smooth white breasts and pink nipples. His breath caught in his throat.

"But I assumed you had been sick. Else why had you not telephoned? I've been in Petrograd for three days now. And tonight I find you with Natalia."

"Natalia . . . how do you know each other?"

"Natalia is my cousin," she said with a hint of frost. "Now look, my dear man, I expect you to call on me. Natalia Vasolova can spare you for one night."

She whirled away then, leaving Evans so dazed that Natalia had to shake his arm when she came up a few moments later.

"What did that witch want with you, Bill?"

Evans shook his head to clear it. "We met once, at a dinner party."

"I can imagine."

Natalia stretched one arm across his chest, then rolled over and licked at his chin. "I liked that. Again?"

"My God, woman," Evans muttered. "Wait awhile at least."

Natalia traced circles on his skin with her fingertips until he grunted and shifted away. Exasperated, she sat up and switched on the light.

"It's Mathilda, isn't it? You're going to see her. When?"

"Huh?" Evans tried to sit up against the pillow, but Natalia pushed him back. The lamplight glowed softly on her fine skin, highlighting her small, firm breasts and sleek stomach. She kept a hand on his chest, holding him down.

"Mathilda is a whore."

Evans pushed her hand away and sat up. "Natalia, for the love of God . . ." They had argued—rather, she had nagged at him—all during the ride back to the hotel. Twice she had demanded that he promise to stop seeing Mathilda, or anyone else for that matter. Only through long practice had he managed to avoid a commitment. He was going to have to do something about Natalia, and soon.

Her expression was bleak as she waited for his response. "Bill, I love you. You know that."

40

God damn it, he thought, she wasn't going to leave it alone. "Natalia, I don't want to listen to any more of your jealous carping tonight!"

"I am not jealous! Only concerned for you. Mathilda doesn't care about you, wouldn't have given you a second look if you weren't an American diplomat!"

Evans laughed at her. "What the hell has that to do with it?"

"Her husband is a leader of the Constitutional Democratic party, the Kadets. She told you they were at their estate in the Crimea, didn't she? Well, she lied. They were in Moscow, meeting with certain generals plotting to assume control of the revolution and she—"

"What revolution, for Christ's sake? A few riots? They're sending troops from the front. The city will be back to normal by the end of the week."

Natalia sat up straighter and looked at him. Evans found it hard to concentrate on what she was saying, and in spite of his exasperation, he did want to make love to her again; but she evaded his hands.

"Normal? Do you think that to freeze and starve during the winter is a normal thing? Do you think prices for what little food there is should be at more than four hundred times what they were before the war? Do you think that countless millions of Russian deaths on the front lines is normal? Do you think a tsar who would rather listen to a charlatan like Rasputin than to his cabinet ministers or the Duma is normal? I was a little girl in 1905, but I remember what happened then. In the countryside they murdered the nobles, burned them to death in their own houses, drowned entire families in their wells.

"Nothing has really changed. Do you think front-line troops will shoot their neighbors and relatives to keep a corrupt government and a foolish tsar on the throne? Today there were reports of troops refusing to fire, even joining the mob. Once that begins, it will spread like wildfire."

She put her hands to her face and burst into uncontrollable sobs. Astonished, Evans did not know how to react. He tried to take her into his arms, but she pushed him away. After a moment she brushed at her eyes and stifled a sob.

"Will you lend me five thousand rubles?"

"Five thousand . . . what are you going to do?"

"I am going to leave Russia. I've made all the arrangements."

Evans gaped at her. "Aren't you taking this a bit seriously? For Christ's sake, where will you go?"

"To Stockholm. I have sent a telegram to a friend saying I am coming. I must leave Russia before the killing begins."

"Now look here, Natalia, who said anything—"

She sat back, her face composed. "In 1905 I saw my father murdered. His own peasants hanged him and then set his body afire. He was still alive when the rope burned through. These were the same people to whom he had sold a large portion of his estate at low cost and no interest, the same people whom he had helped and defended, protected and cared for all his life. It made no difference to them. He was a landlord and a noble."

"Jesus Christ," he muttered under his breath. From the set of her expression and the distant look in her eyes, he knew she was telling the truth.

"They raped my mother and my fourteen-year-old sister. They raped them both again and again. The women only laughed and encouraged the men. Then they whipped my mother to death, beating her one after another with knotted ropes. They impaled my sister on the iron fence that surrounded the house. They would have killed me as well, but I hid. They burned the house and all the buildings to the ground. I can still see those hideous faces leering at my sister as she screamed and screamed until she died." Her tears glistened in the light, and he wanted to wipe them away but was paralyzed by the horror of her story.

"Of course," he finally managed, "I'll lend you five thousand rubles. More if you like."

"No," she said quietly, and slid off the bed. "Five thousand will be quite sufficient." She found her clothes and began to dress. "I leave on the morning train to Helsingfors."

After she had gone, Evans lay awake thinking. Five thousand rubles was a cheap buy-off. He wondered how much she had exaggerated to play on his sympathies. And as far as Mathilda was concerned, what nonsense. General Orbelesky was a fatuous old fool, period. He couldn't lead himself out of a dark room. He grinned at his overwhelming sense of relief. Natalia had solved his problem very neatly by removing herself from the scene. Why the hell couldn't all women be as accommodating?

The military lorries ground to a halt at the intersection of Zabalkansky and Klinsky prospekts in the Moscow District of Petrograd. Captain Nikolai Khristoforovich Sheremetiev swung down from the cab as his company poured out of the trucks and hustled into two lines facing the shop fronts on the western side of the boulevard. He took a deep breath of freezing air and slapped gloved hands together. Looking along the Zabalkansky, he could see trams which had been tipped off the line, private automobiles and even pieces of furniture crammed in with paving stones, benches and rubbish to form a barricade. In the distance he could see the icy sheen of the Obvodny Canal.

Thousands of people were milling about—men from textile and munitions factories in the Vyborg District north of the Neva, from the

Russian-American Rubber Works, railyards and other factories in the Narew District, as well as women and children who had been caught up in the disturbance. Lines of workers had formed up across streets that might have served as exits. Making certain, he thought grimly, that no one could get out. The workers intended to use the presence of the women and children to keep the police from firing on them. Sheremetiev swore under his breath at the fool who had thought of that ploy. It was going to be a bad day, he knew. A very bad day. His men were aware of the women and children.

Sheremetiev took the sergeant major's salute and strode across the street to where a knot of officers stood talking. Cossacks were lined up in the Third Rota, partially hidden by a grayish multistory building. They were Stepnoy Cossacks with the crimson collar patches, pants stripes and shoulder straps of the Ural *Voiskos,* and they looked grim enough for the day's work.

The knot of officers included a gray-uniformed police general and his adjutant, a colonel from the military governor's office whom he had once met, the Cossack commander and several of lesser rank. The police general was hectoring the colonel and pointedly ignored Sheremetiev. The other officers took their cue from the general.

For a week now, since the Troitsky Bridge shootings, Sheremetiev and his company had rushed from riot to riot, arguing, shouting, crowding back the mobs, sometimes at bayonet point and three times with shots fired above their heads. Most of those incidents could have been avoided but for the pigheaded fools, like this general, who seemed determined to goad the workers and the poor of Petrograd into all-out revolution. Sheremetiev chewed at his badly chapped lips. He had already given orders that had resulted in the deaths of his fellow countrymen. He did not think he could do so again, nor did he think his restless soldiers would obey if he did.

The intersection of the two prospekts and the lesser streets formed an open area about a hundred meters wide. Two- and three-story buildings lined each street: warehouses, empty stores and the barely adequate flats of workers and their families. It was a solidly industrial neighborhood, the type of area that would be chosen by a clever agitator.

"You there, Captain!" the general shouted. "Get your company along the east side of the road. See that your men have live ammunition chambered. I want none of this nonsense about firing high. When I give the order to shoot, they are to shoot to kill. Do you understand?"

Sheremetiev stared at the corpulent police general. His face was brick red from cold and high blood pressure, and he was so fat he could barely clasp his hands behind his back. He saw the general's eyes flick to the Cross of Saint George and campaign ribbons on his greatcoat.

"General, there are women and children in that intersection. Surely—"

"Surely, Captain," the general snapped, "you will obey orders without argument. If there are women and children with that rabble, they have chosen to be there of their own free will. They will get only what they deserve."

It was useless to argue, and he spun about and returned to his company. As he passed the Cossacks being mustered into line, not a single man was smiling, and all had carbines slung across their backs and saber knots looped about their wrists. For a moment he toyed with the idea of ordering his company to return to the barracks.

A thin wind whistled along the street, billowing his greatcoat. The Cossack officer mounted his horse and led the troop out onto the Zabalkansky Prospekt. A knot of men had formed up before the main barricade. At the sight of the Cossacks, the workers began to advance, and the Cossack officer leaned forward expectantly. The mounted men exchanged wary glances, and here and there a sword was hefted. Why in the name of God had they not been issued whips, Sheremetiev wondered? There was nothing like a Cossack knout to break up a riot.

A brick flew at the line of horsemen but fell well short. A flurry of assorted objects followed; then the workers fell back, laughing and shouting obscenities. A bravado gesture, Sheremetiev thought. The street was still thick with people, most of them not involved but kept in the area by the worker gangs shutting off the exits. Then, with the telepathic quickness that seems to infect crowds, the people sensed what was going to happen and scattered for the protection of doorways and alleys.

The Cossack officer whipped his sword up and shouted, *"Huzzah!"* Fifty mounted men shot forward, swords raised, and swept down on the rioters. They were in among them in seconds. Sabers flashed, shots snapped and bodies fell. Sheremetiev saw a Cossack throw both hands to his face and somersault backward from his horse. A woman ran screaming, dragging a small child. She lost her grip on the child's hand, turned back and was ridden down by a Cossack who tried desperately to swerve his horse. The animal lost its footing on the icy cobbles and fell on the woman. The Cossack was thrown headlong against the curb, and Sheremetiev heard his skull crack with a sickening thud. The child sat screaming not far from where its mother lay dead.

The Cossacks wheeled and cantered back in ragged lines. Fifteen or more bodies lay in the street. The last worker scrambled over the barricade, and the police general stood at the head of his officers, raging. The Cossack officer galloped back to where his troop had re-formed in two lines, once more facing the barricade. He was shouting obscenities, reviling them for not pressing home the charge. His horse reared, slipped, but the officer held on in a magnificent display of horsemanship. When he had the horse under control again, he wheeled about, and still not looking at the general, who was shaking a fist and pointing at the barricade, he raised his saber and shouted the command to charge.

He spurred his horse across the intersection, directly for the barricade. The Cossack troop wavered; then someone shouted, and horses were curbed. The officer rode directly at the barricade, saber in one hand, revolver in the other, never once looking back. A single shot sounded, and the riderless horse veered. The officer lay dead in the street, shot through the throat.

The police general was shouting commands now, and the staff colonel raced toward Sheremetiev.

"The Cossacks!" the officer screamed. "Shoot the traitors! Shoot them, the bastards!"

Sheremetiev saw only the colonel's immaculate uniform and thin pencil-line mustache, the smooth face which had never seen, nor would ever see, front-line duty, sensed the anger and hatred of the soldiers at his back and knew. Years of frustration, of fear and terror drove him to yank his revolver from its holster and shoot the staff officer dead.

As if released from a bad dream, he pointed at the knot of officers and shouted, "Company! Aim and fire."

Without the slightest hesitation, the volley blasted across the boulevard, and the crowd of officers was swept away. Only the general remained standing, clutching his side and staring stupidly at his bloodied hand. A single bullet cracked past Sheremetiev's head, and the general slumped to a sitting position, still staring at his hand. A dozen rifles fired then, and he collapsed like a broken toy.

A great cheer went up as the Cossacks crowded around the troops, and Sheremetiev was hoisted onto their shoulders. Someone began to sing the "Marseillaise," and the soldiers took it up with a roar and marched toward the barricade, from which the rioters poured to meet them. The two groups came together in a blast of cheering, and Sheremetiev was deposited on a trash wagon tipped onto its side. Instinctively he tore the shoulder boards from his greatcoat and flung them to the crowd, shouting, "Huzzah for the revolution!"

The mansion belonging to General Orbelesky stood on a quiet street in the Rozhdestvenskaya District. The temperature hovered at fifteen below in midafternoon as Evans dismissed his cab. A stiff wind was blowing from the west, and the cold seemed to have calmed the strikers. He had seen no sign of disorder during the drive to or from the Finland Station to see Natalia off.

Evans had not wanted to go. But there were some things one had to do, and seeing a former lover off was one of them. It was clear, however, that Natalia in no way thought of herself as a former lover. She had extracted a promise not only that he would write to her but that he would also visit her in Stockholm as soon as he got leave. Of course, he had no intention of keeping either promise.

A servant in full livery took his overcoat and showed him to a small parlor. Mathilda came in a few moments later and stood on tiptoe to kiss him with icy lips. She had just come in from the garden, she announced, and huddled into his arms for warmth. He could feel her body shivering slightly; her cheeks were flushed, and her eyes sparkled.

"I need a drink. Over there, dear boy. On the trolley."

He held up a bottle of brandy, and she nodded. After he had poured the drinks, Evans carried them to the fireplace and carefully warmed the balloon glasses.

"You came quickly enough. Perhaps you are tiring of Natalia?" the princess asked over the rim of her glass, her eyes suddenly hard.

"She's left, you know."

"Left what?" Mathilda laughed. "Your bed?"

"No. Russia. I've just come from the railroad station. She's left the country."

"From the railroad station?" Mathilda lowered the glass and looked at him. "Why?" Then with mild scorn: "I suppose she's afraid of revolution."

"So she said."

Mathilda was silent a moment, staring into the fire. "She has reason to be."

"I know."

Mathilda walked to the window and parted the curtains. Evans joined her, close, yet not touching. He studied the soft curving profile of her face, closed off now, all animation gone. A single sleigh went past, the horse's head down as if very weary, the driver invisible beneath furs and blankets. The short day was over, and darkness was sliding in from the west. Shadows filled the streets with an evil bluish tinge, and the snow seemed dirty and old.

Mathilda let the curtain drop and turned to him, still without expression. She held out her arms and came to him without a word.

Lili Dehn plucked up her skirts and scurried along the platform as the train began to move. The conductor leaned out, and she grasped his hand and swung onto the steps, laughing.

The train ran out of the Tsarskoye Selo Station through the Petrograd suburbs under a rich blue sky. A brilliant sun splashed from high snowbanks, and as the houses and buildings of the city fell away, distant trees made sharp dark lines against the horizon. The air was crisp, icy cold—the perfect Petrograd winter day.

Lili had received a telephoned invitation less than an hour before, to Tsarskoye Selo for the day. "It's a lovely day, Lili," the tsarina had said. "The girls have asked for you, and I'll meet you with the car."

The train chuffed into the tiny station, and as Lili stepped down

Alexandra hurried toward her, smiling. But her first question was of the riots in the city. Lili told her that although the general strike was inconvenient, she had seen nothing alarming. "One never knows when the grocers will open, and that makes it bothersome for the servants. There are reports of shooting in the newspapers, but I think they are making them up. I certainly haven't heard any gunshots."

The Panhard touring car was waiting, and they drove through the village, exchanging gossip. A detachment of the Garde Equipage, the marines who served aboard the royal yacht *Standart*, was exercising in the fields before the palace gates, and the tsarina ordered the car stopped. The captain of the detachment came across and saluted. Alexandra questioned him closely about the disorders, and he smiled. "There is really no danger, Your Majesty."

Lili thought his tone designed only to soothe a worried woman, but she remained silent.

"The children became sick the night before last," Alexandra told her when they reached the palace. She led the way into a sitting room where tea waited. Anna Vyrubova was there, reclining on the couch, eyes closed and almost asleep. She greeted Lili wearily.

"Anna was up all night with the girls, poor thing." Alexandra smiled at her. "Last week some boys from the military academy came to play with Alexei, and apparently one had the measles. Oh, will it never cease?"

Lili patted her hand and went up to see the girls. Anastasia had not yet contracted the disease, and she was fretting in her room, arms crossed on the window sill, watching the marines as they marched back through the palace gates.

"Oh, Lili, I'm glad you've come!" she exclaimed. "With everyone so sick, there is just nothing to do. Mama won't let me have my friends from the village for fear of making them sick as well."

Lili spent the morning playing games with her until Anna Vyrubova came to say that the girls' fevers were rising alarmingly. They both hurried along to the large bedroom belonging to Olga, now converted to a girls' dormitory. Alexandra was already there, dressed in her Red Cross uniform and holding a glass of water for Tatiana, while the nurse squeezed a wet cloth in a basin and laid it on her forehead. Anna Vyrubova sat down abruptly and put her head in her hand. The nurse took one look at Anna and ordered her into bed as well.

Near midnight Lili was alone in the sickroom with the girls when the tsarina opened the door and beckoned her into the corridor.

"Lili," she said quietly, "I've just been to talk with the commander of the palace guard. There is a rumor that the Litovsky Regiment has mutinied in Petrograd and murdered their officers. The Volinsky Regiment is reported to have followed suit."

Lili stared, her mind refusing to accept what she was hearing.

"It . . . it can't be true. The Litovsky Regiment wouldn't . . . no, it can't be true. I tell you, I didn't see a thing in the city that would indicate—" A servant hurried in with a message that the palace commandant wished to speak to the tsarina again. The officer was standing anxiously outside the door, and Lili saw that his face was very pale.

In the morning Alexandra tried to telephone the tsar at army headquarters near Mogilev but was unable to get through. All calls from Tsarskoye Selo were routed through Petrograd, and the central telephone exchange was thought to be in the hands of the mutineers. Despairing of ever reaching her husband directly, she sent a telegram begging him to return. His answer came later in the day, stating that he would return on the fourteenth.

A few hours later Anna Vyrubova's father limped through the gates, red-faced and out of breath. He sat down on his daughter's sickbed and eased his shoes off. "Petrograd has been taken over by the mob," he announced dramatically. "They commandeered all motorcars. I've had to walk.

"The entire city is in rebellion," he told them, eyes bright and glistening, both from his brisk walk and the perverse pleasure he seemed to be taking in delivering the bad news. "They say that the soldiers are shooting their officers right and left. At the Peter and Paul Fortress, they threw officers into the moat. The fall to the ice killed them." Alexandra turned away in dismay, and Anna scolded him from the room.

For the next two days they remained caged in the palace while the children recovered. Lili was amazed at how quickly everything collapsed, and her fears for the royal family's safety grew as the news worsened. The president of the Duma, Rodzianko, sent a telegram warning the tsarina that she and the children were in danger and should leave Tsarskoye Selo immediately. But the tsar wired an hour later, instructing her to remain and ordering only that a train be made up for the following morning. On Tuesday, the thirteenth, there was a fresh blizzard, followed by a deep, intense cold. Lili watched from the palace windows as the guards stamped their feet and swung their arms to keep warm. Alexandra gave orders to allow them into the palace to warm themselves, and Lili quickly discovered that her kindness had been misinterpreted as fear.

She had gone to the head of the stairway to see the first soldiers come in. All big men, it seemed to her, clad in huge greatcoats and fur hats with their rifles worn upside down across their backs to keep the snow from the barrels. At first she reveled in the attention they paid her, the respectful questions, the smiles. But after a while one soldier, a small, hawk-faced man, began to make remarks about discrepancies between the classes. Instead of angering the others, his comments seemed to make them boisterous. A bearded soldier winked at her and called for her to come down the staircase. Another soldier, a sergeant, she supposed, roared at the man, and he turned away sheepishly; but when the sergeant's back was turned, he winked again and made a shockingly obscene gesture.

The following morning Lili was sitting with Olga and Tatiana, drinking *café au lait* and discussing the events of the past week when word came that a crowd of soldiers in trucks had arrived from Petrograd to seize the palace. The girls scrambled out of bed in their nightgowns, excited at the prospect of seeing actual rebels. The palace grounds were still and close under a fresh blanket of snow. The sun had appeared earlier in the morning; but now it was gone, and a curious, waiting twilight lay over the countryside.

Indignantly Lili chased the girls back to bed, warning them to stay away from the windows. The memory of the bearded soldier's lewd invitation was still embarrassingly fresh, and the sight of the two slender and very attractive young women reluctantly slipping between the covers, figures neatly outlined by their cotton nightgowns, caused her a pang of deep fear. After excusing herself, she hurried along the hall to a small study which Nicholas liked to use when he desired a private moment.

She pushed the door open and peeked in. Empty. Emboldened, she stepped inside and closed the door, shivering in the sudden chill. The fireplace was cold, and she noticed that the hot-air duct to the room had been shut off, by the tsar, she supposed, who was forever turning out lamps and closing the heating system in unused rooms to the despair of the servants. She stood with her back to the door, plucking up courage. Having crossed to the desk where a new series of Sergei Mikhailovich Prokudin-Gorskii's color photographs was neatly stacked, she lifted the top; it fell from her nervous fingers with a clatter that caused her heart to jump. She stood frozen for several minutes until she was convinced that no one had heard.

When she dared open the top again, she propped it up with a book, then opened the top left-hand drawer. The oiled sheen of the small automatic pistol lay half-concealed beneath a folder, and she drew it out. When she was taking coffee one day the previous summer with the tsar, he had shown her the weapon, a gift from its American designer, John Browning. She had no idea how the pistol worked, only that one had to turn down a small lever on the side and pull the trigger. She slipped it into the pocket of her apron and returned to the girls' room.

Nicholas Alexandrovich Romanov, Tsar of All the Russias and the world's last total autocrat, stood at the train window, watching the troops huddled along the tracks in the railyard at Pskov. Snow blew hard on the wind and had half covered the side of the car with frost. The sun had shone earlier, a cold, cheerless sun to be sure, but at least sun. Now there was only the lowering gray cloud, the wind and the snow. They were—had been—*his* soldiers at one time. Even in weather like this they would have uncovered their heads out of respect and given a cheer at his appearance. He was not certain what they would do now. Here and there agitators were trying to harangue them, but no one listened for long. It was that which decided him: The revolutionary movement was spontaneous, independent of political and social ideologies. In a rare moment of insight he realized that those half-frozen men had come to tell him his time had passed.

Nicholas turned back to the group of officers gathered around the map table. They were watching him, as they always did, waiting to see what he would decide before resuming their interminable wrangling. For twenty years, he thought, I have been the tsar, the supreme ruler of Russia, and for twenty years I have been beset by fools and cowards, not one of whom really believes I am more fitted than he to rule, except by accident of birth.

The telegram that ended all his hopes lay on the table. The Duma had assumed power in Petrograd, and the fighting and unrest had spread to Moscow. Now the Duma had sent three incompetent fools to demand his abdication in favor of his brother, the Grand Duke Michael, until Alexei came of age. He smiled wryly. Poor Michael had no intention of assuming the crown, even as regent. They waited there, the three generals, not daring to meet his eye. Beyond he could see lights coming on in the railyard. It was only midafternoon, but the clouds, he supposed, made it seem later.

He thought of his family in Tsarskoye Selo: his son, his four daughters and Alexandra, grown old so soon. Alexei had been the cause of that, had aged them both, yet there was nothing to be done. It was God's will. A little suffering in return for the awesome privilege of ruling Russia. He had tolerated that fool Rasputin for the relief he brought both Alexei and Alexandra. Perhaps he should have been more forceful with the man, but what else could he have done? His first duty was to Russia, and that meant Alexei had to be safeguarded as heir. There was no question of that. Without a clear succession, the reformers would have had their pretext for replacing the monarchy with a democracy—the rule of the mob.

His head lifted at the thought. An expression of disgust crossed his face; the three generals misinterpreted it, although not entirely, as being directed at them.

Russia was not a single nation like Britain or France or America. It was a diverse collection of people, most of whom were too ignorant and superstitious to understand anything but hatred. Russia needed a strong, hard hand on the whip to drive it, to weld it into a single nation. If not him, then someone else, but never a parliament of arguing, ineffectual fools. The Duma, the Provisional Government as it was now styling itself, must soon recognize that fact. Sooner or later the monarchy would be recalled.

In the meantime, he would retire to one of his estates in the country. Another few years, and perhaps Alexei might begin to recover, as the doctors promised. If so, then Alexei could take it up again. If not, then perhaps it didn't matter. Of a sudden, he was aware of how exhausted he was. It was in God's hands in any event, and nothing he could do or say would change that.

The tsar swept the compartment with his glance, and those around the table came quietly to attention.

"Gentlemen, I will abdicate in favor of the Grand Duke Michael, who will serve as regent for the rightful heir to the throne, my son, Alexei." He made the sign of the cross and bowed his head in prayer. The others in the car exchanged uncomfortable glances and followed suit.

IV

Nicholas was oblivious to the afternoon sun that filtered through the trellis of trailing roses overhanging the window to fill the room with soft greenish gold light. The telegram held his entire attention.

EVENTS OF THE PAST WEEK HAVE DISTRESSED ME. MY THOUGHTS ARE CONSTANTLY WITH YOU, AND I SHALL ALWAYS REMAIN YOUR TRUE AND DEVOTED FRIEND AS YOU KNOW I HAVE BEEN IN THE PAST [SIGNED] GEORGE V.

Nicholas shifted in his chair, then stood up and went to the window to stare at the lovely spring green of the birch forests that surrounded the palace. The harsh winter was over and done at last. A gardener was already pushing a mower through the grass that seemed to have sprung to ankle depth in less than a week. Fat white clouds marched serenely across the sky from the Gulf of Finland, promising more fair weather. The breeze, sharp, yet soft and filled with the scent of new growth, came to him through the window, and he drew a deep breath, reveling in that simple pleasure. For just a moment the familiar view, one he had enjoyed every spring for more than twenty years, lifted his spirits. Tomorrow was the twenty-first anniversary of his coronation, he thought, and suddenly the circumstances of their predicament crashed down about him again.

The man sitting on the other side of the desk cleared his throat, and Nicholas suppressed a flash of irritation.

"Your Majesty, at the risk of seeming ill-mannered, I must insist that you avail yourself of the opportunity offered by the English king. At the very least, allow me to send your family out of Russia to safety."

Kerensky could be an arrogant and pushy sort at times, Nicholas thought. But he had no doubt that within his limited sphere of authority the man was doing the best he possibly could. Nevertheless, two weeks ago Nicholas had allowed himself to be persuaded to attempt an escape, and embarrassment at the failure still rankled. They had gathered in the main hall at midnight. The ancient clock had ticked off minutes, then hours, and still the automobiles had failed to arrive. Kerensky's aide had assured him that everything had been arranged, that his own yacht *Standart* was waiting for them in the Gulf of Finland, ready to make the dash to Norway. The German government had secretly agreed to allow them to pass the U-boat pickets. But the automobiles had never left Petrograd, and the palace guard had begun to make fun of them. At 6:00 A.M. he had sent them all off for what sleep they could manage, and the soldiers had become downright rude. Since then a few had been quite hostile.

One of his daughters appeared in the yard below. He strained to see which. Ah, Olga! At once his depression eased. Alexei ran out, laughing at something and calling to Nagorny, his sailor aide. Nicholas still felt a twinge of bitterness when he thought of Derevenko's desertion the week before. For years, Derevenko had shared with Nagorny the privilege of looking after Alexei. But having seen how the wind lay, Derevenko had abandoned the boy, who considered him one of his closest friends, had even forced Alexei to wait on him hand and foot before leaving. It was only with difficulty that Dr. Botkin and he had prevented Nagorny from rushing off to throttle him.

A slovenly guard stepped from the entrance and motioned Olga and Alexei back. Alexei called something to the man, who only waved a hand and walked away. Nicholas saw him turn to Nagorny, who shook his head. The boy wandered disconsolate after Olga.

"Yes," he said without turning. "We will accept your offer."

Kerensky sighed in relief.

Nicholas raised a finger to his lips, and the tense whispering died away. The guards who should have been on the door were absent, and three large automobiles waited in the courtyard, exhausts bubbling. He stepped out into the moonlight, the driver in the lead vehicle nodded and he motioned everyone out. Each had been assigned to a vehicle, and it took only a moment to see everyone safely aboard.

At Alexandra's insistence Nicholas had agreed to keep his family together in the first automobile. Intellectually he knew that dispersing them would increase their chance of escape should anything go wrong; emotionally neither he nor his wife could bear the thought of separation from the children under such circumstances. He went back to the door for a final good-bye to the staff and court officials who had remained loyal during the difficult past two months, then hurried to the automobile and climbed up beside the driver.

The three vehicles moved quickly out of the courtyard and onto the long sweep of drive that led to the boulevard. He was aware of his wife and daughters jammed into the back, and occasionally he overheard one whispering to another.

They turned onto the boulevard, and Nicholas began to relax. If the palace guard, under the nominal command of the Provisional Government, were to have changed its mind, he was certain they would not have been allowed to leave. The night was absolutely silent. The houses they passed were all dark, and many were shuttered. A vague sorrow settled over Nicholas at the thought that he was probably leaving this familiar home forever, but with the rigid self-discipline that had been trained into him from childhood, he suppressed it, knowing that without his family to consider, not even the threat of death would cause him to leave Russia.

As the automobiles drove into the car park, he saw the train standing beyond the railroad station. He helped Alexandra and the girls down. Nagorny came forward quickly to lift Alexei out and settle him on his shoulders; then he picked up a suitcase. Nicholas took two more and waited until everyone was ready. Four servants and two friends, Lili Dehn and the Countess Hendrikova, had insisted on going as well. When they all were ready, he led them quickly up the graveled path toward the darkened train, wondering why the engineer had not gotten steam up.

Nicholas stepped onto the platform, and lights flashed on. Armed men swirled around them, pushing, grabbing at suitcases and shouting for them to put their hands up.

A heavyset man in a worker's cap and wearing a red armband shoved Nicholas against the wall. He smelled the man's rank breath and held his eyes rigidly away from the revolver at his face.

"Thinking of leaving us, Comrade Romanov?" the man demanded. Nicholas yanked his arm from the man's grasp and brushed the revolver away. Surprised, the man stepped back.

"Order your men to release the members of my family," he snapped. "Are they such poor soldiers that they fear women?"

The man laughed, recovering from the surprise of Nicholas's reaction, but ordered his men to stand away from the women.

"A fine one to talk you are," he sneered. "Trying to sneak out in the middle of the night."

"We are under orders from the Provisional Government to leave Tsarskoye Selo this night. I have—"

"We do not recognize the authority of the Provisional Government, Comrade Romanov. "I am sent by the Petrograd Workers' and Soldiers' Soviet to prevent your escape. I have orders to take you to Petrograd, where you and your family will be confined to the Peter and Paul Fortress."

Even as the realization of what he feared most burst through him, Nicholas was distracted by the sound of heavy lorries arriving, and a moment later uniformed soldiers surrounded the platform. He recognized several of the palace guard. A bearded soldier who had once been a sergeant in the Preobrazhensky Regiment stepped onto the platform. He ignored the Red Guards and spoke directly to Nicholas.

"Our soldiers' committee has taken a vote, Comrade Romanov. You are to return to the Alexander Palace immediately."

"Like hell—" the Red guardsman started to shout. The sergeant raised his hand, and there was an instant rattle of rifle bolts. The scene burned itself into Nicholas's mind. The soldiers were far outnumbered by the Red guardsmen, most of whom were bristling with weapons, but their superior discipline seemed to have a telling effect. One at a time, the guardsmen lowered their weapons and shuffled to one end of the platform. The former sergeant nodded to Nicholas, and for a moment he thought he detected regret in his eyes.

"Please have your family and friends follow along to the lorries . . . Your Majesty," he added in a whisper.

When Evans adjusted his watch twenty-nine minutes forward to Moscow time and stepped off the train, it was to see a huge red banner hanging from the iron beams of the Kursk and Nizhni-Novgorod Station. Armed soldiers were everywhere. He trudged the length of the train, searching vainly for a porter, thinking that the revolution had well and truly come to Moscow.

Standing in the square before the station, he surveyed a fire-blackened ruin across the street. The top stories had fallen in, and it looked much like the damage done to the SVNY building in Petrograd when a mob had held off the firemen just to see it burn. As he walked along the streets, he noticed that at each intersection there was a sandbagged machine gun encircled by barbed wire. Sullen soldiers stood about, swathed from head to foot in khaki greatcoats and fur caps.

Finally, he managed to find a cab to take him to the American Consulate. A policeman stood in front of the gate, hands clasped behind his back, and he neither greeted nor acknowledged Evans.

A male receptionist checked his papers, showed him where to hang his hat and coat and took him up to a large office on the second floor, where he was welcomed with relief by Consul General Sumner Madden.

As the weeks went by, Evans found his life in Moscow vastly different from that in Petrograd. There was no time for tennis in the afternoon, and the night clubs had been closed by the Soviet. Bootleg liquor, however, was just as plentiful as in the capital, and he found he was drinking more and more to ease the tremendous pressures they were all under. There was too much work to do and too few people to do it, and more than once he slept on his desk as he struggled vainly to keep up with the volume of work demanded by Madden, the embassy in Petrograd and the State Department in Washington. As a consequence, the brief Russian summer had gone and the autumn rains begun without his even noticing.

Even so, he still found time to pester Boyd by letter for news of the royal family. He pored over newspapers and quizzed consular officials from other missions at every opportunity. But beyond the bare fact that the tsar had been arrested on March 18 by the Provisional Government and confined with his family to the Alexander Palace at Tsarskoye Selo, there was little information available.

The coalition government, sworn in to much acclaim in early May, had, by the beginning of July, foundered badly. The war, as always, was to blame. Kerensky had ordered a general offensive in mid-June to eject German and Austrian troops from Russian territory in spite of widespread and serious sentiment for an immediate armistice, with or without the Allies. Evans, watching the rioting that followed the announcement, suspected that the Kerensky government had made an irretrievable mistake.

A letter, postmarked Washington, D.C., and addressed in succession to his former stations in Stockholm and Petrograd, had arrived at the consulate on July 3, the same day the Bolshevik disturbances began. His application to activate his reserve commission in the Massachusetts National Guard, made the day Ambassador Francis finally packed him off to Moscow in disgust, had been denied. The State Department had blocked his transfer, and he knew damned well who was responsible. Evans immediately went to fire off a cable to his father.

The post office annex was crowded. Evans hesitated just inside the revolving doors, scanning the lines stretching ten and fifteen deep to the telegraph windows. The hell with it, he thought, and turned to go, only to find the lobby filled with armed men. Their leader, a dirty red-bearded man in a torn army greatcoat, roared at the crowd to put up their hands. One of his minions fired a rifle shot into the ceiling, and bits of brick and plaster showered down.

A guard burst from a side room, revolver drawn, and fired a single shot that struck the red-bearded man in the forehead. Evans dived for the floor as the bandits opened fire. He took shelter under a metal writing table until the shooting stopped. He had the impression of bodies everywhere and blood streaking the marble floor. Ragged soldiers herded people through the main doors, and Evans was pushed out with them into the brilliant sunlight. Five of the gunmen ran to the edge of the steps to form an impromptu firing squad. Someone cursed the terrified people as they were shoved against the wall. Everything was confusion, and Evans groped for his passport, only to be clubbed down from behind—undoubtedly saving his life. A volley of rifle fire smashed into the crowd, and raving like demons, the bandits thrust another group against the wall.

A lorry careened into view, and khaki-clad soldiers poured from it to kneel and fire again and again as the bandits broke and ran. Someone eased Evans onto a stretcher, and he fainted.

That evening Evans sat by himself in his hotel room and finished a bottle of bootleg vodka while staring at the newspaper headlines that had styled the abortive Bolshevik rebellion in which he had almost been killed the July Days Uprising.

For the first time in his life he had come face-to-face with death, with the imminence of extinction. He remembered his paralyzing fear, so strong that he had not been able to speak. Was his father right after all? Was he just not worth a damn? What the hell had he accomplished in his life? He was nothing more than a minor functionary in a useless bureaucracy with a record so poor that only his father's influence prevented his being fired in disgrace. And the old man was interested only in protecting the family name. For Christ's sake, he thought, why the devil couldn't he ever do anything right? Every time he tried . . . The army was the answer, he knew. He had been a damned good National Guard officer . . . He'd send that telegram tomorrow. He'd change his damned name if he had to, but he was getting the hell out of the Diplomatic Service with its constant paper shuffling and scraping and bowing. . . .

The great summer offensive was smashed. German and Austrian troops marched through Russian lines as entire regiments threw down their rifles and walked away. On July 6 the coalition government fell on a vote of no confidence. The following day Kerensky, ever the able politician, formed a Government of Salvation of the Revolution. By deft maneuvering, he managed to eliminate reactionary influence, and the new government became entirely Socialist in composition. Inevitably rumors sprang up that Kerensky had caused the offensive to fail in order to bring down the government and put the Socialists into power. Whether true or not, the lines were now clearly drawn between the Socialist left wing and the democratic parties of the middle.

The new government moved swiftly to establish its authority and root out opposition. The death penalty was restored in the army. Leon Trotsky was arrested during a speech in Petrograd, and many revolutionary leaders left the country. Lenin was reported to have despaired of revolution in Russia and fled to Finland.

In late October Evans received a hand-delivered letter from Peter

Boyd asking him to return to Petrograd. Probably to replace someone drafted into the army, he decided. Happy to leave Moscow, he informed the consul general and packed his bags.

The train was two hours late. The Kursk and Nizhni-Novgorod Station was clamorous with whistles, shouts and the scream of air brakes and steam being vented. The place was a madhouse of confusion. Another of the interminable strikes was in progress, and exhausted supervisory personnel struggled to keep the trains running. Troops of various political persuasions, some in uniform, others in civilian clothing with armbands or cockades, eyed each other with suspicion and the civilians with contempt.

An embassy chauffeur met him at the Nicholas Station in Petrograd and led the way to a touring car parked in the Alexander Square. A militiaman started toward them, looking suspicious, but twin American flags mounted on the fenders deterred him from closer inspection.

"Bastards," the chauffeur muttered as he edged the automobile through the crowds. Evans saw the great equestrian statue in the square. Peter Boyd had once pointed out that Alexander II, known as the Tsar-Liberator for freeing the serfs, was astride the monstrous, rearing horse that represented Russia.

"Look at the reins, old boy. They aren't much bigger than a girl's hair ribbon. The horse can be guided only if the reins are intact, and that requires an alert and sensitive hand."

Evans had forgotten how dreary Petrograd could be in autumn. Thick mists flowed in from the Gulf of Finland and filled the city with damp cotton wool. The embassy seemed unchanged, even to the single, unarmed marine guard on the gate. But inside, it was a different story. The place swarmed with American uniforms, evenly divided between army and Red Cross. The middle-aged, lackadaisical receptionist had been replaced by an efficient young man, who guided him to the second floor. The wall between two offices had been knocked out, and two secretaries sat outside, pounding battered Underwood typewriters. Evans cleared his throat twice before one looked up.

"I'm William—"

"Yes, Mr. Evans. You were expected an hour ago. Wait over there." She motioned toward a stiff-backed chair and disappeared into an inner office. The typist continued to ignore him. The secretary bustled out. "He can spare five minutes, no more."

"Well, well," Boyd boomed, grinning from ear to ear as Evans was shown in. "It's damned good to see you, Bill! What sexual misadventures did you manage in Moscow?"

Evans snorted. "Absolutely none. Too busy. Who's the dragon guarding your door?"

"That, my friend, is Miss Belinda Matthews. She arrived in June. Watches me like a hawk to make certain the State Department gets its full quota of my attention."

"She says you can spare me five minutes. From what?" Evans looked at the carpeted office with its official portrait of President Wilson, cream-colored silk wall coverings and rich Turkestan carpeting.

"Ah, you poor innocent lamb, great changes afoot while you were vacationing in Moscow. Great changes now that the USA is in the war to save the world for democracy! For one thing, I am now Major Peter Boyd, United States Army."

"A promotion!"

"The army finally recognized my superior talents. Enough bragging. I've got a new job for you, one for which you are uniquely qualified."

"If you think I'm going back to the Tauride Palace to listen to those nitwits in the Duma again—"

Boyd held up a hand. "Interesting work, I assure you. Besides, they call themselves the Provisional Government these days. Want some coffee?" Evans shook his head.

"When the tsar abdicated in March"—Boyd plopped down in his chair—"the British government expressed a strong interest in his welfare and that of his family. After all, George the Fifth and Nicholas the Second are related."

"So are George and Kaiser Bill," Evans observed.

"True enough. The kaiser, by the way, has also expressed concern over his cousin's welfare. But in any event, Kerensky assured both London and Berlin that the Romanovs would be well looked after. They then began negotiations with the British to send the tsar into exile."

Evans nodded. "I picked up that much on the grapevine." For a moment he did not hear what Boyd was saying, remembering the relief he had felt at the news. It had done much to ease his mind about Olga's safety.

". . . family was held all summer at Tsarskoye Selo while Kerensky maneuvered to get them out of the country. Two weeks ago the British learned that the tsar, his family and servants all had been shipped off to Siberia for safekeeping."

"Siberia! For Christ's sake. Where?"

"A town called Tobolsk, on the Irtysh River. Kerensky told the British ambassador he was afraid the Petrograd Soviet might just decide to try the tsar on its own and shoot him. If it came to a showdown, Kerensky would have no choice but to give in. He claims that each time he tried to get the family out, the soviet got wind of it and blocked him."

"The family is safe then?"

Boyd looked troubled. "As far as anyone knows, yes. But Kerensky's government is damned shaky. His insistence on continuing the war may have helped the Allies, but it's killing him at home. Whoever replaces him will be even more radical. Knowing this, King George has become anxious about his royal cousin since they disappeared into

Siberia, and possibly feels a bit guilty as well that he did not insist that his Government bring the Royal family out before this. Of course, the Liberal and Labour parties would have resisted strenuously anything to do with assuring the welfare of a deposed monarch, especially one with his reputation, deserved or otherwise.

"So the Prime Minister, Lloyd George, can't be involved directly in expressing concern for the tsar. He has asked President Wilson to send someone to visit the family in Siberia. Then if anything can be done to bring them out . . ." Boyd shrugged. "He's relying on Wilson's humanitarian nature, of course.

"Wilson agreed, reluctantly. Ever since 1914 he's made it clear that he sees this as a war between democracy and autocracy. It's plain enough that he was embarrassed by the possibility of Russia as an ally or we might have gotten into the war sooner. In fact, I've heard there were some pretty lively celebrations in Washington, the day Nicholas abdicated."

Boyd sucked at his cigar and exhaled a long cloud of smoke. "With that as background then, the ambassador wants you to visit them."

Evans felt a thrill of excitement at the thought of seeing Olga once more. But he decided to move cautiously. "Why me?"

The telephone jangled, and with a grimace Boyd lifted it just long enough to break the connection. "Miss Belinda," he said with a snort. "Telling me your five minutes are up." He grinned and continued. "I convinced the ambassador that you're uniquely qualified. You know the family personally and will be the best judge of their condition. By the way, he's received favorable reports of your work in Moscow."

Evans accepted the compliment with a smirk, thinking that he'd do anything, go just about anywhere to get the hell out of Moscow and away from that damned desk.

An irate Belinda Matthews poked her head in. "You *were* due to see Colonel Akers at ten. It is now ten-oh-five."

Boyd sighed. "Miss Matthews, I have told you a thousand times that when I lift the hook, it means I do not wish to be disturbed. Colonel Akers will just have to wait or, better yet, come back another time."

"Well, if your friend had been on time, we would not—"

"That will be all, Matthews," Boyd roared, and the door slammed. "Goddamned woman will drive me crazy. Best argument I ever saw against women's suffrage."

That evening they had dinner together at the Hotel Europe, where the kitchen and service were a shadow of their prerevolutionary best. Boyd brought along cigars and brandy, and after dinner the waiter drew the curtains on their private alcove. Boyd poured the brandy and handed Evans a cigar.

"What do you hear from Natalia?" he asked.

Evans used the excuse of lighting the cigar to cover his surprise. "Natalia? Nothing, why?"

Boyd dropped a packet of letters on the table. Each was addressed to him in Natalia's handwriting and postmarked Stockholm. "What are these?" Evans asked.

Boyd shrugged. "They've been piling up in the embassy mail room." He drew on the cigar. "All over between you two?"

"Damn it, Pete, there was never anything there to begin with."

"Is that why you told the mail room not to forward her letters?"

"Look here," Evans snapped in exasperation, "if you're so damned concerned about her, why the devil don't you do something about it? I know you're soft on her."

Boyd poured another brandy. "I tried. I even went to Stockholm a month ago. No dice. She's in love with you and fooling herself that you are in love with her."

"Well, God damn it, I'm not! What the devil do I have to do to make her understand that simple fact!"

"You might try telling her."

They finished their brandy in awkward silence, and when the waiter knocked, they both were grateful for the interruption. Afterward they compared conditions in Petrograd and Moscow and talked about Evans's trip. Neither mentioned Natalia again.

The square in front of the Finland Station was packed; red banners hung from every lamppost, and a steady buzz rose from the crowd. Former Captain Nikolai Khristoforovich Sheremetiev's company pushed their way through the good-natured mob with a minimum of shoving and cursing and entered the station. If possible, it was even more crowded inside. People, mostly workers in dirty clothing or soldiers in slovenly uniforms, stood about everywhere. They had climbed onto everything that offered a vantage point, including the armored trains on the side tracks. Only the single rail line that began at Åbo, in Finland, and ran through Helsingfors to Petrograd had been kept clear.

An officer wearing the armband of the Provisional Government over his tsarist cavalry uniform bustled up. He motioned to a line of baggage wagons.

"Be obliged if you'd take your men and make certain none of this rabble pushes through into the reserved area." He glanced keenly at Sheremetiev, perhaps noting his military bearing. "I say, what rank were you before you exchanged your uniform? Sergeant major?"

Sheremetiev smiled. "Same as yours, Captain. I served in the Vologda Regiment. Before that the Guards Rifles. Three years of front-line duty."

The officer gave him a frigid stare and motioned around the platform. "Must feel right at home then. Plenty of Bolsheviks all about you." He went off without another word, and Sheremetiev smirked. He had encountered that attitude since the day he had joined the tsar's army, first as an up-from-the-ranks officer—what the Americans called a mustang—and now because he had shed his officer's shoulder boards as symbols of repression.

Sheremetiev distributed his company smartly. His shoulder boards might be gone, but he hadn't modified his attitude toward discipline in the slightest. Bolsheviks were they!

He had received orders from the soviet to take his company to the Finland Station and assure that order was kept. There had been no information on who, what or why. Now it seemed that some political dignitary was arriving. A leftist if the profusion of red banners was any indication.

"They say," he overheard one man telling another, "that the Germans gave him an entire railway car and sent him from Switzerland to Sweden."

What nonsense! Sheremetiev snorted.

The train was due in at six in the evening, but darkness had long since fallen and his men were restless and tired when the signal changed from green to red to indicate a train approaching. A curious buzz of expectation ran through the station, and from outside in the square there rose a deep roar of huzzahs.

The train appeared at the bend and slid into the station amid clouds of steam and the squeal of air brakes. Sheremetiev passed the word for his men to look sharp. The crowd jostled forward, mixing hostility and good nature. The door to a third-class carriage a few paces away slid open. Cheers, shouts and boos filled the station as a balding, stoutish man with a goatee and glasses and dressed in a cheap suit stepped out and stood blinking at the crowd as if he did not know what to make of his reception. He stood like that for a moment, then shook hands with each of the men who came forward to meet him. The band struck up the "Marseillaise," and Sheremetiev was amused to see the man's chin come up, his back straighten and a grim smile crease his face.

As the music ended and before anyone could stop him, Vladimir Ilyich Lenin sprang onto a baggage wagon and raised both arms. The cheering redoubled, and he turned, arms spread as if to catch the cheers, and waited until they died away.

"Comrades!" he thundered, and his voice echoed through the immense structure. "The Petrograd Soviet has betrayed you!"

Silence swept the crowd, and Sheremetiev stared in open-mouthed astonishment at this balding, fat man who had sat out the war safe and sound in neutral Switzerland. A swelling, angry buzzing swamped the few half-hearted cheers. Lenin ignored both.

"The Petrograd Soviet is playing into the hands of the Provisional Government, which is composed of capitalist lackeys and members of the old regime!" he bellowed. "We must take power into our own hands! The soldiers and workers must take power at the point of a gun!"

And which are you, Sheremetiev thought sarcastically, soldier or worker?

"I have only one program! The Bolshevik party has only one program!" Lenin roared. "And that is to establish a dictatorship of soldiers, workers and peasants! To that end, we must destroy the Provisional Government! We must take control of the Petrograd Soviet!"

This last was greeted with a fierce roar, and the crowd surged toward the baggage wagon. Sheremetiev snapped an order, bayoneted rifles came down and the crowd paused, uncertain.

"Armed workers must run the factories," Lenin went on. "Armed peasants must take control of the land and build collective farms! Armed soldiers must turn their backs on the so-called enemy and work for the revolution. They must persuade the soldiers of other nations that their true enemy is capitalism and not the Russian people! There can be no deviation!"

The cheering was continuous now, the deep, roaring, animallike sound of a crowd in frenzy. In spite of the confusion, the fear of the mob and the noise that made it nearly impossible to think, Sheremetiev wondered if Russia hadn't found a leader after all, one with the intelligence to realize that only single-minded pursuit of clearly stated goals would allow the revolution to succeed. He did not like the call for a unilateral end to the war, but Sheremetiev knew that unless it was ended, the revolution was doomed.

"There can be no compromise of any kind between the Bolsheviks and any other party! We must take power!"

"He's right!" Sheremetiev found himself shouting.

The journey from Petrograd to Tobolsk was monotonous in the extreme. For days the train rumbled through mile after mile of dark forest lashed by rain. During the day the carriage was overheated and the windows were fastened shut. At night the porter put the fire out and the temperature dropped to near freezing. Russian trains habitually traveled no faster than thirty-five miles an hour, and Evans was learning first hand how frustrating that speed could be in the vast Russian space.

Days later the train crawled into Tyumen on the Tura River where the track ended; to reach Tobolsk, he had to transfer to a river steamer which took a further two days to travel the two hundred miles downstream. The captain, pleased to have a passenger able to afford first-class passage, kept him entertained every moment.

"See, my friend, there. That nice-looking village we are passing. See how prosperous it appears to be? Look at the window boxes. Just count them. If you would measure the wealth of a Russian village, count window boxes and pigs. Well, this village is Pokrovskoye. The name would mean nothing to you, my American friend, but it was the home of that devil's spawn Rasputin." The captain spat over the side.

It was late afternoon when the steamer approached the wharf at Tobolsk. The captain studied the black sky and the dull red furnace to the west, shivered and reminded Evans they would be sailing at noon the following day. "Otherwise, you will have to wait a week for the next steamer." Evans had already resolved to stay at least a week, using the steamer's infrequent visits as his excuse. Buoyed by the anticipation of seeing Olga again, he hurried toward the village.

The governor's house, where the royal family was being held, loomed through the darkness like a North Atlantic iceberg in the fog. Evans stared at the white two-story structure fringed with balconies. A plank fence had been thrown closely about the house, and a single unfriendly guard stood before it, rifle propped against a tree.

The guard refused to look at his papers. "It is forbidden to enter. Go away."

Evans pointed to the signature. "Kerensky, you fool. Do you know who he is?"

The guard snorted at the name but picked up his rifle and sauntered through the gate. A thin rain began to fall, and Evans took what shelter he could beneath a tree.

A sergeant appeared finally, holding an umbrella and muttering to himself. He ignored Evans's introduction and snatched the letter, turning it this way and that to catch the meager light.

"In there." He hooked a thumb. Evans stamped up the path, struggling to keep his temper under control.

The front door was open, and leaves and other debris covered the marble floor. Two soldiers lounged on the stairs, their rifles leaning against the far wall. They regarded Evans's rain-soaked figure without curiosity. The house, or what he could see of it, was filthy. At one time rich hangings had covered the windows; these were now tattered at best, and most of them lay in moldering heaps. A priceless Oriental carpet had been slashed and kicked aside.

On the first floor a servant answered his knock and returned with the tsar. Shocked at his appearance, Evans could barely mumble a response to Nicholas's fervent greeting. There were deep lines running from nose to mouth, and his eyes seemed to have sunk into their sockets. His once-dark hair was uniformly gray, and he wore country corduroys and soft boots run down at the heels. Yet Nicholas was as ramrod-stiff as Evans remembered, and as courteous. He led him into the parlor, and Olga gave a small cry of surprise and pleasure. Evans found himself grinning like a schoolboy.

"My dears, you remember Mr. William Hughes Evans," Nicholas said by way of introduction, "the American we had the pleasure of rescuing from anarchists last autumn? Well, he has come to visit us again."

Evans found it hard to focus on anyone but Olga. She seemed in glowing health and more beautiful than ever in a worn frock and knitted sweater. She smiled and shyly took his hand, her fingers applying extra pressure; then, as if reluctant to let him go, she half turned and called, "Tatiana, Marie, say hello to Mr. Evans."

Those first minutes were a confusion of impressions. When Alexandra entered the room with the aid of a cane, he realized that her physical deterioration was even more shocking than her husband's. Tatiana helped her mother to the table and poured a cup of tea, then smoothed back a lock of her white hair. Olga was still holding his hand, and he forced himself to stop gaping at the tsarina. Then Anastasia appeared, and immediately the dreary atmosphere improved. She saw Evans and, with a glad cry, ran across the room to receive his bow.

"The fairy princess," Evans managed, recalling their private joke, and she giggled.

"Please, Mr. Evans," Nicholas invited, "be seated and tell us about yourself. We receive so little news. How long are you permitted to stay?"

Permitted? he thought. "At least a week, Your Majesty—"

Nicholas expressed amusement at the honorific. "Comrade, please. But I am astonished that you were able to arrange so lengthy a visit. Our guards have never allowed anyone to remain even overnight—" The tsar broke off as a heavy knock sounded in the next room and a booted soldier stamped in and glared at Evans.

"Citizen Romanov, I have been sent to tell you that your exercise period has been shortened to one hour every other day."

Tatiana started to object angrily, but her mother put a hand on her arm. Nicholas stared at the man, saying nothing, until he shuffled his feet and withdrew. The family exchanged anguished glances, and Evans was acutely embarrassed.

"I take it this is not an unusual experience," he growled. "I'm sorry if my presence here makes things worse, but I must tell you that the British government has asked my government to intervene. I am to make a full and confidential report." Evans realized the total inadequacy of his words. "You may be assured that Kerensky will not interfere. He is waiting for sizable loans from the United States, which will not be approved until my report is received," he lied.

They talked for two hours, Evans asking the questions he had prepared and reviewed with Boyd and the ambassador. Nicholas told him that at first they had been very well treated. The guards, in contrast with the militiamen who had occupied the grounds of the Alexander Palace, had been courteous and considerate. But starting in October, they were replaced by younger men, workers for the most part from Moscow or Petrograd, who lacked the discipline of the older front-line soldiers.

Nicholas described the conditions of their imprisonment in dispassionate terms, and Evans was impressed by the picture that emerged of the tsar as a man intensely weary of public life and power, convinced that he had been betrayed by the very people to whom he had dedicated his life.

"I must ask Your Majesty"—Evans consulted his notes to make certain of his phrasing—"whether or not you would be willing to return to the throne in your own right or as regent for your son."

Nicholas did not answer at once. He dragged his eyes away from the meager fire, and for a moment Evans saw once more the Tsar of All the Russias. "If asked to do so by unanimous vote of the Provisional Government, of course. But only the Provisional Government, you understand. They usurped my position, and so they must restore it." He was silent for a moment. "Chaos reigns in Russia. Surely they must see that they will have to restore the monarchy as the only institution that commands the respect of all the people."

Evans had difficulty concealing his smile. Nicholas was either more foolish than he had thought possible or so completely isolated from events that he had no conception of what he was saying. He sought to bring the conversation back to conditions within the governor's house, and Nicholas described the petty annoyances instigated by the two political commissars who had arrived earlier in the month.

One in particular, Alexander Nikolsky, was quite hostile to the entire family; he no longer allowed them to cross the muddy street to the church, and he kept their government allowance, which forced them to rely on personal funds to buy food. Their original jailer, Colonel Kobylinsky, a trusted official of the Provisional Government, had become their chief defender, even though his power had been reduced to insignificance.

The clock had just struck eight o'clock when a soldier stamped into the room without knocking and announced the interview ended.

"We are not finished," Evans snapped.

"You are. Come with me."

Evans hesitated. Nicholas's face was carefully noncommittal. He risked a quick glance at Olga, but she had looked away. Tatiana was watching him with open curiosity. He stood up reluctantly, loath to give in but realizing that he would make it only harder on the family by refusing.

Evans bowed. "My apologies, Your Majesties. Perhaps we can

66

continue our discussion tomorrow." He shook hands with Nicholas and bent to kiss Alexandra's hand. Her glance softened for a moment, and she whispered her thanks. He bowed over the hand of each of the grand duchesses, lingering a moment longer over Olga's, and looked up in time to see tears in her eyes. His withdrawal was a bit unsteady.

The soldier led him down the stairs and along a passageway to the back, where an office had been established in what appeared to be a disused pantry. In contrast with the rest of the house, the room had an air of military neatness about its sparse furnishings. A tall, spare man wearing a curious black leather jacket motioned him to a chair.

"Mr. William Evans, I am Commissar Alexander Nikolsky. My apologies for not greeting you on your arrival. I was in the town on business. I understand that you are here as a representative of the Kerensky government to—"

"I beg your pardon, Commissar Nikolsky, I represent the president of the United States of America." He handed Nikolsky his credentials and his passport from the Provisional Government. The commissar read the letter and barely glanced at the passport.

"The interview cannot be continued," Nikolsky said. He tapped the pile of papers together and stared at Evans.

"I don't understand, Commissar. My papers state my mission very clearly. The authorizations—"

"Are signed by officials of the *former* government and are worthless. The Provisional Government ceased to exist two days ago. It was replaced by a new Soviet of Workers, Peasants and Soldiers. Under the guidance of the Bolshevik party, the soviet is now the sole government of Russia."

"Bolshevik!" Evans exclaimed. "How can that be? The All-Russian Congress of Soviets was elected—"

"The All-Russian Congress of Soviets," Nikolsky told him in a frigid voice, "was merely a tool of the capitalist warmongers. The Bolshevik party, seeing clearly its duty to safeguard the revolution, has deposed the congress and assumed control of the nation. Your credentials from the Provisional Government are no longer valid, and you must leave Tobolsk immediately."

"I will like hell—"

Nikolsky smirked. "Mr. Evans, my position allows me wide discretion. Leave of your own free will, or I will have you arrested and thrown into prison." He paused for emphasis. "As poor as communications are, you will probably remain there for a long time unless, of course, something happens to you which it would be beyond my control to prevent. . . ."

His voice trailed off, leaving Evans in absolutely no doubt of his meaning. For a moment he was stricken with shame at the idea that he could be threatened so easily, but then hadn't he been warned in Petrograd not to endanger himself or the family? This man Nikolsky was in charge at the governor's house and perhaps in the town as well.

He tried one more time. "I have not yet seen the the Tsarevich Alexei. You cannot deny me the opportunity—"

Nikolsky shrugged. "I can and will. There is no longer a tsarevich. He, like his father, is merely another citizen, one under grave suspicion of infamous crimes against the Russian people."

"A thirteen-year-old boy?" Evans cried in amazement. "Of what crimes could he possibly be guilty?"

Nikolsky refused to answer, and Evans thought furiously. He might well be in complete control of the guard, although there was another commissar and the colonel of the guard regiment, Kobylinsky, to consider. Balanced against that was the fact that Evans was a diplomatic representative of the United States, protected by diplomatic immunity, and as arbitrary as the Bolsheviks were, he did not think it likely that Nikolsky would dare imprison or harm him. But his hesitation had been sufficient.

Nikolsky yanked the door open and summoned a guard detail. Two soldiers came into the office and pushed Evans into the corridor where the others waited, rifles sloped. Evans rounded on the commissar, but a soldier menaced him with rifle butt.

Evans stepped back, hands held palms up. "All right, all right. I'll leave, but my government will register a very strong protest in Petrograd, I can assure you!"

Nikolsky turned his back, and Evans was bundled out of the house without further ceremony.

Tatiana moved away from the window as soon as she saw the guards. They had been drinking again, and if they saw her, it would mean a chorus of obscene songs or a bottle thrown at the window. She sank down on the sprung bed and stared with distaste at the room she shared with Olga. Governor's house indeed. The governor of the Cannibal Islands perhaps. Tatiana wished she could cultivate her sister's indifference to their living conditions. But on the other hand, she could endure the insults and taunts that sent Olga weeping to Mama or Papa.

The room was icy, and she drew the worn blanket about the fur coat she wore day and night. Today was the Feast of the Purification of the Virgin Mary, the beginning of February. Three more endless months before the snows disappeared. The parlor would be warmer but crowded. Here at least she enjoyed a measure of privacy. And tonight was bath night! Thank God! Tatiana found being allowed to take a bath only once a week hardest of all to bear. Daily dabs of cold water just weren't sufficient. It wasn't the thought of the icy water—Papa had insisted on cold baths when they were children—it was the inadequacy of it all. She was certain she stank abominably, and all the perfume had been used up well before the end of November.

The letter from Lili Dehn lay on the bed beside her. Tatiana had reread it so often that she had memorized every line. It was the third letter from Lili since she had been released from prison in July and allowed to leave Russia. If only she could see her again, Tatiana thought. Just to talk to her. She missed her more than anything else. The envelope's postmark had been cut away by the censor, but he had stupidly left the English stamp attached. She thought of Lili, probably at Cowes, where they all had visited Uncle Teddy—the late king Edward—years ago. For Tatiana, everything magical was embodied in her concept of England.

An uncomfortable trickling sensation between her legs caused her to swear, using words picked up from the guards. "Not now," she said with a groan. Her period wasn't due to start for two more days. Why did it have to come early this month? The final straw was the queasy sensation in her intestines that told her the cramps would start within the hour.

Still swearing, she rummaged through her suitcase for the carefully washed and preserved rags. She hesitated with one hand on the door latch as she heard boots in the corridor. One of the guards, in defiance of the rules, was using their lavatory again. For an instant the frustrations of past months and the unfairness of it all overwhelmed her, and she had to press her back to the door and bite her lips to keep from bursting into tears. When she was certain he had gone past, she pulled up her dress, dabbed with a dampened cloth at the blood, then secured the clean rag with straps salvaged from a corset she had given up wearing months ago. Tatiana went to the window, fighting back tears.

The boots tramped past again, then hesitated. She turned to see the handle move and the door open.

The bearded, unwashed man who stood there was one of the newest and youngest of the replacements. He leered at her and stepped into the room. Tatiana started to order him out, but he grinned even more and made a suggestive motion with his hands. His crude insult was too much, and her temper blazed. Without thinking, she screamed. The soldier jumped, and so gratifying was his reaction that she screamed again. The soldier panicked and ran to her, both hands flapping in terror. Tatiana screamed again.

"Please, Your Highness," he pleaded, "I meant nothing . . . please don't scream again." He tried to slip a hand over her mouth, but Tatiana got her teeth fastened onto his fingers and bit hard. He yelled as two guards burst in just ahead of her father and Pierre Gilliard. The latter took one look and flew at the boy in a rage. Gilliard was a frail and rather small man, but it took both soldiers and Nicholas to pull him away. Tatiana, now appalled at what she had started, saw that one of the boy's front teeth had been knocked out.

Everyone was talking at once when her father shouted for silence. Old habits die hard, and the three guards snapped smartly to attention. Before Nicholas could say a word, Commissar Alexander Nikolsky appeared in the doorway.

"This uproar will cease instantly," he shouted unnecessarily, and turned to the young guard. "Comrade, tell me what has—"

"I will handle this, Comrade Nikolsky." Colonel Eugene Kobylinsky pushed into the room. For a moment he ignored the startled Nikolsky as he took in Tatiana's flushed face and the soldier's bleeding finger and mouth.

"Comrade Gabvev, you are under arrest. You are confined—"

"Colonel," Nikolsky snapped, "I am handling this situation."

"—to the barracks until further notice," Koblyinsky finished without pause. He hooked a thumb at the door, but the other two guards hesitated.

"What are you waiting for?" he demanded, and with sullen expressions they dragged the soldier out.

"Commissar Nikolsky"—Kobylinsky smiled—"unless you have orders to replace me as commander of the guard detachment, you will not interfere again. Is that understood?"

He did not wait for an answer but gave Tatiana a half bow. "I apologize for the behavior of my guards, Comrade Tatiana Nikolaevna. A hearing will be conducted tomorrow morning. Please hold yourself in readiness to testify." He nodded once to Nicholas and went out.

"Were you hurt, Comrade Tatiana Nikolaevna?" Nikolsky asked. "I will send for the doctor." But his voice was cold.

It was too late to undo what she had done. Perhaps the guards would be less inclined to take liberties now. "I am unharmed," she snapped. "The other guards arrived in time. I do not need the doctor."

The man bowed. "As you wish." He turned to Nicholas, standing pale and silent inside the door. "Citizen Romanov, I have warned you before about allowing your daughters to incite the guards. They are far—"

Tatiana shrieked and flew at him, but he caught her easily and tossed her to Nicholas, who also spoke quickly to Gilliard.

"I did nothing of the kind," she screamed in genuine anger. "He used our lavatory, then came into my room and attacked me! Do not blame us because you are unable to discipline your *mmmf*—"

Nicholas clamped a strong hand across her mouth. "I apologize for my daughter's outburst, Comrade Commissar. She is overwrought."

Nikolsky nodded grudgingly, then glared at Gilliard. "You, sir, will go too far one of these days with your interference."

Gilliard drew himself up. "I am Swiss and not a Russian citizen, sir. Have care with your threats."

* * *

70

When the others had left, the tsar enfolded his daughter in his arms. "Did he touch you?" Nicholas asked.

Tatiana shook her head. Nicholas held her tightly, sensing her fear. Tatiana had always been strong, he thought, and stubborn, like her mother. Once an idea is fixed, it takes heaven and hell to move it. Was that what went wrong? Alexandra had done everything possible to ensure the succession for their son, even while the best minds in Russia had begged him to liberalize. Only the cunning Rasputin had seen that such steps must be taken with care, lest the people expect too much too soon. His own grandfather, Alexander II, had liberated the serfs, and they had killed him with a bomb. Western nations like England and France, Sweden, Denmark and America had evolved over a thousand years. Yet the revolutionaries demanded democracy in a day. Alexandra's fear of the dark people had, however, pushed her too far in the other direction, and he had been too busy with the war . . . ah, God, it was no good making excuses. It was the children who were suffering for his foolishness.

Tatiana sighed and moved in his arms, breaking his train of thought.

"I'm all right, Papa, really I am."

"You were fortunate the other guards were nearby. I shall ask Colonel Kobylinsky for permission to lock your door during the day, but the soldiers' committee will not agree, I'm afraid."

Nicholas stroked her forehead. "Shall I send one of your sisters in?"

It was significant, Tatiana thought, that he did not suggest her mother, who since the start of winter had withdrawn more and more until she was silent and unheeding most of the day. She shook her head.

"No, thank you. I would prefer to rest alone." She kissed her father, and he smiled and went to the door.

"I will be in the parlor, darling girl, if you need me."

As soon as the door closed behind him, Tatiana flew to lock it securely, then ran back to rummage under the mattress for the small cut she had made in the underside. She groped through the rough stuffing until she found the cloth bag and drew out the Browning pistol Lili had pressed into her hand just before she was arrested after their escape attempt in May.

"Keep this, Tatiana," she whispered. "Never let anyone know you have it. You are the most level-headed."

Tatiana had been apprehensive about the gun until now. All of the tsar's children had been taught to shoot at an early age, but with military rifles and revolvers. She had never even held a pistol before.

Tatiana examined the small weapon. She found a knurled switch on the bottom of the butt and pushed at it with her thumb. A clip containing several shiny brass cartridges slid out. Feeling braver now that the pistol was unloaded, she touched the trigger in a tentative manner. It did not give, and she pulled harder. Exasperated, she saw a small catch on one side and remembered vaguely that the top of the pistol slid back and forth as the gun was fired. Pushing down the catch, she grasped the slide and pulled. It slid back easily enough, and she nearly screamed.

Several minutes passed before her hands stopped shaking enough to continue the examination. A cartridge had flipped from the breech when she pulled the slide back. If the safety catch had not been on, the weapon would have fired. Tatiana lay back on the bed, frightened half to death at what might have happened. For a moment the temptation to throw the pistol away was strong, but she forced herself to continue. Soldiers used guns all the time. If a fool like that guard can learn, so can I, she told herself.

It took only a few moments to discover how to replace the cartridge that had fallen out of the chamber and reinsert the magazine. She cocked it and put the safety on. The next problem was where to hide the weapon. A few moments' thought suggested her person as the safest and handiest place. Not once in all the months of imprisonment had the women been subjected to a personal search. She hefted the pistol; it was heavy but compact and certainly much lighter than the Nagant revolver her father and Alexei's sailor bodyguard Nagorny had used to teach them to shoot.

Tatiana unbuttoned her dress and slipped it into the waistband of her pantaloons, but when she stood up, the outline was visible. As she removed the pistol, the first cramp struck, and she gasped and sat down quickly, hugging herself to contain the pain. When it passed, she took a deep breath. This was going to be a bad siege, she thought, worse than the diarrhea that had infected them all after they had arrived and that Dr. Botkin had blamed on impure water.

But the monthly affliction gave her an idea. She pulled up her dress and slipped the automatic into the top of her stocking. The pistol wobbled under the single garter, and she added a second. The two elastic bands held it securely.

Tatiana walked about the room, watching herself in the mirror, but could detect no sign of the pistol. At each step the cold metal brushed against her skin. It would soon rub a raw spot on her thigh; but that could not be helped, and she would get used to it in time. Never again would she be without some means of protecting herself, and her family, if it came to that.

Comrade Nikolai Khristoforovich Sheremetiev, hunched over his bowl of cabbage soup and chunk of black bread in the refectory of the Smolny Institute, ignored the discordant chorus of shouts and clatter—

of conversation surrounding him. The bread was full of weevils, and no amount of knocking on the table would drive them out. Some had been in the bread so long they had died. The one or two wilted cabbage leaves half-submerged in the watery soup lent an illusion of taste. But at least the room was reasonably warm, and that alone made him better off than the majority of Petrograd's citizens. More than once he thought of the comfortable kitchen in Tatrov and his mother's tiled stove. Exploiters, oppressors, the party would call his parents, and they would have been right. Yet in such moments as these Sheremetiev wondered what had become of his mother.

He finished the last of the soup and crammed the bread into his mouth, heedless of remaining weevils. He had been on the move for three days and nights now and was exhausted. Never had he been so tired, not even at the front during the worst of the Austrian bombardments. Maria was off at midnight, and the thought warmed him. They had met during the spring at a Left Social Revolutionary party rally, and he had fallen in love with her like a schoolboy. As if personal considerations mattered. The revolution was all—but he had never suspected the depths of comfort a woman's body could provide. In spite of the revolution and the vast amount to be done, the summer and autumn had been a magical idyll, and he had never been happier.

"Ah, there you are, Comrade Sheremetiev," a man called from the head of the stairs. "Come up, come up! Commissar Tetchov is searching everywhere for you." Sheremetiev groaned.

He found Tetchov, one of the many assistants to Leon Trotsky, minister of war and security for the Petrograd Soviet, shouting into one telephone as he banged down another. He listened for a moment and hung that one up as well. "Ah, there you are, Nikolai Khristoforovich. I know you've been at it for two days—"

"Three days," Sheremetiev corrected.

"Well, then three days. We must all make sacrifices for the revolution. I myself haven't left this desk for a week. In any event, I've a report that the Third Hussars Machine Gun Battalion guarding the telegraph exchange is proving uncooperative. They needed to be persuaded to turn it over to the Commissariat of Communications. Take a squad and persuade them."

Christ in heaven, Sheremetiev thought. A machine-gun battalion! But he nodded and went out, knowing that to protest would do no good at all. If he refused, he would be sent to a labor battalion.

Sheremetiev forced a way through the mass of people crowded into the Smolny. They swarmed through the halls and infested the dining rooms, chattering hysterically. They did nothing but talk. Ask them to do anything, and they were too busy or "engaged on some other task, Comrade, very sorry. Ask Masha over there; he's done nothing for a week now, thank you." If Kerensky should manage to rally just one of the dozen counterrevolutionary challengers and march on Petrograd,

God help them all. This rabble could never hope to stand against trained soldiers.

Sheremetiev found his squad waiting in the courtyard near the playground equipment. How appropriate, he thought wryly. Hardly any of them looked over eighteen. The Smolny, originally a convent, had been a fashionable girls' school until the Petrograd Soviet had kicked them out and set up their myriads of interminably wrangling committees in opposition to the Provisional Government. The Petrograd Soviet was now dominated by the Bolsheviks, and the day following Lenin's speech at the Finland Station Sheremetiev had filed his own application for membership in the party.

Sheremetiev had only lately begun to understand the dynamics of the Bolshevik system of administration. The hundreds of committees maintained the illusion of self-government and kept the masses busy wrangling while a very few select individuals like Tetchov did the real work under orders from an executive committee of real leaders such as Trotsky, with self-granted, unlimited powers.

He inspected his fourteen men, was surprised to find two front-line veterans among them and not surprised to discover that three of the boys did not even know how to load their rifles. Shaking his head, he commandeered two armored cars and loaded the squad, making sure that each man wore a red armband.

The chauffeur was an ex-tram driver who seemed determined to make up for years of crawling along the crowded streets. He drove at breakneck speed, a dangling cigarette showering powdery ash on his clothing and half the cab. The interior stank of stale smoke, vodka and unwashed bodies.

As they passed the Cathedral of Saint Isaac, he had the driver slow and turn off his driving lights. The streetlamps had been shut off in half-hearted compliance with blackout regulations against German Zeppelin raids, but the telephone exchange was well lit. Sheremetiev could see the sandbagged, barbed-wire-encircled machine-gun emplacements very clearly. Sharpshooters were visible in the windows of the top story.

During the ride Sheremetiev had heard the boys boasting of how they would take the telephone exchange for the revolution. The sight of the machine guns ended that talk. Even so, he gave orders to unload all rifles and placed the ammunition in the care of the two veterans. He then sent the second armored car through the side streets to block Pochtamtsky Pereulok just in case the Horse Guards decided to leave their barracks and take a hand. When all were in position, he rummaged about for a white cloth, and leaving one of the veterans in charge, he started toward the barricade, waving the flag.

As he approached, he saw that a heated argument was in progress between an officer and two soldiers, who, nevertheless, kept the barrel of their machine gun pointed firmly in his direction.

Several steps short of the sandbags he shouted, "Comrades, I appeal to you in the name of the revolution to join us!"

"Who's us?" the young officer said with a sneer. "Get back before I have you shot."

"The Petrograd Soviet!"

"Bolsheviks!" the officer replied scornfully. "We want nothing to do with your sort!"

One of the soldiers began to protest, but Sheremetiev's voice overrode him. "Comrades, the revolution is for all, not for a few. I know. I am a former officer. I was a captain in the Vologda Regiment. I spent three years at the front and was wounded three times."

"We have only your word for that!" the officer shouted.

Were the soldiers listening? Heavy cloud pressed on the city, and the wind whirled paper, cardboard, dirt and God alone knew what else along the streets. Like most of the other city services, the street cleaners had gone on strike to claim their share of the revolution.

"If I, an officer, can understand that all must give way to the revolution, then you as front-line soldiers must know it as well! Haven't we all fought for a free Russia? Now we almost have it. Would you let reactionary generals tear it all away? Who was it that reintroduced the death penalty?"

The hussars began to shout in agreement, and Sheremetiev knew he had them. The officer, too young to understand what was happening, climbed onto the sandbags and shouted for silence. The grizzled soldier who had argued with him stepped casually to one side as if to hear better, then, with a nod and a wink to Sheremetiev, smashed his rifle stock across the young officer's knees. The boy collapsed with a scream, and Sheremetiev winced as the soldier reversed his rifle and drove the bayonet into his chest. Sheremetiev could see the astonishment in the young officer's eyes as he stared at the spiked bayonet protruding from his chest. The soldier grunted and tried to wrench the bayonet out for another stroke, but it had caught in muscle and bone. The boy screamed and thrashed, and the veteran pulled the trigger to blast the bayonet loose. The officer convulsed and died.

Twenty minutes later Sheremetiev, having left half his squad at the telephone exchange, returned to the Smolny to report it secured and the Third Hussars firmly in the Bolshevik camp. Commissar Tetchov, already engrossed in another problem, only nodded, and Sheremetiev took advantage of his preoccupation to escape. Something big was going on, he knew. The rumors had it that the First Constituent Assembly was meeting tonight in the Winter Palace. Armed men were everywhere, not only at the Smolny but throughout the city, and the courtyard was filled with motor vehicles, engine noise and gasoline fumes. The elevator was out of order, so he struggled up the four flights of steps crowded with sleeping or arguing people.

Maria Antipova Galitina was leaning through her counter window to listen to an elderly woman when he entered the large office. Even though it was nearly midnight, the line wound around the room several times and out into the corridor. Several people started to object as he forced his way through but stopped when they saw his holstered service revolver.

Maria Antipova gave him a relieved glance and slammed the window down in the middle of a conversation. The old woman stared at the frosted glass in disbelief, and wails of anguish and angry shouts filled the room. Maria came through a side door, pulling on a warm fur coat and fending off protests and complaints with obscenities.

"Damned cattle," she muttered as they hurried down the steps. "Think I've nothing better to do than wait on them all day. I've been there since seven. Let one of the others take over."

She hadn't arrived until nine, Sheremetiev knew, and her shift didn't end until three in the morning. Obviously she had something on the supervisor. He knew Maria was not averse to taking advantage of her position. The coat she was wearing was ermine. Not surprising in view of the fact that her section controlled the issuance of passports for foreign travel. She took his arm and drew it about her, and when she slipped his hand inside to cup her breast, all his misgivings disappeared. She brushed his cheek with cold lips and pressed his hand tight.

The Kansas City railroad depot was jammed to capacity with men in khaki uniforms. Captain William Hughes Evans had finished his eight-week reserve officer refresher course at Camp Funston and was not looking forward to two weeks' leave at his parents' home in Boston. The sudden orders to report to the War Department in Washington, D.C., had almost seemed a godsend.

The trip from Kansas City to Washington stirred memories of his depressing return to Petrograd the previous November. During his absence Boyd had been transferred to London, and no one seemed greatly interested in his report. The Bolsheviks had taken control of the government, ousting the Constituent Assembly from the Winter Palace by the simple expedient of posting machine guns at the door. At the same time Bolshevik Red Guards in one night had secured the post office, the telephone and telegraph exchanges, the Peter and Paul Fortress and every other building of importance to a government and, as Commissar Nikolsky told him, had simply proclaimed themselves a dictatorship of the people.

Starvation stalked the cities, and the peasants hid food to sell at outrageous prices. People died in the streets of hunger and exposure, and the soviets argued and fought. Banditry was worse than ever. No one dared walk the streets after dark, and the Bolsheviks, afraid of a popular uprising, were disarming the citizenry with house-to-house searches. Burglars and bandits followed the Red Guard units, leaving victimized and murdered people in their wake.

In the last week of December the War Department cabled that his reserve commission, at long last endorsed by Ambassador Francis, had finally been activated at the rank of captain. He had packed and boarded the train at the Finland Station, perfectly happy to be leaving.

His one regret was Olga, but then there was absolutely nothing to be done about her or her family. That had been made plain enough to him. He tried once to see someone in authority in the new government. He sat in a crowded anteroom for two hours before leaving in disgust. They were safe enough, he decided. Nicholas would be banished to an estate somewhere in Siberia and then palmed off into exile after the war.

The weather in Washington was unbelievably beautiful even for the middle of April. The streets were filled with traffic, and the area around the War Department annex near the Potomac was jammed. Temporary clapboard buildings, reminiscent of Camp Funston, had been run up, and a marine sentry saluted and directed him along a muddy path.

Inside, the building already smelled of mold, and even though the windows had been opened wide, it was uncomfortably warm; he could imagine what it would be like in August. He was shown to an office at the rear of the building. A middle-aged lieutenant colonel got right down to business.

"I'm afraid, Captain, this is not a social call. We have a job for you and a change in orders. You are being sent as military attaché to the American consul at Odessa, in southern Russia."

"Ah, for Christ's sake!" he groaned. "Why me? There must be a hundred others better qualified."

The colonel held up a hand. "I'm sorry; but as the saying goes, you're in the army now, and that's where they decided to send you. You're the only one we have with any knowledge or experience of dealing with these people."

"I don't understand what the devil this is all about," Evans told him in exasperation. "I've just spent a year and a half in—"

"It's simple enough, Captain. The Bolsheviks took Russia out of the war when they signed the peace treaty at Brest-Litovsk. That freed God knows how many German divisions for service on the western front. American troops are only now beginning to reach France in any significant numbers. The big push will come this summer, most probably in July. If the Germans can continue to expedite the movement of combat troops to the western front at the same rate as during this past month, even the American Expeditionary Force may not be enough to hold them. The powers that be have decided that any chance to knock Lenin and his friends out of Moscow is worth supporting. Intelligence says something is stirring in southern Russia."

"If you mean General Denikin, I doubt it."

"Not Denikin. An old friend of yours. General Fedor Mikhailovich Orbelesky."

"Orbelesky! You've got to be kidding—sir!"

The colonel regarded him with a hurt expression. "General Orbelesky now heads the Constitutional Democratic party. The Kadets are a moderate revolutionary force with democratic ideals, and President Wilson is extremely interested in backing them. They also have the support of a large segment of the Russian people. You said so yourself in a report, um"—he riffled through the papers spread on his desk and came up with a photostated copy—"dated January 22, 1917."

"Colonel, that was last winter," Evans protested. "Before the revolution." He didn't tell him that he had been quoting the general's wife, Mathilda Orbeleskaya, word for word. "At that time they were a viable alternative to the Bolsheviks for the simple reason that almost no one outside the police or the far left had ever heard of the Bolsheviks. But the Kadets had their chance last summer and made a mess of it. Even Kerensky couldn't save the Provisional Government after that."

The colonel pursed his lips and stared at Evans. "I am sorry, Captain, but I have to disagree with you. We have intelligence that suggests that General Orbelesky has a very large following in the south and will be in a position to take the offensive in June. You are being sent to Odessa to assist in coordinating American and Allied aid and, especially, to make contact with the general himself and keep the War Department informed of his plans. The final decision to support the Crimean National Front will be based on the reports you make. So try to be objective. In view of your close friendship with the general you should be in a position to have significant influence over him."

Evans was tempted to tell him of the real nature of his acquaintance with Orbelesky, but the colonel hurried on. "A space has been reserved for you on the noon train for New York, and a Dutch passenger-cargo ship is sailing from Pier Forty-seven at two P.M. day after tomorrow for Port Said, in Egypt. Accommodations will be arranged onward by the British." He tossed a leather bag on the desk, and it hit with a clunk. "There are twelve Mexican fifty-peso gold pieces for expenses. We've been told that currency is just about useless in Russia, but gold is always acceptable. You will have to keep track of it and account for every penny with receipts. Sign here."

Evans glared at him and did so.

The train ran through fields showing the first green of spring wheat. The steppe was giving way to foothills, and if the sky had been clear to the east, the rounded peaks of the Urals would have been visible. A guard passed through the car with a surly glare at the imperial family, and Nicholas watched him from beneath lowered eyelids. For the first time since his abdication he was afraid for his family. He closed the book on his lap, marking his place with a finger. To the west the sky glowed like white-hot iron.

All winter the revolutionaries holding power in the Ural Soviet had demanded his removal to Ekaterinburg, but Colonel Eugene Kobylinsky had resisted, referring all such demands to the new capital at Moscow. Then, a few weeks before, a detachment of soldiers had arrived from Omsk to reorganize the Tobolsk Soviet and eliminate any lingering anti-Bolshevik elements. He recalled how convinced Alexandra had been that the new soldiers were rescuers, and he glanced fondly at his wife, napping across the aisle. This time the commissar from Ekaterinburg had backed his demand for their transfer with guns.

The arrival from Moscow of Commissar Vasily Vasilevich Yakovlev with a cavalry escort of 150 checked the Ekaterinburg Soviet's designs, and Nicholas began to recognize the outlines of a power struggle between the two rival soviets. Yakovlev countered the Ural Soviet's ploy by announcing that the family was to be moved to Moscow.

Alexei had fallen a few days before their departure, and his leg had swollen to ghastly proportions again. Yakovlev had then insisted that Nicholas go alone, confirming his belief that the new Bolshevik government wanted his signature on the damnable treaty signed at Brest-Litovsk that had been a betrayal of everything his Russia stood for. The others would follow after Alexei had recovered. Alexandra had agonized over whether to accompany him but had finally been convinced to go, taking Marie as a traveling companion, while the others remained behind. He had welcomed the journey, feeling that the uncertainty that had plagued him for the last year might finally be resolved. How wrong he had been not to have taken advantage of the arrangements Kerensky had made with the British until it was too late.

Nicholas's mind shied away from their departure: the girls sitting swollen-faced and red-eyed on the couch, Anastasia with tears coursing down her cheeks, Alexei crying upstairs in his bedroom and Alexandra, her lips trembling so that she could not speak, turning and hurrying out into the courtyard where the wagons waited. Even the cynical and unfriendly guards had looked away in embarrassment.

The river was still frozen, and so the journey to the train at Tyumen had been a nightmare of jolting through frozen forests in *taratasses,* peasant carts without springs. The cavalrymen from Moscow formed their escort, and when he jokingly referred to the excessive number of soldiers needed to keep two middle-aged people and one young woman from running off into the wilderness, Yakovlev admitted with some embarrassment that he was more concerned about certain elements who wished to do him harm. That was Nicholas's first intimation that Yakovlev was seriously worried.

The commissar was a puzzle to Nicholas. The man wore the uniform of an enlisted sailor, but he had the manners and refinement one would expect from an officer. He was tall and darkly handsome, and Marie was clearly taken with him. The commissar had treated them with unexpected courtesy, something they had almost forgotten.

They had stopped to change horses in the village of Pokrovskoye late on the Feast of the Assumption. The remount depot, a long, wooden, stablelike structure with a barracks attached, was directly across the street from the two-story house in which Rasputin had lived. When Alexandra overheard one soldier tell this to another, she went rigid. In a low voice that only he and Marie could hear, she reminded them of the starets's prediction that they would one day visit his house. Her eyes shone with new hope as she whispered, "You see, Nicky, even after death, our beloved teacher looks after us. All will be well now." Alexandra and Marie fell to their knees in the mud, and the dim figure of a woman blessed them from a second-story window. Concealing his fury, Nicholas turned away.

Yakovlev sent a telegram to Tobolsk from Tyumen reporting their safe arrival and asking after Alexei's welfare. Later a telegram arrived from Moscow with disturbing news. The line from Tyumen first ran southwest to Ekaterinburg, then turned north and west to Moscow. The Moscow Soviet suspected that Nicholas would be taken from the train at Ekaterinburg, tried by the Ural Soviet and executed immediately.

Yakovlev telegraphed Moscow repeatedly, seeking clarification and instructions, and as a result, the train left before dawn the following morning, traveling east to Omsk and the junction with the southern line of the Trans-Siberian Railroad. It would turn westward again there, passing now through Chelyabinsk and Simbirsk to Moscow.

Ural Soviet troops stopped the train fifty versts from Omsk, outside the town of Kulomzino. Nothing Yakovlev could say, no order that he could produce swayed the soldiers in the slightest. In desperation Yakovlev tried to negotiate with the Omsk Soviet only to discover that he had been declared a traitor to the Bolshevik cause by the Ural Soviet in Ekaterinburg and that Nicholas was ordered surrendered immediately. The Omsk Soviet, in the absence of instructions from Moscow to the contrary, had agreed to the demand. The cavalry escort voted to abide by the decision of the Ural Soviet. His own life now in danger, Yakovlev telegraphed directly to Minister Jacob Sverdlov, president of the Central Executive Committee of the All-Russian Congress of Soviets in Moscow, and was advised to hand over his prisoners.

The train chuffed into the main station at Ekaterinburg in the early-morning hours and was engulfed by an angry crowd.

The cry of "Show us the Romanovs! Show us the Romanovs!" swept through the mob. A bitter taste of fear rose in his throat as Nicholas saw rifles brandished, and one man climbed on another's shoulders to wave a hangman's noose. After a hasty conference between Yakovlev and two local officials, the train was moved back to a station on the outskirts of the city. Nicholas was badly shaken. For the first time he was confronted by hostile demonstrators who were—had once been—his people and not by soldiers or officials of the new regime.

A soldier pushed Nicholas roughly away from the window. "Get your wife and daughter up, Comrade."

Nicholas dressed in his worn uniform trousers, an old plaid shirt and heavy wool coat. He contemplated his battered leather boots. Imprisonment is not enough, he thought. They must humiliate me as well.

He woke Alexandra and Marie and stood guard outside the compartment while they dressed, wondering where Yakovlev had gotten to. The sailor seemed a fervent revolutionary and must have been well thought of by the Moscow Soviet to be entrusted with such a delicate mission. Yet between Tyumen and Omsk, Yakovlev had twice hinted that the family could escape during the night when the train traveled even more slowly than usual because of track conditions. They had only to walk north into the forest, Yakovlev had said, to stand an excellent chance of never being found again. Nicholas had considered the idea, but only for a moment. He was fit and a hardened soldier; hadn't he tested infantry field equipment in forced marches before the war? But he feared Alexandra would never survive. And what about Alexei and the girls in Tobolsk?

Alexandra, followed by Marie, joined him in the corridor. Alexandra's face was pale above the fur collar of her coat, as was Marie's, and he gave them both a reassuring smile.

A chill wind slipped into the car, damp, biting and scented with coal dust and lubricating oil. Feeble gas lamps lit the platform, and he could see a cluster of men in overcoats and fur caps. Guards prowled about, more to keep warm than from any excess of zeal. In spite of their reputed revolutionary spirit, they looked, Nicholas thought, like a raggle-taggle bunch of hoboes with rifles.

Talk ceased abruptly when the imperial family appeared. A spatter of rain fell. A man came to the steps. The engine chuffed once in the silence, and he whipped his head around to glare at the train guard as if it were his fault he had been startled. The train guard's expression of mild disgust deepened.

Ah, Nicholas thought, at least one sympathizer.

"Comrade Romanov," the man said, then cleared his throat to begin again. Does he think about the legality of what he is doing? Nicholas wondered, and smiled to encourage the man.

"Comrade Romanov, it is the decision of the Executive Committee of the Ural Soviet that you be incarcerated in Ekaterinburg until such time as a decision is reached concerning your trial."

"Executive Committee?" Nicholas smiled.

"Executive Committee," the man replied with unnecessary force, but he had the grace to blush when Nicholas nodded knowingly. They both had experience with fearful or obstructive advisers and knew this was the only way to get things done.

"And my wife and daughter?"

The man hesitated. Clearly he had been reading from a prepared script, and this question had not been included.

"They may accompany you or they may return to Tobolsk, as you wish."

Nicholas had not expected that. He thought furiously for a moment, weighing the alternatives. Tobolsk might be safer, at least for the time being. But if Yakovlev succeeded in satisfying the Ural Soviet, if all were together in one place, it would be easier to take them on to Moscow. If the girls and Alexei were to come from Tobolsk . . . In that instant, Nicholas realized how badly he wanted his family with him. It was a decision that would haunt him to the moment he died.

They were driven in automobiles through the muddy streets of the mining city to a stark house on a hill surrounded by still another wooden fence. At the door a lank-haired man introduced himself as Isiah Goloschekin, a member of the Ural Soviet Presidium. He bowed mockingly and indicated the door. "Citizen Romanov, you may enter."

Soldiers stood about inside, a scruffy lot, the tsar thought. Nicholas placed their suitcases on the floor, but a soldier ordered them opened. Nicholas had started to comply when Alexandra shook her head. "This is insulting. I refuse."

"Nevertheless, Citizeness Romanov, you will do as you are told." The soldier smirked.

"You will not touch those bags, young man."

Nicholas put a hand on her arm. "So far," he snapped to Goloschekin, "we have had polite treatment from men who were gentlemen, but now—"

"Be silent!" the new commissar shouted. "You are a prisoner of the Ural Soviet and will be tried for high crimes against the Russian people. You have no rights. And we are not gentlemen but workers and peasants. Blame yourself that we have not had the opportunity to cultivate the manners of polite society. If you continue to act in a provocative manner, you will be isolated from your family. A second offense and you will be awarded a punishment at hard labor."

Alexandra stared at the man in growing fright and snatched her hand from the suitcase as if it were white-hot.

V

The police manning the barriers in the great railway terminal at Odessa wore the uniforms of the tsarist era, but there the similarities ended. Evans's visa was examined closely, and the stamps of the prerevolutionary and Bolshevik governments stiffly noted. Outside, the streets were filled with uniforms of all types and colors, none of which he recognized. Automobiles jousted for space with donkeys, wagons and lorries. Women in veils glided among women in European dress, many in the latest Paris fashion. Over all the sun blazed in undiminished splendor, and when the cab topped a hill, the Black Sea stretched away to the south, east and west. As he watched, a squadron of spidery aircraft passed along the waterfront and turned inland.

It cost fifteen rubles to drive to the American Consulate on Kazarmenni Pereulok. Astounded, Evans tried to argue with the driver, who only shrugged and pretended not to understand. In the end he paid and angrily hauled his luggage up the wide steps and into the building. Vice Consul John Lowden received him briefly, and he was shown along the corridor to an office. Such was his introduction to Odessa and southern Russia.

Three weeks passed during which he wrote several times to General Orbelesky's headquarters in Sevastopol before receiving so much as an acknowledgment. Then, one day he learned that the decision to lend support to Orbelesky had already been made in Washington without benefit of his report or in fact any discussion with the Odessa consulate at all. Thus, half his mission was canceled before he had even begun. Vice Consul Lowden only shrugged when he complained.

"One thing you will learn about President Wilson and his White House advisers, my boy, is that they rarely consult the people in the field before making a decision. They do have some use for you, though," he observed dryly, handing Evans a telegram. "You've been ordered to Sevastopol to serve as direct liaison with General Orbelesky. You will be responsible for accounting for all American supplies sent to the Crimean National Front army. Keep a close eye on them, or they'll steal us blind."

Evans spent most of the twenty-hour trip across the Black Sea reading the stack of newspapers he had bought before leaving Odessa. It seemed that every Russian general had gathered on one side or the other in the military and political struggle that arced two thousand miles from Siberia to the Ukraine. On the White side, Alexeyev, Kornilov, Milyukov and Rodzianko had lately placed themselves under the nominal command of Kaledin, ataman of the Don Cossacks. In western Siberia an admiral named Kolchak had appeared and proclaimed himself supreme ruler. General Orbelesky in the Crimea seemed to hold the balance of power between the two overlords. Clearly, whoever could succeed in pushing the Bolsheviks out of Moscow would be the next ruler of Russia. The Bolsheviks were as poorly organized as the Whites, but they had two things the Whites lacked—central leadership and fanaticism.

If General Orbelesky could lay claim to all Allied aid, the others would have to fall into line. However, the British were still behind Kaledin and were unlikely to change their minds until Orbelesky could prove himself by accomplishing something spectacular. So far, he had done absolutely nothing.

The phaeton driver stopped before a large four-story building adorned with a classical façade. After the heat and glare the interior, full of filtered sunlight and redolent of cleaning fluid and beeswax, was a welcome relief. Cigarettes and a carafe of mineral water were offered, and a few moments later an extremely handsome young officer with a pencil-line mustache and hair gleaming with pomade hurried in.

"I have been instructed to drive you to the general's country estate near Yalta. At the moment he is visiting units of our forces in training camps to the north but is expected to return tomorrow. If you will come with me?"

The drive took more than an hour, but when they finally arrived at the villa, Princess Mathilda Eugenova Orbeleskaya was waiting under the portico. The officer stepped down and bent to kiss her hand. He murmured something, and she nodded, glancing toward the back seat of the car. Darkness was sliding in with a swiftness seen only in coastal areas, and she had to step quite close to recognize the passenger still waiting there. When she did, her surprise and delight were unmistakable. Evans did not miss the officer's scowl.

Supper was served on the veranda by a Tatar butler and consisted of borsch with sour cream, piroshki—a chopped cabbage dish—followed by roast duck baked in apples and served with small potatoes and a cucumber salad. For dessert, large pastry cones of ice cream were served on small dishes, and Evans drew a laugh from the princess and a scowl from the butler when he picked his up to demonstrate how it was eaten in the West.

Afterward they took coffee and brandy in the library and while they talked, Mathilda studied him, eyes full of speculation.

"You can't imagine how happy I was to hear that you had been assigned here. I've missed you terribly," she whispered, and stood up, smiling the impish smile he remembered so well. "I'm tired of politics. Every day for months it has been politics, politics, politics. The general will not return until tomorrow. . . ."

The general appeared after lunch. Evans saw him stomping down the path from the stables, leading two horses. He shook hands with Evans, then, as if it were a ritual they engaged in every day, motioned him to mount. "She's a good, steady beast with a turn of speed." Evans glanced at him sharply, but the general was humming to himself as he adjusted a stirrup. They cantered along the hill, following a faint path that led back into a meadow stretching north and east to the misty outlines of the Caucasus. The sun was warm, not yet hot, although its steamy rays held that promise.

"I have had a long letter from your people in Washington," the general began without preamble as they rested their horses on the meadow's verge.

"To do with my task here, I suppose?"

The general smiled. "I would say that we have underestimated each other. You are not the pleasure-loving nincompoop I took you for, and I doubt if you still think of me as a perverted old fool."

Evans laughed. "I must say, I am glad not to be thought of as a nincompoop."

"You are in a position to be a help or a hindrance to the Kadet cause," the general said, reining his horse around, "which very simply means the survival of democracy in Russia. I would like to assure myself in any manner possible that you will be the former and not the latter."

Evans chose to ignore the rather obvious offer of a bribe. "Simple, General. Just tell me what you intend to do with all the military aid that's pouring in."

The general glared at him. "Kill Bolsheviks, young man."

"And afterward?"

"Mr. Evans, I became a member of the Kadet party in 1886. In 1906 I was imprisoned for my part in the revolution. I have dedicated my life to the democratic principles of the revolution. The Bolsheviks, without the least pretense to legality, have destroyed the Constituent Assembly, the first and only democratically elected parliamentary body in Russia's history. I find that insupportable and will fight to my last breath to establish democratic government in Russia."

Evans nodded. The general had said all the right things so far. No wonder he had convinced Wilson and his White House coterie. "How do you propose to do that, General? The efforts of the Whites, your own armies included, have so far been inept, badly coordinated and largely ineffective."

Orbelesky nodded without showing offense. "I intend to solve the problem by uniting all White forces behind the Kadets. If the Allied governments will ship arms and supplies to me alone, the others will have no choice, Mr. Evans. Can I count on your help?"

Evans hesitated for a moment. Why not? he thought. His stay in this Godforsaken land would be made a great deal more pleasant if he said yes.

"General, I'll be honest with you as well. I've been sent to make certain all that aid is put to good use. You make it possible for me to do my job without any trouble, and there will be no negative reports from me."

Orbelesky chuckled. "Well, now that's settled"—he urged his horse into a trot—"I believe we shall get along very well, Captain Evans."

Evans fell into line as they rode back along the narrow path.

Mathilda moved from the country house closer to Sevastopol, and as usual, General Orbelesky was indifferent. Evans was a frequent visitor, often arriving as early as ten o'clock in the morning and remaining overnight. He saw little of General Orbelesky, and that suited him.

There was little enough for him to do at headquarters. Orbelesky had provided him with a staff headed by Colonel Maxime Rovolovich Obrechev to keep track of the American shipments of arms and equipment that had begun to pour into Sevastopol. The colonel was diligent and worked his staff hard. After the first week Evans began to limit his time in the office to an hour or so in the morning, when Obrechev would brief him on the type and quantity of equipment due in or received the day before. By the end of the second week he had even begun to draft Evans's weekly reports to Vice Consul Lowden in Odessa. As a consequence, Evans was able to spend more time with Mathilda. They rode along the cliffs that lined the southwestern coast and explored the many canyons leading down to the sea. The salty water was warm and inviting, and often after stopping at a deserted beach, they swam naked and later made love in the warm sun.

One lazy, sun-filled afternoon, Mathilda pointed out a large prom-ontory that reared over the dark sea. "Just beyond, my darling, is the site of the ancient city of Chersonesus, which was built in the sixth century B.C. by colonists from Bithynia." She trailed her fingers across his bare stomach. "They were fanatical in their worship of Aphrodite, I understand."

Evans chuckled and kissed her. "Artemis, my dear. They worshiped Artemis, goddess of the hunt. Altogether a different proposition."

One morning in late June Evans stood at the window of his suite in the Hotel Kist, looking down on the Marine Boulevard. The day was already exceptionally hot, and his head ached badly. The Orbeleskys had entertained representatives of Admiral Kolchak's government the night before, and Evans had attended to demonstrate American con-cern for the Crimean National Front. Mathilda and he had ridden out to a favorite beach that afternoon, but a fishing boat was working the surf. With the reception that evening, there had been no time to look for another beach, and they had turned back. That evening he was forced to watch from a distance as she danced and flirted with offi-cers from the Kolchak delegation.

Evans found the bar and proceeded to drink away his tantrum. Sometime later he found himself standing beside his assistant, Colonel Obrechev. They toasted each other, and Obrechev tucked a bottle of Greek brandy under his tunic. "Let's find somewhere private. This stuff's too damned expensive to share with anyone."

They wandered through the spacious villa to a relatively quiet spot on the balcony overlooking the bathing pool and, beyond, the sea. The setting sun had turned the clear sky the color of dark tea with just a streak of orange along the horizon. They toasted the night, Mathilda, the civil war, each of the White front commanders and even the Bolsheviks on the theory that without them, they both might be in trenches fighting the Germans instead of occupying cushy staff posi-tions. The colonel was drinking far more than was usual for him, Evans noted with amusement, and the more brandy he consumed, the more talkative he became. The sight of a naval vessel far out in the bay caught in the last rays of sun started him on a tangent.

"My brother was in the navy . . . commanded a minesweeper at Odessa. Bloody bastards gave him the choice of dying hot or cold."

"Hot or cold?"

"The Black Sea fleet mutiny in February, for Christ's sake. Sailors killed all their officers. Lined 'em all up on the main deck. Had a drumhead court-martial an' sentenced 'em to die. Gave 'em a choice, though. If they chose to die cold, their hands and feet were tied and they were dropped overboard. Cold water, you see. Drowned 'em."

"Good God!" Evans knew only that the mutiny had begun with

the Black Sea fleet and spread to the city, where disorders, looting and lynchings had occurred before it was put down. "What was hot then?"

Obrechev brushed a streak of liquid from his tunic and knocked the brandy glass over. "Damn!" He refilled the glass and raised it to eye level. "If they chose hot, the sailors threw them into the ship's furnaces, alive." He hiccuped and drained the glass.

"Christ! You can't mean they actually did that?"

The Russian nodded. "Bastards! Found bones in the furnaces." His face lit for a moment with a fierce grin. "I commanded the firing parties that shot every one of them, damn their souls to hell!"

Obrechev again raised the glass to his lips; but his eyes rolled up, and he collapsed against the marble railing. Evans staggered off in search of his driver.

Now, watching the traffic meandering below, Evans thought about the fact that at some indefinable point the revolution had become a civil war. His own grandfather had commanded a regiment of Massachusetts infantry during the American Civil War before being wounded at Chancellorsville. Through long association with the old man Evans thought of the War Between the States as a chivalrous pursuit for freedom, a gallant crusade, or so his grandfather, from a remove of forty years, had taught him to believe. But the Russian civil war seemed another matter entirely.

Today he was to conduct a long-scheduled inspection of a naval base at Balaklava, and he knew he was procrastinating. The heat and his headache would make it a miserable affair, but Vice Consul Lowden was becoming very insistent.

He dressed in the new summer-weight uniform Obrechev had arranged to have run up by his tailor and went down to the lobby, curious to see how Obrechev, who always acted as his escort on these infrequent tours, would cope with his hangover. A young subaltern was waiting for him instead.

"I apologize for Colonel Obrechev, sir. He isn't feeling good this morning. If you wish, I can act as your guide."

Evans chuckled at the thought of Obrechev's indisposition. His own was bad enough. As they stepped outside, the sun struck him a solid blow, and he collapsed into the seat, wishing he had canceled the tour after all. The Russian officer only smiled and handed him a pair of smoked glasses.

The movement of the car produced a hot breeze, and Evans closed his eyes and endured. He had seen only bits and pieces of the Crimean National Front army in the few weeks he had been in Sevastopol, but by watching the staff function and observing a few regular units, he had formed a most favorable impression of General Orbelesky's army. The mountains of equipment unloaded at Sevastopol's docks disappeared overnight in shiny new Ford and Reo trucks, and distribution reports were minutely detailed so that every rifle, every round of ammunition were accounted for.

They stopped for lunch at the head of a deep valley. The gourd-shaped harbor at Balaklava lay below. Buff-colored hills, patched with vivid green vineyards and yellow houses, rose steeply on three sides. They ate sandwiches and iced caviar produced from the trunk while the young officer, obviously a student of military history, described the famous charge of the Light Brigade that had taken place on the slopes below them nearly sixty-four years before.

As he talked, Evans's attention wandered to a naval cruiser moving about the mouth of the harbor. Orbelesky had told him personally that he had no intention of honoring the Bolshevik armistice with the Germans, yet here was an important warship in harbor.

After a moment he went to fetch his binoculars from the car. The officer followed and, thinking he wanted to examine the battlefield more closely, began pointing out the various features of the terrain.

"Now, over there is where the British Heavy Brigade waited, just below that rise, where they had an excellent view of the battlefield. The Light Brigade was farther down, and their view was restricted. The Russian batteries were sited here . . ."

Evans wasn't listening. He had focused the glasses on a ship that was just entering the harbor. A merchant steamer, he thought. So that was why the Russian cruiser had moved—to allow her through the narrow harbor entrance. The two rendered passing honors, and for a brief moment he saw an ensign ripple at the merchant's jackstaff. He stared at it in shock, not believing what he had seen. On the dock, activity quickened, and the merchant ship began the turn that would bring her alongside the quay. A light breeze ruffled the water, and he focused on the ship's stern. The breeze stirred, and the German merchant marine ensign billowed.

Later, as the motorcar climbed out of the stifling valley, Evans turned to the young officer. "Does Colonel Obrechev know that you are escorting me today?"

The young man looked sheepish. "Not really, sir. I was sick of the office, and this seemed a perfect opportunity to get away. You aren't angry, are you, sir?"

"On the contrary," Evans told him grimly.

With trembling fingers Tatiana opened the letter from Demidova, her mother's maid who, in happier times, had served as parlormaid at Tsarskoye Selo. It was short and almost devoid of news, except for the line that read, "The tsarina has asked me to advise the grand duchesses that as all are well, they may now dispose of the medicines."

Tatiana stuffed the letter into the pocket of her sweater. A thin rain slanted past the window where only an hour before a bright May sun had streamed. She was so tired of Siberia and its monotonous rain and snow, mud and damp. Would they never be allowed to return to Petrograd? But the answer to that was in the letter. "Dispose of the medicines" was a family code that meant "hide the jewels." Her parents had been searched in Ekaterinburg! Tatiana's worst fears were being realized. When the telegram had come from Ekaterinburg advising Kobylinsky that Papa, Mama and Marie had been taken there, the shock in his face told her that the rumors were true: Papa was in grave danger.

Tatiana thought of herself as made of sterner stuff than her parents and sisters. Somehow, somewhere, she had developed an armor of cynical pessimism that allowed her to face facts squarely. She had thought through their predicament, analyzed the hostility shown them by the commissars from Ekaterinburg and compared it with that displayed by their guards. The result had frightened her thoroughly. The Ekaterinburg commissars had the hard eyes and pinched mouths she had seen in certain of the monks her father received from time to time, madmen who hated everyone and everything except their own perverted beliefs in God. She pressed her thighs together, an action that had become habitual in past months; the hard steel of the Browning pistol gave her a measure of comfort. It was an illusory safety, but while she possessed the gun, she felt she could endure anything. That night, working by the light of a candle shielded by a blanket draped from the headboard of her bed, Tatiana sewed the pistol into her pillow.

On May 11 she was watching from the upper window when a detachment of uniformed men marched through the gate. A sentry tried to bar the way but was pushed aside, and a moment later Kobylinsky hurried from the house. An argument ensued, and she went swiftly to the head of the stairs. The guard who usually stood there had gone, and by crouching at the corner, she was able to hear.

"I don't give a damn, Colonel"—the voice sneered the title—"if Comrade Trotsky gave you your orders personally. I am giving you new ones. The Ural Soviet has relieved you of your command. You will take your people and return to Petrograd. The prisoners are no longer your responsibility."

That evening a thin man clad in a worn brown uniform entered their parlor without knocking. "My name is Rodionov," he said, introducing himself. "I have been sent by the Ural Soviet of Workers and Peasants to command the detachment of guards for the family of the archcriminal Romanov. You all will consider yourselves under my direct orders. Disobedience will be harshly punished."

He looked them over again. "Where is the boy, Alexei?" he demanded. "I ordered everyone assembled here."

Alexei's aide, the sailor Nagorny, rose from a chair and stared at the commissar. "He is in his bedroom, sick," he said finally. The big sailor's rough, heavy voice and protective manner caused Rodionov to back away a step.

"That is no excuse," he snapped, recovering. "You are all to be ready to travel tomorrow, to Ekaterinburg."

"My brother is far too sick to be moved, Comrade Commissar," Tatiana told him in an even voice, not rising from her chair. "If you would care to see him, you . . ."

"Where is the doctor?" Rodionov snarled, and Dr. Botkin stood up.

"I will show you," he muttered, and led the way. Rodionov swept after him without another word.

Between them, Tatiana and Botkin managed to convince Rodionov to delay the journey until the nineteenth, but he would not agree to another hour. Twice Tatiana caught him coming out of Alexei's room, then waiting for a moment before darting back to catch her brother getting out of bed. The first time he looked abashed as Tatiana passed him in the hall; the second time he merely watched her with his cold, hating expression.

On the morning of the nineteenth, Nagorny carried Alexei on his back as they were herded to the docks with what little baggage they had been allowed. Tatiana saw the name *Rus* painted on the bow of the ship and realized it was the same steamer that had brought them to Tobolsk the previous summer. Even the man in the captain's hat staring down at them from the deckhouse was the same. Anastasia waved, and the captain blew her a kiss.

"You all will be locked into your cabins," Rodionov announced as they were assigned staterooms, two by two. Tatiana began to protest, then gave up. It had been the same since Rodionov arrived. The captain of the *Rus* growled a protest when Rodionov insisted on locking Alexei and Nagorny into their cabin.

"The boy is sick, Comrade. How is the doctor to get to him?"

Rodionov, obviously nearing a nervous breakdown under the twin pressures of looking after the imperial family and controlling his unruly guards, screamed at the captain to mind his own business. The captain, a huge man with a barrel chest and arms as thick as Tatiana's waist, started toward the commissar. Soldiers intervened, and the captain stormed away to the bridge.

It rained hard most of the time, and this, as much as Rodionov's orders, restricted them to their cabins. The passage was rough, and everyone was grateful when the *Rus* tied up to the Tyumen wharf. Open carts waited in the downpour to carry them to the railroad station. This proved too much even for Rodionov. Angrily he ordered the drivers to find closed carriages or motor lorries.

The crisis came to a head at the railway station. Rodionov had prepared a list detailing family members to one car and retainers to another, a foul-smelling fourth-class carriage at the end of the train.

Tatiana broke away from her guard and hurried along the platform to where Rodionov was watching the rest of the party board. "Monsieur Gilliard," she shouted, waving. Gilliard turned, stepped down from the coach and started toward her, but a burly guard pushed him back with his rifle. Gilliard stumbled against the carriage and fell.

"What are you doing!" Tatiana screamed, and threw herself past the guard. She knelt beside the teacher, but the guard yanked her up.

"Do as you're told, you bitch!" he roared.

The insult paralyzed her into silence. For an instant, embarrassment suffused Rodionov's face, and he jumped to intervene as the guard shook Tatiana.

"Take your hands away, you pig bastard," Rodionov roared. "Are you an animal that I should have you shot?" At the same moment he spun toward Tatiana, still shouting. "You are the prisoner of the Ural Soviet, do you understand, Comrade Tatiana Nikolaevna? If you interfere again, I will have you punished severely."

The journey to Ekaterinburg was made in silence. The change in the conditions of their imprisonment had come so swiftly that they all were in shock. Olga stared with frightened eyes at the desolate landscape. Anastasia sat huddled into a seat by herself, a book lying open but unread on her lap. Tatiana herself sat across from her older sister, wondering at the changes in her over the last year. Of all the family, with perhaps the exception of her mother, Olga had been the most affected by their imprisonment.

She had always been the sparkling personality, able to charm anyone she had a mind to. She also had a stern will, very much like Mama, Tatiana thought, and when she decided a thing must be done, you knew it would be. Olga had never seemed to have a bad day or mood. Her sunny disposition had been as dependable as the sunrise. But since the American had disappeared, something had gone out of her, and she had slipped with increasing speed into permanent depression. Only last night, after they had gone to bed, she had heard Olga sobbing. She had crawled into bed with her and taken her in her arms to pet and soothe her. She knew she would never, ever forget her sister's anguished cry.

"Tania, they are going to shoot us in Ekaterinburg. I'll never know what it is like to have a man love me. . . ."

Tatiana was worried that her family was collapsing under their increasingly harsh imprisonment. At Tsarskoye Selo, life had gone on much as before and they were hardly more restricted than before the abdication. As conditions worsened, Papa had grown distant, no longer played games with them in the evenings but sat beside the meager fire, thinking, praying? Mama was worse. Religion was her retreat, and now she was lost in it, seeing in every untoward incident a divine plot to free and restore her husband to the throne. Tatiana was religious but totally unprepared to cope with her mother's fanaticism.

In late afternoon the sun broke through the heavy cloud for a brief period, and the world changed. Golden sunlight slanting through purple cloud to the west brought color into the landscape, painting the endless stretches of steppe and foothills with soft but vivid greens. Stands of birch, her favorite tree, had been growing more numerous until now they had formed a forest like those near Petrograd. Tatiana watched entranced as the trees flashed green, then silver in the wind and thought that if she could leave the train, she would run forever through the endless forest.

Nikolai Khristoforovich Sheremetiev had been promoted to major in the Red Army when he was transferred to Moscow two weeks before. He crossed the Teatralni Proyezd and paused before the massive granite building facing Lubyanka Square. The building still wore its original sign, reading "All-Russian Insurance Company," concealing the fact that it was now the headquarters of the All-Russian Extraordinary Commission for Combating Counterrevolution and Sabotage—in short, the Cheka.

He showed his orders to the guard, who motioned him inside. Sheremetiev was frightened. Even though the Cheka had not sent armed men, he knew he might well be going to his execution. More than one Red Army officer from the old regime had disappeared recently, and in desperation, he and many others now wore their service revolvers at all times.

In a top-floor office, beyond a glass partition, he saw a pretty young woman seated behind a desk. She gave him a pleasant smile and glanced at his orders. A butterfly at the center of the spider's web, he thought.

The receptionist spoke into a telephone; then, so gracefully that Sheremetiev wondered if she had trained for the ballet, she rose and opened a heavy wood-paneled door for him.

Felix Edmundovich Dzerzhinsky was seated behind an immense mahogany desk, smoking a cigarette clutched in a thin holder. He nodded as Sheremetiev stopped before his desk and casually indicated a chair. "Tea, Comrade Sheremetiev?" he asked, and laughed when Sheremetiev declined. "Please relax, Comrade. The Cheka is not as bad as rumors would have you believe, unless of course, you are here on 'special business.' " He waved a hand about the sumptuous office that had once belonged to the president of the insurance company. "To borrow a phrase from the former owners, you might say I wish to see you settled with a 'secure future.' "

Dzerzhinsky spoke with a cultured accent that Sheremetiev identified immediately as Polish. His voice was thin, to match his features and build. His hair was jet black and carefully slicked down. He wore a dapper business suit, not at all what one would have expected of a proletarian leader of the ongoing Socialist workers' revolution. In fact he looked more like a member of the Russian upper class—the kind Dzerzhinsky was rumored to shoot nightly.

"A secure future?" Sheremetiev ventured.

"You were an officer in the tsarist army," Dzerzhinsky stated sharply.

"Yes, a captain in the Vologda Regiment . . ."

"And before that, you were a noncommissioned officer?"

"Yes . . ."

"In fact, you enlisted as a common soldier and rose from the ranks?"

"Yes."

Dzerzhinsky smiled. "That fact could save you one day from the firing party. But I wouldn't depend on it."

Sheremetiev's fear returned, sharper than ever. "I'm not certain I understand—"

"Quite simple really. We must not allow the Red Army to be infected by the cockroaches of the reactionary Nicholas. How can we build a truly Socialistic society if the very guardians of that society are contaminated? No, my dear Sheremetiev, the infection must be cut out, ruthlessly, like a cancer. All counterrevolutionaries of whatever stripe must be destroyed wherever they are found. You, my dear sir, are a single cell in that cancer, and as a single cancer cell may duplicate itself to destroy the body, so might you duplicate yourself in others and so destroy our revolution."

Sheremetiev stared at Dzerzhinsky in terror. "But, Comrade Dzerzhinsky," he protested, "if an officer joined the Red Army to fight against the counterrevolutionaries, wouldn't that prove his sincerity?"

"How naïve you are, Comrade Sheremetiev." Dzerzhinsky smiled. "Of course not. If you are a dedicated Socialist, then you are merely doing your duty. One does not expect to be rewarded for doing one's duty, does one? Also, if you are a dedicated Socialist, you will understand instinctively that your continued existence, tainted as it is with prerevolutionary ideas and ideals, is detrimental to the Soviet state, and you will see the need for your own elimination as a part of the counterrevolutionary class. You are certainly aware that in the new Russia, the vanguard of the new world order, the individual serves the state, not the state the individual, as in some decadent Western countries."

Sheremetiev did not bother to unravel Dzerzhinsky's twisted logic.

Nor did it surprise him. It was sufficient that Dzerzhinsky believed what he was saying. With one or two exceptions, there were no towering intellects in the Bolshevik party. It had succeeded because it had guns and did not hesitate to use violence and terror to attain results.

"You are not a member of the Communist party?"

"My application was made in November of last year, Comrade. It is still under review."

Dzerzhinsky smiled. "And will remain so. Sign that." He flicked a piece of paper across the polished desk.

Sheremetiev saw that it was a party membership application with his particulars neatly typed in. Dzerzhinsky's signature was at the bottom. Bemused, he signed with the pen Dzerzhinsky offered and was handed in return a pasteboard card with his photograph in one corner— the photo taken the day he received his first Saint George's Cross in 1914. His membership in the party was backdated to the time of his first application.

"Welcome to the All-Russian Communist party, Comrade. Do not lose that square of pasteboard. It is your passport to life." Dzerzhinsky chuckled. "I might also mention that you are also discharged from the Red Army."

Sheremetiev laid the card on the desk. "What must I do to earn it?"

Dzerzhinsky chuckled again. "A careful man. I like a careful man. But do not be too careful with me, Comrade. I annoy very easily. To earn your membership, you must join me in the crusade to root out capitalism and its slimy corruption. Tell me." He changed the subject abruptly. "Do you know that this woman, Maria Antipova Galitina, with whom you live, sells passports to state enemies?"

The question caught him off guard. Of course he did. Everyone in the civil service had a way to earn extra money. It was the same under the tsars; only now it was more widespread. But if he admitted that he knew, he would be naming himself as an accomplice.

"No!" He pretended to be shocked.

"No matter." Dzerzhinsky waved a hand. "Just as long as you are not involved." He shot forward in his chair, the lazy smile gone, his manner all business.

"I need leaders who understand the meaning of discipline and instant obedience. Your record as an officer is excellent. Your men speak highly of you and do not hold your officer status against you. You are self-disciplined, and you are intelligent enough to understand the root causes and directions of the Communist revolution. Will you join me?"

"Yes," Sheremetiev answered. As if there were any other answer.

Dzerzhinsky shook his hand solemnly and scribbled on a sheet of paper which he handed to Sheremetiev. "This is the address of your first assignment and, below that, my pass. With it, you can go anywhere in Moscow, commandeer anything you wish. If refused, use your revolver. The Cheka brooks no interference. At that address you will find a group of anarchists. They belong to a group calling themselves the Black Guard. They have defied the Moscow Soviet and continue to murder and rob. Arrest and bring them here. Do whatever is necessary to carry out your assignment, and report to me when you return."

A smallish man with a sharp-edged, badly scarred face was waiting for him in the corridor and was introduced by the pretty secretary. "Comrade Sheremetiev, may I present your assistant, Comrade Mikhail Borisovich Chizov?" It was a reflection of the party line, Sheremetiev thought as he shook the other's hand, that the woman had dispensed with their ranks. How much longer could they continued this nonsense and maintain discipline?

"Comrade Sheremetiev has just joined the Cheka, Mika."

Sheremetiev glanced at her; perhaps her smile was not so sweet after all, he thought.

"I have assembled a party in the courtyard," Chizov told him in a peculiarly high-pitched and grating voice which, together with his brittle face, made Sheremetiev think of broken glass.

Once they were outside, Sheremetiev stopped the other man. "My rank is major," he said, "and yours?"

"Sergeant major, sir," Chizov answered promptly enough.

Sheremetiev nodded. "Do not forget it."

Twelve men in black leather jackets waited for them beside two canvas-covered trucks. Most wore Mauser automatic pistols in huge leather or wooden holsters that could double as shoulder stocks. Sheremetiev shone a flashlight into the back of one truck and saw two Maxim machine guns mounted on wheeled carriages.

They drove fast through the Moscow streets. The air was smoky, and the stars less than pale blurs through the shreds of vapor. Anarchists, Dzerzhinsky had said. If the party was moving against the anarchists, it marked a major departure from the relatively cautious attitude toward other "acceptable political parties" Lenin had insisted on since the move to Moscow.

The anarchists had occupied a house in the Petrovsko-Razumousky District and had terrorized the area for weeks. Lately they had taken to patrolling the boundaries of their territory, charging admission for entry and ransom for departure. Houses within the area had been ransacked, inhabitants murdered and beaten and any young woman considered halfway desirable raped or worse. The complaints had swelled to such a volume, according to Chizov, that the Moscow Soviet had asked the Cheka to handle the problem.

Chizov spoke quietly to the driver, and the lorry pulled to the curb and stopped. "The territory occupied by the anarchists lies just ahead, in the next block. They will have guards."

"Describe the area to me, Comrade Chizov."

Chizov took a deep breath. "It will be very difficult, Comrade, you had . . ."

Sheremetiev had opened the door and stepped out onto the running board to study the street ahead. Now he ducked his head and stared at Chizov. "This is not a debating society, Comrade Chizov," he said harshly. "Please describe the area for me."

Chizov blinked. Once an officer, always an officer, the dog, the sergeant major thought. Remember my rank indeed! I'll fix him, by God.

"This section was once filled with rich parasites. Most have been driven away or shot, and their houses converted to flats. The Anarchists have occupied a three-story house on Tslinsky Street, which is surrounded by a decorative iron fence. There is a gateman's house which has been converted to a guardhouse. They are armed with at least one cannon, a breechloader from the Turkish wars, which they have fired. They also have a machine gun."

Sheremetiev made his plans quickly and distributed his men. All had been front-line soldiers. He ordered four into the back with the machine guns. Two had shotguns, American pump-action weapons that were devastating at close quarters, and the rest were armed with army rifles.

The lorries separated to either side of the street and, at his whistle, surged forward to turn in opposite directions. "There," Chizov shouted, and the lorry veered sharply to the left, tipped dangerously and stopped. A cable was thrown about the palings of the iron fence, and the lorry lurched backward. The rusty fastenings snapped in sequence, and an entire section of the fence sprang outward. The second lorry bumped over the curb and surged toward the opening, struck the bushes, held, then ground forward onto the lawn. Rifle shots snapped out. A machine gun was handed down to eager hands. Three steel boxes of ammunition were thrown out, and men ran off with the gun. The second machine gun followed.

The machine gun began to fire. Windows shattered, and Sheremetiev heard the whine of ricochets. The second machine gun was brought into action, and the building shuddered under the impact. Sheremetiev delegated two Chekists to act as a rear guard and with the others raced toward the house. He flattened himself beside the front door, took a stick grenade from his belt, twisted the igniter cap, kicked the door open and heaved it inside. The grenade went off with an earsplitting crack, and the man behind him pressed a second grenade into his hand. He counted to twenty, slowly, twisted the igniter and threw the second one into the room to catch anyone still alive. They stepped into a ruin of splintered paneling and doors and smashed tile. One wall was in flames that licked up the shredded wallpaper hungrily, and in the light Sheremetiev saw three mutilated bodies, two men and one woman.

One of the shotgun men rushed to the first open door, and the gun boomed twice. Sheremetiev kicked open another door and fired at a figure that loomed against a window. An elderly woman clutched her throat and fell, trying to scream as she choked to death. Sheremetiev joined Chizov at the foot of the grand staircase leading up to the first floor. A rifle banged, and a chip flew from a marble bust beside his head.

"Suicide to try to get up there," Chizov muttered.

Sheremetiev hunched down and shouted up the stairs to cease fire.

"By whose orders?" a harsh voice roared.

"By order of the Moscow Soviet," he responded. "You are to give up your weapons and come down with your hands raised."

"Like hell, you tsarist police pig. Come and get us."

Sheremetiev grinned and motioned to Chizov to pull the men back to the front entrance. The fire had reached the ceiling, and as he turned to look, gauzy drapes that had somehow escaped the depredations of the anarchists flashed into flame.

"Then stay here, you fool," he shouted. "The house is alight. Come down or burn to death. Since you don't believe in government services, rest assured the fire brigades won't respond!" He laughed and ran back to the door.

Flames spouted from ground-floor windows, and figures could be seen on the upper floor.

At the back of the house the fire was just taking hold. A white cloth appeared at a second-story window, and Sheremetiev shouted for them to throw out their weapons. A veritable shower of pistols and rifles fell. A woman had climbed out of a window. She lay flat on the roof tiles and slithered down until she was stretched full length over the edge, feeling for the porch railing with a foot. Sheremetiev pointed, and three rifles fired. The woman fell with a dull thump.

A chorus of screams and curses came from the house. "You will come out," he shouted, "through the rear door, hands up. Children first, women next and men last."

Immediately figures appeared at the door: children of all ages in rags, some with smoldering clothing, followed by screaming women and men coughing and choking with the smoke. As each adult left the porch, he was tripped to the ground and warned to lie still with a kick. Nine men, six women and five children had left the house when the first floor collapsed. A few screams came from inside until, with a tearing, screeching crash, the roof burned through.

Dzerzhinsky was waiting in the courtyard when the trucks crammed with prisoners drove through the iron gates. Sheremetiev reported his success, but Dzerzhinsky received him in cold silence. He gave orders to have the children taken to the nearest hospital for treatment, but even though two of the men and one young woman were badly burned, he left the adults by the lorries under the watchful eye of the guards.

"Follow me," he snapped at Sheremetiev. They walked into the building, but instead of going to the elevator, they turned left and went down several flights of iron-fretwork stairs to a damp subbasement. Without a word, Dzerzhinsky led him along a brightly lit corridor patrolled by hard-faced guards armed with rifles. Dzerzhinsky paused outside a cell and took the key from a warder, then waved him away.

"You have done a competent job to this point," he told a puzzled Sheremetiev. "Now we must see whether or not you are a true Socialist, deserving of my trust."

He unlocked the cell door and pushed it open. Tied naked to a stool bolted to the floor, face streaked with tears and hands tightly bound behind her back, was Maria. She blinked at the two men; then her eyes closed and her mouth fell slack with relief as she recognized Sheremetiev.

"Oh, thank God, Nicky!" she moaned. "Oh, thank God! I told them over and over again they had made a terrible mistake. . . ."

Sheremetiev turned to Dzerzhinsky, suddenly afraid of what was coming.

"She has abused the people's trust. She is an enemy of the people, Comrade Sheremetiev. She has no right to exist." Dzerzhinsky smiled. "So you will execute her."

Maria stared at them both in horror and began to struggle against the ropes that bound her thighs to the chair. Sheremetiev could see the marks where someone had beaten her and the black smudges of cigarette burns.

He took a step toward her, and she pressed back, lips drawn into a rictus of fear. His glance swept her body, the body he had spent hours caressing; the hours they had spent making love to each other, the things she did to . . . and a sense of unreality swept over him.

He could sense Dzerzhinsky behind him, watching his every move, searching for the least hesitation, which would mean his death as well. Sheremetiev drew and cocked his revolver. For an instant he had a desperate desire to turn and shoot Dzerzhinsky instead.

Maria screamed as he placed the muzzle against her forehead, and the report slammed back from the whitewashed stone walls as her head snapped away from the bullet's impact.

The ropes held her partly upright, and her forehead showed only a tiny black-rimmed hole where the powder had burned the skin and blown the hair back. Sheremetiev holstered the revolver, averting his eyes from the haze of blood that coated the wall and floor behind the body. He faced Dzerzhinsky. The Pole was smiling a thin, almost gloating smile, and he slipped a small automatic pistol back into his pocket.

"Very good." He smirked. "Now you have one more duty to perform."

They went back up to the courtyard. It had started to rain, a soft, clinging rain that reminded him of spring nights when as a child he had walked with his mother. He took a deep breath as they came out of the building into the courtyard. A tremor of excitement still coursed through his traitorous body; he was tense, expectant, not nervous but anticipatory. His mind was unnaturally clear, and the courtyard and everything in it were sharp as crystal. It was this way in battle, he thought.

As they approached the two lorries where the prisoners squatted, blankets or coats held over their heads as shields against the rain, Dzerzhinsky waved. Around the courtyard, arc lights flashed on and engines roared to life. Sheremetiev saw that even decrepit pieces of junk covered in dirt and mud were running. The courtyard was suddenly rank with gasoline fumes, and the springlike atmosphere was banished. Dzerzhinsky shouted above the noise for the prisoners to stand up. They did so reluctantly, helping each other, and he smiled at them. The rain softened the arc lights' glare, but every corner of the installation was bathed in radiance. Sheremetiev saw Dzerzhinsky's pretty secretary with a shawl about her head and shoulders.

"You have disgraced the revolution," Dzerzhinsky shouted at the prisoners. The badly burned young woman sobbed. When she started to collapse, a guard stepped up and jabbed her with a rifle butt. She screamed but struggled to stay on her feet. A man put an arm about her shoulders, but the same guard knocked it away.

"You must now plead for forgiveness." The commissar laughed and waved his left hand. Guards hurried in and clubbed the people to their knees, hitting one or two several times to convince them to stay down. He looked at Sheremetiev and nodded.

Christ in heaven, Sheremetiev raged, what more does he want? He can't kill all these people . . . one lone woman perhaps and no one would ask or even care, not in Moscow, not in these days. But fifteen men and women after all that has happened . . .

Dzerzhinsky turned to him. "The honors are yours." And he bowed mockingly.

There was nothing else to do, and he drew his revolver again and shot the first man. He walked along the line of sobbing, screaming people as they pleaded for their lives, aiming for the forehead. After the fifth victim he stopped to reload. Dzerzhinsky stood a few feet away, watching him, rather than the prisoners, with a studied expression of indifference. The lorry engines roared, and Sheremetiev understood their presence now; their noise covered the gunshots and screams. The Chekists watched, some indifferently, some with disgust and some expectantly; an initiation, Sheremetiev thought as he cocked the hammer. They all are here to see if I can do the job, to see if I can qualify. Even that bitch of a secretary. My God, she's practically slavering!

He shot the next six prisoners, five more men and one of the women, who spat at him just as he pulled the trigger. Her spittle struck his trousers, and he didn't bother to wipe it off. He reloaded once more, as quickly as he could. There were three people left. One of them, an elderly man with a shock of white hair pushed himself up when he heard the hammer click on Sheremetiev's revolver. A guard swung a rifle butt, but the man evaded it and spread his arms wide and stared directly at Sheremetiev as if to say, "Come on, Comrade, what are you waiting for? Make a good job of it." Sheremetiev hesitated, and the man laughed at him. Suddenly infuriated, Sheremetiev shot him in the face. The man's laughter bubbled into a choking gasp, and he fell backward, full length, struck the lorry and slumped to the ground. His arms were still outspread, and he pointed one finger at Sheremetiev as if to curse him and died.

Of the two people left, one was the woman who had been burned so badly. In spite of her pain, she pushed herself up and started to run. A laughing guard waved his arms, deflecting her in another direction. A second guard did the same, and when she ran toward Dzerzhinsky, hands clasped, babbling for mercy, he knocked her down. Sheremetiev did not hesitate but pressed the revolver against her head and pulled the trigger. He straightened slowly and walked to the last man, who had not moved from his knees. He had bowed his head at the beginning, hands clasped as if praying. He had flinched with each shot but had not looked up, even when the woman had tried to run.

Sheremetiev placed the revolver muzzle on his neck, but Dzerzhinsky snapped, "No!"

"What . . ." Swept up in the orgy of killing, Sheremetiev almost fired before Dzerzhinsky's command penetrated. He looked up, blinking.

"This man will live, for now. Release him." None of the others seemed at all surprised at the commissar's action, and two guards helped the man up, gently. One raised his chin, and the anarchist blinked, eyes widening in astonishment to find himself still alive.

"Show him."

The two guards led him from body to body, turning each over, making certain the man saw the gaping wounds. When they finished, they brought him back to stand in front of Dzerzhinsky.

"Go to your friends," he said in a conversational tone. "Tell them what happened here tonight, what you saw, what almost happened to you, what did happen to your friends."

The commissar waved him away, and the two guards opened the iron doors and pushed him out into the street. As the doors slammed shut, Sheremetiev had a glimpse of him staring back at them as if in a dream.

In his office Dzerzhinsky poured two glasses of vodka and opened a drawer. He placed a new Mauser magazine pistol on the desk. The weapon gleamed blue in the lamplight, and the red property tag attached to the lanyard ring glowed like fresh blood.

"Now you see why we issue the Mauser machine pistol," Dzerzhinsky told him. "It holds ten cartridges. So much kinder to the prisoners if you do not have to stop to reload."

"The soviet has abolished the death penalty, Comrade Dzerzhinsky." Sheremetiev was surprised that his words were slurred, as if he were drunk.

Felix Dzerzhinsky nodded thoughtfully, trying to decide whether or not Sheremetiev was challenging him to explain. He decided not.

"Of course. And with good reason. You will however note that none of the people whom you shot tonight had been tried in a court of law. So there is no conflict. The Cheka is the guardian of the revolution. There can be no mercy for counterrevolutionists of any stripe. We do what we must do in the name of the people. The people will not stand for the antisocial actions of a few. We are their surrogates. We embody the will of the people."

Sheremetiev nodded as if he understood. And he did, but not in the way Dzerzhinsky imagined. He had been forced to kill sixteen people tonight, in cold blood, fifteen before witnesses. And he had been an officer in the tsarist army. His ultimate fate might be the same as any of those sixteen—and, like theirs, awaited only Dzerzhinsky's pleasure.

He picked up the Mauser and opened the slide—empty. Comrade Felix was a careful man. The slide worked smoothly on well-polished rails, and the interior gleamed with fresh oil.

"A trade." Dzerzhinsky smiled. "The Mauser for your Nagant revolver."

Sheremetiev chuckled, unsnapped his holster and removed the weapon. He broke the cylinder and shook out the cartridges, then handed it over. Dzerzhinsky laughed and took hold of it by the barrel, near the muzzle. Sheremetiev had no doubt that his fingerprints would be lifted from the metal, and the pistol locked away as evidence—just in case.

"There is one thing I do not understand," he said. Dzerzhinsky sank into the chair and glanced up at him.

"Why did you release the last man?"

The commissar nodded. "You are wondering if he will talk about what happened here tonight. Of course he will. As I want him to. Terror, Comrade Sheremetiev. Only terror will defeat the counterrevolutionists. The word that the Cheka will permit no deviation from the party line must spread through all elements of society. As for that man, when he has served his purpose, he will be arrested and executed. Now you must really excuse me as I have much to do."

Sheremetiev nodded and, resisting the urge to salute, started toward the door. As he opened it, Dzerzhinsky cleared his throat.

"By the way, Comrade Sheremetiev, in the Cheka we shoot prisoners in the back of the head, not the front. That way the bullet destroys the face, making it difficult to identify the prisoner and terrifying those who come to claim the bodies."

As soon as Sheremetiev opened the door, the odor of her perfumes filled his nostrils. The electric lights refused to work, and he lit the candle she kept for such occasions. The flickering light wavered about the room as he turned slowly, surveying her clothing overflowing the tiny closet, clean and dirty underwear jumbled together in a heap on the floor beside a tiny bureau, the unmade bed— The image of her sweaty body twisting and groaning beneath his came unbidden, and he clenched his teeth and swore abruptly.

He could have stalled, made excuses for her, might even have convinced Dzerzhinsky that she was innocent. He dashed the candle to the floor and flung himself to the window. Dzerzhinsky had played with him, tested him. If he had failed, they both would have been shot. And what was the sense of that? He had not survived three years at the front merely to die at the hands of a power-hungry madman. But what had he gained? The woman he loved was dead, and he had killed her. Was he any freer now than before? No! When his usefulness was at an end, Dzerzhinsky would simply have him shot.

Maria's bruised face, slimed with tears and snot, came unbidden into his mind, her terror as he pressed the revolver to her head imprinted forever. She or he; he was not the stuff of which heroes were made. He remembered the two soldiers he had killed. After four years their faces still haunted him. Sheremetiev turned away from the window. Other faces slipped through his mind, the faces of men who had served in his company, the faces of dead men filling trenches to overflowing or piled before an enemy machine-gun post or sprawled about a shell crater, feet toward the hole, what was left of their heads pointing away. . . . They all were boys straight from a farm or a factory. They knew nothing, not even why they were there. Most arrived without weapons: "Don't worry, boys. There'll be plenty after the shooting starts. Just pick one up."

What harm had the Austrians ever done them; who gave a damn about the Serbs anyway? The tsar? That foolish, selfish old man had caused them all to die. Even he did not hate the Austrians, nor was he insane, only foolish enough to listen to a traitorous wife and her lover, Rasputin. Damn him; damn him to hell! God, he needed a woman now. Someone to help bury all the dead. He pressed his forehead to the cool window glass and stared at the rain-lashed street until dawn.

VI

Peter Boyd stood at the open window, watching the fishing boats tack across the bay in the late-afternoon sun. Evans stopped on the threshold of his office and gaped, all thought of the German merchant ship seen that morning forgotten.

"What the devil are you doing in Sevastopol?" he demanded in astonishment.

"A grand tour, courtesy of the U.S. Army." Boyd grinned. "How the hell are you, you old bastard?" They clapped each other on the back, laughing and talking at once.

"Putting on a little weight, aren't you?" He prodded Boyd's waistline. "Whoops. What's this?" He turned back Boyd's tunic to see a blued automatic pistol tucked into a waistband holster. "Are you still carrying that monster around with you?"

Boyd grinned. "Hell, don't you know we're at war?"

Evans dug his last bottle of scotch out of a filing cabinet and poured. "Why the devil didn't you let me know you were coming? I could have had a dozen women—"

"Easy!" Boyd exclaimed. "I haven't eaten all day."

They drove in Evans's chauffeured staff car to a small restaurant along the waterfront for lunch. The sea breeze had flushed away the heat, and a striped awning was tipped to screen the interior from the declining sun. Evans ordered two vodkas with quinine water and ice.

"British attaché introduced me to it in Odessa. No gin, so he tried vodka. I added the ice, and it makes a capital drink in this heat. Has another advantage." He grinned. "No whiskey odor. No one can tell

104

you've been drinking. I bet vodka stocks go sky-high in the States after the war."

"Maybe you didn't notice in training camp, but sentiment for Prohibition is gaining."

Evans laughed at him. "Prohibition? Pete, you can't be serious."

"I married Natalia," Boyd said suddenly. He looked away as Evans grinned.

"I'll be damned. You went to Stockholm after all, you old bastard. When was the wedding?"

"December tenth. In London."

She didn't waste any time nailing him down, Evans thought, and for a moment he experienced a twinge of jealousy, then shrugged inwardly. Some men learned early that the cheapest commodity in the world was a woman's body. Others never did. Boyd was one of those others. He lifted his glass. "To the bride. You're a lucky man, Peter Boyd."

Boyd responded in a half-hearted manner, and Evans gave him a mocking grin. "Since you can't have seen her in at least three weeks, you must be tired from the trip."

"I guess I am. It was a damned long—" The waiter brought a platter of fresh-water crayfish just then. Evans dug in with relish, but Boyd only picked at his. He tried to draw Pete out about Natalia until suddenly Boyd threw down his napkin.

"Look here, Bill, I don't want to talk about Natalia or hunting or old times. I was sent out to check on you."

Evans put his fork down and laughed uneasily. "They sent you all this way to audit my books? Christ, I write enough reports every month to keep a dozen file clerks busy." The pleasure of seeing his old friend so unexpectedly vanished as the memory of the German merchant ship at Balaklava recurred.

Boyd shook his head. "I've read all the reports." He picked up another crayfish, started to dip it into the hot mustard sauce but instead tossed it on his plate.

"Damn it, there's no easy way to say this, Bill. Something's wrong. The United States has shipped close to seventy million dollars' worth of arms and supplies to the Crimean National Front, and your reports account for every penny's worth. But"—he lowered his voice and leaned forward—"Orbelesky isn't doing any fighting. Every time Kolchak, Denikin or Kaledin asks for help, he claims he doesn't have sufficient supplies or arms. Yet your reports show just the opposite." He took a deep breath. "Either Orbelesky is lying or your reports are wrong."

The long day, the traces of hangover from the night before, the shock of seeing the German ship had made Evans a bit fuzzy. He stared at Boyd, trying to grasp the ramifications of all that was happening.

Facts kept sliding away into shadow, and he took refuge in wounded pride.

"For Christ's sake, Pete, you aren't suggesting I've phonied the reports, are you?"

Boyd's expression did not change. "Bill, someone has. We have irrefutable evidence that supplies sent to Orbelesky are being sold in a dozen different black markets around the world. After you write a report, who else sees it? How is it sent to Odessa?"

Boyd's comment about the black market made everything suddenly clear, and Evans's apprehension increased. His voice shook as he said, "Pete, I came across something today. I've just learned that Orbelesky may be playing a double game with us." He watched Boyd's face, trying to gauge the depth of his suspicions.

"Go on."

"I inspected the harbor facilities at Balaklava just this morning. That's the alternate naval base about twenty miles or so to the southeast. I wasn't supposed to go there today, as it turned out, because I saw a German merchant ship in the harbor."

Boyd's face crumpled. "Bill"—his voice was barely a whisper—"how in the name of God did you come to see a German ship?"

"The escorting officer was a last-minute replacement—"

"An accident . . . Jesus!" He shoved himself back in the chair, unable to believe what he had just heard. "Orbelesky is so confident that a German ship, flying a German flag, can put into a Russian harbor and you discover it only by accident?" Aware that people were staring at them, Boyd made an effort to control his anger. "Lowden kept trying to tell us that you were being conned by Orbelesky, but I buried his reports because I believed he was wrong. God damn it, Bill, I risked my neck for you! Someone on Orbelesky's staff writes those damned reports, right? You haven't the faintest idea of what's happened to all that equipment, have you?"

Evans slumped in his chair, unable to answer him.

"My God, it's true!" Boyd sprang up, knocking his chair over. He flung a handful of ruble notes on the table, yanked Evans up by the arm and pushed him out of the restaurant. They crossed the road to the beach, and Boyd dragged him along the hard-packed sand at the water's edge until they were well away from the bathers before turning on him.

"Bill, I'll tell you what's been going on here, and you correct me if I'm wrong. The general has your work done by a staff officer so that you can devote all your time and energy to representing the U.S. at every useless party and social function they can dream up.

"Damn it, Bill, it's clear enough from your reports that you've never been within a hundred miles of the front. That naval base you were so proud of inspecting today is the same base Lowden's been trying to get you to look at for a month. But you've been too busy. Where's

Mathilda? How many times a day do you lay her, damn you? No wonder Orbelesky wouldn't accept anyone else as attaché. They've suckered you. They've got their own private pipeline, and Orbelesky can tell Washington anything he wants because Bill Evans is too god-damned busy fucking his wife to write his own reports or do his job properly!"

Boyd took a deep breath. "Do you realize you'll be court-martialed for this? They'll charge you with gross dereliction of duty. And this time your father won't be able to do a thing to help. You are going to rot in some army stockade for years." He swung away in disgust.

Evans knew Boyd was right. Obrechev had developed a convenient hangover because he knew the German ship was due. Obrechev had even allowed Evans to get him drunk so that Evans would, in effect, be conniving at his own deception when he winked at Obrechev's hangover. But a superefficient young officer who wanted out of a stuffy office for a few hours had made a mistake, and Evans had seen the ship.

"Just as you ruined every other chance you ever had." Boyd raged at him. "When the hell are you going to grow up? You don't give a damn about anyone but yourself. You're too self-centered to see beyond what interests you. It was the same with Natalia, with every damned woman you ever met. Hell, you even ran like a scared rabbit when a Bolshevik shouted boo and left your precious Olga to rot in Siberia. Or had you already given her up, the way you did Natalia, because she was too damned inconvenient. Might just want to demand something of you for a change?

"You are a classic study in motivationless life. You have no goals and no real interests beyond your own pleasures. You are lazy, and you haven't one ounce of self-discipline."

"God damn it, Pete, I thought you were my friend. I—"

"Me? You son of a bitch!"

Evans stepped back involuntarily, astounded at the depths of Boyd's anger.

"Who the hell got you the Duma assignment when the Foreign Ministry was demanding your recall after that tea party incident with the grand duchess Olga? Who had you sent to Moscow after you insulted a royal princess and made an ass of yourself with Mathilda Orbelesky? She was married, for Christ's sake, and you didn't even have sense enough keep it private. Who was it that got you that special assignment to interview the royal family, which you messed up the way you do everything? That fuck-up cost me my job, you bastard. Did anyone ever tell you that? When the ambassador found out what you did in Tobolsk, he transferred me that same day and wired the State Department to get you out of Russia as soon as possible."

"What the hell are you talking about? I went to Tobolsk and did exactly what I was supposed to do," Evans shouted. "It wasn't my fault the Bolsheviks wouldn't let me stay. . . ."

"Wasn't your fault . . ." Boyd choked. He took a deep breath. "You know as well as I that you were a fully accredited representative of the United States with full diplomatic immunity. The Tobolsk authorities could no more have told you to get out of the province than they could to blow your nose. The Tyumen Soviet advised Moscow that you had been *chased* out of Tobolsk. *Chased.* That was the word they used. It was reported that the Allies no longer had an interest in the tsar and his family, strictly because of your actions."

"Hell, it's true," Evans tried to protest. "No one even read my report. You weren't there. You don't know—"

"The Bolsheviks believe they can now do whatever they choose with the royal family," Boyd interrupted, determined to hammer his points home. "They think the British passed their responsibility to the Americans, who really don't give a damn. God only knows what that family has had to endure because of you or what will happen to them."

Boyd put a hand to his forehead and glared at Evans. "You know I've no choice but to telegraph Odessa and ask for your replacement. I'll have to tell them that Orbelesky has been selling our arms and equipment to the Germans, right from under your nose." He looked away to the beach, a helpless expression on his face. "You will have to go back to Odessa with me."

"Damn it, Pete," Evans protested, "doesn't friendship count for anything?" A thought suddenly occurred to him, and he shouted at Boyd. "You rotten bastard. You're just trying to get even with me because I took Natalia away from you in the beginning. Christ, she didn't even tell me until afterward that you two—"

Boyd hit him hard, and he sprawled in the sand, tasting grit and blood. By the time he regained his feet Boyd was already climbing onto the road. Without looking back, he walked steadily toward the tram stop.

Boyd was not at the hotel. Evans telephoned general headquarters but was told by the duty officer that no American officer had been seen all afternoon. As the sun moved toward the horizon, Evans stopped his feverish pacing and sank onto a chaise longue on the balcony. It was amazing how his world had turned upside down in a few short hours. This morning his greatest concern was not seeing Mathilda until tomorrow. Now he wanted to kill her; he had lost his best friend, and his future held only a federal prison. He emptied the last of the vodka into his glass.

A messenger woke him shortly after seven the following morning. He sneezed twice as he pried his eyelids apart and saw the uniformed orderly standing beside the hall porter, both looking at him anxiously. He had fallen asleep on the chaise. His head ached fiercely as he tried to read the message form summoning him to a meeting of the general staff at ten o'clock.

In the long, high-ceilinged conference room with its whitewashed stucco walls and dark walnut molding, fans turned lazily and fat Crimean flies droned. Only General Orbelesky and Colonel Obrechev were at the table, and the latter gave him a dour grin and rolled his eyes supposedly to indicate that he was still not recovered from his hangover.

"Ah, Captain Evans, excellent. Our timetable for evicting the antichrists from Moscow is being moved up today." Orbelesky rubbed his round, bald pate and beamed at him.

Evans nodded absently. Where was Boyd? He would have gone directly to Orbelesky for an explanation of the German freighter. But what the hell did it matter? He was finished.

"As you know," Orbelesky continued, "soldiers from the Czech province of the Austro-Hungarian Empire have refused to fight and have surrendered to Russian forces in regimental strength. Now they have organized in Kiev and are offering to fight against Austria and Germany on the western front. The Czechs have been in telegraphic communication with the Bolshevik government in Moscow, with Admiral Kolchak in Omsk and now with us. The Bolsheviks, at the instigation of Austria, have ordered the Czechs to proceed to Moscow to be disarmed. Of course, they have refused to do so.

"Admiral Kolchak and I have agreed to a concerted plan of action regarding the Czechs, and our offer was telegraphed to Kiev yesterday, promising free passage along the Trans-Siberian Railroad to Vladivostok, from where the Allies have agreed to provide shipping to transport them around the world to Europe."

Evans stared at the general in open-mouthed surprise.

"Forty thousand trained, experienced front-line troops," Orbelesky was saying, "in eight prison camps. And to a man, the Czechoslovaks hate the Bolsheviks. You will forgive me if I appear to have gone around you, Captain Evans, but you were away from your office—on an inspection tour, I believe."

Even in his anger, Evans still caught the smug nod Obrechev gave the general, and he was suddenly apprehensive. They must know he had seen the German ship.

"However, as I pointed out to the military authorities in Washington, Paris, and London, forty thousand or so soldiers will make little difference on the western front, considering the millions already there. But forty thousand soldiers could make all the difference here in Russia in driving the godless Bolsheviks from Moscow and Petrograd, after which, a new eastern front against the Germans can be opened. As a result, the Allies have agreed and—"

Evans lurched to his feet. "I don't understand any of this," he snapped. "I have had no instructions—"

Orbelesky handed him a buff-colored envelope. Inside was a single yellow sheet of coarse paper, a telegram sent from the American Consulate in Odessa only that morning.

HEREBY RELIEVED LIAISON DUTY ODESSA STOP PROCEED IMMEDIATELY
JOIN CZECHOSLOVAK FORCES STOP EVALUATE POTENTIAL STOP PER-
SUADE JOIN FRIENDLY FORCES CRIMEA STOP DETACHED DUTY CRIMEAN
NATIONAL FRONT [SIGNED] LOWDEN

"We have been informed," Orbelesky said smoothly, "that a British
officer will take your place as liaison for the Allies as a whole rather
than just the United States."

This must have been sent before they received Boyd's report, he
thought. Evans dropped the telegram on the table. "Yesterday afternoon," he growled, watching Orbelesky carefully, "I saw a German
freighter in the harbor at Balaklava." He tried desperately to keep the
hoarseness from his voice. God, how he wanted a drink. "It was being
loaded with food and American weapons and military equipment."
This last was a shot in the dark, but when he looked from one to the
other, he had no doubt it had gone home.

"It was clearly understood in the terms of the aid agreement
signed between the Crimean National Front and the United States
that you would not engage in trade, commerce or communication with
an enemy of the Allied powers."

Again, those maddening stares, as if he were only a mild annoyance to be dealt with. "I have the authority to stop all aid to the
Crimean National Front and will notify the consulate accordingly."

Orbelesky's face had assumed a serious expression. "I beg your
pardon, Captain Evans. But I find what you are telling me impossible
to believe! Surely you are mistaken? A German merchant ship at
Balaklava?" He glanced at Obrechev, who only shrugged.

Evans had expected any reaction but this. "I've already reported
the fact to Major Peter Boyd of the United States Army, who arrived
yesterday to investigate questions concerning American aid which . . ."
Evans let the thought trail off, unable to put into words the fact that he
had failed miserably. "But then, he will already have apprised you of
this fact." Evans stood and picked up his cap. "I think there is nothing
further for me to say."

"Major Boyd?" Orbelesky turned to Obrechev. "I was aware that
an American officer had arrived at headquarters, but he has not yet
been presented to me."

Obrechev shook his head. "Nor to me, General Orbelesky." They
both turned to Evans.

"I spoke with Major Boyd yesterday afternoon and informed him
of my suspicions," Evans said in desperation, aware that something
was wrong. "If he has not come to you . . ." He stopped, not knowing
what else to say.

Orbelesky scowled. "I do not know what you are talking about,
Captain Evans, but we shall find this Major Boyd and ask him. In the
meantime"—he pointed to the telegram on the table—"since you are

now under my command, your orders are as follows: You will accompany Colonel Obrechev to persuade the Czech forces to place themselves temporarily under my command. You will use your influence as the representative of the Allied nations to the Crimean National Front to see that they obey."

Evans had written his report to Lowden and gone himself to the central telegraph office to see that it was sent off. He had spent the afternoon since then expecting Peter Boyd to contact him. He had finished the second bottle of vodka on the shaded balcony and was stuporous with the heat when Obrechev arrived.

"How pleasant it is here. The breeze is delightful," Obrechev observed, and handed Evans a bottle of scotch whisky. "I thought you might need a drink, so I stole this from the general's private bar."

Evans's first impulse was to hurl the bottle at the street below, but he resisted the childish gesture. Instead, he removed the cap and pointedly filled only one glass. Obrechev snatched it up. "Not going to join me?" he asked innocently. Evans poured a second glass.

"Good. You'll need it. I'm afraid I've got some bad news."

Evans laughed. What the hell could be worse than a general court-martial? he wondered.

"We found Major Boyd. He was killed late yesterday afternoon in a traffic accident."

Evans sat down abruptly.

"Apparently he stepped in front of an army truck. He died without regaining consciousness in the municipal hospital. The police did not identify him until a short while ago."

Tears ran down Evans's cheeks, and he cried, unashamed, for his friend's death. There was absolutely no doubt in his mind that he was responsible.

Commissar Nikolai Khristoforovich Sheremetiev faced the members of the Workers' and Peasants' Soviet of the Ural Region calmly and listened to their denunciations of Moscow's policies. For an hour they had taken turns to wear him down, as if *he* had any influence on the Kremlin. It was clear enough to Sheremetiev what they really wanted —a separate government, independent of Moscow. And why not? he thought. This was Siberia. A different world from European Russia. For centuries the Muscovites—one speaker even used that term—had used Siberia as a dumping grounds for political exiles and criminals. Russia had exploited the area's riches, never once giving back to it, and the new Bolshevik government seemed to be on the same tack.

A sudden silence in the stuffy room surprised him. The fat man, Isiah Goloschekin, had stopped speaking, all eyes were now on Sheremetiev, expecting a clamorous defense, he supposed.

The chairman cleared his throat in annoyance. "Comrade She-remetiev . . ."

Sheremetiev looked up to the dais—already they begin to draw the old distinctions, he thought. "Yes, Comrade Chairman?"

"You have the floor, Comrade Sheremetiev. Do you not wish to reply?"

"No, Comrade Chairman."

Someone swore loudly and condemned all Muscovites as counter-revolutionary fools. Sheremetiev shifted his gaze to identify the speaker, a young man with long, greasy hair and a dirty shirt. An Armenian agitator, an anarchist in actual fact. A self-exile because the tsarist courts had refused to accommodate him. Well, Comrade Portunian, never fear, we'll deal with you sooner or later, he promised silently.

"Comrade Sheremetiev." The chairman rapped the dais with his gavel. "For an hour we have listened to charges being made against the All-Russian Congress of Soviets. As their representative, it is your duty to reply. In view of certain of your requests, it is clear the Moscow Soviet does recognize the Ural Soviet as the sole legal, judicial and governmental power in this region."

"I believe Admiral Kolchak and General Orbelesky would take exception to your last claim, Comrade Chairman," he answered dryly.

Immediately the room erupted in shouts and catcalls. The real decisions would already have been made by the Executive Committee of the Presidium, made up of carefully selected members who had mutual needs to fulfill and crimes to conceal, Sheremetiev thought, and so he was not worried about these preliminaries. Merely bored.

"Comrades! You are the members of the Ural Soviet! But first, you are members of the Bolshevik party. You have sworn an oath of allegiance to the party leaders, and they now are speaking to you through me. You must obey. If you fail to do so, you all know the penalty!"

The silence was as deafening as the noise. Sheremetiev stood before them, a tall, rather handsome man with a face as hard as granite and eyes like Neva ice. In spite of the heat, he wore the black leather jacket and bulky holster containing the Mauser magazine pistol that had become the uniform of the Cheka. The Ural Soviet had its own Cheka, but Sheremetiev reperesented both Leon Trotsky, minister of war, and Felix Dzerzhinsky of the Extraordinary Commission for Combating Counterrevolution and Sabotage. It was a bold party member who would dare to ignore one or both. As if to touch their memories with a whip, Sheremetiev smiled.

"Admiral Kolchak and General Orbelesky are on the march to-gether. Without Moscow, you cannot stand against them. The Whites will hang every man and woman in this chamber—families as well."

The chairman looked around the room. He was an old-line revolutionary and one of the earliest Bolshevik party members, having sided with Lenin immediately after the 1903 split in London. He had been a boxer in his youth and tended to see the revolutionary struggle in terms of boxing strategy—the initial rounds to size up one's opponent; the middle rounds for gathering points in case the final-round knockout failed. The Ural Soviet needed the extra points that Moscow's support would add. He could see that but knew the fanatics who lined up behind Goloschekin would not.

He sighed and announced the decision argued so hotly in the Executive Committee session earlier. "The Ural Soviet agrees to the request of the Moscow Soviet. The counterrevolutionary pig Nicholas and his family will be turned over to the custody of the All-Russian Congress of Soviets in Moscow."

The roar of disapproval began in the back benches and swept forward. The chairman glared the members into silence. "We further stipulate," he continued when the uproar subsided, "that they may be returned to Moscow, under your orders, at a time to be specified by the Moscow Soviet—"

"Allow me to interrupt, Comrade Chairman," Sheremetiev broke in smoothly. "The former tsar and his family will be removed to Moscow in four days. Arrangements have been made."

The chairman nodded reluctantly.

Sheremetiev decided to throw them a bone. "You may rest assured, Comrades"—he smiled, turning to include them all—"that Moscow has no intention of allowing the archcriminal Nicholas to escape the people's retribution. The decision has been made to try to execute the entire family for high crimes against the Russian people."

The house that had been selected to serve as their prison had once belonged to a Jewish merchant named Ipatiev. "A bloodsucker," the local Cheka man told him as they drove from the Ekaterinburg opera house. "We gave him thirty minutes to get out. Ran like a scared dog. The damned Jew—"

"In the new Russia," Sheremetiev snapped, "all men are regarded as equal. It is considered quite Jeffersonian."

The man shrank toward his side of the seat and remained silent for the rest of the ride. Sheremetiev knew without asking that before the war he had been a member of the Black Hundreds, the vigilante bands of racist fanatics who had conducted the pogroms that swept the Jewish settlements with monotonous regularity.

The Ipatiev house was a three-story affair constructed in a typically Russian style that would have served better in the Crimea, set squarely on a hill in the midst of a pleasant neighborhood that sprawled along the hills rising out of the Iset river valley. Voznesensky Avenue, a wide boulevard, ran up a slight incline before the house, which was surrounded by two raw board fences. A machine gun had been placed before the gate. The opposite side of the street was lined with two- and three-story houses set back from the road and well screened by a variety of shrubs, trees and iron fences. Not a wealthy neighborhood but comfortably middle-class, the kind of house his parents had aspired to but never managed to achieve.

Red Army soldiers lounged along the street for some distance, but at the gate, two slovenly guards sheltered themselves from the hot July sun in the shade of a single oak.

He stepped down from the motorcar, and the Cheka man, anxious to make amends, roared at the guards. Both jumped to attention, and one ran off to fetch the guard commander.

Sheremetiev lit a cigarette, folded his arms and strolled about until the guard commander, a thin man in a dirty uniform, arrived. Sheremetiev stared at him as he dropped his cigarette and stubbed it into the dirt with the toe of one highly polished boot.

"You are Jacob Yurovsky?" The other nodded, his eyes moving quickly from the black leather jacket to the holstered Mauser.

"My name is Nikolai Khristoforovich Sheremetiev. I have been sent to Ekaterinburg to take charge of the criminal Nicholas Alexandrovich Romanov and his family. You will consider yourself under my orders."

Yurovsky smiled at him. "Comrade, uh, Sheremetiev, did you say? I am in charge here. My orders come from the Ural Soviet. What I say goes, and I say, 'Take your damned—' "

Sheremetiev handed him an envelope marked with the cipher of the Ural Soviet. Yurovsky snatched it away, and Sheremetiev waited patiently while he read the message, seeming to deflate as he did so. Finally, he refolded the paper, tucked it into his uniform pocket and stepped back. Sheremetiev nodded and walked through the gate.

The place reeked. Odors compounded of decaying vegetable matter, sweat, human excrement, stagnant air and dirt assaulted his nostrils the moment he stepped through the door. The afternoon sun struggled through grimy whitewashed windows to lose itself in a welter of shadows. Two guardsmen stared at him without bothering to hide their hostility.

Sheremetiev did not know it and never would, but as a professional military officer he had this much in common with Nicholas: His contempt for the Ekaterinburg guard contingent knew no bounds. Not one of them appeared to have bathed at any time in the past twelve months. Individually they stank; collectively they could compete with frightened skunks. Their uniforms were odd collections of tsarist army, Austrian national contingents' and civilian clothing. One man wore boots; the next sandals; the third was barefoot. Weapons were dirty and uncared for. The house itself would never again be habitable by decent human beings. In places the walls were rotting where the guards had urinated against them. The rugs were more mud than wool, and the wallpaper had been decorated with bayonet slashes, filthy words in several languages and filthier depictions of stick figures in a variety of sexual poses, natural, unnatural and impossible.

"Adolescent children?" He tapped one cartoon, directing the question at Yurovsky. The guard commander muttered under his breath.

As they ascended to the second floor, a guard at the head of the stairs came to attention, having witnessed some of the showdown through a front window. Sheremetiev ignored him. The second floor was a bit cleaner, but the air was thicker, harder to breathe. A long hallway led to the rear of the house, and several rooms opened off it, all with their doors ajar. He clasped his hands behind his back and strode along the hall, breathing as little as possible. There were twelve people in all, seven family members and five retainers or servants living on this floor. A woman curtsied to him. A maid, he thought. Unable to rid herself of class differences.

Nicholas, alerted by the sound of boots on the bare floor, was standing at the door to his room. Behind him an elderly woman sat in a chair, reading a Bible. Beside her on the bed was a young boy, covered, in spite of the heat, with a blanket. His face was pale, and his eyes were bright with fever. Neither looked at him. So that was the tsarina and her offspring, he thought. Was the boy sick?

Sheremetiev studied Nicholas, both shocked and amazed at his appearance. Whenever he thought of the tsar, it was as he had seen him at the military review in Kazan in 1914, mounted astride a spirited bay horse that danced against the slashing wind. Nicholas had seemed to him then the very embodiment of Russia—stern, patriarchal, looming huge against the snow-laden sky. Now he was just a defeated old man with stooped shoulders and gray hair and beard, dressed in baggy corduroys and a peasant's shirt belted with a bit of rope.

He despised Nicholas for his foolishness in leading Russia into a war for which it was not prepared and for the millions who had died needlessly. And he hated Nicholas because he had been forced to execute Maria. The tsar and his family were no more and no less than the millions of other Russians—like Maria—who had been caught up in the atrocities of war, revolution and civil war, for which, in their stupidity, they bore the blame. The Moscow Soviet had decided that the family must be crushed. Personal survival dictated that he carry out his orders without deviation.

The stench and heat were terrible, and he felt faint but refused to let it show. Yurovsky, pacing slightly behind and explaining one thing or another in muttered undertones, was apparently not bothered in the slightest.

The family were allowed five rooms for themselves and the five servants. Nicholas, Alexandra and their son occupied one room, the servants and retainers three, and the four daughters the remaining room. He stopped outside the door to this last and looked in to see the grand duchesses staring at him. The two youngest, pretty things, were sitting on the bed. One of the older girls stared at him without expression, but her sister watched him with a look that would "turn milk," as his mother used to say. Which daughter was she?

After they had descended to the ground floor again, Sheremetiev motioned Yurovsky aside. "It has been decided that the Romanovs will be removed to Moscow for trial and execution in four days' time unless circumstances force me to shoot them all here. You are subject to my orders. Withdraw your guards at exactly three o'clock today. My own men will assume control inside the house. Is that understood?"

Commissar Jacob Yurovsky watched the car drive off and swore aloud at Sheremetiev's arrogance. Commissar Isiah Goloschekin had traveled to Moscow for the express purpose of obtaining orders from the Moscow Soviet concerning the Romanovs and had gotten them from no less a personage than Jacob Sverdlov. Now this bastard had arrived from Moscow with countermanding orders. Goloschekin had warned him that something like this might happen.

But then he came close to smiling at the thought of the preparations that had been made without even the knowledge of the Ural Soviet —that damned debating society full of women and Jews. He and Goloschekin had already picked the spot in the forest where the bodies would be cremated and buried in lye. The small room at the back of the house would make a perfect shooting pit. They all would be bunched together. Just the way the rich did it: Trap 'em in a big net and blast away with shotguns. Anyone left alive would taste a bayonet. He grinned at his own excitement. That was the way to execute traitors, without mercy or finesse.

Lenin and Trotsky wished the Moscow Soviet to accept all the credit for the final elimination of centuries of repression. Well, he would see about that. Trotsky was a damned Jew, and some said that Lenin was, too. He almost laughed aloud as he hurried inside to telephone Goloschekin.

Tatiana tightened her abdominal muscles, but it was no use this time. With a mumbled apology to her sisters she fled the room. The guard greeted her with a grin and, as she hurried past him to the lavatory, guffawed and punched her arm, then shambled after.

"Leave the door open, dearie," he shouted so that the entire house could hear.

Tatiana stopped, appalled. The guards were mostly Letts from the Baltic regions, and peasants as well. In spite of the rules, they used the third-floor lavatory, the only one inside the house. Filthy animals! The

116

seat was broken and smeared with excrement, and the floor was pud- dled with urine. The tiny box of a room stank, yet the window had been nailed shut. Tatiana and one of the maids had tried to keep it clean, but Commissar Avadeyev, Yurovsky's predecessor, had forbidden it, pointing out sarcastically that it was beneath their dignity to do so. Papa had raged at the man, but to no avail, and had lost his exercise priv- ileges for a week.

Tatiana cleaned the splintered seat as best she could, breathing as little as possible of the nauseating stench. The half-drunk guard propped himself against the doorframe and winked at her, waiting. There wasn't anything else she could do, and choking with angry, em- barrassed frustration, Tatiana hiked up her skirt, lowered her patched drawers and gingerly sat down. The guard was leering, bending and twisting to see better, and she shut her eyes tightly.

The cramps were almost unbearable, and release came with a pain- ful rush that brought an involuntary groan. When she opened her eyes, she saw that the guard was stumbling back to his post, a vodka bottle tilted toward the ceiling. Her eyes encountered the graffiti penciled in crude letters and symbols on the walls. Most of it was in a language she did not understand and was probably misspelled, like the Russian versions—filthy poems and couplets concerning Mama or herself and her sisters and Rasputin. One crude drawing showed her mother on her back, thighs spread to receive a monstrously large penis attached to a stick figure in a priest's hat, obviously meant to resemble Rasputin. Dear teacher, she thought, shutting her eyes, unable to restrain her tears at the defilement of his sacred memory.

Of all the astonishing things that had happened to them in the past year and a half, the most surprising and the one that most puzzled Tatiana was the guards' hatred for this holy man of God. What, she won- dered, had that gentle man ever done to deserve such revulsion? She tried to tell herself that the guards were all atheistic Bolsheviks and would burn in hell for eternity for their sacrilege. But how could God allow . . . she tore her mind away from this blasphemy.

"Here, dearie," the guard hooted. She opened her eyes to see him waving the vodka bottle at her. She shook her head. "Better take some, Comrade Tatiana Nikolaevna. It's good for the bowels." And he dis- solved into drunken laughter again.

Tatiana could not put off any longer this most embarrassing part of the ordeal to which they all were now subjected. The only toilet paper was a copy of an Ekaterinburg newspaper which they weren't allowed to read. Even though the food was so poor that they all were infected with dysentery, the guards delighted in denying them proper sanitation. She tore a single page, all they were allowed, into four sections and wiped herself, conscious that her face was beet red with embarrassment. The guard laughed and offered advice, then stumbled toward her.

Of course, there was no soap, had not been any in weeks. She washed her hands as best she could, rubbing them over and over again to remove the contamination that she could feel on her skin, then laved water on her face.

Drying her face on the sleeve of her blouse, she pushed past the guard, who stood in the doorway to block her. The guards were not allowed to touch the prisoners, but that did not prevent them from finding excuses to force the girls to push past them. Tatiana shrank against the doorframe and squeezed past. She felt one hand fumble to tug up her skirt while the other cupped her breast.

Suddenly it was all too much, and with a sudden movement she broke free and ran sobbing down the hall to her room, screaming silently over and over in her mind that this couldn't be happening to her.

Tatiana sat on the bed staring at the painted window. The heat, trapped in the narrow room, was stifling. She put a hand on her pillow and pushed down to feel the unyielding metal form of the pistol. It was all she could do to keep from ripping the stitches open to snatch it out and kill the monster who had violated her with his hands.

Once, when she was fourteen, she had found a paper-covered romance novel in the woods near their estate in Finland. The book, probably hidden by one of the maids, was cheaply printed on pulp paper and even more cheaply written, yet the story held a certain fascination. Tatiana had read pages at random. The heroine was a young French girl, lost in the countryside during the Middle Ages. For days she wandered through endless forests, searching for the path to her home. One scene remained imprinted in Tatiana's mind: The heroine had fallen exhausted into a haystack one evening and awakened the following morning to discover a soldier sleeping beside her. The author described in lingering detail how the soldier caressed her breasts and thighs with his hard hands and tried to remove her dress. But the heroine managed to run away. For days the heroine felt repelled by this *violation* of her body. Tatiana hadn't understood then what this meant; she did now.

She had been violated, just as the lost girl had. That pig had dared put his hands on her. Tatiana's face was hot with shame. It would never happen to her again. She listened until she heard the clink of a bottle, then pulled the stitches apart and slipped the Browning automatic into the top of her stocking. The gun was warm, like the room, and the hard, dangerous feel of its smooth surface excited her. Carefully she tied it against her thigh with a hair ribbon. The next one who tried to violate her or her sisters would receive the surprise of his life.

Colonel Maxime Rovolovich Obrechev slapped Evans from his stupor. The Czech soldiers, who had seen it all before, ignored them.

"You son of a bitch," Evans muttered in English, "stop hitting me." He pushed Obrechev away and reached for the half-empty bottle of vodka, but the colonel beat him to it. Tears of frustration welled in Evans's eyes, and Obrechev turned away, disgusted.

After a while Evans was able to sit up. Sleep clung to his brain, and his movements were as slow and sticky as his thoughts. There were no shadows on the sun-blasted steppe. Noon, he thought, and fumbled the water bottle from his valise to rinse his face.

Outside, the heat made his headache worse. He stumbled along the armored train after Obrechev, and they passed soldiers pulling a canvas tarpaulin off the huge six-inch naval gun that had been mounted on a flatcar. The train was General Otto Mazachesky's proudest possession. He had captured it from a Ukrainian railroad yard the day the Czechs had been turned out of their prisoner of war camp by local Bolsheviks. This armored train and its six-inch gun, he told them one evening at dinner, were their passport to Vladivostok.

He could still recall the evening two weeks before in the dining room of the Hotel Amerikanskaya in Orenburg, now four hundred miles to the south and west. Late-afternoon sun slanted through the dusty window, lending an air of opulence the hotel did not deserve.

"Gentlemen." Obrechev produced a telegram from his tunic pocket. "Now that Orenburg has fallen and our southern flank is secure, we have been ordered to capture the city of Ekaterinburg."

"Ekaterinburg." General Mazachesky snorted. "My soldiers are not interested in Ekaterinburg, only in Vladivostok."

Obrechev went on as if the general had not spoken. "We will act in concert with Admiral Kolchak's southern army. Ekaterinburg is the headquarters of the most powerful Bolshevik soviet east of Moscow. When we drive them out, the way to Moscow will be open. In addition —he paused dramatically—"an objective equal in importance to the capture of the city is the rescue of the tsar and his family."

General Mazachesky shrugged and drained his wineglass. "Send a Russian army to secure their release. My soldiers are also not concerned with preserving the life of bloody Nicholas."

Evans conjured up a vision of Olga as he had first seen her in the Finland Station, tall, cool, lovely, and then as he had last seen her in the governor's house in Tobolsk: lovelier, if anything, but thinner, with deep shadows of worry in her face. For a moment he closed his eyes as the memory of Boyd's accusation of indifference overwhelmed him. He grabbed up the wineglass and emptied it.

"Intelligence reports indicate the Bolsheviks will abandon the city readily enough under pressure. General Orbelesky has assigned your regiment, General Mazachesky, the honor of leading the attack."

The general snorted. "Some honor. We are not interested."

"Ah, but you are wrong, General. The tsar is the spirit of Russia, revered and respected by all the people—with the exception of a minority of revolutionaries and traitors, many of whom are Jews anyway. His person will serve to unite all anti-Bolshevik factions under the leadership of the Crimean National Front. There will then be no further need for your help, General, and all Czech forces will be free to proceed to Vladivostok. General Orbelesky grants his solemn oath . . ."

Two gunners, naked to the waist, lifted a cylindrical shell, rammed it home and slammed and spun the breech block closed. The officer laying the gun shouted the range, and the barrel rose smoothly, hesitated and exploded with a gout of flame clearly visible in the bright sun. The concussion struck Evans a solid blow.

Evans found a ditch beside a road paralleling the railroad track. The thick grass and immature sunflowers thrusting toward the brassy sky cushioned the thumping of the huge gun. The sun was unbearably hot, and he lay for a while, aware of the vodka bottle close to hand. Through half-closed eyes he saw a single sunflower stalk swaying gently in the heat currents.

He remembered Boyd's hotel room: the old Gladstone bag on the rug, the battered camera on the dresser. He had packed his friend's belongings: a dirty uniform, a pair of shoes, the shaving case with the ivory-handled cutthroat he had often borrowed in Petrograd. It all wouldn't fit, and he emptied the bag to rearrange the contents and found the bottle of White Horse scotch whisky. Boyd, who did not like scotch, must have brought it as a present for him. Evans had not been sober since.

Intermingled with his grief were self-disgust and a sense of fallibility; no, that wasn't quite correct, he thought. A sense of failure that touched everything he did or thought, everyone he knew or loved. He had been fooled so easily in Sevastopol. It was as if Obrechev had been privy to Boyd's assessment of him, had been able to discuss all his weakest points with his father. He *was* the failure and fool his father had always accused him of being.

He remembered Mathilda, and a sense of overpowering anger filled him and he sat up suddenly, blinking in the sunlight. He had driven out to see her the day after the coroner's inquest. The air smelled like hot iron—that's what had reminded him of Mathilda. The air had smelled the same way that day.

She was waiting for him on the terrace with a chilled bottle of champagne and wearing only a thin silk dressing gown, which clung damply to her breasts and nipples, thighs and buttocks.

He had tossed off the first glass to clear his throat, and his anger exploded.

"You bitch! You used me!"

She astonished him by laughing. "Of course I did, just as you used me. I waited for you in Petrograd, waited and waited, but you were with Natalia or some other whore. But the day that Natalia left, you came directly to me, didn't you? That very same afternoon. You didn't even let a decent interval pass before you came panting after me. Then you went off to Moscow with the most casual of farewells, and not a word, not a letter until you appeared a month ago, oh, so full of yourself, dispensing your favors again! And you accuse me of using you!"

Mathilda drew herself up. "You are nothing compared to General Orbelesky. You deserve not the least consideration from me, you bastard. Get out of here!" She flew at him, screaming, and he barely avoided her slashing fingernails.

Sitting in the ditch, drunk, running with perspiration, his uniform filthy, he cried with pity for himself.

The train moved on at dusk. Evans slumped in his seat, head pressed against the hard varnished wood of the coach, aching from sun exposure and hangover and listened to snatches of conversation between Obrechev and one of the Czech officers. He gathered that Bolshevik resistance was stiffer than expected and that they had fallen badly behind schedule. Obrechev was furious, but the Czechs only laughed at him as he stormed up and down the train, begging, pleading, threatening.

Olga was somewhere in Ekaterinburg. Would she remember him? How long had it been? Seven, eight months—or was it a year and seven or eight months? He remembered that he had once entertained thoughts of sweeping her away, and his face burned in the darkness at such adolescent fantasies. Christ in heaven, he needed a drink.

Commissar Nikolai Khristoforovich Sheremetiev studied each member of the royal family and their servants and retainers gathered in the small back room of the house. The westering sun shone directly into the room, and with the window shut and the door firmly closed, it had been worse than an oven. The German woman was close to fainting, and all leaned forward to catch the faintest breath of fresh air from the now-opened door.

"I protest this treatment, sir!" The tsar tried to stand, but his legs refused to support him. "This is a despicable act, hardly worthy of a madman." His voice was thin, had become almost a whine.

"Resume your seat, Comrade Romanov," Sheremetiev said without looking at him.

Tatiana leaned forward to tug at her father's sleeve. "Please, Papa," she whispered. "Your heart . . ."

Nicholas was suddenly a querulous old man. He looked at his daughter, expression uncertain, and then his shoulders slumped and every appearance of military bearing disappeared. Sheremetiev was satisfied. He had seen it happen to hardened professional military officers who had faced the worst the Germans or the Austrians could throw at them without flinching, men who had withstood artillery barrages that lasted for days. Loss of dignity and honor coupled with gross discomfort and suspense could often destroy in days what it had taken eighteen months to kill in the Tsar of All the Russias.

"I have been in communication with Moscow," Sheremetiev told them in an even voice. "It has been agreed that you will be moved from this place tomorrow night. You will be taken to a place of imprisonment pending the conclusions of a commission to examine criminal actions committed by you as tsar of Russia." He paused to look straight at Nicholas. "I will tell you frankly that it does not look good for you, Comrade Romanov."

"Will I be allowed to defend myself?" Nicholas asked in a weary voice.

Sheremetiev laughed. "Of course not, Comrade Romanov. What would be the point? Your crimes are well known. What defense could you possibly offer?"

Nicholas nodded. "Indeed."

Sheremetiev stiffened at the sarcasm in the single word. No, he wasn't quite ready, yet. He stared hard at the daughter who leaned forward again to touch his sleeve. Tatiana, wasn't it? The second eldest— the one who had glared at him yesterday. A pretty thing.

"You will be allowed one bag per person," he went on in a voice suddenly harsh. "No servants will accompany you. They will remain here until the Moscow Soviet decides what shall be done with them. You will be ready to leave at seven o'clock tomorrow evening. That is all."

Nicholas raised his head. "Certainly Dr. Botkin will be allowed to go with us. Alexei must—"

Sheremetiev shouted at him, "You have your orders!" and stamped from the room.

Tatiana helped Olga take their mother upstairs. Olga volunteered to remain awhile, and Tatiana continued along the hall to their room. The Ekaterinburg guards had been replaced by the new men from Moscow, disciplined, cruel men who stared at her as if she didn't exist; no, she told herself, that wasn't quite right. As if she had no right to exist.

The bedroom was hot, but not as bad as the closed room where they had been made to wait for so long. What kind of man did things like that? She pressed her forehead to the whitewashed glass. All day she had been worrying about the pistol. There had been rumors they would be moved. If so, would they be searched? If the pistol was found, she was sure they all would be shot immediately. She had awakened this morning fully resolved to get rid of it. But now she was certain they all were to be executed in any event.

"Sheremetiev." She said his name aloud and started guiltily. The guard at the stairs might hear. Why had he looked at her like that? The memory of his eyes, pale behind narrowed lids, caused her to shiver, and she thought about the guard's hands violating her and choked back a sob.

Did he already have orders from those faceless men in Moscow, those jumped-up peasants who had dared displace her father, dared revolt against God? She would never part with the pistol again. All the horrors the young French girl had endured in that novel and all the ones left unspoken, the things a man could do to a woman with his body that no one would ever talk about, frightened her more than the threat of death.

The gunfire had been steady for some time now. It had intruded on Evans's unconscious, bringing him into that half-waking state where one is prey to the terrors of life and dying and time reaches out to hold one for an eternity. The steady drumming sound through the closed carriage windows and the distant flash of the gun muzzle finally brought him fully awake, and he staggered up from the hard bench to find the car deserted.

Outside, the mild summer night full of stars made a startling contrast with the lines of men shuffling by in the darkness with rifles slung. The whole atmosphere was charged with expectancy. He saw light flicker beyond the horizon and thought at first it was heat lightning until the ground trembled. The train jerked forward, and all the cars crashed together in rapid sequence, moved, stopped, moved again and stopped. Soldiers pushed on board, swearing and laughing in Czech, and the train went on for twenty minutes at slow speed. They were well into the city's suburbs. Old buildings, warehouses, machine shops, blocks of flats passed on either side. All around the train were the sound of rifle fire and, occasionally, the boom of artillery.

Twice more during the short night hours the Czechs clambered aboard. The last time the soldiers were subdued, and in the gray dawn light Evans could see that their faces were strained, worried. One man had a long slash across his forehead, and every few moments he wiped a dirty hand along it and stared at the fresh blood as if seeing it for the first time. He resisted any attempt to bandage the wound, and when the train stopped again and an officer shouted, the others went off, leaving him behind.

After a while the man closed his eyes and slumped a bit in the seat. Evans watched him until the train began to move; then he stumbled forward, concerned. In the strengthening dawn the man's face was pale, and his lips had a bluish cast. Evans touched his arm, but the man did not respond. When he tried to turn his head for a better look at the cut, the soldier collapsed onto his side. Only then did Evans notice that the side of the man's tunic was sodden with blood. When he pulled it open, he saw a shell splinter protruding from his chest. Shock had prevented the soldier from feeling it before he bled to death.

Nikolai Khristoforovich Sheremetiev stared at the note and shook his head in disbelief. His fist crashed on the table, and he looked up at the startled messenger who had just arrived from the opera house.

"Go back and tell those fools that I am in charge and will act according to my orders."

"But . . . but," the man sputtered, "that's . . . that's a direct order from the Ural Soviet. It must be obeyed."

Sheremetiev swung his chair around as Chizov opened the door. "Get this idiot out of here," he snapped to the guards. He pointed to a side chair as the messenger was hustled out. "Well, Mika, you'd better have some good news for a change."

Chizov sank down in the chair gratefully and wiped his streaming face. "All bad, I'm afraid. The Sixteenth Regiment has given way to Kolchak's forces in the eastern suburbs. And there's at least a battalion of Czechs coming up the railway from Orenburg who are breaking through the defenses south of the city. They've got a cannon mounted on an armored train. There's not a hope in hell the Red Army forces can hold them after dawn tomorrow. I passed the main depot on the way here. The rats are already running."

Sheremetiev swore silently, but his face remained immobile. "How long?"

"Tonight for Kolchak's forces. Tomorrow morning, at the latest." He jerked his chin toward the ceiling. "What about them?"

"Dzerzhinsky claims the Executive Committee wants them in Moscow for a public trial and execution—for crimes against the people." He snorted in frustration. "But Sverdlov is trying to gain support from the district soviets, and he's ordered me to hand them over to the Ural Soviet. If I do, Dzerzhinsky will have me shot. But if I don't, well, you saw what happened to Yakovlev. The Ural Soviet declared him a traitor and shot him in secret. Moscow didn't lift a finger a stop it, even though he was only carrying out its orders." He slammed a fist on the desk.

Chizov pursed his lips but wisely remained silent.

"I've had four delegations of loyal workers and soldiers so far this afternoon. Each wanted to hang them all from the nearest tree. The Ural Soviet has reneged on its agreement, and that messenger just brought orders for us to deliver them to the opera house immediately. No wonder the bastards refused to let us leave last night."

Again Chizov said nothing.

"Bring the family to the room at nine this evening," Sheremetiev said at last. "If the news is worse, we'll shoot them all ourselves and run for the train. That way everyone will be partly satisfied."

Chizov pushed himself up and started for the door. "Above all," Sheremetiev called after him, "watch out for the bastard Yurovsky. He and Goloschekin are up to something."

The harsh, unremitting faces of the Moscow guards frightened her. They had been sitting for two hours in the same stuffy ground-floor room they had occupied the day before, although it wasn't quite as bad because the servants and retainers had not been jammed in with them. Also, three chairs had been brought in for her father and mother and Alexei. All the while, the two guards watched them closely and fingered their weapons.

Tatiana first heard the guns at noon. For a while she thought it was distant thunder and breathed a prayer of thanksgiving; rain would relieve the horrible heat and cool the house. There had been so little rain this summer. She had rushed to Papa, but his haggard, hopeless face had told her that they were guns, artillery, and that they had come too late. The White armies rushing to their rescue would never find them alive.

In the first hour Nicholas had tried to lead a prayer, but the guard had threatened to beat them all if he didn't remain silent. Alexei had fallen asleep against Papa's knee, and Anastasia was stretched out on the hard floor. Alexandra read her Bible, and Marie sat staring at nothing. Once in a while Tatiana saw a shiver pass across her thin frame. Olga sat beside her father, holding his hand, and Nicholas just gazed at the painted-over window.

Tatiana knew they would not survive the night. It only remained to see how they would be killed. She was afraid of dying but even more of being tortured, or *worse*. Once the guard commander, Sheremetiev, had looked in on them from the doorway, his face expressionless and his eyes deadly cold. His glance had lingered on her, and the single word *violation* began to repeat itself over and over in her mind. Is that what had happened to the French girl in the end? Oh, why hadn't she hidden that book in another place to finish it? At least she would have known what to expect.

She pressed her thighs together against the pistol. The warmth that stole through her body whenever she did so was somehow comforting. She should be praying, readying her soul to meet God . . . yet all manner of thoughts kept intruding, especially her resolve to kill at least one guard before she or any of them were killed. Her abiding hope was that Commissar Sheremetiev would be the one.

The pale square of window faded into darkness. A guard she recognized as one of the younger Ekaterinburg men brought a lamp.

When he noticed Alexandra tip her Bible to catch the last light from the window, he placed it on the table and adjusted the shade. Alexandra smiled, and Nicholas thanked him. Tatiana watched with veiled eyes, thinking that after months of cruelty a single act of impulsive kindness made little difference. And even that was spoiled when he began to collect their rings, brooches and earrings. She flung hers on the floor, and he stooped and picked them up, face flaming with embarrassment. Tatiana ignored her father's gentle reproof.

Sheremetiev sat behind the desk, listening. The guns were much closer now, well into the city suburbs. He could identify them by their sound—the sharp bark of Red Army howitzers, the deeper, growling sound of fieldpieces from the east and the drawn rumble of the Czech cannon.

Ekaterinburg would fall to the Whites before dawn; of that he was now certain. In midafternoon a rumor that the Czechs had pushed a force of mounted men to the west and cut the rail line had swept the city. The stories claimed whole trainloads of people shot down by Czech firing squads and one train dynamited to kill all the passengers when their ammunition ran low.

Sheremetiev automatically dismissed those stories as ridiculous exaggerations; the same stories had been told about Russian trains captured by Austrian and German troops in August 1914. He flung himself from the chair to pace the room. Where in hell was Chizov? Why didn't the man . . . if he didn't return within an hour, he would shoot them all.

The Chekists appeared at midnight, six of them, all armed, and Sheremetiev was with them. Fear, and something else—exultation perhaps—rose in Tatiana. Nicholas stood slowly, resolutely, and Alexandra laid the Bible in her lap, one finger marking her place. Alexei slept on, and Tatiana hoped they would not wake him. It would be so much kinder. The window was thrown up with a sudden clatter that caused them to jump. Two more armed guards appeared outside.

Tatiana had changed her position, moving to the back of the family group, so that she was not clearly visible from the door. She spread her legs, as if stretching cramped muscles, and reached beneath her skirt. Her fingers closed around the hard rubber grips, and she untied the ribbon and eased the weapon free of her stocking.

All were standing now, facing their executioners. Olga opened her mouth to speak; but Nicholas squeezed her hand, and she did not. Tatiana thought she had already reached the absolute limit of her terror, but now she was absolutely frozen with fear. It raged in her chest, her throat, throughout her body like a hot stream of acid. Her mind whirled, and her eyes closed involuntarily; her fingers spasmed, and the pistol nearly slipped from her fingers.

"Have you come to kill us now?" Nicholas asked quietly, his voice taking on the old familiar resonance. He shamed her; how could she be so terrified when he was so calm?

"Come." Sheremetiev spun on his heel and hurried out. The Chekists picked up their suitcases, and one started to wake Alexei; but Nicholas stopped him. Instead, he picked the boy up and cradled him against his chest. Alexei opened his eyes.

"Papa?"

Nicholas shushed him gently.

Tatiana took a deep breath. So they were being taken elsewhere to be murdered. The pistol was still in her hand, and she thrust it into her coat to push it through the opening of her dress and into the bodice of her chemise just before a guard shoved her roughly from the room.

They were led to the side door that opened into what they had jokingly named the exercise yard, a space a few feet wide by twenty long bounded by the house and a high board fence. Tatiana saw that the boards at one end had been removed and two lorries were backed into the yard.

They were going to be killed here. . . .

A door opened behind them, and Tatiana turned. She had only a brief glimpse before a guard snarled, "Keep your eyes to the front."

But in that instant she had seen her mother's maid, Demidova, Dr. Botkin, her father's valet, Trup, and Kharitonov, the cook, and others being pushed into the same room they had just left. She had also seen the guard, the one who had run his hands over her, with a drawn pistol in his hand, and her knees almost gave way. She choked back the scream just as a guard pushed her after the others. They crossed the yard and climbed a makeshift staircase of wooden crates into the back of the lorry. Just before the rear curtain was fastened, two guards with rifles climbed in to stand facing them. Surely, she thought in anguish, they could not expect two men with rifles to kill the seven of them? She bit her lip to keep from crying out.

The truck lurched into motion, swung hard right and rattled over an obstruction before turning again, this time onto the smooth pavement of the road. It picked up speed downhill, and at the bottom the driver braked hard and turned, throwing them against one another.

Her mother began to pray aloud, and Papa and then Alexei joined her. One guard shouted for them to be quiet, but for the first time in their captivity the family, as one, disobeyed a direct order. The guard shouted again, but his companion told him to shut up.

Alexandra was repeating the comforting words of her favorite psalm. The family's murmuring filled the stuffy interior of the truck, and Tatiana cried silently.

*   *   *

The endless ride, coupled with tension and exhaustion, took its toll. Tatiana heard her father whisper to Alexandra that Alexei was asleep again. With that simple family message, a terrible fury engulfed her, and for an instant she would have gladly murdered each of the guards. Her hand trembled as she clutched the pistol grip in her bodice. Why, why, she demanded of God, was He allowing this to happen? They were being taken for butchering. Why? What possible purpose could be served by the deaths of children like Alexei, Marie and Anastasia? What purpose in the deaths of her father and mother? Of any of the family? Or the servants and friends who had refused to desert them? Could any God be so harsh as to allow this to happen? For an instant her thoughts frightened her. Had she committed the gravest of all sins, the denial of God? Not even Job in his . . . She clutched her head in her hands and rocked back and forth on the bench until she felt her mother's arms go around her shoulders and heard indistinct words of comfort murmured over and over.

The truck stopped unexpectedly. For an instant there was only silence; then someone yanked the canvas away. Harsh light poured in, blinding them.

"Get down!" a voice shouted. "Hurry."

Sheremetiev appeared out of the glare, talking over his shoulder to a smaller man. His narrow face turned in their direction, and for a moment his eyes reflected the arc lights like a cat's. Armed guards formed a half circle about them; all she could see were shadowed faces, men staring at them, some with curiosity, some with hostility, waiting only to be told to open fire. She folded her arms and squeezed to feel the pistol hard against her breasts.

". . . strong detachment of Czechs are in the outskirts." The small man was nearly hysterical. "They'll be here anytime."

Sheremetiev's voice roared the man into silence. "Rumormongering and spreading false and seditious lies are punishable by death!" he shouted.

The other voice was silent for a moment, and peering into the glare of the arc lights, Tatiana saw that the man was dressed in rumpled worker's clothes and wore steel spectacles that made his face seem even narrower. He appeared as frightened as she was.

"You are right, Comrade." The man swallowed. "But something has to be done. We are evacuating as quickly as possible." His voice dropped. "The Red Army can't hold out any longer. We've had reports that units have panicked and run away. Kolchak's soldiers are near the city center. . . . By dawn . . ." He gulped and drew a deep breath to steady himself. "They say that the railroad line has been cut to the west. The Romanovs must be shot, now!" His eyes slid in their direction, then darted away in fright.

A fresh surge of fear plunged through her. She wanted to gag,

128

and her stomach was on the verge of erupting. Perhaps worst of all was the burning pain of muscles tensed far too long in her back and legs, in her neck and forehead. Oh, God, please, make them get it over with quickly.

Her glance veered to her father. Nicholas was standing stiff-backed, and beside him was Alexei, also at attention as befitted the tsarevich. Her mother stared calmly at the commissar, Bible in one hand and chin raised. Tatiana felt a rush of affection for them all, especially for this severe, stern woman whom she remembered as so warm, so loving and so beautiful.

"The most beautiful woman in Russia on her wedding day, when all women are beautiful," Anna Vyrubova had once told her.

Tatiana watched the commissar closely, her back straight, as she had been taught. She was the daughter of the tsar of all the Russias, and this night these men, these animals who would murder them, would carry away a picture of her that would haunt them to the end of their days and beyond, to eternal damnation in hell.

Sheremetiev strode away from the man unholstering his pistol. He stopped in front of Nicholas, who faced him without flinching.

"The Ural Soviet has sentenced the Romanov family to death for crimes against the Russian people, the sentence to be carried out immediately."

In spite of her resolve, Tatiana swayed in a half faint at the words. Pistols were drawn and cocked. Her father stepped toward Sheremetiev, as if to shield his family. Tatiana pushed aside the worn fabric of her dress and grasped the Browning pistol. Sheremetiev was standing three paces from her, half-turned to face her father so that his side was presented to her. One step forward, she told herself, then press the gun against his ribs where the bullet would be certain to strike his heart. Her thumb pushed the safety off. Father in heaven, forgive me, she breathed as her head roared and the universe became concentrated in the seam just behind the commissar's arm. The arc lights glared against the black leather.

". . . the Moscow Soviet, for the time being, has overruled this decision," Sheremetiev said. The words began to penetrate the noise in her head. "You will be removed to Moscow at once. But I warn you, a single instance of attempted escape will be punishable by immediate execution. All members of the family, Comrade Romanov, will be shot. Do I make myself clear?"

The words buzzed in her head as meaningless as insects on a summer evening. Hadn't he said they were to be executed? She hesitated, the pistol half-drawn from her bodice.

"Yes, Commissar," Nicholas said in a clear, sharp tone, and several guards exchanged troubled glances.

"Put them aboard the train!" Sheremetiev bellowed.

VII

Evans counted ninety-three bodies beneath the wall. They had been shot down as fast as they could be brought up from the cells, he supposed. The numbers to be executed had forced the firing parties to shoot each batch of prisoners before the last was taken away so that the bodies were piled one on top of another. Even so, there hadn't been time to kill them all. At the back of the prison, in the last two tiers, the Czechs had found thirty-three men and women still alive.

Obrechev had come down as working parties of Red prisoners carried the bodies out into the sunny courtyard and piled them onto carts for burial.

"A terrible thing," he muttered. "But we'll soon avenge them. Five Reds for every one killed!" He threw away his cigarette and nodded to the lines of Red prisoners carrying bodies up from the cells. "Starting with those bastards."

Evans turned away, sickened and badly in need of a drink.

White Army troops belonging to Admiral Kolchak and General Orbelesky had occupied the center of the city by the time the Czechs crushed the last resistance in the southern suburbs and captured the railyard and industrial districts in fierce hand-to-hand fighting. Relations between the two groups were badly strained; the Czechs knew they had been given the worst of the fighting.

A message from Mazachesky was waiting when Evans returned

130

from Orbelesky's headquarters in the municipal opera house, requesting that he come to his office as soon as he returned. There was not even time for a drink, and muttering angrily, he followed the messenger through the corridors of the modern office building.

"We've found the house where the Romanov family was kept," Mazachesky began as soon as he appeared in the doorway. "Apparently they all were shot."

Evans sat down abruptly. His head was filled with a roaring noise that blocked all thought. For a moment he thought he might be sick to his stomach.

". . . . in a small room and shot. The walls and floor have been cleaned up, but I'm told there are still traces of blood and bayonet marks. I want you, as a representative of the Allied high command, to go there immediately."

Evans was driven in a requisitioned automobile through a comfortable neighborhood that could have belonged to any medium-sized city in the United States. Electric streetlamps dangled across the paved road. He noted the incongruity of a British Union Jack hanging listlessly in the heat and read the sign in English and Russian as they passed, "British Consul—Ekaterinburg." The car labored up a slight incline to a big house surrounded by a high board fence. Grim Czech soldiers stood about; the street was otherwise deserted.

A Czech lieutenant saluted Evans's captain's insignia and glanced away from his unshaved face and rumpled uniform. Evans was suddenly conscious that he had not bathed in a week. The officer led him inside. The house was indescribably filthy, and the odor of unwashed bodies, overflowing toilets and human feces overpowering.

As they walked through the house, the disorder and wanton vandalism reminded him of the governor's house in Tobolsk, although that had been mild in comparison. The Czech officer spoke hesitant Russian, and he used it to comment on the morals and sanitary habits of all Russians. Evans let him babble on, shocked himself at the drawings and filthy words that had been chalked, painted and carved into the walls and woodwork.

The officer stood aside to let him enter a small room. The single whitewashed window glared balefully, the only source of light. The room was papered in a striped pattern, and the ceiling arched toward the center. The molding about the junction of wall and ceiling was intricately carved. The floor looked as if someone had used it as a throwing knife target. The wall facing the door had been shattered chest-high, and the diagonal lath work was exposed. A double-doored wardrobe contained a bullet hole in each door. There was no doubt that people had been murdered in this room. He could even see where a sponge or cleaning brush had left rusty streaks as the blood was washed away. The floor was gritty with a mixture of sand and chalk, and the strong smell of pine tar soap that reminded him, fittingly enough, of Rasputin could not quite hide the rich metallic smell of blood that had soaked into the floorboards. He thought of Rasputin's long-ago prediction that he would be the salvation of the royal family. The son of a bitch had been wrong again.

"Bodies?" he asked after several minutes, and the Czech officer who had been standing with his back to the wall, eyes closed in weariness, shook his head.

"No. And no trace of any. We've interrogated some of the neighbors. They reported some shooting about midnight and lorries coming and going all night—as would be expected." He snorted. "No one admits to knowing the Romanovs were here. They claim they thought the prisoners were merely high personages of the old regime."

"The British consular official down the street?"

"He at least admits to knowing about the Romanovs. He claims to have tried to see them many times." The officer shrugged. "He did not hear shots last night."

The officer pushed away from the wall. "I suspect that they all were brought down together, the family and whatever servants were left to them. They must have waited in the room for some time as there are scribblings on the wall. The guards stood just inside the door, and perhaps at the window as well, since there are bullet holes opposite. They finished off anyone still alive with bayonets. Someone must have tried to get away." He pointed to a succession of bayonet gouges in the walls and along the floor, leading to a scarred area hideously marked with dried blood. "The bodies must then have been carted out to lorries and taken away. You can see where they tore down the fence and the tire tracks."

Evans nodded, trying to ignore the pain in his chest and the metallic flat taste burning his mouth. The urge for a drink was overpowering. "You said scribblings. Where?"

"Here." The officer stepped to the window and stooped.

Squinting, Evans spelled out "Belsatzar ward in selbiger Nacht von seinen Knechten umgebracht."

He copied the words in his notebook and stood up, then had to lean against the wall to regain his equilibrium as the blood rushed from his head. The room was making him feel sick, and he went out and hurried through the house to the main porch. The Czech officer followed.

"What do you think?" he persisted.

"Think? About what?" Evans mopped his sodden forehead and looked through the gate in the double fence to the street where the sun had hammered everything to a dull, dust color. My God, won't this heat ever end?

"About the writing, of course. Is it German?"

Evans took the notebook from his pocket and squinted at the scribbled words. "Yes." The words seemed vaguely familiar, as if he might have read them once.

"What do they mean? Can you read German? Surely you don't think Germans shot them, do you?"

Evans brushed the suggestion aside with a wave of annoyance. "Of course not. It means—" and he struggled to translate from German to English to Russian—" 'On the same night Belsatzar was killed by his slaves.' "

"Belsatzar! He was a Babylonian king, in the Bible, wasn't he?"

"Yes." Evans stared at the writing. He had just noticed that the word *Belsatzar* was misspelled. In German, it should have been *Belsazar*. Someone had added a *t* to approximate the German transliteration of the Russian spelling of *tsar;* one of the executioners had a penchant for classical, if grim, humor.

"You have seen the house then?" Obrechev greeted Evans with a suspiciously good-natured smile when he returned to the CNF headquarters. "You will be forwarding a report to your government concerning the murder of the tsar and his family?"

Evans nodded, aware of the curious numbness that gripped him. It was as if he were sitting at a great remove, watching the world through the wrong end of a telescope. Strange, he thought. I feel sorrow for the entire family, but no outrage. The knowledge that Olga was dead, murdered, had initially filled him with a cold fury, but now there was only a great, empty weariness.

"Ah, good. But before you do, you must talk with two Red soldiers whom we captured this afternoon. They were found hiding in an empty warehouse."

Evans started to protest; but Obrechev insisted, and he had no choice but to follow him up to the fourth floor, which was being used as a jail. Makeshift bars had been rigged by the simple expedient of removing the glass from the office doors and nailing wooden slats across the opening. Guards with rifles paced the corridors. Two more stood at each elevator. The two special prisoners were held in a large central room, and each was heavily manacled and guarded by a soldier with a rifle and bayonet.

The two men, one in his late thirties, the other hardly more than a boy, sat against opposite walls. "Letts, both of them," Obrechev said.

"Lithuanian. That's what we are," the older man growled. Evans recalled then that *Lett* was a slang term for people from the Baltic provinces, who were generally considered inferior in intellect, morals and civilized habits to the Russians. They both were dressed in odd bits of filthy uniform, an Austrian tunic and Russian trousers. Both were barefoot, and he guessed that their boots had been taken away.

"Tell him," Obrechev prompted. The elder prisoner hawked and spat on the floor, but the younger one shifted uneasily, eyes darting from his companion to Obrechev and back again.

"Tell him," Obrechev said once more.

"What difference does it make if I tell them again, Petri?" the younger boy begged. "They will kill us anyway. Why not make it easier?" The one addressed as Petri turned away, and the boy stared at him in misery. Evans noticed the smear of blood and the bruises on his face.

"Tell me what?" Evans prompted.

"I . . . that is, we were guards at . . . at the prison where the Romanovs were kept."

Evans was shaken by the intensity of his sudden hatred. "I suppose you helped write all those obscene poems and pictures on the walls?" was all he could think of to ask.

"Ah, no, not me. As God is my witness, not me!"

Petri laughed harshly. "No, not him! He's too prissy for that. Not so good as to refuse to pull a trigger, though."

"I had no choice," the boy screamed. "They . . . you all would have shot me if I hadn't . . ." He gulped and sank down on his knees, huddling his arms about his chest.

"You were one of those who shot the Romanov family?"

The boy's face worked in an expression somewhere between hope and despair. "No, Your Honor. No. You see, the Romanovs were not shot. Only the servants and retainers. The Romanovs were taken away by Chekists from Moscow. The all wore black leather jackets . . . I saw them myself at the railroad yard. I helped the women down from the lorry . . . no, they are still alive, Your Honor."

"Shit!" The older man snorted. "They're all dead. Every one of them." He nodded at the blubbering boy. "Ask him. Ask him how many times he fired his pistol. Ask him how many times he stuck his bayonet in the woman. Killed her, he did. Bayoneted her in the throat. Ask him how he used to spy on them when they went to toilet. He was always there, watching and laughing, trying to get them to pull up their dresses. . . ."

Evans blundered out of the room and leaned against the wall, gasping for breath. Behind, he heard a high-pitched scream and the sound of blows. Obrechev came out a few moments later and clapped him on the shoulder.

"Felt the same way myself. Don't worry. They've already been court-martialed. They'll hang this evening." He sucked on a bruised knuckle and grinned at Evans.

"What about the young one's story?" he asked thickly. Evans was surprised that he had to struggle to force the words out. "He said the Romanovs were taken away. . . ."

134

"Nonsense! A poor story to save his life. You saw the room. Do you have any doubt they were killed? We'll find the bodies soon enough." He took Evans by the arm and led him to the elevator. He clapped him on the shoulder.

"We may have come too late, but all is not lost, by God! A dead tsar's worth as much to us as a live one. Maybe more! He certainly can't interfere and argue over details. Imagine, bayoneting those four young girls to death. It couldn't be better. Come on now, I've still got a bottle or two hidden away, and I need a drink as badly as you do after that!"

Evans rode the elevator down with him, thinking that now indeed, Orbelesky had his *cause célèbre*.

The train moved across the endless steppe in fits and starts or sat motionless in the sweltering heat, both doors tightly closed and locked, the only ventilation provided by two hatches at either end of the roof and the numerous small cracks and crevices in the weathered wood of the wagon sides. Only at dawn and again at sunset were the doors opened briefly. Then two armed guards waited in the shadows, bayonets mounted, as two other guards brought a single pail of food: oatmeal in the morning and a thin, tasteless stew in the evening. Nicholas would hand down the slops pail, and later it would be returned, carelessly cleaned, if at all.

During the day the family tried to amuse themselves with the pocket chess set Alexei had hidden in his tunic or by playing twenty questions or with geography quizzes. At other times they simply lay on the musty straw, enduring the breathless heat. From time to time Tatiana would press her face to a crack and stare at the brownish land or, if they were stationary, at a single cloud and imagine fanciful figures.

Her terror had subsided to a dull ache of constant apprehension, but her sleep was filled with the most terrible dreams in which faceless men pursued her naked through dark rooms filled with menace. At the very least, she thought, they now knew the worst. They *all* had been sentenced to die, and it would happen, sooner or later.

The last few days and especially the last night in Ekaterinburg had taken an immense toll of each member of the family, her father most of all, as if he were blaming himself for what was happening to them all. When he spoke to her or answered a question, his eyes looked past or through, never at her. His answers were vague and often meaningless. Only with Sheremetiev was he stiff-backed and precise. His face had aged terribly, with deep lines below his eyes and around his mouth; he shuffled as he walked, and his hands trembled constantly.

Alexei lay quietly in the straw that Olga and Marie kept banked for him. His right leg was again badly bent at the knee. He had fallen the first night when the train had jolted unexpectedly. The swelling had begun the following day, and there was nothing that could be done to relieve the terrible pain of blood flowing into the joint. He had fallen into a half-waking state in which he tossed and turned constantly. Low moans escaped his lips whenever the train shuddered or jarred over points or a section of bad track. Yet even though the pain must have been excruciating, when awake he did not so much as utter a whimper. What a brave, decisive tsar he would have made, she thought, and immediately felt a touch of shame for the implied criticism of her father.

Olga had all but collapsed. At night she would wake screaming, and during the day she sat beside Alexei, staring at nothing. She had become positively haggard, and her face and hands were covered with dirt and sores. Her long, wonderful hair remained unbound and had developed a curious crinkly appearance. Her skin was blotchy, especially about the eyes. Tatiana could see in her the same destructive changes that had robbed her mother of any semblance of her once-famous beauty.

Marie retreated into her Bible, and Anastasia clung to her mother as if she were a small child again. All traces of baby fat had long since disappeared, and she might, Tatiana thought with bitterness, have been the most beautiful of the sisters.

The train halted as the late-afternoon sun was turning to gold. Tatiana was able to establish only that they had stopped in a railyard. For several hours trains chuffed back and forth, and once she heard the distant shout of a workman. It was almost totally dark outside before the door slid back and a lantern flashed, blinding them all.

"I trust I find you all well?" the familiar voice of Commissar Sheremetiev asked.

Tatiana screwed up her eyes as her father stood up, like an old man. Sheremetiev moved the lantern to take in their worn, unwashed clothing, the tattered straw covering the floor, the bucket which had not been emptied that day and was overpowering in the heated interior.

"I apologize for the harsh conditions," Sheremetiev said quietly. "However, the Russian people are also enduring such tribulations, and I know that you do not mind sharing their burden."

"Indeed not." Nicholas smiled. "But if conditions are as bad outside as they are inside, then they must have worsened since I gave up the throne."

"Insults will not help your case at all, Comrade Romanov."

"Can they hurt?"

Sheremetiev glanced around the wagon, ignoring the remark, perfectly conscious of the tension he was causing. He set the lantern down on the floor and drew out a cigarette, tapped it on the back of one hand

and lit it with a silver cigarette lighter. He inhaled deeply and let the smoke trickle through his nostrils while he regarded Nicholas closely.

"We will remain here for a period of time. You will be allowed out once in the evening for thirty minutes. Where is your cap?"

Nicholas touched his bare head and grinned ruefully. "It has worn out, I'm afraid. The bill came away—"

Sheremetiev handed him his own. "Wear this. It will help disguise your face." He turned to go.

"Can you not tell us where we are? Is this Moscow?"

Sheremetiev paused at the door. "No, Comrade Romanov, you are in Perm."

He blew out the lantern, and a guard rolled the door shut.

The two Ekaterinburg guards were executed that same evening. As a representative of the Allied powers Evans was required to attend. The two men were marched from the opera house to gallows rigged in the square by the simple expedient of throwing noosed ropes over lamp standards. Two stepladders served as platforms.

The older guard, Petri, came out of the building, back straight and contemptuous until he saw the stepladders and nooses. Then he screamed once and collapsed. The boy glanced at him and continued by himself to the nearest ladder while Petri had to be dragged. Evans looked away, embarrassed and disgusted. Obrechev was watching, expressionless. Evans noticed that his hands twitched from time to time as if in anticipation of pulling the ropes himself. General Orbelesky had not bothered to attend.

Two lines of soldiers faced the front of the building. The entrances to the square had been blocked, but even so, people waited in the gathering dusk. Why? Evans wondered. What was so interesting about seeing a man die?

There was no fanfare, no ruffle of drums, no reading of the sentences. Two soldiers helped each man onto a ladder, and the sergeant serving as executioner adjusted the noose about each man's neck. As soon as he was satisfied, he motioned the soldiers away. The older guard, Petri, sagged against his noose, then jerked upright as if galvanized and almost lost his balance. The executioner steadied him, and his gasp of relief was audible in the square. It would have been comical if it hadn't been so fruitless. The younger man's eyes were closed, and he swayed gently on the ladder.

The executioner glanced up at Obrechev, then pivoted and snatched the ladder away. Petri dropped like a stone, and the snap of breaking bone cracked loudly in the stillness. The boy stiffened at the sound, opened his mouth and groaned just as the executioner dashed to the next standard and snatched his ladder away. Evans turned away, sickened. Olga was dead. The killing of two of her executioners hadn't changed that in the slightest.

The following afternoon he walked up the hill toward the Ipatiev house. He had no reason for being there other than the fact that he was too restless to remain in the hot, stuffy office that had been allotted him. There was little for him to do now that the Czechs were pulling out, and he needed another look at the house to describe it properly in his report.

A breath of wind in the hot, still afternoon caused him to look up. In his preoccupation he had walked past his destination and was standing before a two-story house nearly hidden behind an unkempt garden. It was typically Russian in architecture, but with concessions to the harsh Siberian winters. All the usual fretwork standard in European Russia had been eliminated so that the house reminded him of those gaunt structures seen on the wind-swept prairies of Wyoming or the Dakotas. The thought that the residents might have been able to see over the fence from the upper floor struck him.

Curiosity aroused, he pushed through the rickety gate and went up a flagstone walk all but lost in the overgrown yard. Ornamental bushes grew so thick that he had climbed the steps before realizing that a porch ran the entire length of the house. He pulled the bell and heard it ring inside.

The door opened, and Evans saw an old woman peering out at him.

"Good afternoon, madam, I'm sorry to disturb you. May I ask you a question or two?" He smiled again, hoping he hadn't frightened her.

"Are you to do with the government?" she asked, peering at his uniform, and he shook his head.

"No. Not a Russian government in any event. I'm an American army officer."

"An American," she marveled. "I've never met an American before." She beckoned him into a spotlessly clean hall redolent of flowers and polishing wax. In contrast with the afternoon heat, the house was cool and dark. In a parlor crammed with a lifetime of mementos, knick-knacks and potted ferns, reddish light made its way beneath a heavily fringed shade, and he saw that his hostess was an elderly, spare woman who barely rose to his elbow.

"Will you take a cup of tea?"

Amused by her formal courtesy, he nodded. "I would enjoy that."

She bustled away. The massive silence of the house, the warm tones of walnut and oak, the familiar smells, the lacy busyness of the room—all reminded him of his grandmother's house in Boston. Inexplicably he felt better and took a deep breath. The painful need for a drink receded. The oak bookcase, he was surprised to find, held volumes in several languages and included an eclectic range of authors from Bret Harte to Leo Tolstoy, Shakespeare to Kant.

"I see you have discovered the library," she piped as she hurried in with the tea tray. "My husband was an amateur linguist, and he enjoyed reading. He knew twelve languages in all. We spent many winter evenings in this room." She sighed. "They were so enjoyable."

She placed the tray on the table and motioned for him to sit. "Now we must introduce ourselves. My name is Veronica Maximievna Lodoskaya. And you are . . ."

Evans gave his name in turn and told her that he was the military representative of the Allied powers to the Crimean National Front army. At a loss where to start, he made small talk while they sipped the tea. "You have a very nice house."

"Thank you, young man. My husband built it with his own hands, thirty-six years ago. Our only son was born here. Both are gone now. Our boy disappeared in the winter of 1915, and the news killed my husband." She gave a sigh, then handed him the plate of cakes. "I bake them myself, but so few ever visit now. My son, André, loved them. He would have been about your age."

"I'm curious," Evans told her. "Why did you and your husband come to Ekaterinburg, especially so long ago? I can tell by your accent that you're not from Siberia originally."

"For a foreigner, your Russian is very good, young man. You have a definite Petersburg accent and a good ear. We came, or I should say my husband came, on a Romanov passport."

"Romanov passport?"

She chuckled. "You don't hear that term anymore. Not for years. A Romanov passport was a sentence to exile in Siberia. You see, my husband was a student in Smolensk. He took part in a student strike against the previous tsar, Alexander the Third. I do not even remember the reason now. He was arrested by the Okhrana and sentenced to five years at hard labor in Siberia. In those days such a sentence meant the gold mines or the forests. The gold mines were terrible, and many died. My husband was very lucky. He was sent to work in the forests. When he had served his time, he was told he could never return to European Russia. So he found a position with the government geological survey and sent for me."

Peter the Great, Evans knew, was credited with opening the immense gold mines in the region around Ekaterinburg; he was also responsible for the decree that they be worked with serf labor, thus creating a self-perpetuating system. In 1861, when Alexander II freed the serfs, the law was changed to allow the use of convict labor. The readiest source of convict labor until 1906 had been political prisoners.

"Are you aware," Evans asked after a long silence, "that the tsar and his family were held just across the road?"

"Oh, yes, in Professor Ipatiev's house. I remember the day they arrived. Poor Ipatiev and his wife were given only hours to get out. They had to take everything with them. Mrs. Ipatiev and I did not get along very well, and perhaps that is why she declined my invitation to stay here. But the imperial family—of course, I knew they were there. I used to watch them taking the air in the afternoons when the weather was fine. He did not look at all like his pictures. I am sure it was because he lacked a uniform. The grand duchesses were very pretty, but I never saw the tsarina. It must have been very hard for them to live like that."

"You could actually see them?" Evans said, struggling to remain calm.

"Of course. From the window of my bedroom one has a view of the yard they used for exercise. They would appear almost every afternoon."

"What about at night?" he asked, his voice suddenly hoarse. "Could you see anything in the yard at night?"

"Why, certainly, whenever the lights were on, I could see the guards. I am an old woman and do not sleep well. At times I would sit by my window and think about the tsar and all he had done to my husband. At first I was glad he had been imprisoned. But then I began to think that it was not fair to keep his daughters and his son in prison as well, or their servants. And then of course, I realized that it was the old tsar, his father, who had sent my husband into exile."

"Do you know they are gone?" He had almost said "murdered."

"Of course. They were driven away three nights ago."

"Driven away?"

"Oh, yes. Just before the guards started shooting."

"Then there was shooting?"

"Of course. It has happened often enough before. Sometimes they would wake me from a sound sleep, and then I became quite angry. It is hard enough to sleep when you are old."

Evans bit his lips, fighting down the urge to interrupt her digressions.

"Sometimes the guards fired their pistols when they were drunk. They were not really very good guards. Well, three nights ago, about one o'clock in the morning, I would say, there was a great deal of shooting. Right after the lorry drove away with the tsar and his family. The guards were celebrating, I suppose. I can imagine how boring it must have been for strong young fellows like that to be cooped up all day in an old house with no one to talk to. Of course, the girls are pretty, but they were, after all, grand duchesses and not for their sort."

Colonel Obrechev listened to his story with a cynical smile. "An interesting theory, my friend. But you can't expect me to take the word of one old woman?"

140

"Why not?" Evans was aware of the sullenness in his voice. "What would it cost to investigate?"

"Investigate? How may I ask? Assume the tsar is still alive. Where is he? On his way to Moscow to be shot? What could we do for him in that event? The murder of the family has already been announced. The reaction from around the world is more than we expected. It has given the Bolsheviks a real black eye. Even the Germans are reported to be very upset. You can be certain that there will be no more international support for the Bolsheviks."

The room was very hot. Evans had already stripped off his tunic and collar, yet he was still sodden with sweat. Flies buzzed about the room, passing in and out of the unscreened windows as if that were their sole purpose in life. His head ached, and he wanted a drink, badly. The central Urals were in the midst of a heat wave that had already lasted for three weeks, and Evans was heartily sick of it, of Obrechev and Russia in general.

By contrast, the colonel stood with one hand on the door latch, immaculate and cool in his freshly pressed summer-weight uniform.

"Look here, my dear fellow. You seem all in. Get a good night's rest. Lots of work to do in the morning."

"Then you aren't even interested in the possibility they might be alive?"

Obrechev hesitated, then shook his head. "If we had arrived in Ekaterinburg ahead of Kolchak, yes, I would be. In fact, I would be leading the charge if I thought it would do any good. But we have only two regiments in the city, and the Czechs are unreliable. Kolchak has two divisions. If the tsar is found alive, you can determine for yourself who will take the credit. So you see, for our purposes, it is better that the tsar and his family are dead."

He ignored Evans's look of disgust and went out. Evans undressed to his shorts and stretched out on the bed, exhausted and angry, and tried to fit together the disparate pieces of information he had acquired. He had visited the British consul, Preston, after leaving the old woman's house. Preston could supply little more information than she had, although he went on at great length, happy to have someone with whom to speak English. "You would not believe how suspicious the soviet is of me, and as a result, all my Russian friends are afraid to come round."

When Evans, head swimming with heat and nausea, described what Veronica Maximievna had seen, he was surprised that Preston did not dismiss it out of hand.

"Ah, yes, quite a lively thing for one so elderly. Tends to ramble a bit, but sound otherwise." He looked thoughtful. "I wonder," he murmured. "Look here. One of my unofficial contacts, usually a reliable chap, was in the railroad's district manager's office on the night in question. He claims he saw several women, a boy and a man put aboard a goods wagon. He saw it all very clearly because the area was lighted by two arc lamps and there were many armed soldiers about. He thought at first there was to be an execution because of the two arc lamps, but the train left on the Moscow track."

Brooding in the breathless heat, Evans was on the verge of convincing himself that these two unrelated pieces of information could mean only that the Romanovs had been alive when they left Ekaterinburg. He sat up to study the three maps he had stolen from the Czech headquarters. One was a standard Russian ordnance map showing a portion of the steppe west to Perm. The second was a small-scale map of the central Urals region that extended a short way beyond Perm. The third was a standard railway map of European Russia, and it showed tracks diverging beyond Perm, south to Moscow via Vologda and west to Petrograd.

The present White offensive had ended in Ekaterinburg's western suburbs. Between Ekaterinburg and Perm were three hundred and more miles of empty steppe, and he doubted if either side could afford to spare more than a cavalry patrol or two, meaning they would be sticking fairly close to their own lines.

He thrust the map away and went to the window. There was nothing more for him to do here. The Czechs would be gone by tomorrow night, ending his responsibility to the Crimean National Front. That reminded him of the mess he had left behind in Sevastopol. By now Lowden would have sent an investigator from Odessa to verify his report. He'd be arrested the instant he showed his face anywhere near an American military or civil installation. He could expect nothing less than a dishonorable discharge or—at worst—ten years in a federal prison.

Boyd had accused him of being selfish and careless of his obligations to others, and his activities in Sevastopol bore out that charge. But Nicholas Romanov had saved his life once. In return, he had turned tail and run at the very moment when the tsar most needed help. He went back to the table and the maps. Maybe it wasn't too late. After a while he poured the half-full vodka bottle out the window.

On their third day in Perm, Nikolai Khristoforovich Sheremetiev clumped up the ladder into the fetid interior of the goods wagon.

"What is it?"

Nicholas rose stiffly from where he had been sitting beside Alexei and motioned for Sheremetiev to hold the lantern higher. The light fell across the boy, and Sheremetiev stared at him, noting his bloodless, drawn face and thin body twisting feebly from side to side on the straw. He's dying, Sheremetiev thought, and was surprised at the surge of pity that ran through him.

142

"Comrade Sheremetiev." Nicholas addressed him in a steady voice without a trace of its usual quaver. "Your government's quarrel is with me, not with my family. There is no reason for them to suffer. Please take them elsewhere and see that they are given adequate care. My son is very sick."

Tatiana heard her mother whisper, "No!" Olga covered her face with her hands, but Marie only continued to stare blankly through the open door. Anastasia moved to hold her mother's hand. Papa must have reached that decision himself, Tatiana thought. He hadn't even mentioned it . . . why? They all were certain to be shot. . . .

Sheremetiev examined the old man standing before him, so unlike his photographs now, so unlike the man who had sat his horse that day in snowy Kazan, and his lips curved in an involuntary smile at the thought. In a way, he had replaced the tsar in power; he, too, held the power of life and death in his hands. He had only to motion to the guards, and these seven people would cease to exist.

"Your desires are immaterial," he said.

Nicholas hesitated as if examining the wisdom of his next words. "It is evident that I am being made to suffer a cruel form of degradation." He waved a hand about the car. "Perhaps your government sees a reason for it. I no longer care, but there is no reason why my family must be made to endure it with me. If you wish—"

"Enough!" Sheremetiev shouted, angry that the man dared presume. "Your family is guilty. Not only the father and mother but the sons and daughters, brothers, sisters, cousins. All must be rooted out and eliminated. The past must be exterminated if we are to build a new future for the Russian people." Sheremetiev realized that he was paraphrasing Felix Dzerzhinsky's rationale for his own execution. Curiously the words made a certain sense if you looked at them from the proper perspective.

Nicholas gaped at him in astonishment. "What do you know of the Russian people?" he demanded. "You know only how to murder. Will that build a new Russia? You, sir, and your government are fools. Murderous fools. You will destroy this country in your half-witted attempts to build it anew. You are like the anarchists. You don't think, and you have no real plan. You improvise, and the innocent suffer while you destroy. You haven't learned that a nation is a system of laws and that if law exists, it can be changed, added to, subtracted from, and all can be mended." He pointed a finger at Sheremetiev. "But you have no system of laws. You depend on terror and murder to enforce the whims of fools."

Tatiana stared at her father in wonder. He had never, in her experience, spoken to anyone like that before. Even Sheremetiev was astonished.

"That . . . that is nonsense," he sputtered. "The Bolshevik party espouses only the highest ideals of socialism as enunciated by Marx.

Its laws are governed by economic realities and not human emotions and . . ." But Nicholas had turned away and shuffled back to his place beside Alexei. His wife grasped his hand, and Olga hugged him briefly.

Sheremetiev was staggered by this abrupt dismissal and took a step forward, shouting, "Comrade Romanov, I am not interested in your self-justification. . . . I—" He broke off as Tatiana rushed in front of him.

"Get out of here, you murderer! I know what happened to our friends and servants in Ekaterinburg. May you burn in hell for their murders. Get out of here! Leave us alone!" she finished, her voice rising to a scream.

All the frustration of the past six months welled up suddenly in Sheremetiev, and before he could control himself, he had slapped her across the face. In that instant he understood what drove men to madness.

A weird roaring filled his head, and a tremendous pressure seemed to squeeze his brain inside out until he was convinced he was suffering a hemorrhage. As the roaring died away, he was aware of a guard using his bayonet to drive a furious Nicholas back. Sheremetiev stood shaking in the doorway, staring at the family of skeletal figures, screaming and clawing at him from the reddish depths of their putrid hell. He stumbled down the steps, gulping air to calm himself. Tears coursed down his cheeks but were hidden by the dark.

Thank God I've been relieved, he thought fervently. Thank God! Chizov would bear the responsibility in the future. A reinforced guard would be arriving in a few days' time. . . . He stumbled onto the bridge connecting the two yards and sank down against the rough wood of a piling.

What had happened to him, he thought in despair, that he would slap a helpless woman, would act like the most perverted and sadistic of the Chekists? Had he become so debased? It was the terrible conditions in the stifling goods wagon, the sight of the boy dying and Tatiana's accusation. Yurovsky had killed the servants, not he. . . .

VIII

Perm was 1,000 miles and more east of Petrograd, the distance from New York to Chicago, and 311 miles northwest of Ekaterinburg, but the confusion in Perm was as great as in Ekaterinburg. Soldiers stood about everywhere, armed and surly. Evans endured all the passport checks, repeating over and over again his story about searching for three Americans who had disappeared during the evacuation of Ekaterinburg and emphasizing his diplomatic status. Finally, he was released into the heat of early evening, where dust hung in a broad band on the horizon.

An elderly porter, lacking consciousness of revolutionary aims, directed him to the Club of the Noblesse until another porter intervened and gave him directions to the Hotel France. There were no taxis or hacks to be had, and he walked through streets crowded with a mix of uniforms all bearing the crimson armbands of the Red Army.

The Hotel France was full. Behind the desk a man in the dirty clothes of a factory worker laughed at him when he asked where he might go.

"Why, to hell for all I care, Comrade. I don't give a damn if you are an American diplomat, you can't stay here."

Outside he was stopped by a wizened little drunk, incredibly filthy and reeking of vodka. "If ye want a place to sleep for a ruble . . ." Evans shoved a coin into his hand and broke away, seeing himself in a few years. . . .

145

Eventually he found a restaurant where he paid an exorbitant amount for a skimpy meal and a glass of vodka. Afterward another ruble rented him sleeping space on the same bench.

In the morning he found a boardinghouse, a large three-story structure that had once belonged to the owner of a successful dry-goods store. The house was set well back from the street and hidden by a tall yew hedge that served now to disguise the poverty he found inside. Evans introduced himself to the proprietress, a young woman with black circles of exhaustion beneath her eyes, who showed him up to a small, breathless room in the attic, where an unmade bed was covered with dirty clothes.

"You will have to share, I'm afraid. The other gentleman is an official with the government. He . . . I must apologize for the condition of the house. It is difficult—"

"I understand," Evans said, struck by the desperation in her eyes. Every line of her body spoke of total weariness. She brushed back a strand of hair that had escaped the pins drawing it tight to her scalp.

"It must be impossible for you to take care of everything that needs to be done here. Haven't you been able to hire help?"

She laughed, as if he had said something outrageous. "You are an American and so would not know. This is my house, or it was. It was confiscated by the Perm Soviet. I am allowed to live here and operate it as a boardinghouse. All earnings go to the soviet, and I am charged rent, which is deducted from my salary. We are allowed no food for guests, so you must go to the Ministry of Social Services and procure a ration card yourself."

"I see." Evans nodded. "Then you and your husband run this place?"

She gave him a bitter smile. "My husband was shot in March. He was suspected of anti-Bolshevik activities."

For a week Evans tramped the streets of Perm, from river front inland without finding a trace of the royal family, while the two White armies, one under Kolchak and the other under Orbelesky, approached with glacial inevitability. His roommate, the employee of the local soviet, disappeared on the third day, to Evans's endless gratification.

He discovered in Perm the depths, or perhaps the heights, to which the Bolshevik bureaucracy aspired. He and many others, Russian and foreigner alike, had complained bitterly and often that the bureaucrat was the true ruler of tsarist Russia and as such was slowly strangling the country to death. The situation had grown worse under the Bolsheviks.

In prerevolutionary days the bureaucracy had merely resorted to internal passports to monitor the movements of the people. The Bolsheviks introduced the identity card. Every man, woman and child was

146

issued a combined ration, work, residence and tax card by the local soviet. Anyone wearing the armband of Red Guard or the uniform of the Red Army or the militia or any city or county official, party officer or member could demand to see the card at any time. The cards were cross-filed and indexed in a central registry, and at the discretion of some anonymous clerk, an arrest warrant could be issued day or night. The prisons were jammed to overflowing, the courts and tribunals swamped, and the execution squads worked overtime, many suspected, because it was quicker to shoot or hang a person than to try him.

A harried clerk accompanied his diplomatic visitor down into the records center, a basement reeking with damp and the smell of rats. After thirty minutes of asking foolish questions and thumbing through boxes of cards, he left Evans on his own, claiming important work to do.

There were two cards for each person, an original and a carbon copy. The original was filed alphabetically; the second, cross-indexed by address. He went through all cards, looking for the royal family name, and found nothing. Next, he turned to the address cards listed under the Spassky Prison, where he found a card for each prisoner with that person's Christian, patronymic and family names; height, weight, coloring and distinguishing features; a cross-indexed location for fingerprints; and his family background and class. Roughly half the prison cards, he discovered, were marked "inactive," and he guessed this meant the prisoner was no longer a recipient of the state's largess. To test the system, he looked up the name of the clerk who had shown him into the room. Not only was he listed, but each member of his family was cross-referenced as well. The card for his eldest daughter, a child of six, contained a cross reference to all other members of the family, including godparents. A selection of those cards referred not only to the daughter but to every other member of the family. The amount of work involved was mind-boggling, and Evans began to understand how the Bolsheviks could claim that everyone would have plenty of work under their system.

There was nothing in the index to indicate that the Romanovs were or ever had been in the city.

That night he sat before the maps spread on the bed. It had occurred to him that there was no reason why the Bolshevik government might not have decided to handle the problem of the tsar and his family differently. They could have been shot anywhere between Ekaterinburg and Perm and buried along the tracks. The Whites had already announced to the world that the tsar and his family had been murdered.

The heat was stifling in the garret room, and he was running with sweat. From his vantage point he could see over most of the flattish city between the river bluffs.

What he was doing here? he wondered. He had nothing more than the word of a frightened boy facing the hangman, an elderly woman who could not sleep and a vague rumor overheard by a British consul. A red line on the map marked the railroad from Perm to Vologda, where the line divided, one branch going south to Moscow, the other continuing west to Petrograd. The northern route line crossed an immense land dotted with the unfamiliar names of villages, towns and cities—Voznesenskaya, Glazov, Zuyevka, Vyatka, Galich and hundreds more. How in the name of God was he going to search them all?

The heat made it hard to think. He needed a drink so badly his hands were shaking. It had been almost two weeks now. . . . The dresser mirror reflected the room, and Evans saw himself: a tall man with several days' stubble and staring, bloodshot eyes. He was astonished to see how thin he had become. He had been in Perm for seven days now and had failed to discover any trace of the family, and there was nothing to go back to but a court-martial. What the hell did he have to lose?

Leaden clouds frowned across the city, compressing the heat against the burned land. The railroad station was jammed with people desperate to get away from the advancing Whites, said to be less than thirty miles to the east.

The interior of the station was unbearable. He stood in line for two hours, enduring, while the line shuffled slowly forward until he faced the official across the table. The man's eyebrows went up at the sight of his diplomatic passport, and Evans tried to summon energy for the argument. But the official simply stamped the page, scribbled his initials on a ticket and pushed them both across the table. Evans stumbled out onto the platform, mumbling in gratitude.

He sank down on the bench, wishing for a drink. God, how he wanted a drink. He'd overslept and missed the early train, and possibly his last chance to leave Perm. There would be no trains after today, he had been told, and even this one was uncertain. Christ, you've thrown it away again, you bastard.

The station was small for so large a city, he thought, trying to take his mind off liquor. Two lines of tracks between twin platforms connected by a bridge—one platform for eastbound, the other westbound. A signal changed from yellow to red, and a train moved into the station. A plume of steam blew from the air brakes, and the train chugged slowly past to the end of the platform opposite. Three passenger cars were attached; "wagon-lits," he translated the Russian characters. Four men, apparently the only eastbound passengers, got off and went along the platform and into the reception room.

His mind, dulled by heat and hangover and preoccupied with the need for alcohol, was slow in reacting to the fact that both wore black leather jackets and high-laced boots. When it did penetrate, Evans shot to his feet and ran for the stairs leading to the bridge. He came down the other side with a clatter, stumbled on the worn steel steps and pushed into the reception room. Empty! He stepped out in time to see them climb into the back of a lorry.

Evans ran out to look for a taxi. He had last seen that kind of black leather jacket in Tobolsk, worn by the Chekist officer in charge of the guard detail—and the young Lett guard hanged in Ekaterinburg had said the guards who came from Moscow were Chekists and wore black leather jackets. Just maybe . . .

The truck reached the gate as he spotted the Ford delivery truck, a wood-paneled Model T popular in Russia. The driver had just gone into a shed. He ran across the yard, threw his suitcase into the back, reached in to set the spark, ran around to the front where he folded his thumb under, grasped the crank and pulled. And again. And a panicky third time before the engine caught, raggedly. He dived inside, advanced the spark a bit more, released the brake and shifted into gear. By the time the owner came out of the shed he was almost at the gate.

A horse-drawn cart was passing as Evans started into the street, the Ford's screaming owner sprinting only yards behind. He squeezed the horn bulb and picked up speed. The driver of the cart saw that Evans wasn't going to stop and stood up, shouting. Evans cut the wheel hard to the left, and the truck lurched against the wagon. The driver toppled into the road. Evans spotted the lorry with the Chekists dawdling through the intersection and shot after them. A moment later the truck ahead turned into a side street and picked up speed. Evans followed.

Only now did the magnitude of what he had done occur to him. He had just surrendered a seat on the last train to Moscow before the city came under White attack.

The Chekists drove through the southern end of the city toward the river before he realized they were heading for the railyard. Shortly the truck stopped at the main gate. Evans kept on without even a sidelong glance.

Was the royal family in the railyard? But where? Why? Feverishly he increased speed and, at the junction, followed the road that ran toward the river bluffs. Ten minutes later he had crossed a narrow bridge and turned onto a narrower, potholed track that went over the top of the bluffs. Evans picked a stand of trees well off the track and parked the Ford in their shade. He dug his field glasses out of his suitcase and hurried toward the bluff.

All during the endless afternoon he lay in the dry grass, sneezing violently every time a vagrant breeze stirred the dust and pollen. He fought a losing battle to remain awake as he surveyed the railyard below. The sun burned in a pale sky, and the unremitting glare turned his eyes red-rimmed and very sore.

The city of Perm was built along the river Kama, and the tracks of the Trans-Siberian Railroad ran through the southern end of the urban complex. The railyards, nestled below the river bluffs, appeared to have grown haphazardly over the years, and it was difficult to gain an impression of the overall layout. Gradually, however, it began to make sense. The northern end, nearly bare of rolling stock and full of dilapidated buildings, seemed abandoned. In the southern end four armored trains stood on sidings while switch engines shunted more cars to them. A flatcar had been attached ahead of each engine, and machine guns mounted on each.

As the afternoon wore on, a high cloud cover drew in to mitigate the heat but increase the humidity, and he fell asleep twice. A bird call woke him the first time, but it took a sudden burst of activity and noise in the southern yard to drag him back to consciousness the second time. A bout of sneezing helped clear his head, and he sat up, groaning at sore muscles. He rolled over, rubbed his gummy eyes clear and checked his watch. Seven in the evening! He had been asleep for more than four hours, and he was dehydrated and hungry. He focused the binoculars. Three of the armored trains had gotten up steam and were following one another like Chinese dragons around the curves that led east out of the yard.

East, he thought with surprise. He had expected them to go west, to the relative safety of Moscow. Perhaps the Reds were intending to put up a better fight at Perm than they had at Ekaterinburg.

Only one train remained in the northern yard, and in the distance he could hear the familiar bump of artillery. The Chekists must have had other business at the railyard, he decided. Not once had he caught a single glimpse of them. There was nothing to do now but go back to the boardinghouse.

A movement near the train in the northern yard caught his attention, and he picked up the glasses. Although the sun was still two to three hours from setting, the heavy clouds had reduced the light to a dull blue-gray that made it hard to define detail. He fiddled with the focusing knob, and two figures swam into view. The man was in shirt sleeves and carrying a rifle. Evans dipped the glasses to pick up his feet and saw the high-laced boots. He caught his breath and swung his glasses to the other figure, a woman. For a long moment he stared, willing her to raise her head. When she did so, he recognized the grand duchess Marie Nikolaevna Romanova.

The night was very still, and the sky had taken on a peculiar copper color at sunset. Evans scrambled through the wire, and his boots crunched on the cinders as he skirted piles of sleepers, rails and old machinery. The railyard was roughly rectangular in shape, but constricted in the center by a bridge that crossed a creek on its way to the Kama.

150

Evans had chosen a long warehouse close to the bridge. It was oriented somewhat against the grain of the other buildings, and he was certain he could get to it without being seen. Whoever had established the sentry posts had known his business. There was hardly a square foot of the yard the guards did not have under observation, provided they were alert. And Evans thought these Chekists would be very alert indeed.

He skirted from building to building, ever mindful of the guards. The cinders crunched loudly in the abnormally still night, and he stopped to remove his boots. He tied the laces together, slung them around his neck and pressed on, cursing the sharp cinders. The eastern horizon began to lighten as the moon rose. He had counted on the heavy cloud cover to eliminate moonlight. The atmosphere was electric, as if an immense storm were building, yet the sky was clear to the east. He went on, wishing to God he had a gun.

The military yard across the bridge was brightly lit, and he could hear the roar of heavy equipment and men shouting. He crouched in the shadows to study the long-deserted building. The odor of gasoline from the battered can he had found in the Ford was strong, and he had never been so thirsty in his life. What was he doing here? Orbelesky and Kolchak would occupy the city in a few more days at the most; then all he would have to do would be to cable the State and War departments . . . but he knew that was foolish. The Bolsheviks would laugh, would challenge him to produce proof. Which he could not do. Hell, he did not even know for certain the royal family was on that train or, if it was, where it would be this time tomorrow, let alone a week from today.

A voice shouted close by, and he almost bolted for the fence; instead, he forced himself to cross the twenty yards of open cinders in a kind of dance. Evans put his boots back on and edged along the wall to where an empty window frame gaped. The new moonlight illuminated the interior, which smelled of cat urine. Holding his breath, he climbed inside and poured gasoline in a trail from the window, across the floor to the far wall abutting the next warehouse.

Outside again, he lit a match, cupping it in his hands until it was well alight. He took a deep breath and dropped it inside. The whoosh of flaring gasoline startled him. Flame raced across the floor and exploded up the far wall. The structure was so dry that it flamed like tissue. The warehouse burned far faster than he had expected, and across the bridge a fire alarm began to clang.

He hesitated, not certain what to do, then ran, cursing the fact that nothing ever went as planned.

He dropped behind a pile of railroad ties as men burst from the train and raced toward the burning warehouse. He could see most of the train, but the engine was hidden by a small building. The tender and three freight cars glowed in the orange glare. The fire bell's clanging was muted by the roar of the flames, and he could feel the heat beating against his back. The fire had already spread to two more buildings, and as he looked back, the roof of a third erupted. The long hot spell had turned the wood to tinder, and the entire yard might go up in flames. So much the better, he thought grimly.

There was one last open space to cross; Evans got to his feet just as a guard appeared, and froze. Another building caught, and the light was growing brighter—someone would see him damned soon. The guard reached the last car and turned to stare at the flames, then shook his head and disappeared around the other side.

Evans ran. No one shouted, no shots were fired and he dropped into the shelter of the switch house, gasping for breath. The engine was less than five feet away. He pushed himself up on hands and knees, like a runner waiting for the gun. The guard's boots passed between the tender's trucks, and he shot across the gap and up the ladder into the engine.

The compartment was acrid with coal dust and lubricating oil. Quickly he removed a wrench from the greasy tool chest. A footstep crunched on the gravel, and he duck-walked to the footplate and braced himself against the side.

The guard's head did not appear. He hesitated for the barest fraction of a second, then lunged for the tender. A bayonet clanged against the steel plate where he had been an instant before. Evans scrambled onto the coal as the guard swarmed up the ladder into the cabin. Evans looked around wildly as the guard saw him. The bayonet tangled in the whistle cord, and Evans lunged, swinging the wrench. The open end smashed the guard across the face, and he shot backward out of the cab. Evans landed beside him and struck down hard again. The body did not move. He knelt for a moment, head bowed, struggling for breath. The bastard had almost killed him!

Evans dragged the body under the tender, picked up the rifle and ran from wagon to wagon. The first and last cars were open, the middle locked. He ducked under the train to the opposite side—out of sight of those fighting the fire—and hauled himself up onto the door track. The hasp was bolted into the wood, and he tried to lever it open with the bayonet; when it refused to give, he reversed his hold and stabbed at the wood around the hasp, using the bayonet like a chisel. Someone called from inside, but he paid no attention.

He tried again. The wood popped but held. Swearing furiously, he hacked again and again, aiming the point just past the hasp, pounding it into the wood with the heel of his hand and using the hasp itself as a fulcrum. A long splinter broke loose, and he grunted with satisfaction. This time the hasp broke away from the wood, and he jumped down and dragged at the door.

152

"Who. . . ?" the hesitant voice called again. A horrible odor like decaying animal matter rushed out, and he gagged.

The door was slammed shut and locked as the fire bell clanged, and she could hear running feet on the cinders. Only mildly curious, Tatiana lay down beside the wall and peered through a crack. At first she could see little more than a dull orange glow, but then it grew suddenly brighter.

Someone hammered on the door, and she froze. The single thought *They've come for us* shot through her mind. The one candle they were allowed at night glimmered feebly, and she saw her family huddling together at the end of the car. Her father beckoned her, but instead, she scuttled to the door. The hammering started again, then became a scraping noise.

"Who is it?" she whispered. The noise stopped for a moment, and she heard metal rattle on metal and a popping noise, as if someone were straining to break the lock. She heard a voice swear . . . in English! Wood splintered above her head, and the door slid open.

Tatiana shrank against the wall not knowing what to expect. A voice called in Russian, "Your Majesty?"

"Who are you?" she demanded, one hand on the heavy door, ready to run it shut.

"Never mind," the voice grunted. "This isn't the time for introductions. Is this the Romanov family?"

Tatiana hesitated. "Yes."

"Come with me. I've got a motor truck. Hurry!"

"Tania, who is it?" her father called, and she made a swift decision. There was nothing to be gained by remaining.

She hurried to the back of the car. "Papa, someone has come to rescue us. We must go with him." She spoke slowly and deliberately, realizing that if she showed the least sign of excitement, she would frighten them all into immobility.

"Hurry," the man called again. She heard a grunt and the sound of his boots as he tried to climb into the car.

"Tania, perhaps it would be . . ." Nicholas let the sentence lapse. In the dim light she could barely see him, but she had no trouble guessing at his expression. She did not hesitate but grasped her father's arm.

"Please, Papa," she begged, "come. . . . There is nothing else to be done."

Still Nicholas continued to stare at her. He was totally defeated. Tatiana straightened, looking at her sisters and mother and at Alexei . . . and she had an inspiration.

"Come, Papa, and bring Alexei. This is your last chance to save the throne." For a moment the tsar did not move; then she felt his arm flex under her hand, and he bent to scoop up the boy without a word.

"Tania," Olga whispered, and Tatiana went to her knees beside her sister. Olga grasped her hand and kissed it. "Go without me, Tania. Take the others and go. I . . . I can't endure this any longer."

"Hurry, damn it," the voice called from the door. Tatiana ignored him and put her other hand on her sister's shoulder.

"You have to come. I need help with Mama and the girls. I can't do it alone."

"But I can't . . ." Olga whimpered, and Tatiana shook her.

"You must!" she snapped. "They all will die if you don't."

Olga helped Marie get their mother up while Nicholas carried Alexei to the door and handed him down. Tatiana led Anastasia to the door, then ran back to kick the filthy straw into a pile against the wall. She jammed the burning candle into it, and it flared immediately.

"Come on," the voice shouted urgently. "What the hell are you doing?" The fire was well alight now and licking at the walls of the goods wagon. She hurried to the door and slid down, scraping her knees.

"Help me," she panted, and together they ran the door closed. "They might think we burned to death inside—at least for a while."

"Good thinking." The man laughed nervously. "Now come on." He pushed everyone into a line. "Listen to me. I've got a truck on the other side of the fence. Follow me as quietly as you can. Don't say a word. Move quickly. If anyone sees us, don't panic, and for God's sake, stay with me."

Evans slung the rifle and dashed for the corner of the building. The others followed close behind. This was the most dangerous part; they would be in the open with the fire behind. The entire railyard, including the wooden structure of the bridge, was going up in flames. He had underestimated the speed with which the fire would spread, and now they were in danger of being cut off from the fence.

"Go," he snapped, and pushed Nicholas toward the opening. The man hesitated a moment with the boy clutched in his arms and a daughter hanging onto his jacket. Tatiana darted past, detached Anastasia and wriggled through. Olga followed her example; her mother, then Marie and the tsar followed. Evans ducked after them, rifle at the ready, swearing at himself for not taking the guard's cartridge belt as well. He had at best five cartridges . . . if the magazine was fully charged.

It took only a few minutes to cross the sloping field to the trees

154

where he had hidden the truck. His greatest fear was that someone might already have discovered it, but the Model T was undisturbed.

While Evans set the spark and cranked the engine, Tatiana marshaled her family into the back, then ran around to the cab as the engine caught. A few minutes later they were bumping across the field to the road that skirted the city and ran north into the vast steppe.

The old truck bounced and lurched over the rutted road in the dark. Evans didn't dare use the headlamps this close to the city, and the heavy cloud cover made the night seem impenetrable. Only at junctions were the roads lit by streetlamps, and he approached each one cautiously, afraid of military roadblocks.

A jagged bolt of lightning lit the sky from end to end, and rain poured down in a torrent. The Model T had no doors, and he had left the windshield down to improve visibility. The rain swept at them on a tide of wind, and both he and Tatiana were soaked to the skin in seconds. He stopped the truck and struggled with the rusty clamps until he got the windshield up.

"Push!" he shouted over the wind.

"What?" she called back, and he fumbled in her lap for her hand. Tatiana shrieked and tried to push his hand away, but he clamped her fingers on the wiper handle.

"Push, God damn it!" he shouted again, and forced her hand down. The wipers made an uneven streak, and he wrestled the truck into the gear, wheels spinning on the wet macadam.

Waiting on the bluff, Evans had worked out an escape route to the north. He was counting on the fact that they would not be expected to run away from the advancing White armies but toward them. The problem lay in the fact that Perm was shown on the extreme northern and western side of the large-scale map. He could only hope that the same empty steppe land lay to the north of the city as on the south and east.

But he hadn't reckoned on the rain. After a month the prolonged dry spell seemed destined to last forever. In one way the rain was a blessing because it would make it harder to follow them, especially after the paved road gave way to a dirt track that degenerated quickly into a sea of mud.

The Ford topped a rise, and he stopped to look back. The lights of Perm had disappeared in the rain and darkness. For the last twenty minutes he had been driving by luck and constant lightning flashes; but the leading edge of the storm was moving east, and the rain was falling harder. He struggled out and was instantly soaked to the skin. Leaning back into the cab, Evans struck a match. Tatiana huddled as far away from the door opening as possible, her face white beneath streaks of dirt.

"What are you—"

He rummaged in the cab without answering and found a can of carbide jammed under the seat and threw the match away. The contents of the can rattled, and he groaned. God only knew how old it was. He shook it hard to crack the lumps into smaller pieces and powdered it as much as possible with a screwdriver, then coaxed the lumpy powder carefully into the tanks and cupped his hands into a funnel to fill the water container. A steady hissing told him the carbide was forming gas, and he managed to strike a match. The left lamp lit, but the right refused to work. There wasn't even a hiss of gas, and he guessed it was clogged solid. He gave up on it and paused only long enough to cup his hands again and drink until he could hold no more.

The single lamp cast a pale cone that did little more than keep them out of ditches. For an endless time they felt their way through the black, pouring night, rarely exceeding fifteen miles an hour.

At first it was such a novel sensation that Tatiana laughed aloud to feel the cool water running over her head and face, washing away a month's dirt and sweat. But the sensation passed quickly, changing to discomfort as her clothing clung to her body and the cold rain whipped through the door opening. She was cold, terribly so, and as the shivering became prolonged, it sapped what little strength remained to her. Her arms ached dreadfully as she pumped the lever that worked the windshield wipers.

The ride was a nightmare. She had no idea who the driver was or why he had risked his life to rescue them. She thought at first that he was taking them to meet a large force, perhaps White army soldiers. But as the night drew on and it became clear that he was expecting no immediate help, she began to despair.

The Ford lurched into a pothole and nearly stalled. Evans geared down and ground forward. The road was a quagmire and, in places, a small river. Twice the truck slued sideways on the surface as treacherous as ice. Tatiana's pumping flagged; but the wipers were almost useless in any event, and the dreadful screeching of metal on glass where the rubber was broken was driving Evans to distraction.

They passed through two villages, both dark and shuttered against the rain and night. A dog barked in one; silence in the other. A shaky bridge wobbled over a creek that had become a maelstrom, and the Model T truck rumbled across as fast as he could make it go. The bridge swayed alarmingly but held. As the road worsened in the rain, he became desperate to find a way off it before they bogged down hopelessly.

Sometime near three in the morning the pale yellowish blur of the headlamp showed a cart track leading up a rise to the right, roughly eastward. He swung the wheel onto the track and found the ground firmer than the road. The rain was steady but had lost its insistent driving force. The steppe spread about them now, without shape in the darkness. Tatiana had fallen asleep, huddling against him for warmth. In the faint glimmer of light from the headlamp, her hair was plastered wetly about her head and shoulders, and her dress stuck to her back. He could see the curve of a cheek and eyelashes.

He found he was driving into a sparse grove of trees which broke the force of the rain. Weary beyond measure, he drove off the track as far into the trees as he dared. Tatiana mumbled something when he shut off the engine but subsided as he patted her shoulder. He would cheerfully have killed for a glass of vodka.

Evans was awakened by a sudden flurry of wind. Tatiana's head was pressed uncomfortably against his hip, and he poked her until she changed position with a grunt. He remembered the rest of the family in the back, groaned and climbed down. The truck's enclosed cargo space was warm with body heat. The sound of steady breathing indicated that the exhausted family was asleep. For a moment he was tempted to join them; instead, he went back to the cab, shook Tatiana half-awake and led her around to the back and boosted her in. Back in the cab he found a pack of dry cigarettes in his valise, lit one and put on a dry wool shirt and jacket. The trees gave decent shelter from the rain, and gradually his shivering stopped. He flicked the butt away and started to take stock. He had seven half-starved, exhausted people in the back of a truck, perhaps four gallons of gasoline and enough food to keep one person during a two-day train ride to Vologda. And the bread was half sawdust.

In addition, he had one rifle, probably rusting, five cartridges, a pair of binoculars and his diplomatic passport—which they would burn right after they shot him.

Tatiana awoke in fetid blackness to crushing disappointment. For a moment she longed for death as the vivid dream of their rescue faded. Someone moved restlessly and coughed. Only a few gleams of daylight came through the sides of the truck, and she closed her eyes to avoid them. It had seemed so real: the fire, the smell of burning, the cold, the endless hours of bumping across the steppe in the pouring rain.

Thunder rumbled in the distance, and she sat up swiftly. It *was* raining! She scurried on hands and knees to the brightest crack and thrust her hand against the wall. Canvas? Peering through the rent in the fabric, she saw trees beneath the endless gray skies. Oh, God, she breathed, it was true. She pushed the cover aside and jumped down. Wet grass clung to her legs, and as she turned to look at the sky, tears came in a flood of happiness and relief, and she sank down against the wet earth.

157

When she had herself under control once more, she hiked up her skirt to make certain that the Browning pistol and was still tied securely to her thigh, then wandered among the trees, touching, feeling, sniffing the rough bark and the pungent aroma of living things. The grass was high and wet, and her tattered shoes and dress were soaked again before she had gone more than a few paces. But she didn't care; she was like the condemned prisoner on a scaffold who is unable to believe that she has just been pardoned. She thought of a book she had found in her father's study, by an author named Dostoyevsky. He had described a character's thoughts during his execution and last-minute reprieve from the scaffold, and they mirrored her own feelings exactly. She giggled then and the giggle became laughter and she had to sit down in the grass and laugh until the tears and the laughter were so intermingled that even Tatiana did not know which was which.

When the spasm of hysteria had passed, she began to shiver. A misty rain was falling, and the breeze chilled her. She went back to the truck and found the man stretched across both seats asleep. He had curled his body in such a way that his stomach was pressed against the gearshift levers and one leg protruded into the rain while the other, as if seeking shelter, had slid under the steering wheel.

His face had relaxed in sleep, and his mouth was partly open. His short hair was very wet and plastered against his scalp, which looked dead white. The skin under the left eye, the only one she could see, was dark, almost as if it had been bruised. A two-day stubble of beard had sprouted, and she shuddered as she recalled the Lett guards in Ekaterinburg—the first men she had ever seen unshaved and unwashed, even in the military hospitals where she, her mother and Olga had served. For a moment she stared at his face, and then her mouth dropped in surprise. The American diplomat . . . the one who had come to see them in Tobolsk and then had left so quickly. What was he doing . . . why. . . ? A thousand questions raged, and she touched his shoulder, tentatively, knowing she should let him sleep but overcome with both curiosity and a vague unease that was smothering her exultation.

She pushed at this shoulder, harder this time. "Wake up, please."

Evans stirred, shivered, opened his eyes briefly, closed them when he saw her, then sat up quickly, banging his head against the dash panel, and swore vigorously in English. He rubbed his face and shivered. Tatiana stepped back as he grimaced and muttered, "Good morning, Your Highness . . . Marie is it, or Tatiana?"

He pushed himself out of the cab and stamped about, chafing his arms and neck to restore circulation. One foot had fallen asleep, and he kicked it against a tire.

"Are you all right?" Tatiana asked, suddenly conscious of how she must look in her tattered dress with her short hair streaming about her face.

. He ran his tongue about cracked lips. "Hell, no," he began in

English, then stopped and said in Russian, "Not really." He took a deep breath and looked around the grove. "Is anyone else awake yet?"

She shook her head.

"Good. Stay here."

Evans half staggered, half stumbled farther into the trees away from the truck. Tatiana was puzzled until she realized where he was going, blushed furiously, then, reminded of her own bladder, ran in the opposite direction.

Marie and Olga were awake when she returned. Tatiana was grateful for that; she felt terribly awkward with the tall American.

Alexei was feverish, Evans discovered. His skin was tightly drawn, and his eyes were sunk deep into his skull. His right knee was drawn up tightly to his chest and badly swollen. The pain of being jounced all night had taken its toll of the boy's frail body. He was barely conscious, and his lips twitched constantly. It was the first time Evans had ever seen the effects of hemophilic bleeding, and he found it difficult to believe. The child's face, drawn and pallid with excruciating pain, sickened him.

Evans gave them a meager breakfast of bread and sausage. Afterward he took Nicholas aside, and they squatted under the shelter of a large aspen while Evans described their situation.

The scent of wormwood, released by the rain, was astringent and refreshing, Nicholas thought as he listened. It seemed they had met before but he could not recall the circumstances. It is hard to keep one's mind on such matters, he told himself, when one had just been released from death. He thought of all the hundreds of death sentences he had commuted and was very grateful he had. Only when he heard Olga laugh about the strange-tasting sausage at breakfast did he really understand that they were free. It was as if the world were a lantern-slide projection that had suddenly snapped into focus.

"That's the story, Your Majesty," Evans finished. "I believe we have the jump on them. The rain should have washed away any trail we left. But we have little food and less gasoline."

Evans unfolded the wet map with care and spread it on his knee. "As far as I can determine, we are here." He pointed to a spot a few miles past a road junction. "The road turns east in another two miles—excuse me, about three and a half versts, and that's where the map ends. There's bound to be a village somewhere along this way. Roads don't just go nowhere."

Nicholas nodded in agreement. The English word *miles* made him remember. Of course. The American diplomat who had called on them in Tobolsk . . . and whom he had taken aboard his train . . . when? It seemed a long time ago. Was this the Allied rescue that he had waited for so long?

"I dislike stopping anywhere with people about, but we haven't any choice." Evans glanced at the sky. "As long as the rain continues, I think we should move. Can your son stand more riding?"

Nicholas hesitated. His expression reflected his internal struggle to spare the boy further pain and yet to protect his life. "When one considers the alternative," he said hopelessly, "there is no other choice."

The steppe stretched in endless undulating folds in every direction. To Evans's inexpressible joy, Olga had chosen to sit with him in the exposed cab, wrapped in a blanket. He hardly dared look at her at first; when he finally did, she smiled shyly, and he grinned in spite of himself. The girls' hair had been cropped short at the beginning of June, Tatiana had told him. It was beginning to grow out again, and Olga looked very boyish, as did all the girls. Her face was drawn, reflecting months of ill-treatment; but her skin was clear and very fragile, and her violet eyes were daunting when she looked at him.

The short afternoon closed down on them, and the rain died away to intermittent showers. The tsar offered to take the wheel, but Evans did not dare relinquish it. Their lives depended on the truck; it also provided an excuse to be alone with Olga.

As the afternoon wore on, Olga gradually emerged from the frightened shell she had drawn about herself until she seemed once again the laughing, teasing young woman he remembered from Tsarskoye Selo. Evans forgot about the rain, the danger, everything that was not connected with the young woman sitting beside him, and in his eagerness he missed the haunted shadows in her face.

Darkness came prematurely when they stopped for a meager dinner of dried sausage, sawdust bread and water. Again, the family exclaimed with delight, and even Alexei managed a wan smile as he solemnly chewed his piece of sausage. Their reaction to the poor food, even more than the horrible stench in the freight wagon and their physical condition, told Evans how badly they had been treated.

Gasoline was his greatest worry and, after that, Alexei's worsening condition. The boy's stertorous breathing could now be heard in the cab. Evans stopped near midnight, climbed into the back and struck a match. The boy's eyes were tightly closed, his jaws clenched, as if holding back a groan of agony even in his sleep. His leg was still contorted at an unnatural angle, and his fingers worked spasmodically. When Evans turned his head, his eyes met the tsarina's. She stared through him to her son, barely aware that he was beside her. Evans blew out the match. Nicholas cleared his throat as he backed out.

"He is becoming worse," he said without inflection in his voice.

"He needs a doctor and a hospital," Evans muttered, at a loss for anything else to say.

He felt that tsar's trembling hand touch his shoulder. "No matter what happens," the tsar said quietly, "I will never cease to thank you for the lives of my family. Your reward in the next life is assured." Embarrassed, Evans drove on.

Former Sergeant Major and now Commissar Mikhail Borisovich Chizov tugged the rain slicker about his chin and studied the hissing remains of the goods wagon. Only the trucks, the twisted iron framework and the metal rods remained, and the stench of burned wood was nauseating. The fire had destroyed most of the yard before the rain began. Too late for the Romanovs, he thought. It must have been a horrible death, as horrible as some he had witnessed in the front lines during the four years of the tsar's war.

"Commissar Chizov! We've found Gorshonov. He's dead." Sudden apprehension cut short the pleasure he felt at being addressed by his new title, and he rounded on the man. "Dead! What the hell do you mean, dead?"

"He was under the tender. His skull was crushed, and his rifle is nowhere to be found."

For an instant Chizov's mind refused to grasp the implications of the guard's words; then he had a sudden vision of a Mauser pistol pointing at his head.

Almost as quickly as it had come, the paralysis evaporated. "Rig arc lights," he roared. "Sift through those ashes. There will be bones and metal parts of their clothing and luggage. Find them."

The guard stared at him as if at a madman. "But, Commissar, the ashes are still hot . . . how can—"

"Do it!" he screamed.

The Ford's engine sputtered to a stop an hour later. A peal of thunder sounded in the west, and a flash of lightning lit the sky. Evans climbed down, grunting at stiff muscles, and extinguished the carbide lamp. A cold wind whipped the grass about his legs, and he shivered. Nicholas loomed beside him.

"Where are we?"

Evans rubbed his face with both hands. He was so damned tired that it was hard to think straight.

"I don't know, Your Majesty. We've run out of gasoline. There has to be a village of some kind along this road. We've come nearly sixty miles."

"I will go on foot," the tsar said decisively, but Evans caught his arm.

"Thank you, no! You had better stay with your family. Besides,

I'm in better physical condition." He handed Nicholas the rifle. "Take this, just in case."

Nicholas started to object, then nodded and took the rifle. Evans shut off the carbide lamp and started along the road.

"Be careful," he heard Olga whisper. Startled, he reached out and caught her arm. He felt her lips brush his cheek and gathered her into his arms without thinking. She came as if she had been waiting, and her lips melted against his. For an instant everything was gone from his mind, leaving only the fact that he was holding her and that she was responding. Her body pressed, and her arms tightened around his neck so that she was almost lifted from the ground. He could feel the liquid firmness of her breasts and the curve of her hips and abdomen pressed against his when she shuddered. His lips opened involuntarily, and as his tongue encountered hers, she gasped but did not break away.

Evans came over the ridge well past dawn. A thin ground mist obscured the lower end of the village, but buildings and fences emerged reluctantly as the road climbed a hill. It was a typical steppe village of the kind he had seen along the railroads. A house or two with pretensions but reduced to gray disorder by the steppe winters; the rest little more than huts of brick or timbers rafted in from the forests to the north. The single unpaved road, mud in the rain, dust in the heat, furnished forage for pigs and chickens and a playground for small children. At the end of the village was a dilapidated church with boards nailed across the door and the paint on the wooden dome peeling badly. Bolshevik territory, he thought. More than one of the huts showed signs of neglect, a roof fallen in here, a shed collapsing there, a crumpled brick wall where the rain had eaten away the foundation. War, revolution and civil war had laid their hands upon the village.

Evans identified the merchant's house, a two-story clapboard affair with pointed gables. He was also concious of every eye in the village following his progress as he stamped up the rickety steps and pushed into the house, shaking the rain from his hat.

"God bless this house." He bowed to the shopkeeper, a wizened little man with a pinched face and a shrewd look. The curtain behind the counter moved slightly, and he had the impression of an immensely fat woman watching him.

The interior was stifling hot, and an assortment of clothes and kettles steamed on the huge stove. The windows were running with condensate, and the labels on canned goods had loosened and were falling away.

"I need food, blankets and gasoline."

"Gasoline?" The shopkeeper scurried to the window. "I did not hear an automobile."

The woman entered at that moment and wriggled around the

162

counter to the stove, where she gathered up dry items. She exuded a fine mist of perspiration and an unwashed aroma that caught at his throat before she retreated to the back without a word or change of expression.

"My automobile ran out of fuel on the steppe," Evans explained, and that seemed to satisfy the man.

He selected canned goods, a thick loaf of black bread, tea, a twist of sugar, a small can of honey and two cans of condensed milk for Alexei. The merchant then led him around to the back of the house and filled a large tin with gasoline. Inside again, the merchant totaled the bill, and Evans was astonished at the high price. But he was in no position to argue. The man watched him narrowly, stroking his chin as Evans counted the remaining notes in his wallet. He hadn't enough. Reluctantly he removed his belt and slipped two of the Mexican gold coins from the recess. The merchant's eyes lit, and he smiled at the sight of the coins. They haggled over the exchange rate, and the merchant capitulated quickly, leading Evans to believe that he had held out for too low a rate. He pocketed the handful of Kerensky rubles that remained.

Two hours later he steered the Ford truck along the muddy road, avoiding the deeper puddles, to the combination house and shop. All pretense had been dropped, and it seemed that the entire village had turned out to watch, unmindful of the persistent rain. Apparently motorcars were rare enough that the appearance of one was a major event. He had made certain that the back curtain was securely tied to conceal the royal family, but even so, he was barely in time to prevent two young boys from cutting the knots. As he poured the last pail of gasoline into the tank, an elderly uniformed official trotted down the road, waving his arms and shouting for him to stop. Evans tossed the pail aside and cranked hard, praying the motor would start without trouble. It did, and he got in quickly. The children scattered, shrieking, and he roared up the hill, leaving the official behind, screaming imprecations.

"You will release my men immediately," Chizov snarled at the military official of the Perm Soviet, who stared at him with a bland expression.

"Calm yourself, Commissar Chizov." He leaned back in his chair and rubbed his eyes wearily. "Here I give the orders. And don't threaten me with Moscow. It's unlikely that I'll live to experience its displeasure." He indicated the rain-drenched city through the broken window. "You can hear for yourself how near the Whites are. They are attacking from two directions, and I haven't enough troops to defend even half the front. Those Red militia units from Moscow are worse than our own gutter sweepings. The first time they hear a rifle fired, they piss their pants and run away."

He smiled at Chizov, the kind of smile a cat would show a mouse. "And you ask that I release trained soldiers because you wish to search for mysterious escapees." He smacked the desk with his fist. "White Cossacks burned that railroad yard, Comrade. Your Chekists didn't stop them then, so now they can serve the people at the front. There will be no more discussion! Your people have been requisitioned for front-line duty by the Peasants' and Workers' Soviet of the district of Perm. Go find your escapees yourself. I've heard the Cheka is invincible!" The officer regarded him for a moment, then grimaced. "Tell you what, Comrade. I'll let you keep two of your men. You can't say then that the Perm army command isn't understanding." He laughed and dismissed a fuming Chizov.

Chizov drove the requisitioned Renault touring car into the village in late afternoon, when the sun had broken through the clouds in horizontal columns. Chickens strutted, and a sow lay in a mud hole, forcing him to edge cautiously past to avoid getting stuck in the muddy verge. Alerted by the motor, the two Perm Chekists stepped out of the magistrate's house and stood beside the wattle fence.

Both were of Kalmuk origin, and the sunlight accented the brown-yellow cast of their skin. The shorter man had a cruel saber scar that ran clear across his face from temple to opposite cheek. The scar had drawn the left eye down, and when he blinked, the two lids did not quite meet. The taller man pointed across to the merchant's house.

"The magistrate says a man came into the village on foot early this morning. The same man came again two hours later, in an automobile. He refused to halt when the magistrate commanded him to."

Chizov swore and turned to look at the elderly, potbellied official, who bobbed a small bow in his direction. "And what was the fool doing that he wasn't aware the motorcar had arrived?"

The Kalmuk shrugged. "He had not yet risen for the day."

Chizov snorted in disgust and crossed the road to the house. As he started up the steps, he saw a curtain twitch and, in reflex, unbuttoned his holster flap. The two Kalmuks cocked their rifles and hurried on ahead, kicked the door open and bounded inside. Before he entered, Chizov turned to see all the villagers gathering opposite. Good, he thought. They would learn a valuable lesson.

An elderly, bearded man watched anxiously from behind a counter, and Chizov regarded him with distaste. A damned Jew, of course. The bloodsucker.

"I am Commissar Mikhail Borisovich Chizov of the All-Russian Extraordinary Commission for Combating Counterrevolution and Sabotage," he announced in pompous tones.

The man paled and clutched the counter, and Chizov smiled to think that even here, in this backwater, the reputation of the Cheka was well known.

"We are hunting a group of escaped prisoners, two or more men, five women and a boy. To give aid and comfort to the enemy is punishable by death."

"No, Your Honor." The man hiccuped. "No one like that passed—"

"You damned liar!" One of the Kalmuks sprang at the merchant and cuffed his head.

The man threw up both arms and crouched, uttering little cries of terror.

"Don't lie to me," Chizov warned, "or it will be all the worse for you."

"No, Your Honor . . . I mean, yes . . ." the man blubbered. The other Kalmuk tore down the curtain and yanked an immensely fat woman through. She staggered across the room, struck a shelf and collapsed in a flurry of boxes and cans. Groaning, the woman heaved and struggled to get up. The shorter Kalmuk shoved her down again, grabbed one huge breast and squeezed. The woman squealed in pain and terror.

"Ah, to climb on this one." He winked at Chizov. "It would take you all night to get in, and then you might get lost!"

Chizov ignored him and stepped closer to the terrified merchant. "Why do you say I am wrong when your good neighbors report the truth and the magistrate confirms it?" he asked softly.

"I saw . . . only . . . a single man . . . Excellency."

"Only a single man," Chizov mimicked. "And what would a single man need with so much food and eight blankets?"

"I didn't . . . question . . . him, Excellency. Business has been—"

"Don't tell me about your business," Chizov roared in his face. "My business is seeking out and executing counterrevolutionaries. And I've found another, one who places his own interests ahead of the people's!"

The merchant rolled his eyes to where the two Kalmuks were tickling and pinching his wife. One began to slice the buttons off her dress with a curved knife. Chizov punched his nose and drew blood when he protested her treatment.

"Never mind that cow! Answer my questions."

"But, sir, I remained here . . . the man carried down the supplies. I saw nothing. . . ."

"But you sold him gasoline?"

"Yes, yes. His motor truck had run out on the steppe—"

"Are you not aware that the district soviet has forbidden the sale of gasoline?" Chizov demanded, banging the man's head against the counter for emphasis.

"Mercy, Your Excellency . . . I didn't know!"

"You lie!" Chizov screamed in his ear.

His wife groaned aloud as one of the Kalmuks cut away the last of her dress, exposing her mountainous dead white body. He shouted happily and fumbled at his pants.

"And what did this enemy of the people, this escaped counter-revolutionary, tell you?" Chizov asked quietly, stepping to one side so that the merchant could better see what was happening to his wife. "How did he pay you?"

"With Kerensky rubles," the man moaned, shutting his eyes as one of the Kalmuks succeeded in separating her immense thighs with his knife point. The other Kalmuk had knelt and clamped her head between his thighs.

"She smells terrible," one laughed.

"Please, Excellency," the merchant pleaded. "My wife. Don't let them—"

Chizov slapped him hard, and something clanked on the floor. He picked up the coin and whistled. The small Kalmuk was laughing now and shouting encouragement at the larger one, who was grunting with effort. The merchant had forgotten all about his wife's choking squeals and was blubbering in terror. Chizov held up a gold coin he had never seen before. "He gave you this, did he?"

The merchant's head wobbled, as if he were no longer in control of his body.

"What other lies have you told?" Chizov asked in a pleasant voice.

"None, Excellency . . . none." His voice was almost a whisper. The Kalmuk finished with the woman, and she lay still, an inert mass of slug white fat and skin, shuddering occasionally. Chizov turned to her, and the Kalmuks backed away with smiles of anticipation.

"The private ownership of gold is forbidden, and the penalty is death. You have lied to an official of the people's Cheka, and the penalty is death. I am empowered by the All-Russian Congress of Soviets to administer the sentence." He drew his Mauser, slipped the safety off and cocked the hammer. The man watched in growing horror as he aimed at one fat breast and fired. The merchant fell to his knees and crawled toward Chizov, blubbering for mercy as the woman's screams pierced the room. The old man banged his head against the muddy floor and screeched his truthfulness.

Chizov laughed, bent over and carefully fired a second bullet through her left breast, ignoring her thrashing efforts to fend him off.

"What else?" he demanded calmly, and the man lifted a tear-streaked face to him.

"I swear by all that is holy, Your Excellency, there was nothing more. I saw nothing more . . ."

166

Chizov nodded; the man probably really did not know anything more. He shot the screaming woman through the forehead, and she gave one convulsive flop and was still. The man stared at her in disbelief until Chizov put a boot against his back, pushed him down and shot him in the neck.

They dragged the bodies out onto the slope in front of the house for the entire village to see. It had begun to rain again as Chizov sat in the passenger side of the lorry and questioned each villager. Whenever he felt he was not getting enough information, he would nod and the Kalmuks would beat the individual. They shot two people, a man and a woman, for refusing to cooperate, and their bodies were turned over to expose the ruined faces, mute examples to the rest.

By dusk he had learned no more than the merchant had told him. The lorry with one man driving and no passengers to be seen had driven out of the village on the road east.

After they burned the merchant's house and refueled the Renault, they drove hard all through the night. Chizov was confident they would catch up with the lorry by dawn at the latest. And then, he thought grimly, he would attend to bloody Nicholas and his family. In a gesture of reassurance, he touched his breast pocket, which contained the much-folded Moscow telegram giving him permission to shoot the family if they were in danger of being freed by counterrevolutionaries. There would certainly be no question about it now.

The road had degenerated to a muddy cart track, and twice the carbide lamp flickered and went out, the last time for good. Evans cursed himself for not including carbide in the list of supplies; it never seemed to make any difference, he thought, how carefully he planned; he always managed to leave something undone. He coasted to a stop and shut off the engine.

The silence was oppressive. He lit a cigarette with hands shaking from lack of sleep. He had driven steadily since leaving the village with only a single stop hours before to eat a quick meal. How long would it have taken that magistrate to contact the authorities? Twice he almost restarted the engine, only to stop when better sense prevailed. It would do them no good to go another few miles if they became hopelessly stuck.

A soft rustle in the grass made him start with fear. Christ! He sat rigid for a moment, shielding the cigarette end with his hand, imagining Red soldiers closing in on them in the darkness. A breath of wind touched his face, and he heard the sound again. His breath whooshed out in a relieved gasp.

At least the family was asleep. He could hear Alexei's hard breathing clearly through the canvas sides and wondered if the boy was not developing pneumonia. He slouched back in the seat and rested his arms on the steering wheel. Another cigarette would help him stay awake, he decided.

Olga was shaking his shoulder.

"Jesus, what . . . ?" But Olga grasped his face with both hands and kissed him soundly.

"We are safe!" She laughed. The kiss drove all other thoughts from his mind, and Evans pulled her close, relishing the soft crush of her lips against his, the hard enamel of her teeth against his tongue and the shock when her mouth opened suddenly and her tongue thrust against his. Her response so overwhelmed him that it was several seconds before he noticed Nicholas speaking to three mounted men.

When he did, Evans vaulted from the cab and snatched up the rifle, pushing Olga behind him. A horseman saw him, wheeled his mount and aimed his carbine. Evans dived headlong into the grass. The snick of the rifle bolt galvanized Nicholas, and he ran toward Evans, shouting, "Friends, they are friends. Cossacks from the Kuban." He pointed to the three men. "They are part of General Orbelesky's forces. . . ."

One of the Cossacks shouted and pointed to the west. At the top of the hill an automobile had stopped, and a man was studying them through his field glasses. One Cossack galloped off, and the other two dismounted. The smell of horse sweat, oiled leather and tobacco swamped Evans; their greatcoats were damp with rain, and the crimson piping on their uniforms had faded to dull brown long ago. Both carried Japanese-made rifles slung upside down across their backs to keep the bores dry.

The automobile moved toward them, and Evans swore. How many soldiers inside? The two Cossacks glanced at his rifle.

When the automobile had closed to one hundred yards, two men jumped out and raced to either side with the obvious intention of flanking them. Evans steadied the rifle on the Model T's hood and sighted carefully at the window on the driver's side. The Renault lurched just as he squeezed the trigger, and the bullet smashed the windshield, but too high. The Cossacks laughed.

Bullets whistled at them from the flankers, and Evans shifted his aim to the man on the right and fired. The thought occurred to him that this was the first time he had ever been shot at, and he was surprised at how calm he was. He fired again, and the man disappeared into the grass. The Cossacks began to shoot, concentrating their fire on the man to the left, and he scampered back to the protection of the motorcar. The automobile suddenly described a large circle, barely pausing to pick up the other flanker. Evans fired the last cartridge in the

168

magazine and turned to see a Cossack patrol galloping toward them. By the time they thundered past the auto had lurched back over the crest of the hill.

Evans sat down and leaned his head back, fighting a sudden nausea. He hadn't been quite so calm after all. The Cossacks grinned at him, and one even clapped him on the shoulder.

The officer in charge of the patrol examined Evans's papers and raised an eyebrow when he demanded to be put in contact with Colonel Maxime Rovolovich Obrechev.

"So you want to see Colonel Obrechev, do you? Do you know him then?" Evans assured him that he did and that the personages he was escorting were of the very highest importance. The officer pursed his lips, glanced at the family huddled beside the truck like refugees and snorted.

They were taken to a small village farther east, and Evans asked Nicholas to sit in front with him.

"Ah . . . Your Majesty," Evans began when the escort had drawn far enough away that they could not be overheard. "I hope you won't be offended if—"

"Offended!" Nicholas turned to him in amazement. "My dear boy, you have saved the lives of my family. How could I possibly be offended by anything you might do?"

"Thank you, sir. In that case, I'll speak plainly. I would recommend, as strongly as possible, that you conceal your identity until we are certain . . ." His voice trailed off at Nicholas's sudden, angry frown. Couldn't possibly be offended, he thought wryly.

"I am not certain I understand, Mr. Evans. With the help of your government, I—"

"Don't count on help from the United States, sir. Or any of the Allies, for that matter."

Nicholas stared at him. "But then why did they send you to help us?"

"*They* didn't. I came on my own." Evans wanted to say more, but he kept silent.

"Are you telling me that in all this time the Allied governments have never—"

Evans shook his head grimly.

"But last winter you yourself came to Tobolsk to see us. You said then that your government was concerned, that loans would be held up."

"That was last winter," Evans said gratingly. "A lot has happened since then, and nothing was done on my return. By anyone. Not the British, the French, no one."

"My God," Nicholas breathed, plainly distressed. His face was a study in misery, and he was silent for a long moment. "I . . . I sacrificed an entire army in Galicia in 1915, to save France," he mumbled, as if not quite believing what he had done. "And again in 1916. Oh, my poor country . . . what have I done?" He drew a shuddering breath. "You must be wrong," he said in a harsh voice.

Evans shook his head. "No, sir. This war is seen in the West as a battle between autocracy and democracy. There were celebrations in Washington and London when it was learned that you had abdicated."

Nicholas stared rigidly ahead, his expression now revealing the full extent of his sense of betrayal.

"My devoted friends," he whispered.

After a long while he raised his head and looked around at the empty steppe on either side of the road beneath the endless gray sky. Evans felt an immense sympathy for the man, yet at the same time was dumfounded that Nicholas could be so naïve as to expect a foreign government, a faceless bureaucracy, to jeopardize its interests, real or imagined, for any individual, no matter who that person was or had been, no matter what he might once have done for them.

As if their minds were working in parallel, Nicholas nodded slowly. "I see now that I made a grave mistake when I agreed to an alliance with France and England. Perhaps now it is time I think solely of Russia. It must be extricated from the morass my foolishness has created. Perhaps it is time I put aside the idea that I can ever attain a measure of privacy, and return to the throne."

Alarmed, Evans objected. "Your Majesty, conditions have changed—"

"Changed how, sir?"

Evans took a deep breath. "You will find very little sentiment for the return of the monarchy. Russia demands a democratic form of government."

"What foolishness!" Nicholas exploded. "How could they possibly when disorder and anarchy are the result?"

Evans tried to make him understand. "Look, Your Majesty, neither the Bolsheviks nor any of the White forces under Denikin, Kolchak or Orbelesky have based their appeal for support on the return of the monarchy, just as none has the slightest intention of allowing more than a token democratic government. General Orbelesky's interest in your restoration as tsar *was* simply as a figurehead. The real government would be invested in a supreme council, which he would appoint and direct. In short, a dictatorship similar to the one employed by the Bolsheviks. His concern for you was based strictly on your usefulness as a rallying point for rightist forces. But since he has now gained that support in any event, I think you might prove an embarrassment to him."

"That is your opinion then?" Nicholas asked in a frigid voice. "And what do you suggest?"

"I can arrange for you and your family to be granted political asylum in the United States, sir."

"You ask me to leave Russia now, in its gravest hour? I think, Mr. Evans, that you underestimate me and my Russian people. When it becomes known that the royal family is still alive, that the Tsarevich Alexei will succeed to the throne, the Russian peasant will rally to us as always, and together we will sweep the accursed Bolsheviks from Moscow and the nation. I will never again consider running away, Mr. Evans. My son will obtain his rightful heritage."

Nicholas turned away at that point and refused to answer or acknowledge Evans for the rest of the journey.

Olga's smile was strained, and she kept the screen door of the hotel closed. Evans blinked at her, wondering if this was the same young woman who had reacted so passionately to his kiss on the steppe that morning.

"I am afraid I must tell you good-bye," she said. "Tomorrow we will start for Sevastopol. The danger is past. General Orbelesky has extended the warmest possible welcome to us and has assured Papa that he will do everything in his power to see that he is restored to the throne. Then this terrible civil war will end——"

"Olga, please listen to me," he said urgently. "I know how your father must feel, but I know General Orbelesky. I served as the American representative to his staff, and I know exactly how he intends——"

"We are aware that you know General Orbelesky, and his wife, intimately," she broke in with just the slightest emphasis on the word *intimately*.

Evans cringed. "Olga"—he tried to open the door but it was latched—"you must listen to me. When your father learns what Orbelesky really wants him to do he——"

Olga slammed the front door shut, and when he tried to wrench it open, the guards shoved him back with their bayonets.

Evans had been impressed at the speed with which Colonel Maxime Obrechev arrived. A small airplane circled the village less than an hour after their arrival and landed on a meadow north of the village. Staring morosely from the second-story window of the house where he had been quartered, he reflected that his approach to the tsar could not have been more wrong if he had deliberately chosen it.

Nicholas had been trained from birth to rule. Three hundred years of family tradition backed that training. To tell him that he had been repudiated by the whole of Russia had been foolish in the extreme and only proved to Nicholas that while his rescuer might have the best possible intentions, he was still a foreigner and knew absolutely nothing about the mysteries of the Russian soul, which Nicholas, as the father-tsar appointed by God, understood perfectly.

Toward midnight Obrechev burst into his room, wrapped his arms around Evans and laughed and cried in the grand Russian manner.

"I had mounted patrols searching the countryside about Ekaterinburg for miles in every direction, old friend. I was afraid that you had been captured by the Bolsheviks and shot." Obrechev flung himself into an overstuffed chair and waved his hands to clear away the dust that flew up.

He tilted his head to one side. "How I grieved for you. We had already notified your government of your disappearance. Happily we can now correct that error. I will give the proper orders in the morning! Ah, the trouble you have caused. Every Red prisoner captured on the Perm front is interrogated for news of your whereabouts."

Evans's smile grew strained as he listened to Obrechev's lies. But he knew that if he antagonized the man, he would never stand a chance of seeing Olga again. He apologized for leaving Ekaterinburg without a word of explanation. "But I knew if I told you, you wouldn't let me go. . . ."

Obrechev spread his hands wide and jumped up, shouting, "But I was wrong, and I admit it. Now we must have a drink to celebrate."

The temptation was great, but Evans shook his head. "Not for me, Max. I've given up drinking."

"Ah, but just one, old friend. You would not insult me? There is much to celebrate. Your promotion, for instance. You are promoted to major by your government for your accomplishments, and the tsar wishes me to tell you that as soon as possible he will personally decorate you with the Saint George Cross, our highest honor for gallantry. And tomorrow we go to Chelyabinsk and a hero's welcome for you!"

The vodka gurgled into metal traveling cups, and Obrechev pushed one into Evans's hand. "To the tsar!"

The sickening motion had stopped. That fact took a long time to penetrate the alcoholic haze bathing Evans's brain. He lay perfectly still, thinking that if he didn't move, everything would be all right. A dim light penetrated the blinds covering the compartment window, and he had a terrible need to urinate. Reluctantly he sat up, cringing at the pain that shattered his skull, and clutched his head with both hands, willing blood to his brain to cleanse away the alcohol. When the pain subsided after an endless time, he stood up slowly, hanging onto the walls as the floor spun away. His mouth was as dry as the sunburned steppe, and his stomach churned madly.

He shuffled along the corridor, thankful it was deserted, to the smelly, filthy compartment at the end that served as the lavatory. The urinal was a clogged metal tank that drained directly beneath the car. He fumbled his pants buttons opened and sighed with relief. The faucet dispensed only a stream of tepid, rusty water, and the sliver of soap refused to produce lather. Nevertheless, he washed his face and neck as best he could, dried them on his sleeves and staggered out, nearly overcome by the stench.

The car was the last in line, he saw when he climbed down to the track bed and discovered that it was early evening and that they were in a railyard. He raised his face to the cooling mist and closed his eyes. Voices startled him, and he scurried back inside, in no condition to see anyone or to be seen. Two men stopped on the platform on the opposite side of the coach. One voice was louder and more dominating than the other, and after a muffled exchange which he could not make out, Evans identified Obrechev's voice issuing instructions to clear the track as far as Chelyabinsk and to exchange the guard and train crew.

Nausea gripped him, and he stumbled back along the corridor, clutching his stomach and swearing. He vaguely remembered Obrechev's laughter as he had steered him away from one compartment door last night—this morning?

"Ah, no, my friend, that is my compartment. Yours is over here. . . ."

His compartment. Evans stopped. Obrechev always traveled with at least one bottle of vodka in reserve. If he could get a drink, it would settle his stomach, and then he could sleep. He opened doors along the corridor until he saw a khaki tunic with a colonel's insignia hanging on a hook. A pair of dirty socks lay on the floor, and a battered valise was shoved under the bunk. He drew it out and rummaged through the contents until his hand encountered something solid wrapped in a towel. Grunting with satisfaction, he drew it out.

But instead of a vodka bottle, he unwrapped a gleaming Colt .45 caliber automatic pistol. Where in the world had Obrechev found that? he wondered. He held the gun closer to the window and saw the British proofs on the part of the barrel visible through the ejection port. The slide was marked "COLT Automatic Calibre .45." Where the devil had he seen a pistol like . . . his hands began to shake.

It was Peter Boyd's pistol. He remembered the day Boyd first showed it to him in the duck blind—so long ago. As if in a dream, he drew out his penknife and removed the screws holding the left walnut grip panel. Scratched into the wood were the initials *PB* and the date, *5/12/14*.

How had Obrechev got hold of it? He himself had gone through Pete's effects, had found only the bottle of scotch . . . the lorry driver had sworn that . . . Boyd had gone that afternoon to, where? To challenge Orbelesky? To send a telegram to Odessa? Evans's head pounded, and he clutched his temples, trying to ignore the pain, forcing himself to think. Pete was wearing the pistol the afternoon he died—he had kidded him about it.

A Colt automatic pistol was literally worth its weight in gold in Russia. A policeman or a hospital attendant would have stolen it . . . unless the person who killed him had taken it first. He pulled the slide open. There was a round in the chamber. He ejected the magazine and counted the cartridges—five. Pete had distrusted safeties and never left a cartridge in the chamber. The magazine held seven cartridges when full. One shot had been fired.

Evans slipped the pistol into his belt, put the spare magazine in his pocket and went to his own compartment. He was completely sober now, and he sat staring at the countryside disappearing into the evening gloom.

The overcast was breaking up, and he could see the Urals behind. Immense columns of cumulus clouds marched in rank toward the mountains, which were wreathed in a smoky blue dusk. At sunset a soldier banged on the door and clattered a tray of cold meat, unidentifiable vegetables and a bottle of vodka on the floor. Evans carried it inside, opened the window and forced himself to pour the vodka out. He struggled to eat the nauseating food and watched the endless grasslands of Russian Siberia stream by. A deserted junction went past, and a single line of track led away northwest to the distant mountains.

It was dark when he awoke to the murmur of voices. He had fallen asleep in the seat; his neck was stiff, and his back ached horribly. The headache induced by the hangover had disappeared, but he remained weak and shaky. The train was stopped in the middle of nowhere, and a huge bonfire burned near the base of the embankment.

"You in there, come out!" The command was coupled with a sharp bang on the door. Evans opened it to see a soldier step back and motion with his rifle. Other figures were leaving the private car ahead, and he heard Obrechev's voice, full of assurance, as he came along the corridor.

"There is some trouble with the train, Bill. I felt it best to have everyone out until the problem is resolved. The air brakes, you know. Food and hot tea are being prepared, and I have had the guards light a fire. Please join the others."

Evans hesitated. Something was wrong, but the combination of hangover and muzziness slowed his thinking. The soldier pushed him with the rifle, and he stumbled down the embankment, arms flailing to maintain his balance. As he started toward the fire, muttering, he heard the muffled click of a rifle bolt, saw the royal family, completely dressed beside the fire and Obrechev walking toward them, carrying a revolver. Like a thunderclap, it burst on him, and as he shouted a warning, he remembered and yanked the Colt from his belt.

Nicholas turned toward Obrechev, one hand out as if seeking an explanation. Obrechev shot him in the chest. Rifle shots spattered the group; Evans whirled and shot a soldier aiming at him. He fired twice more at the soldiers, who had advanced to within fifteen paces. One screamed and fell, legs jerking spasmodically. As Evans scrambled through the grass, cursing, Marie and Anastasia were flung against each other by a third volley.

He saw Obrechev aim at a slim figure in white as she ran to her father. Evans screamed at Olga to get down just as Obrechev pulled the trigger. Olga fell headlong, and Evans turned on Obrechev; but the Russian went to his knees, clawing at his back, mouth open in a spasmodic scream. Tatiana ran up, and as Obrechev turned, she fired point-blank into his face.

There was no time to wonder; a soldier pivoted toward him, rifle at his shoulder. Evans threw himself to one side and killed the man from five paces. The slide locked open, empty; he shoved the pistol into his belt. The last soldier ran toward the fire, shouting. Alexandra flung herself across Alexei, and the soldier jammed the rifle toward her chest and fired. Mouthing obscenities, he cocked the bolt and aimed at Alexei. Evans heard the striker fall on an empty chamber, and the man lunged forward and drove the bayonet into the boy's side. Alexei fell back with a scream, and Evans slammed into the man from behind. They went down together, and Evans wrenched the rifle away.

The man scrambled up and whipped out a thin-bladed skinning knife. Evans brought the bayonet-mounted rifle to the guard position clumsily as the soldier feinted, sneering at his ineptitude. The soldier feinted again to draw him in, but Evans stepped back, pivoted the rifle stock and struck the man full in the face with the butt plate. As he stumbled back, clutching his broken mouth and nose, Evans reversed the rifle again and drove the bayonet into his throat, grateful suddenly for the long, cold hours on the bayonet course. He bore in on the blade and twisted, screaming obscenities, wanting the bastard who murdered women and children to die slowly, horribly. The soldier pawed at his collar as blood spurted, trying to scream. The knife fell from his fingers, and he slipped to his knees and bowed forward until his head was touching the earth, twitched spasmodically and died.

The scene was etched indelibly in Evans's memory; he would always be able to recall the least detail of the huddled bodies and staring faces filled with shocked disbelief: Nicholas lying on his side, one hand stretched out as if to Olga; Alexei beside his mother's body, blood seeping through his fingers; Anastasia and Marie side by side as if asleep; Tatiana kneeling by herself in the middle of the carnage, deep in shock.

Smoke belched from the engine, and Evans dropped the rifle and ran. Only by the most desperate lunge did he manage to catch the ladder of the last wagon-lit carriage and pull himself up on the platform. As the train gathered speed, he worked his way around to the back and climbed the ladder to the roof.

The firelight faded behind. There was no time to think, and he ran forward over the slick wooden roofs, skirting the mushroom-shaped ventilators, leaped the swaying gap between the cars and jumped down into the coal tender. The fireman heard him, shouted a warning and swung his shovel. Evans avoided the blow and fumbled the Colt from his belt. The fireman swung again, and in panic Evans leaped aside and scrambled up the mound to the top. Somehow he ejected the empty magazine and rammed home the fresh one as the fireman rushed toward him, shovel back for a skull-shattering swing. Evans found the release, the slide slammed forward and he pulled the trigger. The blast inside the metal walls deafened him, and the fireman was flung to the bottom of the car.

"Back . . ." he finally managed to shout at the engineer, now crouching over the dead fireman.

The tsar's body drew him. He knelt down beside the man whose only crime was that he had never learned to see the world as it was rather than as he wanted it to be. The tsar's eyes were open, and Evans closed them, disconcerted by their shocked stare. A short distance away Tatiana wept over her mother's body. The engineer huddled by the fire, hands and feet tied with wire Evans had found in the engine tool box. He picked up a flaming brand and walked into the darkness.

One of the soldiers was still alive. The man lay on his back, gasping with pain, hands clutching his stomach. His tongue flickered across his lips, and his eyes darted from the flames to Evans's face.

In a level voice he asked, "Did you know it was the tsar and his family you were to murder?"

The man stared at him. He tried to speak but could not. His eyes slid away, and he managed to shake his head.

"You liar."

The man's eyes were filled with pain and fear, but he shook his head again. "Water . . ." he whispered, and died.

Alexei was still alive. The bayonet wound was deep and had certainly entered his lung. Tatiana knelt beside him, took Evans's handkerchief and pressed it against the wound. The cloth reddened in seconds. The boy's breathing was shallow, almost nonexistent, and his face was pasty and damp with shock and pneumonia. His eyes were open, but Evans doubted that he was conscious.

He closed his eyes for a moment, gritting his teeth against a burst of nausea. Why? he demanded silently. It served no purpose to torture and kill a man who was as much victim as victimizer; less still to torture and kill his wife and children. The firelight tinted the boy's face a ruddy orange, and traces of blood coated his lips. Evans gently wiped them with his fingers. Tatiana read the realization that Alexei was dying in his expression and covered her face with her hands.

Olga lay beside her father. In death she had relaxed, one arm pillowing her face. Like a child asleep. The light played with her hair so that it seemed a vagrant breeze was blowing. He knelt beside her for a long time, oblivious of the tears that ran silently down his face. Yet even as he mourned her, he recalled her abrupt dismissal of him the previous night outside the hotel. She had cared for him only so long as he had been useful and, when he was no longer needed, had discarded him without a thought. Much as he himself had done to her in Tobolsk and to so many others.

Evans handed the engineer a shovel and led him away from the track. After the grass was hacked away, the damp soil was relatively easy to dig. When the two graves were deep enough, they dragged the fireman, Obrechev and the soldiers to the first and smaller and dumped them in without ceremony. They carried the others to the larger grave and laid them side by side, Nicholas and Alexandra together and Anastasia and Olga on either side, each wrapped in a blanket taken from the train.

Tatiana dropped a small pistol into the grave, and he wondered how in the world she had managed to get hold of it. The engineer took off his cap and prayed until Evans nudged him roughly, and they began to fill in the hole. It seemed to him a useless exercise to pray. If there were a God, if the Christian religion had had any validity, such an atrocity would never have been permitted.

Afterward Evans tried to ask Tatiana where she had obtained the gun to shoot Obrechev, but she did not even look at him. Shock, he thought. He wondered how long it would be before it wore off and how she would react then.

For a few moments he stood beside the dying fire, eyes fixed blindly on the frightened engineer. Panic and confusion roiled through his mind as his own reaction set in. In the space of an hour everything had changed completely. He was alone on the steppe with the two survivors of the royal family—one certain to die within hours—a frightened engine driver and a special train. One of the most powerful contending factions in Russia had succeeded in killing the tsar and his family. How could he hope to conceal the fact of a survivor, even if he killed the engine driver?

"We must get your brother aboard the train," he told Tatiana, and when she did not protest, he picked the boy up, surprised at how frail and weightless he was, and carried him up the embankment and into the private car. Tatiana moved ahead without a word and opened doors. He laid the boy on a bunk and in the dim light saw that blood was seeping in greater quantities between his lips. Alexei was bleeding to death.

As he stooped over the child, he experienced something of what Nicholas and Alexandra must have felt whenever they looked at him and knew they were helpless even to relieve his pain. For the first time he understood how Rasputin could have gained such power over them with merely the promise of the child's relief.

177

Outside again, Evans kicked the fire apart. The engineer watched his every movement, plainly expecting to be killed. He cringed as Evans pushed him toward the engine.

"You will drive the train as I tell you. Make one mistake, and I'll kill you."

The train jerked against the weight of the cars and began to move backward. The engineer tried to convince Evans that they would be struck by another train, but Evans, remembering Obrechev's order to clear the line as far as Chelyabinsk, snarled at him to shut up.

He watched the engine driver closely until he was certain he could manage the train himself. Screw valves opened and closed the boiler lines that fed steam to the pistons, and above it was the throttle. The brake pedal seemed to work much like the mechanical brakes of an automobile. After an hour he ordered the train stopped.

The engine stood panting in the vastness of the steppe while, groaning with fear, the engine driver climbed down and stood with bowed head and clenched fists, waiting for Evans to shoot him.

After a moment Evans told him quietly, "Run." He spun the steam valve screw, and the train began to move. Evans leaned far out of the cab as the engine gathered speed and watched the lone figure frozen beside the track until he disappeared in the darkness. He knew then that he should have killed the man. To leave him alive was stupid. . . . Resolutely he turned his mind away. So? He would live with the consequences.

By dawn the track was so badly eroded that their speed was reduced to a crawl. The switching gear at the junction was badly rusted, and he despaired of moving it at all. But oil and a great deal of hammering persuaded it to shift. After he moved the train onto the spur, he struggled for another ten minutes to set it back to the main line. Before going on, he climbed into the private car. The door to the bedroom in which Alexei lay dying was open. A single lamp with a green glass shade illuminated the child's face, accentuating the skull-like hollows of his eyes.

Tatiana sat beside him, clasping his hand. His breath came in ragged gasps, and every few seconds a shudder passed through his body. When he could not stand it any longer, Evans left and returned to the engine. He shoveled coal against the grate and began to fill the firebox, working like a madman, so great was his anger.

The line ended abruptly. Steep slopes rose on either side to frame a summer sky clear of any trace of rain. Evans climbed down from the cab. A deep valley wound into the distance, and above, he saw the weathered buildings of an abandoned mine. He climbed back into the cab and opened all the steam vents. The boiler fire would burn out within the hour, he guessed.

Alexei died just after dawn. His skin had taken on the waxy color and texture Tatiana knew so well from previous bleeding episodes. He woke just before the end and smiled at her. She felt a gentle tightening of his fingers in her hand; then he drew a shallow breath, closed his eyes and died.

For a long time Tatiana sat beside the couch, holding the lifeless hand, numbed by the night's horror. She must have fallen asleep, she thought, because the train had stopped and the American was standing beside her. Gently he disengaged Alexei's hand, and she stood aside for him to wrap the body in a green felt rug.

Evans climbed down onto the roadbed and nodded toward the engine. Tatiana understood. Before he reached the small stream on the slope, she caught up to him with the heavy coal shovel. A hundred yards below the track, they found a lichen-covered boulder. Sun streamed through the newly washed foliage, and the brook danced with light.

Evans dug, and Tatiana washed Alexei's body. The coal shovel was wholly unsuited to the task, but the ground was soft after three days of rain. Had it only been three days? Three days ago at this time he had been waiting in Perm for the train.

When the grave was finished, Evans lowered the blanket-covered form into the pit. Afterward he stood a little way off, watching while Tatiana knelt and prayed.

The air was soft, and the stillness absolute. The stream rippled, and a faint breeze stirred the scent of growing things. Tatiana sprinkled a handful of dirt in the grave and went back to the train while he filled it in and replaced the sod. The Romanov ancestors lay in marble vaults in Moscow and Petrograd. Yet, Evans felt, Nicholas, Alexandra, Alexei, Olga, Marie and Anastasia Romanov had the best of it. They lay in the land they had loved too dearly to flee.

They abandoned the train at midday and walked down into the valley leading north. The map showed few and scattered villages on the eastern side of the Urals, and they would need supplies. Evans had gathered a few pieces of clothing, most belonging to the dead guards or to Obrechev, a few tins of food, soap, a sewing kit, two sheepskin jackets, maps and what other useful items he could find, but there was little enough and practically no food suited to their needs.

He had taken a rifle from one of the dead guards the night before. Only one man had been equipped with the Mosin-Nagant Russian army rifle; the others had carried Japanese Arisaka rifles, and he had left them behind because he could find only a few rounds of ammunition.

Late in the afternoon they entered a village that was little more than a huddle of four farms. An old gaffer sat in the sun, smoking and watching children play on a swing. In the fields three more men worked.

Evans charged the rifle's magazine to capacity with five rounds, then slipped the cartridge belt under his jacket. He also removed the captain's insignia from his jacket and cap. His uniform had once been a passport through recalcitrant officials on both sides, but now it would only attract unwanted attention.

Evans slung the rifle conspicuously over his shoulder. Curtains fluttered, and one or two women came to stand in their dooryards. There was no store, not even a church, and he guessed that there was a larger village nearby. Preferring to stay away from population centers, he struck a one-sided bargain with an old farmer for three horses—an ancient gelding and two mares, equally as old—two worn-out saddles and food, mostly rye bread, three strings of sausages and three round hams, in exchange for the last of the Kerensky rubles obtained from the merchant and one Mexican gold coin.

They left before sundown, declining an offer to remain overnight, and struck off in the direction of the main village. But once out of sight, he led Tatiana back up the slope and circled to the north. The horses plodded dutifully along, expecting nothing better from life.

During the next several days they followed a route that led generally north and west to open as much distance as possible between them and the spot where they had abandoned the train. Tatiana spoke only when he asked her a direct question. To have endured so much, to have escaped as they had done and then to see it all end . . . He blamed himself as much as Obrechev, or even Nicholas. If he had not gotten drunk, he might have seen what was happening, might have been able to stop it. Evans rode silently, crushed by what he saw as his responsibility for so many deaths. Without verbalizing the resolution, he came to the realization that he would never drink again.

As sunset of the fifth day drew shadows across the shallow valley into which they had ridden, Tatiana urged her horse closer to Evans's. The silence was unbelievable. The sky was full of huge gold- and rose-tinted clouds, and the air held the last mild heat of the day.

Tatiana cleared her throat. "Where are we going?"

Evans glanced at her. She had been quiet for so long that the sound of her voice came as a surprise. Pale and slender, she looked like a waif in a dead guard's oversized clothing.

"Out of Russia, as quickly as possible—when I figure out how. Until then we keep moving."

"Then I will leave you now," she said without the least change in expression.

"You what?"

180

"I will leave you now. Russia is my country." She turned her horse aside.

Evans caught at the reins. "Look here," he protested, "General Orbelesky will have search parties out by now. They'll have found the engine driver. You don't think friend Obrechev was acting on his own, do you? Both sides have signed your death warrant—"

She shook her head. "I . . . I don't care." She tugged at the reins, and confused, the old mare shied. Evans released his hold, and Tatiana rode off without a word.

He watched her ride back the way they had come, suddenly relieved that she had gone. He was sick and tired of Romanov ingratitude. Her family had been murdered because Nicholas wouldn't listen to him, and now she would be shot for the same reason. Well, he thought, it would serve her right. Maybe that's what she wants.

He found a spot to camp a mile farther on beside a stream that chuckled and laughed its way along a graveled bed. After he had eaten some of the bread and ham, it occurred to him that she had not even taken a share of the food. Hell, she wouldn't even last long enough for the soldiers to find her.

An errant thought slipped through his defenses as he fell asleep. Why had Tatiana survived when Olga had died? He wondered in a vague way if he was still in love with the myth he had created for himself.

Evans awoke shortly after dawn, chilled by the dew that had settled on his blankets. He built a fire and stood over it until the sun cleared the treetops to the east. A thin wind swayed among the leaves, and the sky was filled with high scattered clouds. It was only the second week in August, but autumn would come early in the mountains.

He was not surprised to find that Tatiana had not returned during the night. As he cooked and ate some of the sausage, he studied the map again. Without her, his task was simplified. The Ural mountain chain ran north to south for fifteen hundred miles and marked the boundary between Europe and Asia. East of where he now sat were four thousand miles of Siberian forest, tundra and desert. Approximately eight hundred miles to the south lay the Persian-Afghan border. Four hundred miles north was the Arctic Ocean, and six hundred miles west lay Moscow and the center of Bolshevik power.

Orbelesky held the south, and Kolchak the east, leaving north and west the only directions open to him. He had no illusions that even in revolutionary Russia he could elude White agents long enough to reach the American diplomatic mission at Odessa. West to Moscow was the shortest way out of Russia, and there would be no reason for the Bolshevik government to stop him. He was, after all, an American diplomat.

Evans broke camp and rode a good mile before he reined in the horse and, with an oath, retraced his route. It took two hours to pick up her trail. When Evans rode into the clearing at midmorning, her blanket roll was badly tied, and her horse had wandered away. For a long moment they stared at each other; then he pulled his horse around and went in search of the mare. When he returned, she was still sitting where he had left her.

"Let's go," he said gently.

After the train Tatiana could remember only the barest details. Obrechev's face was etched into her mind at the instant she shot him, and she recalled quite clearly the unexpected kick of the Browning pistol against her hand. But she had only disjointed images of her father and mother, of Olga and Anastasia and, for some reason, no memory at all of Marie. But her worst nightmares were reserved for Alexei. The ghastly sight of the horrible wound in his side, his moans of pain, even though he was unconscious, and the hot, dry feel of his skin. Why had this tall American risked his life for them? For Olga, of course. And now she had to go with him because she didn't know how else to survive. As they rode through the clear, warm afternoon, a bitter taste like hot metal filled her mouth.

They rode and walked to rest the horses from sunup to sundown each day, moving steadily but without haste. Evans had immediately abandoned his plan to turn west. Instead, he had, after a great deal of thought, decided to travel north. Allied forces were in strength in only three places in all of Asian and European Russia—Vladivostok in the Far East and Murmansk and Archangel in the extreme north. Archangel was the closest—fifteen hundred miles rather than four thousand through the forests of Siberia. Evans did not doubt his ability to complete the journey or to live off the land after his years in Wyoming. He described the plan to Tatiana in some detail, but she only nodded apathetically.

Fifteen hundred miles were not as bad as they sounded, he thought. St. Louis to San Francisco. There were people still living who had ridden and even walked that distance not so long ago. There were numerous rivers; the Pechora alone could shave several hundred miles from the journey. And the Bolsheviks would be thinly spread in the north at best.

As the days passed, Tatiana began to come out of herself, and through diplomatically phrased questions, Evans learned how inhumane their treatment had been during the last few months of imprisonment. Tatiana found to her surprise that talking about the ordeal had an emotionally cathartic effect. The more she talked, the more she wanted to tell him, to make him realize how hellishly her family had suffered.

"We were quite close, as you may have observed," she told him one afternoon as they rode across an open meadow. The sun beat down, and the afternoon was absolutely still. They might have been the only two people in the world.

182

"I was a little girl in 1905, but I still recall very vividly the way my father and mother reacted when the revolution began. They would be talking, and suddenly they would stare at each other in silence, and then Mama would burst into tears for no apparent reason. My great-uncle, Grand Duke Alexei, was killed by an anarchist's bomb. Papa was so fearful that someone else in the family would be hurt."

She talked for a long time, describing the precautions that were taken, the raising and equipping of special units of Cossack body-guards recruited from the finest Don and Kuban regiments. As she did so, Evans began to understand the completely insular life the royal family had been forced into by the constant threat of assassination.

The summer weather held. Golden days followed one another, and indigo blue skies were filled with towering clouds. Silk skeins of mist wove through the trees at dawn, and overhead vast wedges of geese and ducks fled south.

One day in late August Evans hissed at her to halt. He dismounted and pointed down a grassy slope, where Tatiana saw a small deer herd grazing on the edge of a clearing. The wind was northeasterly, toward them. Evans knelt, and before Tatiana could stop him, the flat, hard crack of his rifle sent echoes spreading for miles. The deer disappeared, and Evans scrambled down the slope. A brown form lay half-hidden in the meadow grass.

Tatiana refused to speak to him for the rest of the day. Evans paid even less attention to her than usual. That evening he wove a grill of green willow branches and placed two steaks on it above the fire. In the still air the smoke rose in a straight column, and the smell of roast-ing meat filled the clearing. Tatiana watched him eat, resentment and anger struggling with hunger. Evans forked the second steak onto a hastily carved wooden plate and handed it to her.

"Better eat, Your Highness. You'll need the strength."

Tatiana shook her head angrily.

"Look here," Evans said gently, "the deer I shot was old and would not have survived the winter. The wolves would have taken it. I gave it a clean death. We need the food to survive. I'm going to have to hunt, and you are going to have to eat the results. It's that simple."

After a moment Tatiana accepted the plate.

The deer kill brought home to Evans the precariousness of their existence. They had not seen another human being in a week, and vil-lages were becoming fewer as they pushed deeper into the mountains. He calculated they had traveled two hundred miles since leaving the train, far slower than he had anticipated. The fine weather would not endure much longer, and the horses, poor to begin with, were deteriorat-ing badly. Reluctantly he decided they would have to turn east and ride out onto the steppe to find a decent-sized village.

IX

The forest had been cleared well past the village boundaries, and one had the impression that it was surrounded by a vast meadow. The village consisted of perhaps twenty houses, only one of substance, and a scattering of outlying farms. Maples flamed with color and gave a false impression of well-being. Evans had learned to look for signs of poverty: broken equipment rusting in a yard, window screens torn and unmended, silent children who squinted between inflamed eyelids, matted thatching on the roofs or an empty barnyard.

They rode into the yard of the farm that seemed most prosperous, hoping to find what they needed without having to press on into the village proper. Evans heard the sound of a hammer on steel and nodded to Tatiana, who, in a well-practiced gesture, let her shoulders slump and tugged the battered military fatigue cap lower on her head. With the shapeless military sheepskin coat clutched about her and a little dirt rubbed on her face, Evans doubted that anyone in so remote a place would ever recognize her as the daughter of the dead tsar.

He dismounted, and she remained on the mare, which dropped its head wearily and began to crop the thick grass. The hammering stopped, and a heavyset man with a permanent scowl came to the doorway, carrying a blacksmith's hammer and wiping his face on a piece of waste. He eyed Evans narrowly, noting the rifle slung across his back.

184

"We want to buy supplies and horses. Three if you can spare them," Evans told him, striving to imitate the heavy accent of a Ukrainian.

The man studied them with contempt until Evans dug a gold coin from his pocket. "I can pay."

The blacksmith's face creased in an obsequious grin. "Running?" He nodded at the worn horses. "Red or White, you're all the same to us. The more of you that run away, the fewer there are to take our grain." He hawked and spat. "I'll sell you the horses and supplies. Tell me what you want."

Evans had prepared the list carefully this time. He ticked off flour, oats, bacon, dried sunflower seeds, tobacco, a bolt of cloth, two axes, two hammers, a saw, a file and a host of other things. "You might have come away better prepared," the blacksmith grumbled. "You'll need a pack saddle for the third horse."

Evans agreed, and the man, after a few minutes of rumination, set the price at three of the gold coins. Evans was surprised. The cost was lower than he expected. He accepted at once, before the man could change his mind. Business settled, the man stumped across the yard to the house and returned with a bottle of vodka and two large metal cups. Evans's mouth went dry at the sight of the colorless liquid, and only with great effort did he shake his head. It had been five weeks since the night of the executions, five weeks since Obrechev had got him drunk. He refused the proffered cup, and the blacksmith scowled. When he shook his head a second time, the man dashed the contents to the ground and stamped off in disgust. Evans leaned weakly against the doorpost, conscious that Tatiana was watching him with a puzzled expression. Evidently the blacksmith's curiosity was greater than his anger because he returned shortly to ask about the war.

"Plenty of fighting in the south," Evans told him, guessing where he did not have facts. "The Whites under Orbelesky and Kolchak are said to have taken Perm. Denikin has raised the Don Cossacks and the Germans have occupied the Ukraine."

The blacksmith peered at him. "It is true they shot bloody Nicholas?" he asked suddenly.

It startled him to hear the question put so crudely. "In Ekaterinburg in July." He saw Tatiana waiting tensely for the man's reaction, but the blacksmith only grunted and turned away.

While supplies were being brought out, the blacksmith led out three horses, and they haggled over the merits of each. Two were acceptable, but the third, proposed to serve as the packhorse, had a sore fetlock. Evans noticed the barest hesitation in the horse's step as a small boy led it around the muddy corral. The blacksmith grabbed up the hoof and showed it to Evans. "See." He pointed to a spot of mud which, when he rubbed it away with his thumb, proved to be a hole. "I drove a nail into the hoof so the horse would limp when the Reds came last. A little soreness, that's all."

Evans refused and continued to refuse to take the horse until the furious blacksmith led out another which was acceptable. Evans caught him eyeing Tatiana furtively as she helped pack the gear and saddle the new horses. The day had grown quite warm, and Tatiana had removed her sheepskin. Uneasily he noticed the way the blacksmith's eyes kept sliding from her face to her figure, which even the oversized uniform pants and shirt did not conceal. He suspected that White soldiers were not far behind and only hoped that they did not think to ride down out of the mountains to search the fringing villages. He doubted the blacksmith would soon forget this woman traveling with a deserter.

They left the village as soon as possible, riding east and circling north before turning west to the mountains again. That night they dry-camped on the steppe deep in a grove of aspen and rode on at dawn. The new horses had been well cared for, and the novelty of open steppe and unlimited grass infected them with energetic restlessness. At mid-morning Evans gave up trying to rein them in and, with a shout to Tatiana, let his horse have its head. She followed suit, and they galloped across the steppe, laughing like children suddenly released from school.

They camped that evening near a quiet stream deep in the foot-hills. The gallop had done them both good, he thought, as foolish a stunt as it had been. Her cheeks retained the color the ride had put in them, and she was quick to smile at him and once even laughed at a joke. But her good humor dulled his; for the first time in days he thought about Olga, and after a while he wandered away from the fire-light and sat smoking for a long time, listening to the stream while he tried to sort his conflicting emotions and square them with fact. Tatiana, watching from beside the fire, guessed at his thoughts and turned away, suddenly overcome with grief, as much for herself as for her murdered family.

For two days they had followed the stream deep into the mountains. The terrain began to rise, and the horses, cleansed of their exuberance, settled down. Tatiana watched him pensively. The relatively dry weather so late in the season had shrunk the river. In spots the horses splashed across with the water hardly up to their knees. The sun grew warmer, and sweat trickled down her back and chest, making her acutely uncomfortable. She felt as if something were crawling inside her clothing, and at midafternoon, when they came across a relatively wide, flat spot along the bank, well screened by trees and with a small water meadow on the far bank, she demanded that they stop.

"I," she announced imperiously, "am going to take a bath. We will camp here for the night."

Evans started to object but gave in when he saw her stubborn expression. Tatiana threw her greatcoat over the saddle and went off along the bank, clutching a small piece of soap.

She tore a small branch from a tree as she walked and stripped the leaves away, crushing each in turn to sniff the heavy scent of green life. When the leaves were gone, she chewed the stick, delighting in the minty flavor. The sun was hot, and the shadows were deliciously cool. There would not be many more days like this, she knew. Soon the rains would begin, and this far north they would quickly turn to snow. What would they do then? But she refused for the moment to speculate on the future. For the first time in weeks she was beginning to feel at peace.

Tatiana pushed through a stand of willows brushing the crystal water where it lay against the bank and saw that a few feet on, the stream widened. The water slid smoothly over a sandy bottom. The place was so private and perfect that she smiled, undressing slowly, relishing the touch of warm air on her bare skin. She took a deep breath and lay back against the moist earth. The contrast between land and sun, cool against warm, was heady, sensual, and she repressed a voice telling her that pleasures of the flesh were wrong. A scrap of sermon against sexuality preached years before by dear Grigor slipped into her mind. For an instant she heard the words combined with an image of a crude cartoon on a wall in the Ekaterinburg house showing her mother and Rasputin as stick figures in sexual attitudes, and she sat up with a gasp, then dashed into the stream and dived under.

The water was unexpectedly cold and deep. For a moment she couldn't find the bottom. Her head went under; then, almost before she could react, her foot brushed sand, and she kicked to the surface and waded onto the bank, gasping for breath. A patch of sun-warmed moss spread outward from the base of a tree, and she lay down and began to laugh at herself. I'm an excellent swimmer, she thought, yet I'm frightened by a pool not much bigger than a bath.

Feeling better, she fetched the last piece of French soap Evans had taken from Obrechev's luggage and, standing on the warm moss, soaped herself completely, massaging her hair and skin with the suds. This time she was ready when she dived, curved to the surface, gulped more air and dived again. She had never before swum naked, and the sensation was wickedly exhilarating.

She thought of swimming back for her shirt to serve as a towel; but a larger patch of moss on the far bank drew her, and she stretched out at full length, arms and legs spread to the sun to warm away the chill. A languorous feeling of heat suffused her body, and she was content to watch red whorls come and go against her eyelids. To take such pleasure in her body was surely a sin, but for the moment she didn't care. Almost without her being aware of it, her fingertips caressed a nipple, and the guilty pleasure that flooded her body was insupportable.

She pressed a tentative hand on damp pubic hair at the same time, wondering at herself. The sun pressed down with an almost physical sensation, and she spread her knees, clenched abdominal muscles and groaned.

The splashing alerted her, and she sat up quickly to see two mounted men on the far side of the pool, watching. One grinned.

"Look, Mishka," a heavy voice rumbled. "She's warming herself up. Let's deal with her first."

She screamed and darted into the trees. Behind her came a shout and the sound of horses splashing across the creek.

Evans unsaddled the horses, hobbled all three and turned them loose to graze in the meadow. The sun was warm, and the forest silent in the waning afternoon.

A bath was a good idea, he decided, and hung the pack with the food from a tree branch, draped his saddlebags across and walked off in the opposite direction. He found a spot less than a hundred yards distant, peeled off his clothes and waded in. The icy water was delicious against his skin, and he ducked, splashed himself thoroughly and rinsed his hair. After he had washed his clothes, he climbed onto a large granite boulder with a flattish top and rolled a cigarette. He lay watching the smoke curl into the still air and let his mind wander.

In spite of whatever he told himself to the contrary, he hated Tatiana, hated her not because she was who she was but because she had survived and Olga had died. It was stupid, he knew. Stupid and adolescent, but he was unable to shake the emotion. As long as she had remained silent and withdrawn, had done exactly as he had told her to, he was able to control his feelings. She was just another chore, like caring for the horses, packing the gear properly. . . . Evans shrugged irritably and stubbed out the cigarette.

The sound came from upstream. Half-asleep, he opened his eyes and listened. This time he heard the scream clearly.

Evans leaped from the boulder and raced back along the bank, swearing at the sharp rocks that jabbed his feet. In the clearing, the horses were grazing quietly. He yanked the saddlebags down, fumbled inside for the Colt pistol and ran along the stream in the direction Tatiana had taken.

The willows were thick and mingled with poplars that came right down to the bank. He ducked inland, ignoring the slashing branches. Less than a quarter of a mile on he spotted two horses on the far bank, and a sudden chill struck him when he saw Tatiana's clothing nearby. The bank was churned with hoof marks leading into the water. Evans

188

quickly waded across and found a small, bare footprint on the far side surrounded by the marks of men's boots.

Evans's fear for Tatiana threatened to choke him. His bare feet moved soundlessly on the damp leaves, and the forest was darker, more shadowed now as the sun moved toward the ridge. How had Orbelesky's soldiers found them so quickly?

He heard Tatiana scream again, and a man laughed not far away. Soldiers . . . deserters? He cursed himself for not bringing the rifle and broke out of the trees to discover that he was on an island. The far bank was thirty feet away, and alders and poplars blazed in autumnal splendor against a rising wave of dark green firs. The sun gilded the ridgetop for an instant, and then the warmth went and cold shadows fled over the river.

She was hardly aware that she was in the open again when one of them lunged and caught her foot, throwing her into the water. A hand wadded in her hair, and she was dragged onto the sand. In reflex, Tatiana squeezed her eyes closed and rolled into a tight ball; but her arms were yanked away, and she was slapped twice across the face. The man's hands were like hammers, and her brain whirled at the force of the blows.

She screamed again, and the smaller one dropped onto his knees and caught her head between his thighs, fumbling at his belt. "I'll stuff her mouth so she can't scream," he said with a cackle.

"Here now, none of that!" the bigger man roared, and shoved him back. He winked. "You wait until I've had my turn. Then you can do what you want with the sow." He leaned over Tatiana. "You might as well make up your mind to enjoy this, Your Majesty." He laughed when Tatiana gasped. How could they possibly know?

He had knelt ponderously and spread her tightly clenched legs without effort, rubbing and prodding with a huge, dirty hand.

"The dunking seems to have cooled you." He leered. "I'll have to warm you again."

The hand was hard and hurt, and Tatiana tried to squirm away; but he gathered a handful of pubic hair and pulled. She screamed at the sudden pain, and he roared at her to lie still. Even at that moment she was aware that her body was responding to the friction of the man's hands, and she flushed with shame. He knelt above her, like a massive tree trunk undoing his belt. Tatiana realized what was going to happen. The book—the French girl had been terrified when the soldier had unfastened his belt.

Evans saw Tatiana on her back across the stream. One man knelt on her arms while his hands roughly massaged her breasts. The scene had the unreality of a dream. It was the blacksmith from the village who crouched between her legs, unfastening his belt. He whipped it off and, before Evans could shout, flicked it like a lash across her thighs. Tatiana screamed, and he laughed and tossed the belt aside and unbuttoned his pants. As he turned, he saw Evans and roared in surprise.

The other man leaned forward to see better, one dirty hand splaying across her breast. A hunting knife appeared in the other hand, and he grinned and touched it to her throat.

"Comrade," the blacksmith rumbled as he stood up. "I admit I lied! We *are* Communists! We've come to share your grand duchess . . . and your gold. There's posters all over the district, you know."

He took a step forward, and the tableau fractured. Evans saw everything with the utmost clarity. The blacksmith was the distraction. The other man's arm whipped back to throw the knife, and Evans, moving with deliberation, brought the Colt up in one smooth motion, centered the thin blade in the U notch just under the man's heart and squeezed the trigger. The recoil took the pistol high enough to show him the man sprawling backward, a look of comical surprise on his face as he died. Evans turned slightly to his right, bringing the pistol down as the blacksmith charged across the river. He fired without haste, and momentum carried the blacksmith on after the bullet had smashed into his head. Evans stepped aside as he stumbled past and fired once more, directly into his neck.

The gunshots were unreal. Even the body falling backward to free her head confused her. Images flickered; the man she recognized now as the blacksmith from the village was lying in the water. Then Evans was holding her tightly, and she sobbed against his bare shoulder, knowing that the terror was beginning again.

Both realized they were naked at the same time. Tatiana closed her eyes, suffused with embarrassment. Evans felt her face flush hot against his chest and released her. He tugged the evil-smelling coat from the dead blacksmith and wrapped it about Tatiana's shoulders, then turned to make certain that the blacksmith's companion was dead and to take his coat.

Tatiana took a deep breath. Darkness was flowing into the valley, and the air was cold. She was surprised rather than embarrassed at the sight of his body. He seemed a much larger man than when clothed. His shoulders were quite broad, and his back and chest deep. She had never thought of him as being well muscled. He drew on the coat, and she looked away hastily. She had never seen a man naked before. In the past she had attended army and navy gymnastic competitions where the men had worn abbreviated costumes over tight one-piece garments, but she had never been close enough for a proper look. The rough sheepskin lining rubbed her nipples, and she flushed again.

"I don't think there are any more of them," he said as he took her arm and guided her across the stream. "I was afraid they might be General Orbelesky's men." He hesitated for a moment, staring toward the trees. "They knew who you were, and he said something about posters. Orbelesky must have circulated your description, probably offered a damned large reward. Christ," he finished softly.

"They . . . the bodies . . . ?" she began, but he shook his head.

"Leave them for the wolves. The bastards don't deserve to be buried."

He gathered up the three horses, and by the time they reached the clearing opposite the water meadow it was dark. Their own animals had moved apart to graze but were still in sight. Evans hobbled the new horses and turned them loose, then built a fire. He murmured something about his clothes and handed her the pistol before disappearing into the bushes.

Tatiana suppressed a surge of fear at being left alone and laid the heavy pistol in her lap. After a moment she threw off the coat and walked into the stream, shivering at the touch of the water that now seemed icy cold. Even so, she submerged herself and scrubbed hard wherever they had touched her. Afterward she dressed slowly in fresh, if not clean, clothing from her saddlebag. The bath had been more symbolic than anything else, but she felt cleaner for it.

A scrap of a sermon, preached long ago in a church on their Finnish estates near Imatra, came back to her. The priest had thundered against the sins of the flesh, promising God's retribution for all eternity to those who ignored His commandments. God had ignored her, she told herself, and was immediately shocked by her blasphemy. But wasn't it true? God had deserted her. If there was a God. How could there be a kind and loving God if all that had happened to her . . .

"Tatiana?"

Evans's voice startled her. He had dressed—she could see that his clothing was still damp. Preoccupied with her blasphemy, she shivered. He stooped over the saddles, unfastened his blanket and laid it over her shoulders. For some reason he refused to meet her eyes—he was thinking about Olga, she decided—but walked off again into the darkness. Hugging the blanket to her, enveloped by his odor, Tatiana heard the rhythmic thud of the ax. The growing feeling of excitement she had experienced as she lay on the mossy bank and touched her breast and her . . . Tatiana glanced wildly about the clearing, seeking something to distract her mind. But the feeling had returned, only stronger now. She clenched her knees involuntarily and gasped at the sensation.

Evans reappeared with an armload of firewood. When he had it going to his satisfaction, he mixed mince with water from the stream, tore off part of a loaf of black bread and set both to warm by the fire.

They ate, huddled in blankets as the air turned crisp and stars blazed overhead. "Autumn," Tatiana murmured, and he nodded.

"Are you all right?" he asked quietly, and she nodded.

"They didn't . . ."

"No. You came in time. Again." She said this last so softly that he almost didn't hear. He grinned uneasily and started to get up, but Tatiana stopped him with a hand on his arm.

"No, please. Three times now you've saved my life. You did not have to come back for me that day." She lowered her head, and Evans caught the glint of tears. She took a deep breath. "It would have been so much better for you, for both of you, if Olga had lived instead of—"

"Don't say that!" Evans snapped. "Ever!"

Her eyes shimmered in the firelight, and suddenly Evans felt overwhelming pity for her. Her world had gone; she had no one, was completely alone. He started to take her hand, but the memory of her fierce sense of independence stopped him. He didn't want another rebuff.

Tatiana forgot about the two men, forgot about the terror, forgot even about the religious strictures that had bounded her life. Something had happened to her in the past few weeks, and she did not know what, nor did she want to explore the causes. She needed to be comforted; she was frightened, lonely and desperate. "Will you hold me?" Tatiana whispered.

All of Evans's preconceived notions shattered in that moment.

"Please," Tatiana whispered.

She lay with her arms hugging her breasts, legs rigidly extended. Sensations flooded her body. Pain, fear, pleasure coupled with excitement, fading to self-disgust. The sensations were confusing and seemed to her inadequate.

The way he had touched her face with his fingertips, so gently, her shoulders, back and, finally, her breasts. She could still feel his body pressing hers, crushing her as his hands slipped to her stomach, her abdomen, into the junction of her thighs to press. She had tried to pull away, nauseated because his hands were like the blacksmith's.

The pain was sharp at first, like a flame twisting inside. Then a warm flood of emotion swept her body as tension built until she was afraid she would scream. He was thrusting harder and faster into her. Tatiana was overwhelmed with sensation: his crushing weight, his breath against her neck, his hands pulling her to him. It was hard to breathe, and her body was twisting, pulling, tightening to unbearable proportions until she knew she would scream. Suddenly Evans groaned and shuddered, and a moment later he collapsed onto her. Tatiana gasped and struggled to hold the tension, but it faded inexorably. He groaned again when she prodded him and rolled off onto his back, throwing one hand across his eyes.

Tatiana lay for a moment, certain she had been on the brink of an astonishing discovery. Then, as she huddled into herself, any gratitude she felt faded into an instant's hatred that left her shaken.

But as the moments passed and the intensity of the feelings faded, so did the hatred, overwhelmed by the vestiges of excitement and pleasure she had experienced. Evans touched her hip, and she turned quickly into his arms. After a while she fell asleep as he stroked her flanks and back.

They crossed the spine of the Urals into European Russia the following week. To Tatiana, the journey was symbolic of her coming of age. Thoughts of her murdered family no longer occupied her every waking hour, and nights spent in Evans's arms all but banished the nightmares. After years of speculation, she delighted in the thought that she had mastered the mysteries of the human body. The little French girl was no longer her mentor, and as she and Evans learned about each other, their lovemaking began to take on a physical intensity that was satisfying in itself. To Evans's surprise, he found he was taking great pains to satisfy her. He had never considered doing so before with any woman.

The weather continued fine during the rapidly shortening days, but the nights suggested winter. Evans spent hours poring over the map, trying to decide what to do. Shelter was their most immediate problem. He had thought to find an isolated village, but the Urals were at once more sparsely inhabited and better organized than he had expected. The tiniest village seemed to have its own council, or soviet, and there was still the matter of Orbelesky's posters. He decided finally they would have to move into Bolshevik-controlled territory, which held its own dangers.

They had traveled nearly a hundred miles from where he had killed the two men and were within a week's ride of a village near the base of the mountains. He still had six Mexican gold pieces, and even one would guarantee them a winter's comfortable lodging if he should decide to risk leaving the safety of the mountains.

Evans finally decided that they should give themselves as much time as possible to investigate the area, and they started down in mid-September. At noon the following day the sun abruptly vanished behind dense clouds, moving in quickly from the northwest. The firs bent to a whistling wind, and the beauty of the mountain forest disappeared. They shivered in quartering blasts that veered unexpectedly, and the worn horses plodded on with drooping heads until they entered a narrow valley and the wind was suddenly gone.

Evans reined in and glanced around, half expecting a storm front to come roaring down on them. Instead, he saw canyon walls rising to break the force of the wind. Farther on birches and alders lined the banks of a wandering stream, and even in the overcast they blazed with reds and oranges, doubly vivid against white trunks. The valley floor was carpeted with grass, and the stream widened to a marshy area that gave way to an immense water meadow. Stands of scattered trees came together as the land rose to meet the ridges, and the forest flowed like a dark carpet onto the rocky heights.

The beauty of the place could prove deceiving, Evans thought. He reined his horse into the cover of some trees on the crest and took out his field glasses. Tatiana urged her mare alongside. "What's the matter?"

Evans shook his head and examined the valley. "Best we start being a little more careful. We're bound to meet more people." Tatiana bit her lip, a habit he had noticed recently whenever something bothered her. Smiling, he brushed her cheek with a kiss.

Evans estimated the valley at close to five miles long but less than a mile wide. They had approached over the southern and higher rim; to the north the slope was shallower. They rode slowly along, following the creek to where it made an oxbow with a deep, blue-green pool to one side. Across the pool the water meadow began, graced here and there with stands of flaming birches. Willows and cattails were in abundance, and in the muddy bank Evans saw evidence of deer.

"Bill!" Tatiana caught at his arm.

He wheeled at the alarm in her voice, tugging the rifle free of its lashing under his leg. Tatiana was pointing to a hut, all but hidden in the trees; he didn't wait to see more but grabbed her reins and kicked both horses forward. They spurted up and out of the bowl into the forest, where he wheeled the horses into cover and dismounted. Tatiana followed suit, and he pulled her down with him behind a fallen tree.

"Keep your head down," he snapped. Tatiana spat out a mouthful of dirt and dead leaves and tried to push his hand away, but he gripped her sleeve tighter. "Damn it, lie still!"

She did as she was told, and they remained that way for some minutes before he stood up slowly. "You stay here," he muttered.

The hut—cabin, rather—was built of unpeeled logs jammed upright in the ground and lashed together with rope. The interstices had been plastered with mud, and there was a roof of long poles covered with bark and a layer of sod. The eaves reached almost to the ground. No wonder they hadn't seen it before, he thought.

He approached at an angle, ducked under a low branch and sprinted across to the cabin wall, where he squatted and duck-walked rapidly around to the front. The cabin door was partly open. He pushed at it with his rifle muzzle and, when nothing growled or rushed out, kicked it open.

Dirt covered everything a finger's span deep. A shutter over a window had sagged off its leather hinges, and the table beneath was smothered in years of rotting leaves. The top had warped and one leg had broken under the burden. The cabin was full of disturbed rustlings —mice.

He stepped outside and called to Tatiana. When she reached him, he waved a hand at the cabin. "Our own Winter Palace," he joked.

Tatiana stared through the door, eyes widening. There was no stove, merely an open fireplace of fieldstone mortared with mud. A stand with a rusted bowl filled with sour mud stood before the back wall, and a bed had been constructed Russian fashion over an oven. Two badly carved and fitted chairs were overturned and half-buried in the debris that covered the bare dirt floor. The interior was black from years of smoke.

"You can't be serious?" she managed to ask.

"The overriding consideration is concealment," Evans explained as they ate a midday meal of dried venison. "This place is damned isolated. There's good water, plenty of firewood—there must have been an avalanche down the ridge because I noticed a lot of downed trees pointing in the same direction—and there's bound to be plenty of game on the ridges. With winter coming, Orbelesky's troops will be concentrating on the villages."

"But the dirt—"

"We'll clean it."

"The horses—"

"Plenty of grass in the meadow. We can cut enough for the winter, and there's bark to strip as well."

"But someone lives here—"

"Not in years. Just look at the place. Tania, we can stay here through the winter with no one the wiser. For all intents and purposes, we'll have vanished." Evans left her to think it over while he tended the horses. When he returned, Tatiana had cut a pine branch to use as a broom and the air was full of dust.

A brief spell of wet weather set in, and Tatiana was glad they had chosen to remain. Evans repaired the narrow bunk atop the oven, and that night, as the rain pattered on the roof, they lay together, making love on a mattress made of two blankets sewn together and stuffed with fragrant meadow grass.

The rain lasted for several days and was followed by a period of fine Indian summer that ran well into October. Grateful for the respite, Evans and Tatiana worked from dawn to dusk, cutting meadow grass for the horses and vast quantities of firewood. The first days were an agony of blistered hands and aching muscles; but the rim of flesh around Evans's waist melted away, and the shadowy gauntness that had followed Tatiana since Perm disappeared. Long, hard work supplemented with plentiful food caused her to bloom, and Evans was struck one brilliant afternoon by the fact that she was an extremely desirable and beautiful young woman.

A dependable food supply, he had learned long ago, was the key to winter health. He showed Tatiana how to construct a Hudson's Bay figure four deadfall—a precarious but effective assembly of sticks and a heavy log. One stick was notched in mid-length, pointed at both ends and thrust into the ground beside an animal run. The other two sticks were pointed at one end and notched near the other. The horizontal stick in the backward figure 4 rested in the notch of the upright. The pointed end of the angled stick rested in its notch, and its notch in turn rested on the top end of the upright. The bait was fastened to the horizontal stick—the trigger—and the assemblage held in place by the weight of the log balanced against the end of the angled stick. When the bait was disturbed, the log collapsed and brained the animal.

Tatiana was curious to see if the trap really worked and made the rounds with him the following morning. Her enthusiasm did not survive the first kill, however, and it became Evans's job to reset the traps thereafter.

Evans also showed Tatiana how to loosen and pull up the cattails fringing the pool for their potatolike roots, and they gathered watercress, dandelion and chicory as time permitted, building a store of dried greens, wild mustard, clover and nettles. A constant diet of meat had quickly palled, and Tatiana was amused by the vigor with which she had attacked a salad of boiled dandelions and wild mustard. And one memorable morning Evans surprised her with a tin mug of coffee—ground dandelion roots mixed with chicory.

Their arsenal had grown to four weapons. The dead blacksmith and his friend had supplied two army surplus .42 caliber rifles, last used by the Russian army in the 1880s, and a pouch of black-powder cartridges. He had only ten cartridges left for the bolt-action Mosin-Nagant rifle; the rest had been expended in hunting, and three cartridges remained in the Colt pistol.

Evans was long to remember that Indian summer as one of the finest and happiest periods of his life. The weather held mild and clear, the sky the cleanest cerulean. The aspens and birches blazed, and in the evenings they would sit by the stream where it flowed to form the pool and watch the leaves like colorful boats floating across the darkening water as Tatiana talked about her life before the abdication. One thing he quickly learned was not to discuss the monarchy. For Tatiana, her father was a hero, and no matter what, he never wanted that to change.

It was during these quiet talks that he came to know an unsuspected side of Tatiana's personality. It was as if finding the cabin and the isolated valley had released all her fears. She began to laugh, easily and quickly. She told jokes and played jokes, stole his clothes when he went out to bathe, stuffed his shoes with grass and hid his tools in the evening so that he would pay attention to her.

The weather broke in mid-month. The first hint was a sudden chill in the late afternoon. Both looked at the sky to see pewter clouds sliding over the northern rim of the valley. All color abruptly disappeared, and Evans heard the wind roaring among the trees. By the time they stored the firewood they had cut that day it had begun to rain.

When he woke shortly before dawn, wind prowled about the cabin. Reluctantly he scurried across the icy floor to build up the fire and add another log to the oven. Drafts whistled through the walls, and a conical pile of snow had built near the door where the mud chinking had fallen away. Through the window the world was lost in a featureless gray whiteness. He could sense the wind raging through the valley, thrashing trees and spewing snow, and the full impact of their complete isolation swept over him. They remained in bed most of that day, luxuriating in the absence of physical labor for the first time in a month.

The first weeks of confinement declined into a period of unexpected pain for Evans. The enforced idleness brought a craving for alcohol he had thought finished. The need was so intense, so painful that he sometimes sat beside the fire for an hour or more, pretending to be thinking or studying the maps, teeth clenched to keep from screaming, his stomach churning with nausea. At night his dreams were crowded with images of Pete Boyd, and he saw over and over again Boyd's battered face on the morgue table. He concealed his distress from Tatiana as best he could, fearing that it might open secrets better left untold.

Tatiana was also affected by the wind's constant howling and the never-varying white beyond the single window. The endless hours spent on horseback or engaged in physical labor, coupled with the intense sexual passion she shared with Evans, had kept her mind too occupied to brood about her family's ordeal and murder and her own denial of God. Now, as Evans withdrew into himself for reasons she was at a loss to understand, the malevolent wind seemed to search her out.

The storm is the reminder of God's power, she heard Rasputin's bass voice proclaim in the depths of one howling night. Behind him, her favorite icon of the Virgin and Child glowed softly, candlelight shading its ancient varnish. *The storm at sea that is the terror of mariners, the storm of the steppe that whips the grasses to frenzy and humbles the mightiest tree, the mountain storm—all are reminders of the all-powerful God!*

197

That night she heard the words again as a particularly vicious blast set the spruces to screaming like condemned souls. The words seemed so clear that she was certain she had called out to the beloved starets. The wind raged like an insane beast, slapping the cabin walls, causing the door to shudder on its leather hinges. Something flapped suddenly against the roof, and she started in terror.

Cold is hell as well as flame, Rasputin intoned. *There are depths into which the greatest sinners are cast where the wind howls with a ferocity unimagined and the snow flies like shot, and they must wander shrivering and crying against a pain fiercer even than that of the eternal fire. They are the sinners who cursed God.*

If she had confided in Evans, he would have explained that Rasputin had plagiarized a thirteenth-century Italian poet and perhaps eased her mind; but she did not, and the fragment of sermon festered in the depths of her subconscious.

The first blizzard ended and was followed by a day of unearthly stillness. The snow was deep and soft. The forest was sheathed in powdery whiteness, and the meadow had disappeared beneath an endless blanket the exact shade of the overcast sky. The pool lay slate gray and still, ice thickening about its edges, while the stream had carved a sluggish passage through the snow overhanging its banks like cake icing. Animal tracks appeared in the untouched snow, and Evans spotted deer sign. That afternoon he followed the tracks toward the ridge on snowshoes fashioned from spruce boughs, laboriously steamed to shape and laced with willow. Tatiana watched as the trees swallowed him up, and the silence crushed her. Sky and valley pressed in, and she found herself gasping for breath as she fled to the cabin.

October melded into November, and an unseasonal thaw arrived in mid-month. Where the wind had prowled about the cabin as they fell asleep, the sound of dripping water woke them. For the first time in weeks they saw the sun as more than a pale disk. It flooded the valley, and a mild south wind warmed them as they stood gaping in the doorway. The temperature rose, and snow disappeared from the meadow.

Tatiana's good humor returned. On the second day of the thaw she found herself tempted beyond endurance. Evans heard her scream and ran outside to find her naked and shivering at the edge of the stream, nerving herself for another plunge. The iron-cold water bit at her skin, and she screamed again as she dived in and came up laughing and crying at the exhilarating pain. Evans rubbed her blue, shivering limbs with a blanket and then decided to bathe as well. Tatiana displayed more imagination than he had in restoring his circulation.

The thaw ended in a blizzard of immense proportions that blew for an entire week, driving snow into every crevice of the cabin, banking well above the roof and darkening the interior even after they had tunneled outward from the door and window. Evans rechinked the logs and strengthened the shed that sheltered the horses.

December dragged into a series of blizzards. Evans's recurring longing for alcohol during periods of enforced idleness began to subside as he found work about the cabin to keep his hands busy, but Tatiana began to retreat into herself again.

It took him some time to notice what was happening to her. He would look up to see her sitting cross-legged at the fire, staring into the flames, while the piece of clothing she was mending sat untouched in her lap. More and more she was unresponsive when he made love to her, and once she turned him away. In the morning his anger disappeared when he saw the dark circles and drawn look that signaled another sleepless night. He connected her moodiness to the weather and did not worry because he had seen the same phenomenon attack otherwise stable, happy Swedish friends during the long winter months. In Wyoming they called it cabin fever.

The Christmas holidays were ushered in by bright sunshine and crisp weather. Temperatures rose above freezing during the day, and immense icicles dripped from the roof. While Evans hunted, Tatiana stripped bark to eke out the dwindling stock of hay. After nearly a month of constant confinement the horses had begun to fail, and Evans was worried. The poor diet, intense cold and close quarters of the shed were taking their toll.

On the Feast of the Epiphany they exchanged gifts. Evans gave her a mink and fox jacket made from skins taken in the deadfall traps. Tatiana had fashioned a pair of mittens from softly tanned deerskin and shyly admitted having chewed the leather to soften it. Astonished, he slipped his hands into the supple leather, filled with cattail fur for insulation. The workmanship was marvelous, and she had decorated the mittens with intricate stitching.

Evans saved the best gift for last. In midafternoon, after a huge dinner of fresh venison and a salad of dried greens, he dragged in a bathtub he had been working on since he discovered her bathing in the half-frozen pool, and Tatiana screamed with excitement. The tub was made from a single spruce log hollowed by a slow fire and a great deal of ax work to smooth the interior, and it was big enough to sit in comfortably. Evans put it near the fireplace and filled it with water drawn from the creek. It took several hours for it to warm to the point where it was bearable, and Tatiana could barely wait to throw off her clothes and plunge in. A moment later he joined her.

They were sitting in front of the fireplace one evening near the end of January, Evans entertaining Tatiana with a long, involved story about his consulate days in Italy, when the door slammed against the wall and a snow-covered apparition, clutching a rifle, stumbled in. Evans snatched up the ax as Tatiana screamed. His rifle was leaning against the wall by the bunk, and the pistol hung on a nail beside the door. With a gloved hand, the intruder thrust back his fur hood to reveal greasy hair and reddish eyes glaring from inflamed sockets. The man wore a heavy pack slung from his shoulders, and a long skinning knife was sheathed at his belt.

"Hold," the man mumbled in a thick voice. "I'm near frozen."

He pushed the door closed and staggered to the fire. Tatiana scrambled out of his reach, eyes wide with terror.

"Caught . . . blizzard. Never . . . thought to reach here."

"Who the devil are you?" Evans demanded. He moved swiftly and grabbed the pistol from its nail. The man leaned his rifle against the fireplace and sank down as close to the flames as he could.

"Sergei Petrovich Blyekov," he rumbled. His fur parka began to steam and exude a sour smell of badly tanned skins and long-unwashed body. His beard and hair were unkempt, and a scar crossed one cheek to his left eye. Beneath the scarred lid Evans saw the milky whiteness of the globe without a defined iris.

When Blyekov thawed sufficiently, he drew a shuddering breath. "I go to the village twice a year," he told them, pronouncing each word as if it were a novelty. "For supplies. The storm caught me." The man moved restlessly, then, as if aware that he was making them nervous, remained still.

Evans pointed to the kettle on the hook. "There's food. . . ."

Blyekov flashed him a look of gratitude. He ate steadily for a long time and, when he was satisfied, sat back and wiped his mouth with his hands. He looked at them for a moment, then dug into his pack and produced a bottle of vodka.

The clear liquid flared red in the firelight, and Evans felt his mouth flood with saliva. The desire was stronger than ever before. He started to reach for the bottle, then abruptly shook his head. Blyekov shrugged, offered the bottle to Tatiana, who also declined. He put it away in his pack, and Evans sank down on the bed, weak beyond belief.

In response to their questions, Blyekov told them he was a trapper, originally from the Ukraine, the village of Vielst. "At sixteen I went into the army. I became a sergeant. My regiment was in action against the Austrians in Poland. I saw there what fools our commanders were. I was wounded in the leg and so survived. I was wounded again in 1915, but the last time, in 1916, I received this sword cut"—he touched his face—"from a Russian officer. Imagine!"

When he saw the skeptical expression on Tatiana's face, he explained. "I was ordered to take three men and enter a village held by the Austrians in order to draw their fire. It was suicide. I refused, and he cut me down with his sword."

Tatiana uttered an exclamation.

Blyekov smiled. "Perhaps you do not believe me? Imagine how I felt when I saw that sword whistling at me. I was turning away when he struck. I tell you, I earned two Saint George crosses for bravery, but I know better than to throw away life, which is both foolish and a mortal sin. I was told I was to be court-martialed when I recovered. Because of the mutinies in the French army, they resolved to shoot me as an example to others. So I escaped."

Evans could see that Tatiana wanted to challenge the man's story, but he put a hand on her arm and said quickly, "Is there any news of the civil war?"

The hunter nodded. "There is talk that the Bolsheviks have been pushed back on all fronts. In the Don region the Cossacks and the Germans have cleared them out. They say that General Orbelesky and Admiral Kolchak will drive to Moscow in the spring; but they failed to take Perm, and the Bolsheviks are said to be sending reinforcements with every train. The Germans have occupied my native Ukraine, and there is talk they will sever it from Russia. Perhaps then I could go home again."

For an instant there was such an intense expression of longing on his face that Evans looked away in embarrassment.

"The war in the West is over. An armistice in November."

Evans gaped at the man. The war over? He wasn't certain he heard right. But the hunter repeated the news and swore it was true. "I saw newspapers."

The war was over! Evans's momentary regret that he had not been involved, really involved, was submerged instantly in memories of real war as he seen it along the Trans-Siberian Railroad and at Ekaterinburg. Real war meant dead bodies bloating in the sun, the smell of corruption and blood, burning farms and houses, raped women, men's bodies swinging from makeshift gallows or thrown like discarded rag dolls into pits, one atop the other, no longer needed. He remembered the burial parties hauling bodies from the prison cellar in Ekaterinburg. War was an individual's existence snuffed out because a political theoretician in Moscow or Petrograd or London or Washington or Paris or Berlin or wherever had decreed that those who did not *believe* must die.

The hunter slept beside the fire and left with the first indication of dawn. It was still snowing quite hard, but the wind had died during the night. Evans went with him for a short distance on his snowshoes. He noticed that the hunter was wearing skis, but that rather than the usual long pole balanced crosswise, he used two, smaller poles, one in each hand to propel himself. Evans had first seen the new technique in 1914 in Norway.

When he returned, Tatiana was clearing snow away from the

window. She turned as she heard him coming, and the reddish fox fur framing her face emphasized the paleness of her skin. She seemed at that moment so fragile, so much in need of protection that he wondered why he had ever thought of her as stubborn. Tatiana saw him watching her and smiled, and suddenly Evans was overwhelmed with a feeling of tenderness for her that surprised him with its intensity.

In the first week of March an early springlike thaw began but was quickly submerged in fresh blizzards. As the month dragged on, two of the horses died, but the remaining four improved with the extra fodder.

The dreams that had been triggered by the howling storm winds still troubled Tatiana a great deal. Religion had been so much a part of her life for so long that she still bowed her head at the thought of Christ's name, her hand still twitched to make the sign of the cross and the idea that she had once forsworn God, denied His existence troubled her often. The fact that she had done so in the throes of extreme emotion and grief was not, as far as she was concerned, a mitigating factor. She began again to wake at night, filled with the same kind of terror she had experienced in the train at Perm.

For a while Evans's hard body beside her was a comfort, but then the knowledge that they were living in mortal sin began to produce a kind of fear that threatened at times to drive her mad. Often her dreams resulted in a lingering depression that Evans was helpless to relieve.

By mid-April the thaw had begun in earnest. Evans, convinced now that winter was ending, began preparations to resume the trek north. The horses, freed of the confining shed and corral, cavorted happily in the water meadow and put on new flesh.

They left the valley in the last week of April. A pelting rain had fallen all week; but that day the sun was bright and warm, and the fresh-washed air mild with spring. They had erased every trace of their occupation from the cabin, even tearing down the corral and scattering the posts in the forest. What they could not take, they burned or buried, and Tatiana cried as her bathtub was rolled into the creek to form part of a beaver dam. By the time they rode away, the cabin appeared as run-down and abandoned as when they had discovered it in the autumn.

Evans had spent weeks deciding on a route. The map showed the town of Nadezhdinski Zavod, a two-week ride away on the eastern side of the Urals. It had been in Bolshevik hands the previous autumn, but with a suitable disguise, Tatiana would be safe enough. As far as the Bolsheviks were concerned, the royal family was in White hands. And they needed news of the civil war, in particular, of operations in the north. The question of whether or not Allied forces were still at Archangel had troubled Evans all winter. If not, they would have to turn east for the unimaginably long journey to China.

They rode into the mining town of Nadezhdinski Zavod late one cold spring day. People, horses and motorcars cluttered the streets, filling them both with apprehension and lending authenticity to their portrayal of backwoods dwellers.

Evans found a small boardinghouse run by a wizened old woman with a shrewd eye and a sour odor that permeated the house. She pushed a yellow card and a stub of pencil across the desk and watched as he filled in the information demanded: name, place of birth, nationality, religion, height, weight, coloring, military service and political affiliation. Evans affected only the most elementary ability to write and read. The old woman peered at the card with near-sighted intentness and motioned Tatiana to fill hers in.

"Can't read or write," Evans muttered. "Ain't no need." He completed her card and roughly helped her mark an X.

Satisfied, the landlady accepted three Kerensky ruble notes and led them up to a room which was as dingy as the appearance of the house promised. Dirt was evident in the corners, and the threadbare bedding was filled with fleas. Evans grimaced and made up their bedrolls on the floor. Tatiana sat on the window ledge, staring out into the gray afternoon.

When he came in after seeing to the horses, her face was a study in misery, and he thought he understood: The filth, the mean people, the walls pressing in—she was in the house at Ekaterinburg again. He touched her hair, and as she tilted her head against his side, he slipped an arm about her shoulder.

"Tania, tell me. What's bothering you?"

She pressed against him for a moment; she wanted to tell him about the dreams, but she couldn't find the words. How to make her beliefs sound reasonable to someone who did not even profess a religion? She had struggled with the problem all winter, and still, she could not tell him that she was afraid to go on living with him in mortal sin. Evans coaxed her gently, and she forced herself to smile.

"I'm just tired, that's all."

"There isn't anything else?" He knew there was; but he also knew that she would tell him only when she was ready, and in any event he was anxious to go out for the supplies before dark. When she shook her head, he did not press.

After he had left, Tatiana went down and knocked on the landlady's door. She heard a sullen groan and the shuffling of carpet slippers, and the door opened a crack. A suspicious eye full of rheum squinted at her.

"What do you want?"

"Please, may I talk to you?"

"From there, dearie. I let no one in." A wave of overheated and evil-smelling air washed out, and Tatiana was almost glad the woman had refused.

"Please, can you tell me where I can find the nearest church?"

The woman hissed in surprise. "There are no more churches! Go away!" she whispered, and slammed the door as Tatiana started to plead with her.

Evans strode along the narrow streets in the cold glare of the setting sun. Telegraph poles festooned with layer on layer of wire skirted the road, and the wind sang through them. It was extremely cold, and underfoot, the mud had frozen into miniature mountain ranges. A factory whistle blasted, and the street was suddenly filled with people.

In the next block a light glowed in the window of a general store. An old man wearing a felt skullcap and a gray coat greeted him politely when he entered.

Evans muttered a response and drew out a crumpled piece of paper. "Supplies."

The old man turned to the shelves, and Evans glanced at the Moscow newspaper he had been reading, a two-month-old copy called *Pravda,* "Truth." He scanned the headlines as the old man hummed to himself and took down boxes and cans from the shelves. The newspaper spoke glowingly of Red Army victories on all fronts, of great gains being made by volunteer units in Siberia. There was even a lengthy article that made it sound as if the Red retreat at Ekaterinburg were actually a victory. The logic was so transparent that Evans marveled at anyone's being expected to believe it.

". . . we are in a narrow valley," the shopkeeper's voice broke into his thoughts. "So it remains cold here much longer."

Evans let him ramble for a few moments, then interrupted to ask if the fighting had reached Moscow yet.

The bell over the door jangled before he could answer and two hard-faced men entered. Both wore uniform coats with red armbands and carried rifles. The shopkeeper greeted them respectfully, but they ignored him and eyed Evans closely.

One gestured at his rough clothing and sheepskin jacket. "Down from the mountains, Comrade?"

Evans nodded.

"A hard winter," the other remarked sympathetically. "I wouldn't want your life."

The first man, the older one with a hawk's hooded eyes, stared at Evans. "I don't remember seeing you before, Comrade. Been at it long?"

Evans forced himself to nod. "Since 1915," he grunted, cursing as he suddenly remembered he had left without the Colt pistol.

"No service in the German war?"

Evans nodded, thinking quickly of the trapper's story. But he could not recall the name of any battle. Desperately he snatched at one. "Wounded. Tannenberg, 1914. Released."

"Tannenberg, eh? My brother fought there. Died there. The officers saw to that, the sons of bitches! Maybe you ran across him. Servov. Mikhail Leonidonvich Servov. Sergeant in the Smolensk Regiment?"

Evans shook his head.

The militiaman nodded. His face was hard and closed, carved from granite. He had the look of a miner, someone used to dealing with the elemental earth on its terms, whereas his companion was soft and round, almost buttery. A clerk, Evans decided, or a shopkeeper before. He might be the worse—he would have to prove himself.

"Still and all, I don't remember you. Let's have your papers."

As soon as they walked in, he had known it would end like this. What the hell would Tatiana do? The older man was standing expectantly, one hand out, but the other was tucked inside his coat, as if for warmth, and Evans knew it gripped the butt of a revolver.

"I don't have papers."

"Your discharge papers then," the man barked, but Evans shrugged again, eyes darting about the shop for an escape route. The icy edge to the man's voice had caught the attention of his companion, who stepped away from the counter, fingering his rifle sling.

"Those!" Evans snorted in contempt. "I threw them away when they dragged Daddy Nick from his throne. Why would I need his papers?" Fear was rising quickly, and he could feel his hands trembling.

The guard seemed to relax a bit, even though he still eyed Evans closely. "The Nadezhdinski Soviet issued new papers to everyone in the district in February; otherwise, how would we know you're not a deserter, a counterrevolutionary or maybe even a White officer?"

Evans forced a laugh at the idea. "I . . . I was in the mountains then. I didn't know."

"Listen," the younger man snapped, his fierceness assumed for the benefit of his companion, "it's no joking matter. You can be shot for not having the proper papers."

The old man intervened at that point. "Comrade Milyukov, I vouch for him." His voice was mild enough, but Evans saw that he was watching the two militiamen narrowly. "He has come to my shop each spring since 1915."

The man hesitated, then nodded. "I advise you to get your papers in order before you leave." He took a pack of cigarettes from the counter and went to the door without paying.

"Another piece of advice," he shouted as he threw the door open. "If you deal with Jews, you are bound to be cheated."

Laughing, he slammed the door, and Evans sank down onto a wooden crate, weak with fear and relief. He had been a fool to come without the pistol.

"Thank you," he managed. "Another minute and I would have been arrested."

The old man nodded.

"You may have bought trouble for yourself."

"So?" He smiled. "Life is trouble."

Evans had noticed a rack of men's trousers against the wall, and when he stopped shivering, he got up and selected two pairs in the smallest size, two shirts and a sweater, then pointed to a hairbrush and comb. "And soap," he muttered.

The old man smiled. "For your wife. Then I suppose you are an officer?"

Evans laughed, feeling an edge of hysteria as he did so. "Is that what you took me for? A White officer?"

"No. You aren't even a Russian. But don't worry." The old man chuckled. "Few would ever notice. I am a Jew. I have lived among Gentiles all my life. My accent has always made it plain I am a Jew." He shrugged. "I listen to accents. You have a foreign accent, but very faint. At first I thought you might had lived as a child in a foreign country." He shook his head. "But you are a foreigner. A word here, a pronunciation there."

Evans thought of the old woman, Veronica Maximievna Lodoskaya, in Ekaterinburg. She had commented on his accent as well, but then she and her husband had been amateur linguists. He added several pieces of hard candy as a surprise for Tatiana, and the old man calculated the total at 227 rubles and he whistled at the price.

"Inflation is very bad," the man apologized. "I am allowed only five percent profit. Of that, the soviet takes three rubles in every five for taxes. To support the Red Army, they say."

Evans drew one of the Mexican gold coins from his money belt and laid it on the counter.

The old man shook his head vigorously. "It is forbidden to own gold." He glanced at Evans and noted his stricken expression. "An amnesty period was allowed in the autumn. Now it is a serious offense. You were lucky the militiamen did not search you."

Evans drew a deep breath. He felt as if the wind had been knocked out of him. Illegal to own gold! How in the name of God would they ever get to Archangel? He lifted the package of candy from the box and offered the two rubles he had left from his encounter with the blacksmith the previous autumn.

The shopkeeper's expression softened. "I will pay you three hundred Kerensky rubles for the coin." He sighed. "It is worth far more, but the risk is great. However, I do not think a police spy would buy candy with his own money."

Tatiana ran to him as he opened the door. Laughing, Evans held her until she shivered against his wet jacket.

"Tania . . ." he began, but she sank down on the narrow bed, face in her hands and shoulders heaving with the violence of her sobs.

He shed the sheepskin quickly and knelt beside her. "Tania, tell me?"

She twisted her hands together, and he clutched them to keep them still. For some reason the action caused him an almost physical pain. He kissed her fingers. "Tell me."

"I . . . I thought something had happened to you, that you had been arrested—" A sob caught in her throat, and he drew her into his arms again.

"Tania, Tania," he crooned softly. "Nothing will ever happen to me. Nothing. I've got you to take care of. Don't worry about me." But the words were meaningless as he remembered the hard-faced militiaman demanding his papers. Evans petted and soothed her until gradually her shivering stopped and she fell asleep. He turned the oil lamp down and for a long time watched her as she slept.

He woke Tatiana well before dawn. The boardinghouse was still except for the occasional racking cough of a miner in a nearby room. He packed and saddled the four horses quietly and led them out of the slowly collapsing stable behind the house. Tatiana rode close behind him, longing for the illusory peace and security of the winter cabin. Today was the day she had hoped to confess to a priest and receive absolution for her mortal sins, but the landlady's reaction and the terror of Bill's late return had driven all such thoughts from her mind. All she wanted now was to return to the safety of the forest.

X

The steppe began to give way to upland grasses and trees as the train climbed into the Urals. Behind, horses stamped, and the murmur of men's voices over cards and the smell of tobacco were reassuring. He was free, for a while at least. A cooling breeze, stirred by the train's passage, blew in the window, and the sky burned across the grass with sunset. Who was it that once wrote the "steppe was like the sea"?

Two weeks ago Commissar Nikolai Khristoforovich Sheremetiev had been shooting counterrevolutionaries in the Don region. A week ago he was in Moscow, and today he was on his way to Ekaterinburg. But anything was better than the endless executions of endless counter-revolutionaries who were nothing more than misguided old men, foolish boys and more than a few women. In other times a whipping, a term in prison or the mines would have been sufficient. Under the last tsar only the most recalcitrant of criminals had been executed. Whose way was better, he wondered.

The summons to Moscow had come from no less than Dzerzhinsky himself. The office in the Lubyanka was the same; only the blond secretary was gone, replaced by a middle-aged woman with a permanent frown. Dzerzhinsky had been pleased to see him, he had thought, because there were vodka and cigarettes on the desk as well as surprising news.

"The Romanov family escaped from Perm last August."

He had gaped at Dzerzhinsky, who was ejecting a cigarette butt from its holder. "A week after you handed over your command, fortunately for you. Your replacement, Commissar Chizov, claimed to have followed them until they joined a White guard unit some sixty miles north and east of Perm. There was the suggestion that Chizov may have betrayed the revolution and sold the Romanov family to the Whites. In any event," Dzerzhinsky had finished with sudden savagery, "he was recalled to Moscow and executed."

Sheremetiev had sat very still. Dzerzhinsky's rages were legendary in the Cheka.

"It was assumed that when the spring offensive began, the Kolchak government would brandish the tsar like a banner. They have not, thus bearing out certain rumors. There is, however, little to back them up." He had flipped something bright and shining across the desk, and Sheremetiev had caught it by reflex.

"A gold coin, the ownership of which is illegal. Chizov had it in his possession when he was arrested. He was persuaded to tell us that he took it from a Jewish merchant in a village northeast of Perm. A foreigner who was with the royal family was supposed to have given it to him in exchange for supplies." Dzerzhinsky had looked thoughtful for a moment. "Perhaps he told the truth, or perhaps the coin was part of the payment he received for betraying the Russian people."

Sheremetiev had studied the coin, noting the Roman characters which he could not read, then had looked up.

"A coin from Mexico, a fifty-peso piece, worth currently six hundred rubles, provided it was legal to own gold coins. I daresay that on the black market you might get ten times that amount." He had screwed a fresh cigarette into the ivory holder and lit it with a small silver lighter.

"Comrade Lenin has asked me to investigate this matter, and I am assigning you to the task. If the family or any member remains alive, you will carry out the orders of the All-Russian Congress of Soviets and execute them, immediately."

"We may know where the Romanovs are." The Cheka lieutenant, Sergei Dolrov, told him as they walked along the Ekaterinburg railroad platform to the automobile. It was raining lightly; but the air was mild with spring, and Sheremetiev breathed deeply, thankful for the absence of decaying bodies, cordite and burned huts and sheds.

The source of their information proved to be a young Kadet officer captured by Red militiamen. Disguised as a common soldier, he had tried to escape the collapsing Kadet front to the southeast of Perm. The man—a boy, really—was filthy and unshaved, and his eyes were full of blank misery. He proved extraordinarily grateful for the cigarette Sheremetiev offered, and while Lieutenant Dolrov hovered menacingly by the door, Sheremetiev politely drew out his background.

The boy was the son of a Tver merchant and had attended a

military academy from his twelfth year. At seventeen he had gone immediately into the army with the rank of Coronet in the 137th Guards Machine Gun Regiment. He sucked greedily on the cigarette, and Sheremetiev poured a measure of vodka from his pocket flask and watched as he gulped it down.

"Comrade Lieutenant Dolrov, please bring this man a plate of food. Hot, if you please, and a mug of tea with plenty of sugar. Honey will do otherwise."

Dolrov started to protest but stopped abruptly at the senior officer's expression and went out.

"I don't suppose they've fed you well, the swine," Sheremetiev said with regret. "There isn't any reason to treat you like that. I was an officer myself."

The boy stared distrustfully.

"Why so surprised?" Sheremetiev smiled. "We each do what we must. Is that any reason to think the less of a man? People like him"—he hooked a thumb at the door—"give us a bad name. But their time will come. Their crimes will be found out, and the Soviet system will deal with them as it has dealt with others."

He asked a few innocuous questions until Dolrov returned with the food and tea. Sheremetiev cautioned the boy to eat slowly so as to avoid making himself sick and more than once placed a warning hand on his wrist. As expected, the young officer was absurdly grateful and began to answer Sheremetiev's questions without reservation, responding to the small kindnesses like summer-baked land to autumn rains.

The story was simple enough. His machine-gun company had been transferred from the Ukraine after the Crimean National Front had reached an accommodation with the German occupation forces. It had taken no part in the battle for Ekaterinburg but had replaced a Czech regiment on garrison duties before being moved up to Perm to replace a regiment that had been continually in action for six months.

"The day before we went into the front lines, a Cossack patrol brought in eight people who had been driving about in a motor lorry stolen in Perm. Two parents, four daughters and a son and a tall man in a foreign military uniform. The following day an officer from Genneral Orbelesky's own staff arrived by airplane, and they all left on a special train."

Sheremetiev eyed the young officer. "It this how you repay a kindness?" he asked lazily, waving his cigarette. "The information I am seeking will not harm your cause or you. Why do you lie to me?"

The boy stared at him with stricken eyes. "I'm not lying," he whispered. "I'm telling you God's own truth."

Sheremetiev shook his head in regret. "You are lying by omission. Ah, well," he said as he got to his feet, "it wasn't important. Take another cigarette before I go."

"Wait . . . no, please, sit down again. You're right . . . there is more."

Sheremetiev resumed his seat with a polite expression and glanced at his wrist watch. "Well, I do have a few more minutes." Behind him, Dolrov growled as if on cue, and the boy glanced at him quickly.

"The staff officer was Colonel Maxime Obrechev. I don't know his patronymic. I . . . I think the man, the older man with the beard, was the tsar, Nicholas Romanov. I wasn't certain at first; but my sergeant major said he was, and he had been personally decorated by him once." He drew a deep breath as if resolving to continue. "I later recognized one of the women as the grand duchess Olga. She visited our military academy at the beginning of the war. No one was allowed to go near them, and they all left on the special train the following morning."

He stared thoughtfully at the empty plate for a moment. "No one credited the rumor that they were the royal family. Everyone knew they had been shot the month before in Ekaterinburg—" He looked up with a stricken expression. "I . . . didn't mean to imply . . ."

"Where did the train go?"

"Here, to Ekaterinburg, I suppose. After that I don't know."

"And if it was the tsar, why do you suppose your people have not announced that he is alive?"

The boy looked startled. "I . . . I hadn't thought of that."

Outside the cell Dolrov nodded in satisfaction. "Excellent job of interrogation, Comrade Sheremetiev. He never told us that much."

"No, he wouldn't." Sheremetiev snorted. "There is an old saying, Comrade Lieutenant. English, I suppose. 'You catch more flies with honey than with vinegar.' "

Dolrov glanced at him in bewilderment. Educated officers are a pain in the ass, he thought.

"What about him?" Dolrov nodded at the cell.

"He's told us all he knows. Now tell me about these other rumors?"

"When the victorious Red Army retook the battered eastern part of Perm Province and the city of Ekaterinburg, it seems that a mass grave was found some twenty miles east, beside the railroad. It was some weeks before the graves registration detail got around to it, but when it did, it discovered that there were actually two graves. One contained the bodies of five soldiers in the uniform of the Crimean National Front army, one of them an officer, and one civilian. The other grave was empty."

A fine spring rain was falling, and Sheremetiev adjusted his collar and walked to the pits. It was as desolate a spot as he could imagine in which to die. Mud glistened in the uncertain light. To one side of the smaller grave there lay six bodies. The corruption stage had apparently passed before the ground had frozen and the bodies were in a poor state of preservation. A rusted service revolver and a Browning pistol lay with three Japanese rifles.

The other grave had apparently been dug up long before, and the bodies taken away. Why? To be reduced to the handful of bones and bits of clothing the Whites claimed to have recovered at Ekaterinburg? If those bodies were as badly decomposed as these, identification would have been all but impossible; bits and pieces would have been better. And the bodies were said to have been recovered from a lime pit by White guard investigators. They had been burned and soaked with acid, ostensibly by their killers to disguise the victims' identities.

He had to admit that it was a clever ploy. At one stroke the Whites had confirmed the Ural Soviet's own foolish announcement and cemented responsibility by producing a few parts that bore out their version. Who ever would think that the Whites would murder the tsar? Not that it mattered. Moscow was happy enough to accept the responsibility.

Next to the larger grave was a small pile of articles that had been overlooked. Among them were one or two buttons, a small boot, a torn piece of cloth and a cap. Dolrov stomped up, wrinkling his nose at the odor of mud and decay.

"The boy was right. The officer was one Colonel Maxime Rovolovich Obrechev. Intelligence has confirmed that he was a member of General Orbelesky's staff and was used for special assignments."

Sheremetiev snorted. That was the euphemism employed on both sides to describe what in normal times would be called murder. He brushed mud from the cap. It was his own, the one he had given Nicholas in Perm.

"And," Dolrov went on, "they've identified the bullets taken from the bodies." He indicated the rotting remains. "The officer was shot twice at close range with a seven-point-sixty-five-millimeter pistol, probably the Browning found in the grave with him. It's too badly rusted to tell more. Three of the soldiers were killed with a very heavy-caliber weapon. The bullets are copper-jacketed and short, so they must be from a pistol. The caliber is apparently very large, measuring eleven-point-two-five millimeters. One of the men was a civilian, possibly a member of the train crew. He was killed with the same weapon." He handed Sheremetiev two of the bullets. "I telegraphed the information to Moscow, and they suggest they might have been fired from an American Colt pistol, of forty-five caliber, whatever that is."

"Point four-five hundredths of an inch. An English system of measurement," Sheremetiev murmured. How interesting, he thought. There were a number of puzzles. One, how many died here? Two, why was the officer shot at close range with a small pistol? And three, how did an American pistol come to be used to shoot down three soldiers?

"This as well." Dolrov handed Sheremetiev a military telegraph form. Rain spattered it instantly.

EXAMINATION OF ARTICLES FOUND IN LARGER OF GRAVES SUGGESTS FIVE PEOPLE BURIED STOP ONE ADULT MALE STOP FOUR FEMALES STOP FIND MISSING FEMALE AND MALE CHILD STOP [SIGNED] DZERZHINSKY

Now he stood in the doorway of a goods wagon, remembering his last encounter with Nicholas Romanov. It was the last time he had pitied anyone. He had striven hard to think of the family as the enemy. All members of the old ruling class were being systematically exterminated, those, in any case, who had not the wit to leave Russia. The royal family was the last major artifact of the old regime, the old evil of capitalist exploitation and murder. How curious that they should be killed by representatives of that regime.

The train slowed abruptly. Sheremetiev leaned far out. An abandoned engine was visible through a tunnel of overhanging trees. White smoke swirled across the line, obscuring his view for a moment, and then the line straightened and the trees closed in again. He smiled at his own excitement and, from the corner of his eye, saw Dolrov shaking his head in disgust at losing ten rubles to him.

Where else could they have gone? he thought. They had only a train for transportation, and whichever way they went, more killers would have been waiting for them. It was plain enough that the spur line north offered the only escape.

The rain had stopped, and the sky was filled with broken clouds. A thin wind whined through the trees as they followed the course of a stream into a shallow valley. It felt good to be on horseback again, and Sheremetiev breathed deeply of the spring air, conscious of a surprisingly good humor.

The village was only four houses but seemed prosperous enough, even though there was no stock visible. The villagers apparently were not so isolated that they did not know what a troop of mounted horsemen signified. Sheremetiev dismounted, and an old man edged out of a hut with obvious reluctance and trudged to meet him, carrying a crust of bread and a twist of paper.

"God be prai—" he began, then saw the red stars on their caps and flushed. "Welcome, Comrades." He offered the bread and poured salt from the paper into Sheremetiev's hand.

"If you have come to requisition our grain or more of our cattle, you are too late," he quavered. Then his anger overcame good sense, and he shouted at them, "One of your damned thieving bands came last week and took all they had left the month before. We have barely enough now for ourselves. We—"

"Calm yourself, Daddy," Sheremetiev snapped. "We aren't here to requisition food. We want information." He motioned, and Dolrov handed the old man a roll of sausage wrapped in cheesecloth and a bottle of vodka.

"Come, sit here with me." Sheremetiev indicated a bench beneath an oak tree. "Answer my questions truthfully, and no harm will come to you or the village." He nodded to Dolrov, who issued orders to start the search.

"What information?" the old man asked, watching the Chekists stride toward the huts. "Where are they going—?"

"To have a look around, Daddy. Don't worry. Now, a train has been abandoned at the old mine."

The old man nodded and twisted the cork from the bottle. He took a long pull and offered the bottle to Sheremetiev, who declined. He glanced around, then cut a piece of sausage from the roll and began to chew vigorously with his few remaining teeth. The piece was so large that tears started to his eyes and ran down his seamed cheeks.

"The people who drove it—did they come here?"

The old man tried to speak but had to content himself with a nod. He took another pull at the vodka bottle to make the meat easier to chew.

"Did anyone come to the village last autumn, any strangers?"

The old man swallowed noisily and cackled. "Plenty of them. White and Red alike. All running like chickens, scampering . . ."

Sheremetiev pressed the muzzle of his Mauser pistol against the old man's nose, forcing his head back against the tree. From one of the huts a woman screamed, and another ran out into the yard. A Chekist standing by the door knocked her down.

"I haven't time to waste on your jokes, Daddy. Answer my questions. Otherwise, we'll burn the village and shoot everyone in it, just to keep our hand in."

The old peasant tried to nod against the pistol, then settled for blinking his eyes rapidly.

"Very good. A man, a woman and a boy. The woman in her early twenties, the man a few years older, perhaps a foreigner. The boy would have been sickly. Did they come to your village last autumn?"

"Ah . . . ah . . . ah . . ." Sheremetiev eased the pressure, and the old man gasped for breath.

"Two . . . such as you describe. In August, just after the Feast of the Assumption. They bought horses and food. But a man and woman. No boy."

Sheremetiev studied the old man for a moment. But what would he have to gain by lying? Few in the Urals would give a damn for Nicholas Romanov and his family.

"How many horses and how much food? Were they armed? What were they wearing? Where did they go? Speak up, old man, my patience is wearing thin!"

The old peasant's eyes darted about the village as three of the

Chekists pushed people into a compact mass while others searched the huts and sheds.

"Three . . . three horses. All we could spare. Enough food for a few days, but then they had a rifle. The man wore a uniform." He shrugged. "It . . . it, I know little of such things . . . they rode farther into the mountains." He waved a hand vaguely.

"And they paid for everything?"

"With no-good Nicholas rubles, damn their souls." A cunning look had come into the old man's eyes, and Sheremetiev knew there was something more. He called to Dolrov and pointed to one of the women clutching a baby. Dolrov dragged her to the tree and pushed her onto her knees. The woman was terror-stricken and, when Dolrov aimed his revolver, buried her face in the baby's blanket. Her terror communicated itself to the child, who began to howl.

"How did they pay?" Sheremetiev asked again. The woman was shaking so badly that she wobbled, but the old man only stared at her. Sheremetiev knew that he would let her die before answering. He signaled to Dolrov, who lowered his pistol and raised the girl's chin.

Sheremetiev said in a sad voice, "The old fool was going to let you die, you and the baby, by refusing to answer my question."

The girl looked from one to the other for a moment, then with a screech, flung herself on the old peasant, screaming and scratching for his eyes. Dolrov laughed and dragged her off, holding her back easily with one hand. The baby encumbered her; but she still managed to kick the old man on the shin, and he roared with pain.

"Which is his hut?" Sheremetiev asked, and the girl pointed at the largest house in the village, not the one from which he had emerged, but a whitewashed hut with glass in the windows and two chimneys. Behind stood a long shed and a well-fenced cattle yard.

Sheremetiev smiled at the peasant and turned to Dolrov and pointed. "Burn that one."

A Chekist hurried into the hut. When he returned, he was splashing paraffin oil liberally about. The old man fell to his knees, crying and pleading for mercy.

"Perhaps now you are ready to answer truthfully?"

The peasant dug into his trousers and produced a filthy cloth bag. He fumbled inside, and his hand shook as he showed the gold coin to Sheremetiev.

A Mexican gold piece—fifty pesos, he thought in surprise. English sovereigns, gold rubles, Maria Theresa silver dollars and American double eagles were fairly common, but he had never seen a Mexican gold coin until Dzerzhinsky had shown him one. He slipped it into his pocket and waved to the Chekist, who struck a match and tossed it through the doorway.

As they rode away from the village, he could see the young mother kicking the old peasant. Another man, her husband presumably, was running toward them with a wooden beam. As they started onto the slope, Sheremetiev looked back to see the beam rising and falling methodically as the husband beat the old man, presumably to death. People's justice, he thought with a laugh. Dzerzhinsky was right. The Cheka was only an extension of the people's will.

With the discovery of the bodies on the steppe, the abandoned engine and the Mexican gold coin, Sheremetiev sensed he was moving in the right direction. He even suspected strongly that one of the fugitives was an American; the circumstantial evidence was strong. He had executed hundreds on less.

He worded his report to Dzerzhinsky carefully, laying out step by step exactly how he had reached his conclusions. Having protected himself against later accusations of adventurism, he had only to find the fugitives or, failing that, incontrovertible evidence of their deaths.

They returned to Ekaterinburg, where he arranged for Dolrov to be detached to his command along with five of the best woodsmen the local Cheka could produce. He also compiled a circular listing a description of the two gold coins so far recovered, the woman, Tatiana, and whatever vague descriptions of the man he had been able to put together. These he had sent to all local Chekas throughout the Ural region under Bolshevik control. They left Ekaterinburg a few days later.

As spring moved into summer, they traveled deeper into the Urals, trailing the couple from village to village, following the smallest lead in long, hard rides until his men were on the verge of revolt. Only then did he agree to return to Ekaterinburg for a few days' rest, after which they rode out again.

Spring rushed along the mountain slopes after the severe winter like a lover long denied. Overnight the aspens were laced with green, and streams full of melted snow tumbled and slashed through valleys, flooding great tracts of meadowland. Marmots whistled and chattered at the horses, and beavers hobbled about their dams, clucking at the winter's damage. Deer flicked from sun-dappled clearings at the slightest sound or scent, leggy fawns tied to their does by invisible cords.

After the darkness of winter the long days filled with crisp sunlight were a revelation to Tatiana. The periods of depression, the nightmares filled with retribution and images of punishment disappeared. She became gayer, more carefree than Evans had ever seen her, more so even than during the Indian summer days of the previous autumn.

Their lovemaking had lost some of the greedy passion of the autumn and all of the sense of duty that had crept in during the winter. She had also lost a good bit of her Victorian primness. But most of all,

Evans noticed the lack of depression, the gray, moody states that had at times driven him to distraction and that he had begun to consider self-indulgent.

Evans was certain now the search for them had ended. For all intents and purposes, they had disappeared into the winter, and there was no way they could be traced. He was not even worried about the incident in Nadezhdinski Zavod. Neither the militiamen nor the shop-keeper knew who he was, nor had they any way to identify him.

To spare the horses, they traveled in easy stages of ten miles a day. During the winter Evans had spent endless hours with the map, planning their route to Archangel, measuring, estimating and reestimating the number of days needed to reach the city before the blizzards began in October. The past winter months had taught him a healthy respect for Russian winters, as Peter Boyd had once predicted.

The Urals that summer of 1919 were a wonderland, and Tatiana recalled her wistful thought on the train from Tyumen to Ekaterin-burg—was it only a year before—when she had longed to ride forever and ever across the empty land. To Evans, the high mountain air was headier than any liquor, and he realized the immense freedom he had lost when he allowed himself to be drawn away from the Wyoming ranch and thrust into the pin-striped regimentation of the Diplomatic Service.

In mid-June they rode west out of the Ural foothills into the sloping, forested valley of the Pechora River, having traveled more than three hundred miles since mid-May. Archangel lay a further six hundred miles north and east. Plenty of time, he thought happily as they rode across sloping meadows festooned with summer flowers.

He had not expected the river's vast flooding. The area drained by the Pechora was heavily forested with a mixture of pine and birch. Land was low-lying, flat and swampy, and the river had flooded the surrounding area for several miles. Minor streams had become raging torrents; marshes had swelled to lakes, exploding with vast clouds of mosquitoes, midges and flies which, as much as the flooding, drove them back into the foothills.

Evans began to see in the deep folded valleys evidence of harsh glaciation, and the land was far less hospitable than it had been farther south. Trees felled by storms, snow and disease formed tangles of spiky branches fastened into place by the riotous undergrowth to weave an impenetrable virgin forest. But by the first week in July the last of the spring flooding had subsided and the Pechora resumed its normally placid course.

Just after noon one hot day Evans and Tatiana rode into an isolated settlement where a sternwheeler river boat was loading at the dock. They were subjected to the frankly curious stares of the inhabitants, a swarthy-skinned, dark-haired people similar to the Lapps Evans had seen in Sweden. A few spoke Russian with a curiously lilting accent. The huts were single-story affairs of log construction, raised on piles to avoid the spring floods. Rack after rack of drying fish stretched along the riverbanks, and the smoky peat drying fires caused Tatiana to cough and sniffle.

The captain of the river boat, a stocky White Russian named Kuznetsky, studied them with grave suspicion until he saw the gold coin in Evans's hand. They settled on two Mexican fifty-peso coins for the horses, Tatiana and himself. After Evans led the horses aboard and settled them in the makeshift stalls, he rigged a tent against the stern rail, and there they spent their first night together aboard the boat. Fortunately Kuznetsky and his crew were carousing in the village.

The river boat sailed at dawn, belching volumes of smoke from twin stacks as the paddle wheel churned the shallow river into mud and the steam whistle blasted to the cheers of the villagers. Kuznetsky sought midstream, and the pestiferous clouds of insects disappeared. Thereafter he slouched on a canvas stool atop the tiny deckhouse and, despite his raging hangover and generally debilitated body, steered with the ease of long experience. At midmorning, looking back along the placid river, Tatiana could see their wake slowly spreading to either shore in half curves as they avoided snags and emerging sand bars.

The enforced idleness of the voyage made Evans restless. By the end of the first day he was pacing the deck like a caged tiger. It became even worse that night, when they discovered that there was no way they could make love on the small steamer without every sound and movement's being heard below. Evans fell asleep long after Tatiana, still muttering curses.

The trip was not, however, without positive benefits. No one had recognized Tatiana or even given her a second look for any but frankly sexual reasons. Evans was certain they had passed into a section of the country where she would be relatively secure from accidental discovery.

Every other day they stopped along the bank to load wood from piles stacked by woodcutters, who received small packets of provisions in return. While Tatiana exercised the horses, Evans volunteered to help, and Kuznetsky was delighted to accommodate him. The first evening and every evening thereafter they enjoyed a lazy argument, Evans demanding that Kuznetsky reduce their fare, while the captain countered by demanding an increase for providing "diversion and exercise."

The trip upriver lasted two weeks. Each settlement along the way had to be visited, and trading completed, before they could move on. Consequently, it was mid-July by the time the church domes of Ust-Usa came into sight.

The town itself was disappointing, hardly more than a lumber camp. There was ample news of the civil war, however. White advances had ground to a standstill, and the Reds were going over to the offensive. Kolchak, with Orbelesky on his southern flank, had menaced the lower Volga region for a short time, but a swift series of reverses, caused as much by the old White curse—lack of cooperation—as to an improving Red Army, had sent him reeling back into Siberia again. Only Denikin had had a measure of success, forcing his way out of the Ukraine and capturing almost all of southern Russia as far as Tsaritsyn.

As Evans judged the situation, neither side had an upper hand at the moment. He was relieved to hear that the Allies still held Archangel and Murmansk, but with the war in France over, their excuse for remaining was gone. Accordingly, Evans was anxious to move on.

He and Tatiana had discussed the advisability of continuing north on the steamer as far as Naryan-Mar, where the Pechora debouched through a wide delta into the Barents Sea, in the hope of finding a ship willing to take them along the Arctic sea coast to Archangel. But Kuznetsky warned him that a strong, pro-Bolshevik soviet had been set up there during the winter.

After Ust-Usa, the terrain of North Russia changed as the river closed the Arctic Circle. Dense, tangled jungles of fir had given way to more open forests of birch and fir, and Evans had noticed the separation between trees growing day by day until finally, stretches of barren tundra began to appear. He had been following their progress closely on a new map purchased in Ust-Usa, and when the steamer reached the point where the river began its long curve to the north, he had Kuznetsky edge up to the bank.

"So you're going after all?"

Evans gripped his hand. "Thanks for all you've done for us."

Kuznetsky waved away his thanks. "If the truth be known, I've enjoyed your company. The river's a lonely life, and those two"—he snorted and hooked a thumb at his two crewmen, who grinned back—"haven't a complete brain to share between them." He hawked and spat and glanced around the sky.

"Well, good luck to you both. I can guess you might want to avoid the Reds. I've no wish to encounter them either, but my conscience is clear."

They watched the boat until a bend in the river hid all but the plume of smoke from sight. A last blast of the steam whistle evaporated into the vastness without a trace. Tatiana shivered at the sudden silence and mounted. Evans followed suit, and without a word they turned southwest.

It rained that night, a sudden downpour that caught them before the tent was fully rigged. The rain was warm, however, and the horses and gear already under cover. Tatiana laughed, breaking the thrall of silence that had held them all day. She stretched her arms to the sky, then threw off her shirt and trousers to stand naked and laughing while the rain washed away the day's sweat and tension. Suddenly elated, Evans joined her, and as the rain began to ease and before the insects swarmed, they made love for the first time in three weeks on the spongy moss floor of the birch forest.

The days that followed were a reprise of the spring and early summer in the Urals. Evans forgot his worries, secure in the knowledge that they had escaped all pursuit. They laughed and talked and—freed from the constraints of the cramped steamer—made love at all hours of the day and night. Less than four hundred miles of the journey to Archangel remained, and there were still three months of excellent traveling weather.

Infused with a peculiar fatalism, Commissar Nikolai Khristoforovich Sheremetiev cantered through the muddy streets of Nadezhdinski Zavod. To have to admit failure always galled him. To have to admit failure to Dzerzhinsky might well prove fatal.

The fugitives had disappeared without a trace. Everywhere the story was the same: A man and a woman had passed through the previous autumn, followed days to weeks later by White soldiers, asking much the same questions as he. After mid-October all such reports ceased, but the White soldiers had continued to search as late as December. He was therefore certain the fugitives had not been recaptured, rather had died of exposure or been murdered by bandits. But Dzerzhinsky would want proof, not speculation.

The horsemen dismounted in front of the former Ural Mine Works Association, now the headquarters of the local Cheka. Sheremetiev stamped inside, weary, dirty and saddlesore, followed by Lieutenant Dolrov. A rabbit-toothed clerk saw the Mauser pistol beneath his unbuttoned sheepskin jacket, and tea was produced immediately. A Captain Vernodsky hurried from his office, all smiles and cordiality.

"Ah, Commissar Sheremetiev. I've been wondering when you would come!"

Sheremetiev stared at him, nonplused. "Why would you expect me at all?"

"A telegram from Moscow, just two weeks ago." He sent the clerk running for a copy of the message. "I assumed you had the message already."

Sheremetiev put the teacup down and took the message form.

IMPORTANT YOU CONTACT VERNODSKY NADEZHDINSKY ZAVOD STOP HAS NEWS OF SUBJECTS YOUR INVESTIGATION STOP [SIGNED] DZERZHINSKY

220

He looked up to find Vernodsky waiting anxiously. "I sent telegrams to all our soviets throughout the Urals, Commissar. But apparently you—"

"Apparently. Now tell me what this is about?" He picked up the tea again and grimaced at the bitter taste of willow bark. At this moment he wanted a real cup of tea, Darjeeling, say, worse than he had ever wanted anything in his life.

"We arrested a local man in possession of an illegal gold coin. A Jew."

He stared at Vernodsky for a moment before the significance of his words penetrated his utter weariness. The circular, of course!

"What kind of coin?" He jumped to his feet. "Where is this man?"

"A Mexican coin as described in your circular!" Vernodsky grinned in triumph. "We are holding the Jew in an isolation cell. Come with me if you please."

Sheremetiev and Dolrov followed so closely that they trod on his heels.

Sheremetiev studied the old man standing calmly before him. His face was bruised, and a smudge of blood dirtied a corner of his mouth. Even so, his expression was serene. Vernodsky handed him a thick file, and Sheremetiev skimmed it, noting with surprise that the first entries had been made by the local Okhrana in 1895. He began to understand his apparent calm. The man was an old hand at this sort of thing.

Levi Shemuel was born in the Pale, that region of the Ukraine set aside as a vast concentrating area for Jews. Having shown special promise in the village school, he had attended a secondary school in Kiev and won a place at the Vladimir University in Kiev. In 1882 he became active in the Narodnaya Volya "The People's Will"—composed of idealistic students who wished to help the peasants by living among them and teaching agriculture, sanitation and political awareness. Shemuel had returned to his home district to work among the peasants during the repressive reign of Tsar Alexander III. For injudicious criticism of a district official, he was arrested, judged a danger to society and exiled to Siberia in 1884. He served his ten years in the gold mines in the central Urals at a time when the average survival rate was three years. After his release in 1895 he was exiled to Nadezhdinski Zavod.

Studying his face, Sheremetiev could see traces of the great strength he must have once possessed. Shemuel's frame was now shrunken and stooped, and his cheeks were hollow. Most of his teeth were missing, evidence of age as well as years of poor nutrition, but his shoulders were wide-spaced, even if his chest was pinched.

It would be useless to attempt to break this man, he thought. His internal strength would sustain him to death, never far away in one so old. He had seen his kind before. Only the torture of someone close would work. And Shemuel had never married and, of course, had no relatives in the district.

"Comrade Levi Shemuel," he addressed him respectfully, "I will not attempt to fool you. Instead, I appeal to you as a fellow revolutionary, as one of *us*."

"*Us?*" The old man laughed. "I am not one of you. You are butchers, not revolutionaries." His voice was that of an old man, the quaver a sign of age, not fear.

"We are revolutionaries." Sheremetiev smiled. "But as you yourself discovered, revolutions demand hash methods to stamp out old and malign influences."

The old man chuckled. "You are referring to my membership in the Narodnaya Volya. To tell the truth, it was all so long ago I don't remember much about it." He smiled again, then stared shrewdly at Sheremetiev.

"But I do remember this, young man. A true revolutionary is patient. He changes by teaching and persuasion, not by killing and torture. No, your method will only establish a new and more terrible tsar, one who is so morally sure of his position that no crime will seem too great. He will always justify himself in the name of the people."

He sounds, Sheremetiev thought, like Nicholas the last time I saw him, at Perm. I wonder what Shemuel would think of that.

"I will be frank with you. We are hunting a man. A man who bought food from you two months or more ago. A man who paid for the food with a gold coin, a Mexican coin."

"Ah him!" The old man nodded and waved at Vernodsky as if he were of no consequence. "If this fool had told me that, I could have helped you without delay."

"You will tell us?" Sheremetiev was astounded.

"Of course. Why not?" He gave an expressive lift of the shoulders.

"But you lied to the militiamen who saw him in your store. You told them you knew him from previous years?"

Shemuel chuckled. "A reflex action. A policeman is a policeman. Or perhaps I recognized a fugitive as I was myself once. Red authority, White authority, what's the difference? Your authority is no more derived from God than was the tsar's. I only took pity on a fellow-man."

"So you are willing to help us now," Vernodsky snarled, angered at being made to look bad in front of a superior to whom Felix Edmundovich Dzerzhinsky in Moscow sent personal messages. "Perhaps you wish to save your life. Well, I can tell you it's too—"

Sheremetiev silenced him with a gesture, and the old man smiled and told him the little he knew.

After they had left the cell, Vernodsky swore. "I'll enjoy putting a bullet in the Jew's head tonight!"

222

"You won't take into consideration his own revolutionary background?" Sheremetiev asked, more to bait him than from curiosity.

"Of course not!" Vernodsky protested. "What were the Narodniki anyway? Students with foolish ideas, the sons of rich men working to ease guilty consciences. Those who lived became Social Revolutionaries, curse them all. What is an SR but a White anyway?"

Sheremetiev walked alone to a small park and found a bench shaded from the hot sun. The city was shut out by trees and the lazy hum of insects. He lit a cigarette with hands that were trembling from chronic exhaustion, drew the smoke deep into his lungs and closed his eyes.

This life is killing me, he thought. For a moment the quiet fastness of the mountains absorbed him; the urge to abandon everything—search, party, the struggle—was deeply compelling, but then he realized that option was no longer his to consider. Dzerzhinsky had seen to that. He might escape death by leaving Russia, but he knew he could never do that.

His mind turned inevitably to his work. How far they had come, he thought, since those winter days of 1917–18, when he had refused ever again to put down a workers' revolt. How far? he demanded bitterly. Already the revolution had been betrayed. Old Shemuel was right. A new and more terrible tsar was being established. Lenin was carved from ice and so preoccupied with his theories of revolution that he did not care about the types of men filtering into positions of immense power, as long as they hewed to the party line, which he defined. Dzerzhinsky, for one. A ruthless, cold-blooded madman concerned only with what he termed purification while the party and government tottered.

In the east, Kolchak; in the south, Orbelesky and Denikin; in the Ukraine, the Germans giving overt aid to counterrevolutionaries; in Poland and Finland, local uprisings; and the Don, where he had nearly killed himself with work this past winter, was again in revolt. The Allies were at Vladivostok in the Far East, at Murmansk and Archangel in the north. And what was he doing? Acting as an extension of Dzerzhinsky, a hand to be used until no longer needed and then amputated mercilessly.

A factory whistle shrilled in the distance, and a train clicked across a trestle behind the park. A child's voice laughed over the creak of a swing. Sheremetiev opened his eyes suddenly. The Allies in the north . . . of course! Why hadn't he seen it before? They were fleeing north. Everything pointed to it. They had been in Nadezhdinski Zavod six weeks before. That meant they had wintered in the mountains after all. Where? Had they found someone to take them in, a small village he might have missed? No! He'd stake his life on that. Alone

223

then? The storekeeper had seen only a man—but he had bought for a wife. The boy must be dead. A hemophiliac in the mountains? Living rough?

He imagined a map of European Russia in his mind. It was a bold undertaking, he thought with admiration. Risky, very risky . . . no, he amended; if one knew how to survive in the mountains, how to live off the land, the route was far less risky than if they had struck east along the Trans-Siberian Railroad or south to Turkey or Persia. They would encounter few people, and those few would be fiercely independent, like old Shemuel, not inclined to betray one to the authorities. Siberia and northern Russia were filled with two hundred years of political exiles and the offspring of political exiles. Hatred of the central government was endemic.

Sheremetiev felt a renewed surge of energy. The outlines of a plan were already forming. Now that he had an objective again, the depression of the past few days began to slip away. He took a pencil stub from his pocket and began to compose a telegram to Dzerzhinsky on the back of an envelope, outlining his deductions and proposing that he continue the pursuit north from Nadezhdinski Zavod to pick up the trail again. Then he would go to Archangel, via Moscow, while Dolrov continued the pursuit. They would catch and smash them in a vise, by God!

Early in August, Evans and Tatiana passed through the settlement of Borlowskaya. Even here there was a village soviet, although as far as Evans could ascertain, it professed no strong allegiance to any government on neither side. As they had no papers, he did not bother to register, and no one insisted. They stopped just long enough to buy supplies and a handful of rifle cartridges. Ammunition for the Mosin-Nagant rifle had become Evans's greatest concern. The 7.62-millimeter cartridges had practically disappeared from the civilian market at the start of the war, and the demands of the civil war made them all but impossible to obtain this far north. In the end, anxious to leave the village, Evans traded the rifle and his four remaining cartridges for sixty more rounds of .42 caliber Berdan for the two old rifles.

At the end of the week Evans decided on an extra day's rest. He had the impression Tatiana was tired, and he was afraid the constant traveling might wear her down. They camped on the bank of a small stream, and in the morning he was up early to fix breakfast. As a treat, he carved a generous slice from the bacon slab and fried the last of the chicken eggs. When the food was ready, he crawled into the tent with the pan to wake Tatiana.

Even before she was entirely awake, Tatiana's nostils flared at the wonderful odor of real coffee. She threw back the blankets and sat up. And she vomited. Startled, Evans dropped the pan and caught her bare shoulders as she retched. When the spasm had passed, he helped her to the stream to wash. Twice more, she gagged and vomited until her stomach delivered only bitter fluid. She rinsed her mouth without swallowing and lay shivering in the early sun. Evans ran back to the tent for blankets.

By midmorning Tatiana appeared to have recovered. The reddish flush had gone from her skin, and her temperature was normal. She gave him a shaky smile and waded into the river to bathe. Watching her, Evans was suddenly aware of how little he knew about disease or first aid and how helpless he would be if anything happened to either of them. The magnitude of their undertaking struck home then, and the fact that they had crossed almost fifteen hundred miles of wilderness was suddenly very daunting.

Tatiana stepped out of the stream, brushing water drops from her skin. He noticed then that her abdomen was ever so gently rounded and that her breasts were fuller than usual. Bluish-tinged veins were visible around the nipples. Delight and shock struck him at once.

He got up slowly, not knowing whether to shout for joy or damn the bad luck. "Tatiana, are you pregnant?"

Tatiana poised, one foot on the bank, the other still in the water. He thought her magnificent at that moment. Her slimness proclaimed the steel he knew to be in her. Her chestnut hair had grown long again, and it fell in coiled ringlets around her shoulders. Naked, she was more beautiful than any woman he had ever seen.

"Pregnant!" she gasped.

"When did you have your last menstrual period?" He grinned.

Tatiana blushed furiously and protested in embarrassment.

Evans gathered her into his arms laughing. He tended to forget how sheltered she had been and, as a consequence, how little she really knew about sex and the related functions of the human body, other than what he had taught her.

"Tatiana," he told her in a soft voice, "it's nothing to be ashamed of . . . just a perfectly natural body function." Even so, he felt himself blushing as the strictures of his own childhood came into play. He drew her down beside him and kissed her wet hair where it clung to one perfectly shaped ear. Still embarrassed by the question, she drew her knees together and turned away.

"Listen to me," he prompted gently. "When was your last period? Anytime in the last month or so?"

She shook her head, still not looking at him.

"Why didn't you tell me?"

Tatiana half turned away, and he drew the blanket around her shoulders. She hugged it to her, grateful that it concealed her nakedness.

She had never been entirely comfortable naked with him in the daylight, even though she delighted in having him caress and kiss her body.

"Why?" he prompted.

"It never occurred to me . . . I thought it was because we were riding so much. It used to happen . . . before . . . when I was younger . . . if I rode too much. Lili told me that often happened . . ."

"Did Lili tell you anything else?"

Tatiana turned to him, and he was surprised to see tears glistening in her eyes. Overcome with tenderness, he bent to kiss her, but she fended him off.

"Tell me what?" she demanded.

"What else not having your monthly period might mean?"

She shook her head, staring at him with wide eyes. Again he nearly laughed at her ignorance until he remembered that the entire family had been cut off from the mainstream of normal human relationships and the daughters had been surrounded with a myriad of strictures and taboos that were to the advantage of court officials and government ministers to maintain. How else could the family have been so totally out of touch with what was happening in Russia, so completely unaware of the rumors and gossip, the activities and outrages committed by Rasputin and his coterie? And the Tsarina Alexandra had, with her Bible and long hours at prayer and her innately conservative—no, reactionary—outlook, probably embodied the most repressive aspects of Victorian virtue. No wonder her daughter was so naïve. Even after more than twenty years of marriage and five children, how much had Alexandra really known about sex? Fielding's passage describing the conception of Tom Jones occurred to him, and he had to turn away to hide a smile.

At first Evans had watched for signs of pregnancy in Tatiana as he always had in every woman with whom he had had sexual intercourse. After a while he assumed that for whatever reason she was not going to become pregnant and ceased to think about it. There was little they could have done in any event other than to refrain, something neither had been inclined to do. The curious thing, he supposed, was that not once during the entire year had either broached the matter of children—he because he did not want any, at least now; Tatiana, because she, as he now suspected, did not necessarily equate sex with conception and pregnancy.

Even knowing her background, he found it difficult to believe that in the second decade of the twentieth century a woman her age could remain unaware of the connection between sex and conception. But then he recalled the wild rumors and misconceptions he had believed as late as his first year at Harvard, when a combination of biology classes and an incredibly educational weekend in New York had taught him about the true state of affairs. A good many young women—and men as well—in the United States had never had a chance at that kind of education.

He tipped her chin up, kissed her gently and explained.

Tatiana tried to absorb what Evans was telling her even while a fresh bout of nausea roiled her stomach. All the smutty jokes from their imprisonment in Ekaterinburg had long ago made sense to her as far as sex was concerned, but why, she wondered, did the jokes never contain any reference to the end result, human birth?

She and Olga had often giggled over sex, had even speculated that babies were produced in some way by the process. Dear Lili had attempted more than once to teach them about sex, but Tatiana saw now that in her way Lili had been just as inhibited as her mother. Evans had taught her that sex was far from shameful, but she vaguely suspected that those lessons were constructed on the sands of an inept moralism impressed on her by the church, her mother, the functionaries of the court and even a conspiracy among the servants who would have thought it improper for a daughter of the tsar to know what every serving girl knew by the time she reached puberty.

"That's why I need to know when you had your last menstrual period."

Tatiana drew her fingers through the fine sand of the riverbank. The sun had warmed her, and the shivering had stopped. A fly buzzed lazily, and a light breeze rustled the birches. The silence was sudden and intense. Tatiana turned to see Evans watching her, his expression expectant, and impulsively she thrust the blanket away and threw her arms about him.

Evans felt her arms lock, her body strain against his. He brushed her ear with his lips and murmured for the first time, "I love you, Tatiana Nikolaevna."

The tension melted from her, leaving in its place a feeling of satisfaction and warmth such as she had never before experienced. She closed her eyes to the sunlit morning. She had been unaware until now of how deeply she longed to hear those words, even if deep in his heart he was still in love with her sister. No longer was she completely isolated in a hostile world whose only objective was her death.

Evans in turn was amazed at himself. This was not the first time he ever told a woman he loved her, but it was the first time he had ever meant it. And that surprised him more than it did Tatiana.

After a while she murmured, "It's been three months," and then smiled at the fact that she no longer felt embarrassed. The thought that she would bring *their* child into the world filled her with such happiness that she fairly glowed.

That happiness abated quickly. Tatiana was sick again the following morning. They were able to start only at midday, and then, after an hour in the saddle, she began to vomit. They dismounted, and this seemed to help somewhat; but her reserves were quickly dissipated. By midafternoon she was exhausted, and they had gone only four miles. The next day Evans helped her walk, but even so, by noon she was begging to ride. She clung bravely to the saddle until Evans again called a halt at midafternoon, and she lay in the tent, shivering and retching weakly. Evans refused to go on until she recovered.

By the third day Tatiana had begun to regain some of her strength, but even so, Evans could see that deep hollows had formed beneath her eyes, that she had lost weight and moved deliberately, as if every joint pained. She could keep down nothing but sips of water. Nausea was a constant affliction, and even walking a few steps induced retching. And they still had nearly three hundred miles to travel. Evans knew that this close to the Arctic Circle snow could begin as early as mid-October. Yet to continue was not only to chance a miscarriage but to endanger Tatiana's life as well. As the mild summer days passed, he grew more and more desperate.

On the sixth day of their enforced halt he cut two straight trees, trimmed the trunks into poles, then wove willow branches into a lattice connecting them. He harnessed the poles to a horse with lengths of rope. He wrapped Tatiana in a blanket and carried her to the travois, kissed her forehead and strapped her in.

They made slow progress during the following days, and Evans's anxiety increased daily. Tatiana became withdrawn, and weight fell away from her until she was hardly more than a skeleton. Her skin was stretched so tightly across her face as to seem grotesque. She was able to keep down only a small portion of weak broth, and every two or three hours he built a small fire and warmed another few spoonfuls for her. In between, he could not always tell whether she was asleep or unconscious.

Something was wrong with the pregnancy, he knew. The constant movement was killing Tatiana, yet if they stayed in the forest, they both would die before the baby was due. There wasn't enough time to build a real shelter, cut firewood and hunt and forage for enough food to last them through the winter. He knew nothing about delivering babies, and the very idea that he would have to assist her terrified him. They needed help, a doctor, a midwife.

The immensely tall trees rearing about them like the arches of a magnificent cathedral, the land, which in its very emptiness had protected them for so long, had now become their enemy. It was as if the Russian land itself were determined to see that she should not escape retribution for the crimes, real or imagined, of her parents and the system they represented but certainly never controlled.

228

XI

AUGUST 1919–APRIL 1920, THE TAIGA

The village was a collection of dilapidated wooden huts leaning against the forest. Fields had been chopped out of the trees, and a few hunched figures could be seen in the distance, cutting and spreading hay to dry. There were nine huts, built in the Russian manner and spaced haphazardly along a muddy track that widened in front of the church to form a village common. The ubiquitous church stood at the end of the road, a wooden hut slightly larger than the rest, with an onion-shaped dome that had once been painted blue, now turned as gray as the lowering sky.

It was mid-August, and already at night the temperature was edging toward the freezing point. During the day the sun continued as warm as ever but was often hidden behind gray overcast that filled the sky from horizon to horizon. The wind was from the northwest, sweeping out of the Arctic across the Barents Sea.

Tatiana muttered something, and he urged the horses forward, glancing anxiously at her pain-twisted expression. As they crossed the shallow ford and clopped along the mud track that wound between the huts toward the church, people began to appear. Elderly women, or women so worn by the harsh life of the forest that they seemed elderly, stared after them without expression. An old man shuffled from a cabin to the road, shouting unintelligibly and waving his arms. Evans's horse shied, and he unslung his rifle. The old man scurried back inside, and Evans heard a woman screaming at his foolishness.

A priest in a dirty cassock waited for them on the log steps of the church. He squinted suspiciously and combed fingers through his untrimmed beard. Evans laid the rifle across the saddle and eyed him carefully.

"My wife is very sick. She needs care and rest. I can pay, and I can work."

The priest studied him for a moment, then hobbled down to look at Tatiana. Evans watched his face for the least sign of recognition, but he only grunted.

"There is an empty hut at the end of the village." His voice was harsh. "I will send a woman to help. How much can you pay?"

Evans dug a gold coin from his pocket and held it up. The reddish gold gleamed softly in the gray light, and the priest sucked his breath sharply and held out a hand.

Evans shook his head and pocketed the coin. "When she has recovered."

They had come across the village purely by accident, following what he had taken to be a game trail. He doubted if there were another within thirty miles. Tatiana had sunk into a deep apathy and become so listless that Evans had to feed her like a child, then hold her against the deep bouts of nausea that invariably followed.

Their hut was a tumble-down log shack at the end of the village. The roof was covered with a mixture of sod and poles and in far worse condition than the Ural cabin but it provided shelter. Evans knew he could make it habitable, but the thought of having to spend another winter bound to a tiny cabin was almost more than he could bear. By spring, if the trend in Bolshevik victories he had foreseen earlier in the summer continued, the Allies might well have abandoned Archangel, trapping them in a hostile country.

That evening an old woman entered without knocking while Evans was preparing broth for Tatiana. The fireplace flue was clogged with leaves and pine needles, and he had built the fire under the cabin's only window after knocking the rotted shutter open.

The old woman filled the musty cabin with an odor of dirt and decay. Her clothing was a filthy collection of rags, and her feet were bare and black with dirt. She glared at Evans and went straight to Tatiana, who had fallen into a stuporous sleep, and pulled back the blankets. When Evans objected, she waved him away and thereafter ignored him.

With a tenderness he found a stark contrast with her manner, the old hag undressed Tatiana. Then, laying her ear against Tatiana's abdomen, she pushed and prodded and felt while Tatiana gasped and writhed against her insistent fingers. When she was satisfied, the old woman spread her thighs and ran her filthy fingers over hips and probed into her vagina, nodding and emitting a chuckling sound of satisfaction.

The old woman next pushed Evans away from the fire, sniffed the broth and dumped it out, still ignoring his protests. She crumpled a handful of leaves into the pan, poured it half full of fresh water and set it to boil. As she waited, she rocked back and forth, muttering to herself.

When the mixture boiled, she added water to cool it, then carried the pan to Tatiana, soaked a corner of the blanket and placed it between Tatiana's lips. At intervals she remoistened the blanket until the infusion was gone. Tatiana's restlessness seemed gradually to leave her, and she lapsed into a deep sleep. The old woman left the cabin then without a backward glance. Evans sat beside the makeshift bunk, holding Tatiana's hand until he finally fell asleep himself.

In the morning Tatiana seemed more alert. The morning nausea was there, but she did not vomit. The old woman appeared again, prepared another pan of the infusion and helped her drink. At first Tatiana was apprehensive, afraid of the filthy woman who refused to speak, but Evans soothed her and persuaded her to drink the bitter liquid. Afterward she fell asleep, and since the old woman did not leave, he went out to see to the horses.

He had hobbled all four the day before and turned them to graze in the narrow meadowland that lay between the cabin and the stream. No one had disturbed them, and there was plenty of grass and shade. When he returned to the cabin, Tatiana was still asleep and the old woman crouched by the fire, lost in some world of her own. Evans took the ax and set about cutting new poles for the roof, the most urgent repair required if he was to make the cabin livable.

By evening he had dragged away the debris inside, cleared the flue and replaced the roof poles, lashing each with willow fronds. The old woman remained all day, and when Evans knelt beside Tatiana that evening, she was alert, if very pale.

"How are you feeling?"

Tatiana forced a smile. "Better. That horrible drink . . . seems to help. The nausea isn't as bad. Perhaps tomorrow I can help you. . . ."

"The devil," he growled. "You'll lie right here until the baby's born if necessary."

Tatiana closed her eyes and sighed.

A week passed before they had an additional visitor. Evans was fencing a corral for the horses when the priest appeared on the mud path. Evans straightened, grunting at the pain in his back, and drew on his shirt as he walked to meet him.

"You are not Russian," said the priest, who introduced himself as Father Vissarian. Surprised, Evans shook his head. The priest muttered something and pushed past him into the cabin. Tatiana was dozing, but the flapping of his broken boots against the dirt floor woke her. The priest leaned over the bunk Evans had built and regarded her with near-sighted eyes as Tatiana shrank back, plainly frightened of his stark, crowlike appearance. Satisfied, the priest shot a question at the old crone, who nodded.

The priest straightened and motioned Evans to follow him outside. "You are not to interfere. The old woman will do what is necessary. I am the head of this village, and I am the priest. My word is law. Obey and you may stay, for payment. We are a communal folk, and there is millet to be gotten in and hay to be stored. You will be apportioned your share in relation to the work you do. Is this understood?"

Evans nodded, and the priest held out his hand for the gold coin.

Summer faded imperceptibly into autumn. Tatiana improved slowly. She managed to keep the cabin livable and to do some of the cooking. The old woman watched as silently as ever from her corner by the fire, her only duty being to prepare the horrible infusion which Tatiana dreaded but which had probably saved her life, and certainly the child's. Evans was in the fields before dawn or repairing the hut against the coming winter until darkness drove him inside. Often he was too exhausted to do more than eat and fall into his blankets.

The dark forest, the oppressive cabin and her continuing weakness weighed on Tatiana's mind. All the old religious strictures began to haunt her again as she lay for hours, staring at the log walls, ever aware of the presence of the mad crone watching her with the avidity of a kestrel. For some reason the image of Rasputin hovered on the edges of her mind, finger raised in the familiar posture of admonition. Evans's awkward confirmation of the cartoons and jokes she had heard in Ekaterinburg perplexed her. How could such a holy man have preached God and salvation through prayer and exemplary life as he had done, yet wallowed in a morass of sin? It was impossible, she told herself.

As the weather worsened and the cabin grew dark, the answer came to her one day, an answer so simple she did not know why she hadn't seen it before. They were *wrong*. The guards were wrong, the people of Russia were wrong and Bill was wrong. And why not? Hadn't her family been victimized by false information? Hadn't her father been portrayed as a blood-sucking leech and her mother as a traitor? Evil elements in Russia, jealous of their position and power, had struggled for years to persuade the people with horrible lies to destroy her family. The civil war was proof of that. It and the revolution were brought about by the antichrists, the Bolsheviks, even as Rasputin had foretold. What better way to turn the Russian mind from the teachings of Christ, to bring about the anarchy and destruction they demanded, than to bear false witness against Gregory Rasputin, the anointed one of God?

Winter came in mid-October, as Evans had expected, and was far worse than anything they had experienced in the Urals. Blizzards howled from the northwest for days on end, and the temperature rarely rose above zero unless it was snowing. But in mid-November the weather underwent one of those startling changes so common in the Subarctic. The storms ceased, and the sun shone for a few hours at midday, lighting the forest and turning it to a wonderland. The depression that haunted Tatiana evaporated with the sun. The brief hours of light brought about profound changes in her: The gaunt hollows in her cheeks disappeared, and she began to gain weight.

Tatiana no longer felt the oppression of the semidarkness and the dank cabin. The specter of Rasputin and her mortal sins no longer filled her with nameless terrors. An urge to keep her fingers occupied replaced her former listlessness, and she sat for hours spinning thread on a make-shift bobbin and wheel Evans had built for her. Afterward she knitted clothing for the unborn infant.

The village shunned them. The only villager Tatiana ever saw was the old crone, while Evans could add the priest and one or two other village men with whom he worked, but always in silence. No one ever spoke to him.

At first Evans was puzzled by Father Vissarian. Fat and slovenly, he ruled the village with an iron hand, and the only service he held was a Sunday mass. In the beginning Evans thought him at best barely literate, yet one or two remarks he made as the weeks passed, caused Evans to wonder if the priest was not, in fact, better educated than he.

The villagers were a strange lot, even for peasants so completely isolated. As far as Evans could tell, there was little social intercourse among them. They cooperated only grudgingly on common tasks and only under the priest's stern eye. They seemed all of a kind: the men with long faces, receding chins and wispy beards, gaunt almost to the point of emaciation; the women heavyset, stocky and uniformly silent. He was impressed by the fact that there were few young women in the village. Female children seemed to grow immediately into middle age. The struggle to survive in the harsh forest with its poor soil and killing winters sapped their very existence. In all the long months of autumn and early winter he never saw another outsider, not even from one of the neighboring villages he knew to be scattered through the forest.

At the beginning of December, when the blizzards had become infrequent and the snow had turned to névé, permitting travel without the necessity of awkward snowshoes, Evans laid out both rifles and ammunition on the bunk one morning. Tatiana lowered herself awkwardly onto the stool by the fireplace and watched. He had completed all the necessary work on the cabin, and piles of wood cut during October and November were stacked against the windward side as further insulation. He had even split sufficient logs to lay a rough floor, and the dampness had disappeared at once.

He cleaned both rifles and the hundred rounds of ammunition.

He took the Colt automatic pistol from its oiled cloths and checked it over, remembering the duck hunting and the fine weather the first time he had seen it.

"Why are you smiling?" Tatiana asked.

Evans rewrapped the pistol and sat down beside her. "I was remembering the first time, no, the second time I saw you."

"The second time? When? At the palace?"

He shook his head. "No. The second time was aboard the train."

Tatiana wrinkled her nose in puzzlement. "If that was the second time, when was the first?"

Evans squeezed her hand. "On my first day in Russia. I had just arrived at the Finland Station, and you and your sister were being escorted to your train by Countess Hendrikova, I believe, and a squad of Cossacks."

"When was that?" Tatiana demanded in surprise.

"September fourteenth, 1916. I'll never forget that date."

"September fourteenth. Was I with Olga? Perhaps that was a day we were in the city for our weekly Red Cross nursing duty."

Her expression took on a faraway look, and a smile played about the edges of her mouth. Evans decided not to mention that his strongest memory of that day was the Cossack striking the young soldier. He kissed her fingers gently, repressing a deep longing. "I didn't know who you were then, but I remember thinking that if all Russian girls were as pretty as you two, I was going to like Russia very much."

"I remember you now!" Tatiana turned to him, excitement gleaming in her face. "Olga saw you looking at us. You were wearing a straw boater. We thought you looked very funny, very foppish!"

The silence of the forest, the feeling of being alone were a tonic to Evans. For the first hour he strode through trees heavy with snow, not caring where he went or how much noise he made. It was being alone that counted. Even the intense cold did not deter him, nor was he disgruntled when he returned empty-handed as the midday twilight faded. Every day that week he went out, studying, memorizing, cataloguing until he knew the snow-covered forest intimately for at least five miles in any direction. At the end of the first week he shot a small reindeer.

From then on he hunted at least twice a week, husbanding his cartridges and spending long hours on stands within sight of the game trails. Snares and Hudson's Bay deadfalls produced rabbits and not a few minks, once even an ermine. Trotlines dropped through holes cut in the ice covering the stream supplied fish. At first he butchered the animals he shot and stored the surplus in a natural refrigerator constructed by raising an animalproof shed on the back of the hut, but when the surplus grew too great, he began to deliver the meat to the church, leaving it to the priest to make the distribution.

234

In this way he came to know one of the younger men, a tall, silent boy, hardly eighteen, with a harelip. Evans had first noticed him during the autumn harvest, when the boy worked by himself, well away from the others. One day in mid-December, as Evans started into the forest, he saw the boy watching from the door of the hut where he lived with his mother. The following day the boy followed him at a distance, moving even more silently than Evans and obviously at home in the woods. Once the boy turned aside and disappeared only to return with a rabbit tied to his belt. Evans decided that the boy had set traps of his own.

After a week of this Evans waited just inside the trees for the boy to appear. When he did, Evans silently handed him the spare rifle. The boy took it carefully in his bare hands and ran his fingers over the smooth brown metal of the barrel. Evans showed him how to load and how to cock the firing bolt. The boy nodded and pantomimed inserting a cartridge to show that he understood, then raised the rifle to his shoulder, steadied it with one hand grasping the forearm and gently squeezed the trigger.

Evans asked his name.

The boy reddened and ducked his head. After a moment he grunted once and shook his head. Evans clapped him on the shoulder to show he understood, and without another word they set out. He later learned the boy was called Sasha when he overheard his mother speak to him one day.

Sasha proved to be an excellent hunter and tracker. He showed Evans a myriad of game trails he would never have seen otherwise. Often a bent branch or the scraped bark on a twig protruding through the snow was the only sign marking the passage of a small animal.

As the child grew within her and her health improved, Tatiana came to see her rejection of God after the murders of her family as nothing more than a hysterical outburst in a time of great emotional stress. She longed to confess her sins and receive absolution and holy communion, and in time she overcame her fear of the crowlike priest. The child was due around New Year's, and on Christmas Eve she told Evans she wished to attend Christmas Day mass. He agreed absently.

Evans was awakened that night by Tatiana's restlessness. Her skin was hot, and she was perspiring freely. The fire had died to a bed of ashes, and the dull red glow gave off almost no light. Shivering violently in the below-freezing cabin, he piled on more wood. As the fire produced more light, he saw that her eyes were bright with pain.

"Tania?"

She tried to smile, but another spasm twisted her face into a grimace of pain.

By Christmas morning the pains were regular and agonizingly powerful. Tatiana writhed on the bunk, tangling the blankets. He boiled water for tea, but she could drink no more than a sip or two before a fresh spasm gripped her.

When the pains were coming at short intervals, he ran to the church. The single bell had begun to toll, and the priest was putting on his vestments as Evans burst in and babbled his story. The priest shouted, and the old woman shuffled past without a sign of recognition. The priest stared at him for a moment, then made the sign of the cross. Startled, Evans turned and ran back to the cabin.

When he entered, the old woman had already bared Tatiana's swollen abdomen and was watching the progress of a painful contraction. When the spasm subsided, she pointed to the small pile of logs beside the fireplace. Evans nodded and went out to cut more.

He filled the woodbox, but when he started to remove his jacket, the old woman pointed again at the door. He hesitated and glanced at Tatiana twisting on the blankets. The old woman's eyes blazed, and she hurled a stick of wood at him. He left quickly.

The day dragged on. The villagers filed from the church after the Christmas service, and Evans watched from the far end of the path, where he had taken up a stand in the shelter of a grove of pines near the hut. The sky was overcast, and the temperature had risen slightly. The air seemed mild after the intense cold of the past weeks, and he wondered if this was the beginning of a thaw. Toward noon he began to hear Tatiana's agonized cries, low moans at first, then screams that drove him wild. Once he tried to reenter the cabin but found the door barred.

During the long hours of waiting Evans had time to think about Tatiana and about their relationship. She had come to mean more to him than anything in life. The usual words *love* and *devotion* were entirely inadequate to express what he felt. If anything happened to her . . . He swore at himself for such thoughts, but they haunted him all the long day.

By midafternoon the blue darkness was complete and a bitter wind had sprung from the north. Not once during the day had any of the villagers expressed the least interest in Tatiana's labor, even though her cries were audible throughout the settlement. The cold drove him to pace the icy path to keep warm, and the wind swirled birch smoke among the trees, producing an acrid, not unpleasant scent that spoke of warmth and hot food. A light glowing in the single window of the church drew him like a lodestone. Frozen and half-famished, he pushed the door open.

The interior was sweltering and close with the smell of unwashed bodies. Father Vissarian nodded and pointed to a rickety chair beside the fire.

Evans removed his hat and jacket and chafed his hands together. The priest pushed a plate full of stewed meat toward him and indicated

236

a cup attached to a water bottle. He made no effort to speak, and Evans was too exhausted and far too worried about Tatiana to care. He ate the stew slowly, washing it down with cups of water.

The room was cold, and the fire had died to a sullen glow. "Wake up, I tell you!" The priest shook him roughly. "The child has been delivered. Go to your wife."

At first he saw only Tatiana's pale face, surrounded by damp hair. A bundle lay at her breast. The overheated cabin smelled of sweat, fear and blood. Evans approached the bed almost in shock. Tatiana's face was so pale, her lips almost blue. But her eyelids flickered when he whispered her name, and her lips responded when he touched them with his own. As carefully as if he were handling a bomb, he picked up the bundle and folded back a corner of the cloth. A wrinkled, very red forehead and two tightly closed eyes appeared. He smiled and unwrapped the infant to see that it was a girl. He laid the baby again in Tatiana's arm and bent close to her ear.

"A daughter," he whispered, and laughed with sheer joy.

Tatiana's lip curved in a tired smile, and her breathing became even and steady. Evans sat with her for the rest of the night, alternately dozing and watching, perplexed, proud, fearful and astounded.

Tatiana's recovery was rapid. By the following day she could sit up and smile at the child at it began to nurse at her breast. Evans drank in the sight with an avidity that surprised him. They named her Alexandra after Tatiana's mother and she seemed to have inherited her namesake's domineering personality.

Father Vissarian called at the hut late that evening. He stomped in, brushing snow from his rusty black garments in a miniature blizzard, and appropriated the only chair. He regarded Tatiana long and quizzically, then turned his attention to the baby sleeping in the handmade cradle.

"Daughter?"

Evans nodded.

"We will christen her on the Sabbath."

The priest's voice was high and rather unpleasant, Tatiana thought, and he made her uncomfortable with his close scrutiny. She wished he would go. Muffled as he was in a black greatcoat and scarf, he reminded her of the scarecrow that had frightened her long ago at their estate in Finland. Her father had gathered her into his arms to soothe her, but she had dreamed of that broken-limbed figure, black against the bright sun, for years. If only they dared tell him they were not married, Tatiana thought. She could confess her sins and he could marry them and . . . She sighed inwardly. They had discussed it often enough, but both were afraid that the old priest would throw them out of the village without hesitation. It had happened before, Tatiana knew, in these isolated districts, and they could not chance Alexandra's life that way.

Alexandra brought a joy into her life that was beyond anything Tatiana had ever known. The horror-ridden dreams began to recede, and the formless presence within the trees that had haunted her all through the autumn was gone. Her mind was filled with the child and with memories of her family: the times they had spent together at Tsarskoye Selo or at Livadiya in the Crimea, her favorite place in all the world; the summer house in Finland; Baltic cruises aboard the royal yacht *Standart*. And even a lingering fear of punishment for fornication could not spoil her happiness, until one night in early March, when she woke suddenly to the howl of wind and snow. Weird shadows danced about the cabin walls as the wind drew the fire in the chimney's draft.

She was gasping for breath, and the lingering pain of iron fingers about her throat was real enough that her trachea convulsed and she retched and gasped for breath. Tatiana huddled in terror against the log wall until the choking spasm passed.

She had dreamed that the commissar Sheremetiev had come for her. The dream was so vivid that for hours afterward she was almost convinced of its reality. He had entered the cell where she was being held, a Cossack's knout in one hand. Without a word he had set about whipping the child. He beat the blanket-wrapped bundle with grunts of exertion until the child's screaming stopped and the blanket was stained red with blood. But the real horror lay in the fact that she could have halted him with one word, could have prevented the death of the child, but had not. And Sheremetiev leered at her, knowing. She had sinned, and the child, the fruit of that sin, was also the means of atonement. As he moved toward her, his face altered subtly, and he became Rasputin. His hand reached out and tore away her shift, exposing her naked body. He raped her without a word, cruelly, as if exacting revenge.

The dream stayed with her into the daylight, and toward midmorning she forced herself to the window. The storm-lashed birches were bare of leaves. Their silvery trunks appeared dirty and worn, and the snow-covered forest wavered before her eyes. For days Tatiana could not rid herself of the images in that dream. She was being punished for her sins, for denying God. In His infinite goodness He had allowed her the opportunity to live; in reply she had spurned Him, denied Him and committed mortal sin.

A thaw began in April, seeming to presage an early end to the winter. Water dripped incessantly and formed massive icicles. A warm sun beamed day after day from a cloudless sky, and in the meadow the snow retreated to slushy piles and the brown grass, freed of its weight, began to stir and green.

One morning Evans left at dawn to hunt, and in midafternoon Tatiana bathed Alexandra. The child, half-submerged in the warm water, wriggled like a fish, and she tickled her tiny stomach and laughed for the first time in days.

The door slammed against the wall, and soldiers crowded into the hut. Alexandra screamed with fright at the blast of chill air. A rifle butt struck Tatiana between the shoulders; a laughing soldier picked Alexandra out of the basin and crushed her tiny head against the wall. She scrambled across the floor, still not understanding. One man grabbed her by the feet and dragged her back, while another lifted her by the shoulders, threw her onto the bunk and tore her dress away.

The dream was fulfilled as the soldiers raped her in turn, hurting her badly, kneading and punching her breasts, driving hard into her until she screamed with pain. There was an impression of boots, of horses, more men. Icy water and patches of snow. She screamed for Alexandra, saw the priest twisting on the ground nearby. Her head was yanked back painfully, and she saw a knife glitter as it swept toward her throat.

Midafternoon shadows crept across the snow, and the air had turned crisp. Sasha had spotted a reindeer browsing in a forest clearing and taken it with a single shot through the heart. He and Evans had butchered the animal, wrapped the meat in its skin and started back, each carrying a hindquarter. Evans, preoccupied with the fact that they had only twelve cartridges left, did not see the bootprint pressed in the muddy path.

The high-pitched crack of a rifle startled them both into immobility; then, without conscious thought, they ran soundlessly through the trees, broke out of the forest and ducked between two huts to a log pile from which they could see one end of the village. Before Evans's hut, four horses stamped and snorted. A man wearing a heavy sheepskin coat and a fur cap with the earflaps tied up prodded a shapeless bundle writhing at his feet. Nothing else in all the village moved. When the man raised his head, Evans saw the red star on his cap, and a stark terror raced through him.

He heard a scream, and before he could react, three men burst from the hut, dragging Tatiana among them. She was half-naked, and her hands had been tied behind her back. They dropped her in the mud, and one soldier knelt beside her and drew a long curved knife from his belt. He yanked Tatiana's head back by the hair to expose her throat, and Evans shot him as he raised the knife.

The unexpected attack startled the Chekists. Sasha shot a second man even as Evans flipped the breech open and jammed in a new cartridge. He slammed it shut, cocked the bolt, aimed and fired in one smooth motion, killing a third man. Sasha's second shot missed the man with the star on his cap as he hurtled into the trees.

Evans ran to Tatiana, reloading as he went. A bullet screamed past his ear, and Sasha fired again. Tatiana writhed as another shot splashed mud across her face. Evans vaulted her body and ran into the trees, almost colliding with the officer. Evans jinked left and banged the barrel of the old Berdan rifle against the Mauser's receiver just as the man fired. The bullet tore his hat away. The Chekist's eyes went wide with terror as Evans pivoted, using the long barrel for leverage, and slammed the metal butt plate into his face. He dropped onto the Chekist's chest with both knees, jammed the rifle barrel across his throat and pressed down with all his strength. The Chekist struggled, clawing at his face and eyes and the man's heels drummed the earth as his face turned black. Spittle drooled from his mouth, and his blows became feeble and finally stopped. When he was absolutely still, Evans dragged himself back to where Tatiana lay.

She was on her knees when Evans reached her. He cut the bloody cord that bound her hands, and she pushed past him and ran into the cabin. He staggered after her and for an endless moment could not understand why she was kneeling beside the wall. Then he saw that she was holding their daughter. The child's skull had a curiously lop-sided appearance. As if in a dream, he gently loosened Tatiana's hands and took the tiny body and laid it in the cradle. He helped her to the bed and, dazed, wandered out to where the first Chekist he had shot lay face down in the mud. Sasha crouched nearby, watching, his eyes flat and empty.

Evans kicked the man over on his back, ignoring his screams.

"Why?" he demanded. "A child and a woman, you bastard!"

The man's face twisted again, but this time in contempt. "Blood-sucker," he whispered. "She's the daughter . . . of . . . the tsar."

Sasha sucked in his breath and turned to Evans.

"Jesus!" Evans breathed. How had they found them? What kind of people hated like that? Sasha got to his feet and peered at the cabin, then glanced at Evans and ran. Harelip or not, the story would be all over the village in minutes.

The Chekist groaned as a new spasm of pain tore at him. "Do . . . it, for the sake of Christ. Kill . . . me . . . the pain . . ."

Hating him as he had never hated anyone or anything in his life, Evans kicked him again. "How did you find us?"

The Chekist cursed. "We've followed you . . . all . . . across . . ."

"How many more of you are there?"

The man tried to laugh, but a spasm of pain caused him to scream instead.

"How many more?" Evans demanded, and kicked him again.

240

"None . . . one died. We . . . kill me, for Christ's sweet love. The pain is . . ."

Evans spit at him and turned away. Only then did he see the priest lying beside the path. Father Vissarian's face was gray and his breathing uneven. A tumbling Mauser bullet had torn a gaping wound in his stomach, and his gnarled fingers clutched and kneaded the blood-soaked cloth around the wound.

"I . . . tried . . ." he whispered. The old woman pushed him aside and knelt beside the priest. She made the sign of the cross, and gently Evans picked the old man up and carried him to the church.

Tatiana lay staring at the ceiling, eyes unfocused. The feel of her daughter's lifeless body and lolling head would be with her for the rest of her life.

The Chekists had raped her, Evans saw. He warmed water over the fire and sponged away the dirt and blood, then stripped off the torn dress and drew a blanket over her. He built up the fire and sank down on the stool and cried.

Tatiana awoke in the early evening. She saw Evans's swollen face and tried to smile. He took her hand and pressed it to his lips.

"They killed Alexandra," she said distinctly. The words seemed to come from a great distance, and she felt as if she were drawing slowly, steadily away. "Why?"

Evans felt tears running down his cheeks again and could only shake his head.

"They are antichrists," Tatiana said with conviction, then nodded as if confirming a long-held suspicion. After a while she withdrew her hand from his and closed her eyes. Soon, her breathing deepened and she was asleep.

Evans, alert to Tatiana's every movement, slept little. When he stepped outside into the dawn and felt the warm breeze from the south and the sun flooding the forest with golden light, he cursed the world that produced such beauty while it killed his daughter. He took a spade and walked into the forest to a clearing within sight of the hut. He had dug too many graves; this last, for his own daughter, was the hardest.

An ominous stillness lay over the village as he returned to the hut and gathered up the blanketed form of his child. He hesitated, then woke Tatiana.

For just an instant the bright flood of light swept Tatiana with relief and happiness that the horrible dream was finished. Then she saw the tiny bundle in his arms, and it was as if she herself had died. Without a word she dressed and followed him to the clearing.

He laid the body in the grave, and Tatiana watched in silence, enduring a terrible sense of *déjà vu*. How many more times? Her face was expressionless, and her eyes were half-closed. She did not say a word, and there were no traces of tears that Evans could see; but in spite of his own grief, he felt the sense of her terrible loss.

"I'll bring the priest later," he began, then remembered that the priest had been shot as well.

Tatiana cringed as the first clumps landed on the body. Evans finished the terrible task and stared helplessly at the grave. There was no marker he dared place; instead, he broke a tiny willow branch and laid it on the mound. All through the Urals and across the taiga the Chekists had followed them. He cursed himself horribly, overwhelmed by his own inadequacy. If he had killed the engine driver the graves would never have been found and his daughter would still be alive.

Tatiana stared at the fire. She ate a bit of the boiled millet he placed before her; then her hands fell to her lap, and she stared at the flames. Everything was so far away, so dim, she thought, and was surprised that she no longer felt any pain at all.

When Evans told her to dress warmly, she did so without a murmur. Slowly, almost as an experiment, he had her make the bed, sweep the floor and build up the fire. She did everything without protest. But when he tried to draw her out, to discover what actually had happened, she refused to answer. When he stopped directly in front of her, there was no sign of recognition in her eyes, and eventually her gaze slid past him.

He saw with a pang of fear that her depression was a thousand times worse than it had ever been, as if Tatiana had forsaken reality, leaving only her body behind. When he took her hand, she allowed it to rest in his but eventually disengaged it. When he kissed her, there was no answering movement of her lips or change of expression. After a while he retired, baffled and with a feeling of subdued anger as she sat patiently, staring at nothing. His anger grew, and he cursed the Bolsheviks, the Whites, the Cheka, Russia, God.

Evans could not remain inside. At the door he paused. Tatiana had not moved. The bodies lay where they had fallen. No one had helped the man with the shattered pelvis, and he had frozen to death during the night. Evans felt not the least trace of pity. He saw that all the weapons had been taken away, and a chill of premonition went through him as he walked to the church.

The interior was dark. His eyes adjusted slowly, and he found the priest lying on a pallet below the altar, as if he were another sacrifice to a demanding God. The old woman crouching beside the pallet raised her head and watched him with glittering, unreadable eyes.

The old priest was dying. Even in the poor light Evans could see the grayness in his skin. Beads of perspiration wet the old man's forehead. His breathing was harsh and uneven, and blood from the chest wound had soaked though the blankets in a dark stain. He knelt beside the pallet, and the priest's eyelids fluttered.

"You've come," he whispered. "I hoped you would." A thin line of spittle coursed down his chin, and with surprising gentleness, the old woman wiped it away.

"You must go. The villagers . . . hate you because you are different. They . . . they will hate you . . . even more now that the"—he gasped and closed his eyes for a moment against the pain—"that the soldiers have come."

"But why? I've fed them all winter."

"Listen." The priest's hand scrabbled at his jacket. "When I . . . was a young man, I was an aide to the metropolitan of Moscow. We argued one day, a trivial matter, I . . . I don't even remember. To teach me humility, he sent me here for one year. The metropolitan died not long afterward, leaving no written instructions. My enemies convinced his successor that this was intended to be my permanent post. That was in 1887."

The old man lay back, gasping for breath. "They do not trust me, have never accepted me after . . . all these years . . . more years than I remember, with no one to talk to . . ." He gasped and tried to sit up, as if that would ease the terrible red-hot wire drawing more tightly about his heart. Evans supported his shoulders, ignoring the sweetish odor of decay.

He tried to soothe the dying priest, who only shook his head. "Listen . . . they were messengers . . . Satan . . . antichrists . . . tried to . . . to . . . he laughed and shot me." The priest coughed harshly, and Evans held him tightly to ease the spasm of pain.

Why was he doing this? his mind shrilled. The old priest meant nothing . . . He hated this. He never . . . Evans got hold of himself. The old man's eyes were closed, and his lips stained with blood. There was no color in his face, and for a moment Evans thought he had died.

But then Father Vissarian opened his eyes and said in a surprisingly clear voice, "I know who she is."

Evans felt a pang of fear.

"But I never told anyone. . . . You must leave the village. Now that the soldiers have come, now that they know who she is, they will kill you." He closed his eyes and groaned. Evans eased him back down on the pallet. "You must leave . . ." he whispered. "Quickly. Go . . . I tried—" He closed his eyes and lay still. His chest rose and fell twice, and a shudder passed through his body. After a moment the old woman drew the blanket over his face, and Evans closed his eyes against the hot flood of tears.

This angry old man, who had driven him like an animal through the fall, had baptized their child and with his own body had tried to protect Tatiana and Alexandra from the killers. How many more must die?

"You must go," the old woman said. Her voice was thin but cultured, with the lilt of Moscow. "He was quite right. They will kill you."

He stared at her in amazement, and she regarded him calmly.

"I am—was—his sister. When he was sent into exile, I took a nun's vows and followed. Now he is dead. The villagers need my healing skills and will not harm me. But they are little more than animals."

She paused for a moment, then whispered, "He had such a brilliant mind once, such a promising career. He might have become metropolitan of Moscow." She sighed deeply. "Our family was quite well-to-do. I had forgotten."

Evans tried to say something, but the old woman shook her head. The intelligence in her eyes faded again, and all trace of sanity disappeared. He stumbled from the church, shuddering at the horror of such a life.

He found one of the Chekists' horses along the track where its bridle had caught in a tangle of briars. There was no trace of the others. His own four animals were in satisfactory shape after the long winter, and he went in to pack their few belongings.

Tatiana dressed silently when he told her to. Before leaving, he slipped the Colt under his coat and took the undamaged Berdan rifle to the hut where Sasha lived with his mother. He pushed the door open and went in without knocking. The hut stank of animal and man. Sasha sat on the mud stove, cleaning one of the Mauser rifles, and his face twisted in surprise. His mother crouched against a back wall, her eyes filled with fear.

Without a word Evans laid the Berdan rifle and the handful of cartridges on the table and gathered up the four Mausers and their ammunition pouches. Sasha's twisted mouth worked silently, but he did not attempt to stop him. Still watching Sasha, Evans backed to the door. The boy slid down and followed, eyes glittering with hatred.

When they rode out of the village a few minutes later, Evans had slung a loaded Mauser rifle across his back. Sasha was standing on the church steps with the Berdan. Evans reined in his horse and stared at the boy, trying not to focus on his twisted, cleft mouth.

"I'll leave three rifles and ammunition in a clearing ten versts from here." Sasha did not respond, nor did the hate pouring from him ease.

It suddenly occurred to him that Sasha had helped kill the Chekists simply for their rifles. And I taught this bastard to hunt with a rifle, he thought, gave them all the best winter they ever had. Now they want to kill me. He started to ride on, but a flicker of movement caught his eye. He threw himself to the ground as the Berdan rifle boomed in the morning stillness. The horses bolted, and Evans twisted aside, yanking the pistol from his belt. He saw Sasha through a flurry of legs and snow, crouching as he jammed a new cartridge into the rifle. Evans rolled away and, as Sasha straightened, killed him with a single shot.

He stood over the boy's sprawled body. For an instant as he remembered how the peasants had ignored them, refused to help ever, even when his child was being murdered and his wife raped, the urge to burn the village and shoot everyone in it was overpowering. Abruptly he turned and went after the horses.

She knew her daughter was dead. She remembered the grave, remembered watching Evans place the tiny body inside. For an instant Tatiana felt a desperate desire to follow, to climb into the hole, to feel the safety of the earth close about her. In that instant all her sins were before her with the crystal clarity of an apocalyptic vision, and she understood the form and substance of the menace that had haunted her for so long: It was her own damnation, and that of her child. Like her mother, she had suffered a monstrous joke in the person of a child.

The murder of her daughter, her own rape and beating by the Bolshevik Chekists nearly destroyed Tatiana. Satan, not God, had played with her. The antichrist had triumphed. She had been right: The forest menace was the Bolshevik antichrist after all.

Tatiana no longer allowed herself to feel anything, not terror, not pain, not cold, not thirst or hunger. Everything receded from her. She was in a safe world without feeling, without fear. If she remained very, very still, neither Satan nor God could find her. As long as she did not feel, she would be safe. Tatiana shut away all thoughts of Alexandra and Evans and took refuge in her sanctuary of featureless white, so much like the marble hall at Livadiya that led to the nursery where she and her sisters and brother played as children.

As afternoon shadows grayed into darkness, Evans turned from the trail and rode another mile before he felt safe. It was unlikely that any of the villagers would follow, but Evans was no longer taking chances. He chopped a hole in the ice of the first river he came to and thrust the extra Mauser rifles into the water.

He cursed himself bitterly for not having taken the most elementary precaution against such a surprise attack, even while he was utterly amazed that the Cheka had been able to track them through this subarctic wilderness. It wasn't possible that they had been discovered by accident; in the six months they had spent in the village there had not been one visitor. He could only marvel at how much the Bolshevik government feared a single woman.

He made camp deep in the trees, cutting limbs carefully from the pines throughout a wide area to make a shelter. He banked a fire against a reflector made from logs and had Tatiana crawl in and wrap herself warmly in the blankets.

She worried him deeply. She hadn't spoken once since the burial.

He had endured her depressions before, but this was vastly different. It was as if—he sought the right words to describe what he felt—as if she were no longer there. Tatiana seemed to have withdrawn so far into herself that nothing he said or did, nothing her body experienced could touch her. Perplexed and fearing for her sanity, he prepared food and had to order her to eat. When he took the tin plate away, she sat staring at nothing, hands in her lap, until he told her to wrap up in the blankets and sleep.

The relatively mild weather lasted through the middle of April. In a way it was a blessing because they were able to travel more rapidly than he would have expected. They covered, he estimated, a good seventy miles through the forest. Birches and aspens began to appear among the firs with increasing regularity. The temperature remained low enough that the ice in the frequent streams and rivers stayed frozen, but not so cold as to make travel impossible.

Still, good weather was also an enemy. If they could travel swiftly, pursuing Chekists could travel faster. He did not know whether the four dead men were all of them or not, but he was not taking a chance. Evans thought more than once of waiting in ambush but discarded the idea as foolish. The Chekists were trained soldiers, while he had only the benefit of a three-month officers' training course and the National Guard's drilling and drinking routine. They would be heavily armed, and he had only a single Mauser bolt-action rifle and a Colt pistol with three rounds of ammunition remaining. No, he decided, their best chance was to keep as far ahead as they could for as long as possible.

The weather broke at the end of April. At sunset one evening Evans stared long and anxiously at the northwestern sky. Iron gray clouds had obscured the setting sun, slowly smothering the winter red light that for a brief moment had turned the forest to a fairyland. An arctic air mass was moving in from the Barents Sea, advancing like a curtain of artillery fire. As the light faded, he walked back to their makeshift shelter and began to cut more firewood. The horses were twenty yards away. He checked their hobbles and squatted down to smoke a cigarette, knowing his presence was reassuring to the animals. Grass from the previous year lay thick in the tiny clearing, and he decided against feeding them precious hay or millet.

Tatiana lay on her side, eyes open, watching the fire, and he described the approaching storm and his preparations. Evans had fallen into the habit of talking to her as if she were normal. She did not seem to hear him, but even so, he hoped that his voice might serve as a link to reality.

By midnight the wind had risen to gale force. The trees thrashed and roared like angry demons. Evans banked the fire; but the flames fluttered close to the coals, and drafts swept the shelter. From time to time he struggled out to check the horses. They cowered among the trees, crowding together for mutual comfort, backsides to the wind, enduring. They stamped and rolled anxious eyes at him as he soothed and petted and calmed them. The trees broke the worst of the wind, but still, snow filled the clearing and banked up against every obstacle.

The storm did not abate at dawn but rather increased in fury. Snow obscured the dead gray sky, and for the first time Evans experienced the full fury of an arctic gale.

The hours dragged. The continuous whine of the wind was unnerving, and he found himself starting at every sound. Pale daylight flickered with the driving snow, and he began to imagine movement where there couldn't possibly be any. The cold was insidious and seeped through their furs as if they did not exist. He brewed cup after cup of birchbark tea and forced Tatiana to drink and eat to keep up her strength. At midday he took her with him to tend the horses. She huddled against a tree, while he saw to their needs and tried to sweep the snow off the grass with a broken branch. He might as well have tried to empty an ocean.

The second night was worse. Evans slept fitfully, awakened again and again as the wind backed and filled. He could detect no slackening in its velocity, and the cold, if anything, was deepening. He was forced to build the fire higher to maintain even the semblance of heat in the shelter.

And again with dawn, the storm increased in ferocity. Wind slashed across the forest, driving snow before it like cannon shot, and the temperature dropped steadily. In the afternoon Evans wove more branches into the walls of the shelter and built a second fire. He moved Tatiana so that she lay parallel to the fires to absorb maximum heat. The wind had become a steady howl, terrifying in its intensity. Beyond the opaque curtain of driving snow Evans had an impression of trees bent horizontally against its blast. Once he laughed without mirth. After all they had endured, to die in a blizzard . . . life was a grand joke!

At sunset a curious stillness fell over the forest. Snow continued to fall, but he could see it now as individual flakes eddying in the wisps of breeze. The light was flat and fading quickly, and the loom of the forest was unearthly. He crawled out of the shelter, kicking away the wind-driven snow that had partially filled the entrance. Their supply of firewood was dangerously low, and he worked like a demon to gather immense piles of fallen branches.

The thick stand of pines had shielded the horses from the worst of the wind, and the animals had trampled the snow inside so that they were in effect surrounded by a corral. He fed them each a bit of millet, and their warm bodies pressed against him as they ate.

The wind began again soon after dark, building with the terrifying speed of an adiabatic storm. He wrapped Tatiana and himself in the same blankets. She was as oblivious to him as to the storm, and he made no attempt to keep her awake. He had decided that the kindest thing he could do would be to let her die peacefully. He was convinced now that they would not survive the storm.

By dawn of the third day the wood was gone and only a meager bed of coals remained. He was too weak even to shiver in a vain attempt to induce warmth. They were dying, and he did not have the strength to struggle further. At times it was difficult to know for certain when he was conscious. Tatiana had not moved in a long time.

He closed his eyes, and snatches of dream and memory played across his mind. He was in the backyard of the Beacon Hill house near dusk on a spring evening. He could not have been more than six or seven years old. In a rare moment of indulgence his father had agreed to play baseball with him but had insisted he learn to catch without a glove.

He could still hear his father thundering at him, "Do what I tell you, damn it! Stick your hand out there. Don't give up! Act like a man!" He remembered how stubbornly he had resisted, how he had bawled and shouted until his father walked away in disgust.

A coal snapped, and he opened his eyes. After struggling out of the blankets, he crawled to the entrance and pulled himself out, reeling drunkenly, for some reason furious. His body refused to work, and his legs buckled. He had thought he could feel no more pain, but the wind ripped through the sheepskin coat as if it were made of tissue. Shouting obscenities, Evans cursed and raved at the universe, at the storm and at God, raved for all the pain and terror that Tatiana had endured, that he had shared, however lightly in comparison, with her. He bellowed into the storm but could not hear his own voice.

Somewhere deep inside, he refused to die, refused to let his body slip away to the warmth and comfort of sleep and death. Evans stumbled forward, arms outstretched, effectively blind. He collided with the side of the shelter and fell. Pine needles and sharp, whipping branches scratched his face. Beneath the drifted snow were the branches he had piled there earlier. His mind worked with grotesque slowness, and he struggled to pull one free, felt his way back to the entrance and all but collapsed inside. He had only enough strength left to drag the branch toward him across the fire.

Heat seared him awake. In reflex he scrabbled back, panicked, unable to make sense of what was happening. He collided with Tatiana and half turned, shielding her while he tried to clear his mind.

A fire blazed at the entrance, filling the interior with heat. The branch had landed in the wind-scattered ashes, he saw, and burst into flame. Evans dragged Tatiana clear and began to chafe her arms and

248

legs. In the strengthening light, he could see the bluish cast to her lips. As he struggled, his own strength began to seep back, and by the time the pine needles burned away Tatiana was moaning and trying to pull away from his hands. He set a pan of snow on the ashes to melt and stumbled out for more wood.

By midmorning he felt strong enough to check the horses. The wind still showed no indication of flagging. It had grown worse, if anything, and he was forced to crawl blindly, following the rope he had stretched between the shelter and the clearing.

One horse was down, and the others were in a bad way. There was nothing he could do for the horse that had fallen. It hadn't the strength left to raise its head. He fed the others millet, pouring it into the skirt of his greatcoat, and they crowded listlessly about him, snuffling the grain. Afterward he made the trip again, this time carrying the rifle. He tried to get the fallen horse up long enough to lead it away, but the poor animal barely stirred.

Evans was afraid the shot might cause the others to panic, and he took off his sheepskin. The cold struck him with the force of a blow, and he staggered, coughing, as he tried to wrap the jacket around the rifle muzzle. He did the best he could and pressed it to the animal's head and pulled the trigger. The muffled shot was snatched away by the wind as the bullet tore a neat hole through the leather.

When he woke hours later, the fire was low again. He lay without moving, badly disoriented. It was night once more, he realized after a while, and surprisingly, the shelter was filled with warmth. Tatiana sat against one wall, staring at the coals and stirred the fire with a stick. "I'll be damned," he muttered. Evans pushed himself up. The wind had stopped! He stumbled into a soundless night, where the silence seemed as fragile as crystal. The sky was clear and blazed with stars, and the motionless forest was ghostly bluish white in the starlight. A horse whickered softly, and the silence resumed.

They were alive!

The blizzard proved to be the last hurrah of winter. They remained camped for two more days while Evans cut forage and allowed the horses as much time to recover as possible. Tatiana stayed in the shelter, staring with empty eyes unless he told her what to do, and then she performed the duty mindlessly before returning to the fire.

When they rode on through a wonderland of snow-sifted trees and bright, diamond-sharp sunlight, she sat her horse as expertly as ever but offered it no guidance.

Tatiana was certain she had escaped. The white hallway was shrouded in mist at either end, effectively hiding her, and she was satisfied. Occasionally a memory of Alexandra or the sound of Evans's voice would intrude, and she would push it away, convinced that if she stayed perfectly still, refused to allow herself to feel or think, she would never be found.

The hall reminded her of Livadiya. The nursery had been at the end of one wing, and her mother's sitting room at the other. From the windows of the nursery they had a glorious view of the Black Sea, and from her mother's boudoir the snow-capped Caucasus was visible in winter when the air was washed by rain. The nursery had a terrace that led to the lawn and the beach looked so warm.

In mid-May the forest began to give way to tundra. Evans felt distinctly uncomfortable without the concealing trees, but there was nothing for it but to go on. More than once he had the feeling they were being followed, and when they came on a sparse grove of winter-stripped aspens, they camped an entire day while he spent long hours with the field glasses searching the horizon for horsemen.

There were two horses left to them now. The bay taken from the blacksmith the year before had begun to flag soon after the storm. When Evans went to feed the horses one morning, the bay had not the strength to come to him. It stood to one side, head hanging and shivering. Evans stroked its neck and whispered words of encouragement. He saddled the other two and led them aside without removing their hobbles, then took the rifle and shot the bay quickly.

That night he heard wolves and realized that he had made a mistake. But what else could he have done? he asked himself. There was no way to dispose of the horse's body. The tundra was a frozen marsh. He built the fire higher and slept fitfully, remembering all the horror stories he had ever heard about Russian wolves.

He saw the first one the following day. The gray animal loped along parallel to their course and a hundred yards distant. When he stopped, the wolf did so as well, and looking back, Evans thought he saw movement in the distance. The wolf was wary and trotted away as Evans dismounted. He untied the Mauser; the wolf was 150 yards distant, and he adjusted the sight. The animal was difficult to see against the sere tundra vegetation. The rifle cracked viciously, and the wolf jumped, twisting in midair. Evans remounted and, taking Tatiana's reins, rode toward the dead animal, quite proud of what was for him extraordinarily good shooting.

The horses shied away before they were within twenty yards, and Evans gave in and stopped. Through the field glasses he could see the rangy animal twisted in an odd manner. His shot had broken the wolf's spine. Searching back along the horizon, he found no trace of the pack. For an instant a primitive fear caused the hairs on his neck to ripple, and he shivered violently. That night he built a large fire and hardly slept. Toward midnight he heard them moving softly about the perimeter of the firelight. The horses stamped and whinnied nervously. He resisted the urge to shoot blindly into the darkness. Until they reached Archangel, still at least two hundred miles distant, every cartridge was irreplaceable.

Tatiana wasn't certain why, but the marble walls of her sanctuary had been growing translucent for some time. Occasionally sound penetrated: a voice and perhaps the whinny of a horse. But mostly it was a voice. There was something familiar about it, but she did not pursue the matter, fearing to stir interest. She plunged instead into her memories . . . her father and mother as they were when she was a small girl at Livadiya. She could smell the salty tang of the Black Sea and, as they drove out along the dusty October road, of high mountains and dried grass from the Caucasus. On their left were the sheep pasture and the old shepherd who had waved to them for as long as she could remember.

The sun was bright, not yet hot, as it would be later in the day. Olga wriggled beside her, and she pushed her back to make certain she didn't take more of the seat than was her due. Olga protested, and Mama admonished them both. Marie was snuggled into a blanket on her lap. Ahead of the carriage rode their escort, a single Cossack with bristling mustaches, wearing his olive drab uniform. She wished he would wear his scarlet coat, but every time she asked him to, he only laughed and promised to do so at the next parade.

The day was bright and cold, and she shivered. The sun flashed on the ice between the hummocks, and the grassy tufts were bare. Only a few patches of snow remained. A cold wind swept at them, and her horse curved its neck and whickered softly in complaint. Evans rode a few paces ahead, sitting easily in the saddle. Once he turned to glance at her, but Tatiana had already retreated.

Evans shot a second wolf a week later. He had awakened in the night to stir up the fire and saw a shadow of movement near the horses. He sprang up, shouting, and the wolf turned toward him, teeth bared. The animal was torn between its fear of the fire and the urge to attack. The hesitation was time enough for Evans to snatch up the rifle and fire. The wolf screamed an almost human scream and disappeared in the darkness. Evans threw more fuel on the fire, cursing the winter-dried reeds that were all they had. For two days now he had not seen a tree.

"Bill, what is it?"

"A wolf, Tania, go back—"

Evans froze. Even the wolves were forgotten for the moment. He knew he had only imagined Tatiana's voice, but when he turned, he saw her leaning on one arm, watching him. She nodded, lay back and closed her eyes.

In the morning she seemed no different from the way she had been since the day they buried Alexandra. But as time passed, Evans began to discern signs that Tatiana was emerging from her mental hibernation. She seemed to look around her more and even began to do things for herself without having to be told.

A week later they camped for the night in a stand of birches. The trees had begun to appear again, sparse and stunted, but trees nevertheless. They were less than one hundred miles from Archangel, five to seven days' riding at most if the weather held. So far it had remained cold enough that the tundra had not begun to thaw until late in the day. But the ice in the frequent rivers was his greatest concern.

The clump of birches stood beside just such a river. The stream was perhaps ten yards wide and, like all tundra rivers, was shallow but with a fast and dangerous current. Clear water could be seen along the banks, and he had decided to wait for dawn. In a day or so he expected to strike the Dvina River, which they would follow to Archangel.

Now that they were approaching the end of the nearly two-year trek, he forced himself to think about what they would do once they reached the city, if the Allies were still in control. They had had no news of the civil war since leaving Ust-Usa ten months before, and anything could have happened in the interval. He realized that all during the long winter months he had avoided thinking about the possibility that the Allies might already have withdrawn from Archangel.

Tatiana sat across from him, staring at the ice-crusted river. As he often did, he was outlining his apprehensions to her in a running monologue when he noticed her tears. He sat perfectly still, hardly daring to breathe. Tatiana raised a hand and wiped her cheek.

"I miss her so, Bill," she said softly.

"So do I," he managed to say after a moment.

"She was so small, so harmless."

He put an arm around her, and she leaned her head against his shoulder and burst into convulsive sobs. He held her for what seemed like hours.

"You will always have me, Tania," he murmured softly over and over until she raised her face to his and he kissed her gently, afraid to say anything more.

"Always, Bill?"

"Always."

That night she slept in his arms, and he knew her long silence was nearly over. He lay quite still, his heart filled with so much love he thought it might break.

XII

Moscow was a charnel house. Epidemic after epidemic had swept the city during a winter made worse by famine, municipal service strikes, mass arrests and anarchy. Crime was rampant. The public, totally disarmed in sweeping search and seizures the summer before, was completely at the mercy of the ruthless criminal gangs who had replaced the anarchists Sheremetiev had helped destroy. When he was finally released in February to go north to Archangel, he paused barely long enough to exchange his Mauser pistol for a more concealable Luger and to pack his few belongings.

He endured a final interview with Dzerzhinsky, who had not lost his predilection for late night summonses. "You will not leave Archangel until you are certain the Romanov woman is dead," Dzerzhinsky told him. "Do not attempt to return her to Moscow. There is growing pressure to make use of her in a propaganda campaign against the counterrevolutionaries, but there is danger to the Soviet state in that course that I do not care to risk. You will report directly to me as before, but through agents whom I will send."

So, Sheremetiev thought, it was true. Dzerzhinsky had lost ground against Sverdlov over the disappearance of the royal family. The danger he saw in using the woman was to himself. Alive, she was a festering reminder of Dzerzhinsky's failure; dead, of Sverdlov's.

Dzerzhinsky considered him closely for a moment. "Do not fail—this time," he warned.

The railroad was in operation north to Archangel, but he left the train at the last Soviet-controlled barricade north of the scraggly village of Shura, which consisted of three bars, two cafés, a handful of cabins and a log railroad station. In the misty distance was the gray dome of a monastery. The border guards took several passengers off at gunpoint, and the train rolled on.

A Red Army officer showed him into the cramped station, where soldiers clustered about the empty buffet counter, laughing and joking. The arrestees squatted against a wall, waiting to be sent back down the line to the district center for trial. Parasites, he thought. Bourgeois running for their stinking lives with their jewels and money. One man glared at anyone who came near. He reminded Sheremetiev of his father except that he was too well dressed to make his living by his own efforts and his face was choleric with anger and fear. The good life he had formerly enjoyed still showed in smooth jowls and plump belly bulging against a camel's-hair overcoat. Too lazy to disguise his origins or to circumvent the border patrols, who purposely confined themselves to the checkpoints, allowing refugees to flood through the forests, he had let his class arrogance lead him to believe that he could bull his way through in comfort. Well, they'd make short work of him at the district headquarters. They'd have him against a wall before midnight.

That night, dressed in rough clothing, Sheremetiev left the village and made his way into the forest. The following day he joined a throng of refugees traveling north to Archangel.

Sheremetiev found a pickup job on the docks that earned him sufficient money to pay for a bed and meals in one of Archangel's refugee centers. His papers had been forged in Moscow, but they were so badly out of date that he burned them. There were thousands of people in Archangel without documents, but in the week it took to make the proper contacts, he moved circumspectly so as not to attract the attention of the Provisional Government's militia.

He discovered quickly that the local Bolshevik apparatus was riddled with informers. He had been given the names of three reliable contacts before leaving Moscow, but after watching each for a few hours, he destroyed that paper as well. Two were paid informers, and the third was a fool.

Sheremetiev changed jobs twice before he found an appropriate recruiting ground in a pulp mill. He had decided to dispense with help from Moscow whenever he could, especially local help he had not vetted himself. The Provisional Government's counterintelligence organization was not particularly effective, but it was widespread. More important to Sheremetiev, the less Dzerzhinsky knew about the details of his activities, the safer he was.

All during March he developed his plan for identifying and disposing of the fugitives should they escape Dolrov, who at the least would prove a welcome addition to his forces when he arrived. Twice weekly Sheremetiev checked the refugee message board outside the main post office, as they had arranged the summer before in Ust-Usa, before they had split up and he had returned to Moscow.

In the meantime, he continued to build his organization, even though appalled at the poor quality of potential recruits. In a city filled to overflowing with refugees from the Communist government, there were few candidates with the correct mental make-up. Most were anti-social malcontents who would have rebelled no matter what the form of government.

Spring sunlight glared through the wide windows overlooking the Dvina River. A forest of masts and spars, cranes and smokestacks screened the far bank from view. The commissioner of roads and public works, one Victor Vasilievich Esinberg, studied him through the smoke of his imported English cigarette and smiled.

"Your proposal, Comrade Sheremetiev, is rather provocative. But what would keep me from making one telephone call to the militia? They tend to shoot Bolshevik spies without trial."

Sheremetiev smiled. "Only a fool would refuse to admit that when the English leave Archangel, the Provisional Government will collapse. It backed the wrong horse when it chose Admiral Kolchak."

"Perhaps." Esinberg tapped a finger on the telephone's base. "Tell me once more."

Sheremetiev knew he had him then. "You may choose to live anywhere in Russia, free from interference or prosecution by the Soviet government. Or you may have a new passport issued by the Soviet government when the Provisional Government falls. You will receive written permission to leave Russia for any destination you choose."

The fat man chuckled and leaned back in his chair. "A very modest reward for what amounts to treason, Comrade Sheremetiev. Putting you, a Bolshevik officer, in a position to spy on the British checkpoint and keep track of the military patrols that come and go could see me shot if you were discovered."

"There are millions who would give all they own for the choices I have offered."

"Hmmm. Perhaps you are correct. However, I feel the need of a bit more security than the word of the Bolshevik government." He sat up quickly for a man of his bulk. "The passport must be usable immediately. There must be first-class passage on a neutral ship leaving Archangel no later than, say, July thirtieth. And there must be ten thousand pounds British sterling deposited in a Rome bank account in my name." He leaned back. "When those conditions are met, then you will have the job. As you can see, I don't trust you or your government. Once Red soldiers have occupied the city, it will be too easy to renege on a verbal promise."

Sheremetiev held his temper with difficulty. He had no choice. He was taking an unwarranted chance just in being here. "Agreed. I will have the documents for you within a week. The money may take a day or so longer."

Esinberg smiled. "Not too long, I hope, Comrade Commissar. "By the way," he said as Sheremetiev stood up, "I am not stupid enough to believe everything you tell me. You may be assured that I will take precautions: a letter to be mailed to a friend in the Provisional Government in the event of my disappearance that will name you as a Bolshevik spy."

Sheremetiev nodded, trying to look suitably impressed at the man's astuteness. Outside he heaved a sigh of relief. It had been easier than he had anticipated. Esinberg would not disappear. Nor would he board a ship for Rome. Instead, he would spend a few months in a Lubyanka cell. He would still be alive and able to reassure his friend that he was in good health and enjoying himself in sunny Italy. Once the Provisional Government fell, Esinberg would be redundant. In the meantime, Sheremetiev would be safely ensconced as supervisor of the public works department's maintenance depot.

They saw Archangel at midafternoon. For a week now the land along the Dvina had been as flat as if scraped to the exacting measurements of a surveyor. Only since yesterday had the terrain begun to ripple into gentle hills thick with pine forest. Pale sunlight filtered reluctantly through heavy clouds. The horses stood blowing and shivering, and Evans, in a burst of happiness, caught Tatiana's gloved hand and pressed it to his lips. She moved closer, and something like a smile showed as she lifted her face to his. Her kiss was tentative, but Evans was content.

Tatiana emerged a bit more each day from the shell she had drawn around herself. She knew she still had a tendency to turn inward at times; but such spells were becoming infrequent, and when they did occur, it was possible for Evans to pull her out of them.

At the sight of the Union Jack flying above the wooden hut, there washed through him a wave of relief that was so great his legs gave way, and he sat down abruptly. Tears filled his eyes, and Evans dashed at them with gloved hands, swearing at his weakness. Tatiana laughed at the comical spectacle he created and knelt beside him. A tommy leaning against the gate nudged his partner and nodded toward the two figures who were alternately laughing and crying as they hugged each other in the middle of the muddy road.

The officer, a young lieutenant with a small patch of blackened skin on his forehead where the frost had bitten deeply one terror-filled night at Kilometer 343, stared at the two of them. Both wore sheepskin coats rank with wood smoke and horse sweat, and their felt boots were tied on with rags and bits of string. The man's jacket even had a bullet hole in the left side. Their horses were scarecrows that trembled badly and looked as if they had not been rested or fed properly in months.

The man peered at him from frost-blackened eye sockets. A thick beard hid his features, and his bony shoulders protruded against the sheepskin. His eyes were as wet as the roads, and he was grinning like an idiot. The woman with him was in little better shape. Her sheepskin was bound about her with a leather belt. Her face, what little of it could be seen between the scarf tied around her mouth and the hood pulled low on her forehead, was dirty. Strands of oily hair had crept out from under the hood, and she brushed at them nervously.

"I am William Hughes Evans, major, United States Army," the man said, choosing his words carefully, as if he had not spoken English in a long time.

"I beg your pardon?"

"I am Major William Hughes Evans," he repeated. "I am, was, the American military attaché to the Crimean National Front under General Fedor Mikhailovich Orbelesky at Sevastopol. We've come overland from Ekaterinburg."

The lieutenant's understanding of Russian geography was limited to Archangel and its immediate environs, but included a hazy idea that Moscow was somewhere south a few hundred miles. Sevastopol was a name he remembered from third-form history, but Ekaterinburg was meaningless.

"Do you have identification?"

Evans dug through layers of clothing and produced two metal tags suspended from a brass chain. The lieutenant peered at them and wrinkled his nose against the rank body odor. Dog tags, the Yanks called them.

"I'm afraid this is all I have."

The lieutenant's instructions were to allow anyone to pass if he was unarmed and asked for asylum. He was empowered to confiscate weapons and record names and former addresses only. This man looked and sounded more Russian than American. The lieutenant's only contact with Yanks had been with the American 339th Regiment—part of the North Russian Expeditionary Force. It had been recruited mostly from the western states, and a Boston accent did not sound Yankee to him. He decided to play it smart.

"I'm afraid I haven't anyone just now to escort you . . . sir," he added just in case. "But I will telephone for someone to come get you."

Evans laughed. "If you will just give me the address, Lieutenant. We'll find it."

A clerk recorded his name and nationality on a card, accepted the name Evans gave him for Tatiana and watched as they surrendered the rifle and remaining ammunition and trudged off down the muddy road toward the town. He stared thoughtfully at the papers before him, then lifted the telephone receiver and gave the exchange the telephone number of the road maintenance office along the road. There was trouble with the lines, and by the time the connection was made, the two had disappeared from sight. He gave the man's name and described them carefully.

"How bloody long ago, you damned fool?" Sheremetiev slammed down the phone when he heard the answer. He raced down the stairs, shouting for the four men lounging in the yard, and gave them rapid instructions as he struggled into his coat.

Even before the war Archangel had been growing in importance as a seaport. A narrow-gauge railroad had been extended north from Vologda with the intention of being expanded later; but the war had invoked typical bureaucratic indecision, and the result was that even as Archangel became the nation's major receiving port for Allied war aid, the Ministry of Railways canceled the expansion plans, citing lack of manpower and scarcity of materials. Three years later the backlog was enough to equip an army corps. Ostensibly to prevent the supplies from falling into German hands, British, French and American troops had been sent into northern Russia after the Bolshevik takeover in Moscow. In addition, there were 100,000 or more refugees packed into the city— almost half again the native population—that stretched for more than five miles along the banks of the Dvina.

Evans and Tatiana walked along the road, leading their exhausted horses. Low wooden cabins and huts lined the muddy thoroughfare, and men and women stood in slushy yards, offering everything imaginable for sale. The city was narrow, hardly more than a dozen blocks wide, but after endless months in the mountains and taiga, the press of people was daunting. Tatiana clung to Evans's hand, and he stalked along, glaring at anyone who came near. The horses snorted and tugged nervously at the reins.

They reached the Troitsky Prospekt, the main boulevard of Archangel, as the overcast began to disperse and sunlight strengthened. The street was wide and filled with people, but the only vehicles were Allied lorries. They saw no horses, or dogs either for that matter, and before they had gone five blocks, Evans sold both horses for an unimaginable sum—two thousand Kerensky rubles. Laughing, he pressed it all, and the last two Mexican gold coins, into Tatiana's hand after they turned down a side street.

"The first of the riches I'll bestow upon you, my princess," he whispered. Not until later did it occur to him that both horses were probably butchered and eaten before nightfall.

Sheremetiev swore bitterly. He had stopped opposite the post and telegraph office at the intersection of Naberezhnaya and Finlandskaya. So many people milled about that it was impossible to find them. He had expected to spot them by the horses they were supposed to be leading. That damned fool of a clerk had said they had been directed to the American Military Mission. Sheremetiev visualized the city map he had studied so assiduously and, with great reluctance, split his force. There were only two routes they could follow, and his instructions were simple. Find and kill them both. He took one man and hurried in the most likely direction.

Men and women, some elegantly dressed in furs and feather hats, others pushing bicycles, picked their way through the ubiquitous mud. Evans and Tatiana stared in awe at the throng moving up and down the boulevard like swarms of lemmings. He hadn't seen so many different uniforms, so much brightly polished brass, since Odessa. The Troitsky Cathedral reared above them with five immense gilded domes. Farther on were the custom house and the district court. The crowds were better dressed here; but Evans sensed hopelessness, and he suspected the majority were refugees, striving desperately to stay alive and find a way out of Russia.

The crowd pressed closer, and Evans drew Tatiana away and down a side street. According to the directions given them by the British lieutenant, the American Mission was only a block or two farther on. Evans stopped opposite a small church. It was nearly six in the evening, and the long twilight had begun. The sun would dip below the horizon briefly near eleven o'clock, but there would be little real darkness.

Evans knew that once they reached the mission, it would be a madhouse. Better to ask now.

"Tania, will you marry me tomorrow?" In his nervousness he rushed on without waiting for her answer. "We'll find an American or British minister, and that way there won't be any question. You'll be a citizen and entitled to the protection of the American government, no matter what the State Department and the president say."

Tatiana, confused by the crowds and the unbelievable knowledge that they had reached a destination so long anticipated that it hardly seemed real, did not at first understand what Evans had asked. Then something deep inside seemed to fade abruptly, and a certain coldness that had gripped her central being for so long was gone.

"I . . . I, of course, Bill." She looked up at him, features grave, and he burst into laughter and kissed her soundly.

"What a solemn body you've become. All right then, tomorrow we get married, officially, legally, morally." He kissed her again. "I wanted to marry you that time in Nadezhdinski Zavod. I had intended to look for a priest, but the Cheka started sniffing about. Damned Bolsheviks!"

Yes, Tatiana thought. If we had married, there would have been no need for Alexandra to die. . . .

"God damn!"

Evans pushed her hard and she fell against the curbing. Someone shouted; she had only the briefest glimpse of men clinging to him, striking over and over again. There were shouts, and three men ran off.

She scrambled to where he lay in the muddy street, half-curled onto one side. Soldiers with rifles materialized around her, great rough men in olive drab uniforms.

Tatiana's voice came to him from a great distance. His chest was on fire with pain. Only an instant's warning, the flash of a knife as one of three men walking past veered abruptly. There hadn't even been time to reach the pistol. . . .

"Bill! Please . . ."

He opened his eyes and saw her bending over him, face wet with tears. When he tried to take a breath, the pain flared, and he gasped. "Tatiana, I . . ." His head was spinning, and it was difficult to think. The sun had gone, leaving her face in shadow. He wanted to see her so badly, to touch her, to touch her lips with his fingers. . . .

A soldier pushed Tatiana away and knelt beside Evans. He saw the brass chain, tugged out the dog tags and whistled.

"Hey, Corp, you better take a look. This guy's an American."

The corporal sent a man running to the American Mission for an ambulance. He unbuttoned Evans's sheepskin jacket, wrinkled his nose at the smell and the dirt and used a pocketknife to cut away his sweater and shirt.

"Jesus," he muttered. "This guy's dirtier than I am!" He ripped away the last of the shirt, exposing Evans's chest, and sucked in his breath. Blood was seeping from two stab wounds, one near the stomach and the other high on the right side of the chest. He was barely breathing, and his skin was pale and very clammy. The corporal recognized shock when he saw it and hastily drew the shirt and jacket together. He shrugged out of his own greatcoat and covered Evans.

"Ryan, get that hunk of wood over there." A soldier brought a length of board, and the corporal eased it under Evans and propped the end on the curb so that his feet were above his head.

He glanced at the curious crowd. "Anyone see what happened?"

he yelled in English. Tatiana stared at him in shock. His English was harsh and difficult for her to understand.

"Goddamned Russian bastards! Wouldn't say so if they did," the corporal muttered. The four members of the patrol he had sent after the fleeing attackers returned empty-handed. God almighty! he thought. An American, and a officer—if that dog tag wasn't stolen. Tatiana again tried to kneel beside Evans, but he yanked her up and pushed her away. "Stay the hell away from him, lady."

Tatiana twisted her arm from his grasp and pleaded in English, "Please, I am—"

The ambulance roared up, bell clanging, and the noise drowned her words. The corporal helped lift Evans's stretcher into the back. A bewildered Tatiana tried to follow, but the corporal shouted, "Damn it, I told you to get away!" He pushed her aside again. "Goddamned whores," he muttered, and shouted at the driver to move off as the soldiers began to disperse the crowd.

Son of a bitch, the corporal thought as he waded into the press of people, I hate this place. Some half-assed American dressed like a Siberian clown gets himself knifed and his whore's screeching like a banshee 'cause she isn't gonna get paid.

Tatiana tried again to speak to him, but her Russian-accented English was almost as foreign to a corporal from Kansas as his was to her. In the confusion he brushed her aside again and marched his patrol off toward the center of the city.

Sheremetiev hit the man as hard as he could, heard cartilage snap and felt it crumple under his fist as the shock jolted his elbow. The second man jumped back, covering his head in reflex, and Sheremetiev kicked him in the crotch. The man screamed and fell as the other disappeared through the door.

"Three of you," he raged, "could not kill one man and a woman!" He swore obscenely. "A year's work ruined because of your stupidity. Where did they take him? What happened to the woman?"

The man on the floor was screaming in short gasps as he hugged his genitals. The one with the broken nose cowered, and Sheremetiev grabbed a handful of hair and slammed his head against the wall so hard that his eyes rolled up.

"What happened to them?" he shouted. "The soldiers, were they British or American?"

"I . . . don't know . . . we . . ."

"You ran away!" he screamed. "You bastards, you cowardly . . ." Words failed him.

First the fool clerk at the checkpoint hadn't bothered to walk across the road, instead waiting for the phone service to do its job. If there had been more time, if that damned clerk had used his head, if he did not have to depend on fools like these . . . he gave up. By God, he'd settle with the clerk tonight.

For a moment he considered executing these two as well . . . they were worse than useless. Only the fact that gunshots would draw unwelcome attention prevented him from doing so. Scum! He grabbed them both by their hair.

"Listen to me and listen carefully. You will go to the American Mission. You will watch the gate. If one or both leave or reenter, you will kill them immediately. Do you understand? Do not wait for further instructions. Do not come running to tell me first. Just do it. And make certain they are dead. If you fail me again, I will kill you both myself."

The American Military Mission building near the docks looked, appropriately enough, like a fort. Sheremetiev stopped at the end of the street and lit a cigarette. A bitterly cold wind had sprung up to refute the notion that spring had arrived. Crystal stars burned in the cloudless sky. Fewer than the usual number of people were in the street because of the cold, and for that he was grateful.

He found himself thinking of the woman, Tatiana, as she had been that last night in Ekaterinburg, when it was almost necessary to execute the family. She had known. He was certain of that. He recalled the way she had stared directly at him, face pale, chin lifted, expression contemptuous. She had courage. The entire family had for that matter, but she more than the rest. Sheremetiev sensed then that she was a realist and understood that sooner or later they all were going to die.

What had she thought this afternoon when the two of them passed through the British checkpoint? That she had won? He ground out the half-smoked cigarette savagely. His own survival was at stake. If he should fail, Dzerzhinsky would make good his unspoken promise, and if he were very lucky, there would be a bullet in the back of his head. If he were unlucky . . . Sheremetiev had learned one thing of central importance in three years of world war and three of civil war: His personal survival was of paramount consideration.

He stopped beside the man watching the gate and was absurdly pleased to see that his nose had swollen to twice normal size and his eyes were very black. God, but he needed Dolrov.

"No one who looks like the woman has gone in or out," he muttered sullenly.

Sheremetiev lit a fresh cigarette, conscious that his hands were shaking. Fear or anger? he wondered.

"Look here, lady," the sergeant said, "how do I know you're his wife? Hell, I got women comin' in here all day long tellin' me they're married to soldiers just so they can get to the States!"

Tatiana struggled to hold back her tears. Why wouldn't they listen to her? For three hours she had been trying to make them understand. Like the corporal's, this man's English was heavily accented, and she could barely understand him.

She tried once more to explain what had happened, but the sergeant wasn't interested in her story; he was interested in Tatiana. The outer office was thronged with people: soldiers stamping in from patrol or getting ready to go out; tearful civilians explaining to a bored officer why they should be allowed to leave Russia on an American troopship, and Provisional Government militiamen who should have been patrolling the streets but who instead were warming themselves at the stove. The room was stifling, and Tatiana had removed her sheepskin coat. The sergeant was paying far more attention to her breasts than to her words.

"God damn it, lady, I can't hear a word," he growled. "Too much noise." He grabbed her arm and took her into an empty office. He sank down on the battered couch the regimental adjutant had installed and regarded Tatiana with a grin. "Cigarette?" Tatiana shook her head.

"Please," she begged, "I must find my husband." She spoke slowly and clearly so the sergeant would understand. "He was stabbed only this afternoon, a few hours ago. The soldiers took him away in an ambulance. To the hospital here."

"Know something?" The sergeant grinned. "You're a looker under all them duds. Why don't you just make yourself comfortable?" He patted the couch.

Tatiana was confused by his slang. "Duds?"

"Clothes," he told her impatiently. "It's hot in here." He pantomimed removing a coat and wiping his forehead.

"Yes, it is hot," she agreed. Tatiana did not like the way the sergeant was looking at her. "My husband . . ."

The sergeant stubbed his cigarette out and patted the cushion beside him again. Tatiana hesitated, then sat down, folding her arms over her breasts.

"It's like this. We think the guy's an American, but we're not sure. He's got military tags around his neck, but then he could have picked them up anywhere."

He was making little sense to her; the slang words were especially confusing, but Tatiana did not dare interrupt.

"Now supposin' he is American. Then what? You come in here, claimin' to be his wife, but hell, you don't even have a wedding ring. Shit, we get twenty, thirty women a day claimin' to be someone's wife just so they can get a free ride to the States. See what I mean?"

Tatiana did not and said so, and the sergeant swore in exasperation. "Look here, damn it. You got nothin' to prove this guy's your husband. Nothin'. Not even a scrap of paper. Just sayin' so don't mean diddly. If that guy lives, if he's an American and if he still wants you hangin' around, then you get in touch with him, and it'll be his problem.

"But"—he studied Tatiana carefully and grinned—"I bet you ain't nothin' but a whore tryin' to get outa here. Right? Now you and me, maybe we could come to the same kinda arrangement."

He rested a hand on her knee and smiled. "I kinda like you. I could probably help if you were nice to me."

Tatiana struggled to understand what he was saying. The heat of the room, the sudden shock of the assault, hunger and exhaustion combined to make her nauseated. The room had a tendency to slide away, and she passed a hand over her eyes. Immediately the sergeant's hand fumbled at her breasts. She tried to push him away, but he cuffed her hands aside and pushed her back on the couch.

The door opened, and the sergeant jumped to his feet, face red with embarrassment as a senior officer glared at them. "The next time you bring one of your whores into my office, Sergeant, I'll personally kick your ass from here to Moscow. Get her off this post now."

The sergeant dragged Tatiana into the courtyard, and soldiers standing near the gate hooted as he hustled her across the parade. The sergeant swore bitterly—at Tatiana, the adjutant, the U.S. Army and Russia in general.

He pushed open a gate that led to the storerooms and hurried down the frozen path. The sergeant's long strides and iron grasp forced Tatiana to run. As they reached a door, he snarled at her. "One word outa you and I'll break your damned neck." He grabbed at her jacket and missed when Tatiana flinched. She wrenched her arm from his grasp and fled. Headlights glared, and she saw a gate swinging shut as the truck drove through. Tatiana darted after it into the alley and did not stop running for several blocks. She had no idea where she was or what to do next, only that she dare not go back. Shivering, as much with fatigue as fear, she drew the sheepskin jacket tightly about her.

Evans watched the bar of light slide down the wall opposite. He had no idea how long he had been awake or even that he had been unconscious for that matter. It seemed that he had been watching the light forever.

After a while he was aware of others in the room. He heard a cough, a muffled groan, the swish of cloth. Once he heard footsteps. But he did not turn his head. The bar of light began to diminish, and he concentrated on the amazing phenomenon. It was shrinking from the bottom up at a slow but steady rate. The last sliver of light gleamed so brightly he looked for smoke to curl from the wall. When the light slipped away, its reddish brown afterimage glowed for a long time.

"You gave us all a scare the other night."

The man had been standing beside the bed for some time before Evans was aware of him. He wore a white collarless jacket and had iron

264

gray, wavy hair framing a square face. Eyebrows matched, and a prominent, slightly bulbous nose presided over a firm chin. The man smiled.

"We didn't think you were going to make it."

"Who are you?" he whispered.

"I'm a doctor. We had to operate two days ago."

"Tatiana . . . where is she?"

The doctor frowned. "I'm afraid I don't—"

Evans stared at him in terror. "Tatiana! She was right beside me." He struggled to make the doctor understand before his strength gave out, but the blackness took him again.

The next person he remembered was a nurse, a severe, painfully thin woman in a gray dress buttoned tightly to her neck. Her white cap showed a red cross, and she was holding his wrist, counting his pulse. The room was in semidarkness.

"Where am I?"

"You are in the medical clinic of the North Russian Expeditionary Force," she told him. "You were stabbed two weeks ago. Since then you developed cholera and nearly died. Please do not ask any more questions. You need all your strength." She laid his arm down and drew the blanket over it. Surprisingly she touched his face and smiled. The smile transformed her. "You will be all right now."

Sheremetiev was as close to despair as he had ever been in his life. For three weeks he had maintained his watch on the American compound. The woman, Tatiana, had not left, yet according to an informer, she was not inside either. The only good news was that the American, William Hughes Evans, had contracted cholera and was dying. Knowing the man's name did him little good.

He read again the innocuous two-day-old message that had been brought to him that morning. Although he had sent only a brief report to Moscow, Dzerzhinsky proved to be entirely too well informed about his failure to eliminate the fugitives. As if to make that point, Dzerzhinsky was now suggesting that the Americans might be hiding her, might even know her true identity. Since it was one of the first possibilities he had considered, that any sane individual would consider, he knew that it was a warning and not a helpful suggestion. Dzerzhinsky did not make helpful suggestions.

By now, however, he had discounted that possibility. The Americans could not have concealed her this long. They had too little finesse in such matters. Everything the Americans did was a matter of public record, whether they wanted it to be or not. If the Romanov woman was in their custody, it would be impossible for them to keep it a secret. His spy inside the compound was matched, he was sure, by those working for the city's Provisional Government, Kolchak's Siberian government, the English, the French, the Finns and probably the Germans. No, she had slipped past them; of that he was certain.

There were more than 150,000 refugees in Archangel now; how to find one damned woman?

And what in hell had happened to Dolrov?

Confirmation of Evans's status as an officer of the United States Army arrived at the American Mission on June 15. Colonel George E. Stewart, commanding the 339th Infantry Regiment, which, with the 310th Engineers and the 337th's Field Hospital and Ambulance companies, formed the American North Russian Expeditionary Force, walked across to the hospital and showed the cable to the doctor.

"I'll be damned." He read it through again. "It doesn't leave us any choice, does it?"

Colonel Stewart shook his head. "None. When can he leave?"

The doctors glanced at his chart. "It's touch and go whether he will even live. The cholera on top of the stab wounds will probably kill him, so I don't suppose a voyage to England will do any greater harm."

The colonel shrugged. "If he dies, it'll save the army a lot of trouble in the long run," he replied in a grim voice.

Evans was partially conscious when his stretcher was carried down the gangway and onto the quay at the Millwall Docks. A bright June sun shone, the first warmth he had felt in months. Nurses and orderlies swarmed about, and he was lifted and carried and put down again and again. Once he thought he heard someone say, "London." When he woke again, it was dark, and he knew he was aboard a train. The car swayed gently, and the wheels clicked in cadence.

In the third week of his convalescence at one of the last American military hospitals in England, his memory began to return. By then his strength was such that he was able to sit up for an hour or more a day, although the ordeal left him shaking with fatigue. He had been placed at one end of a long ward where huge windows turned the corner so that he had an excellent view in two directions across the sweep of green lawn to what a nurse told him were the Berkshire hills.

The first time the orderly helped him undress for a shower bath, he gasped at his reflection in the mirror. He looked like one of the dead men they had taken out of the Ekaterinburg prison—a gaunt skeleton covered with drumtight skin.

266

"Don't worry, sir," the orderly, a boy with young-old eyes who had served in the trenches as a corpsman said, "they all look like that after cholera. You'll put meat back on, don't worry."

They had shaved his head at some time, and the doctor commented on the scar that ran from his neck halfway up his skull. "Must have been a nasty gash. What happened?"

Evans shook his head. "I don't remember. I . . .." He frowned, and the doctor nodded and passed on.

Evans lay back on the pillow, struggling to remember. The images were hazy, just beyond reach. The ward was quiet, and outside rain slanted down and the lights reflected from the streaked windows. The heavy gray sky only accented the deep, velvet green lawns.

He remembered a hot day and the smell of water and cattails, a duck that had struggled for height. Something English, he thought. Where? Here in England . . . no, a . . . pistol. Peter Boyd's pistol. He remembered then, the hunting trip taken the third week after he arrived in Russia.

Thunder rumbled, and the lights flickered. Someone laughed nervously, and rain fell harder, hissing down so that the sound came clearly through the opened windows. A cool breeze swept through the ward, damp and delicious.

He remembered the little Russian doctor, Botkin. The man had died in . . . Ekaterinburg? Four women in a train compartment, a man of middle height with a carefully trimmed beard wearing old army pants . . . a body lying in the snow, and suddenly it all came back with a rush. The scream was torn from his throat. "Tatiana!"

Evans had to be strapped to the bed and sedated.

He was arrested on August 1. A young second lieutenant ignored the rows of wounded men as he and a squat sergeant wearing a military police armband and holstered pistol followed the sister down the aisle. She stopped by Evans's bed, glared at the officer and flounced away. Evans lowered the magazine he had been staring at for the past half hour without absorbing the slightest bit of information.

"Captain William Hughes Evans?" the lieutenant asked.

"I'm *Major* William Evans, Lieutenant. What can I do for you?"

The officer stared at him in confusion. "I'm sorry, sir, but it says here Captain. You are William Hughes Evans, ID number three-oh-six-nine-two-four?"

Evans nodded. "Yes, that's my serial number, but my rank is major."

"Your rank is captain," the officer said decisively, "and I must inform you that you are under arrest for murder, embezzlement and desertion."

That afternoon a tall man with a clipped mustache and Philadelphia Main Line accent came into the ward. "You must be Captain Evans. I'm Captain Thomas Ardoyle." He shook hands and drew up a chair.

"I am to be your defense counsel. Of course, you may select someone else if you prefer." He paused and, when Evans shook his head, continued. "I assume you were informed of the charges when you were arrested this morning."

Evans's mind still tended to confusion under pressure. "I was told only that I was under arrest for murder, embezzlement and desertion, not why or who or anything else."

Ardoyle sighed. "Sorry. Since the war ended, it has been simply impossible to get anything done properly. Hard enough even then." He withdrew a sheaf of papers from an expensive leather portfolio. "It's really quite simple, Captain. You were assigned as military attaché to the American Consulate, Odessa, in May 1918. From there you were reassigned to Sevastopol as military attaché to the Provisional Government of the Crimean National Front. Certain irregularities appeared in accounts of equipment given over to your charge, and a Major Peter Boyd was sent to investigate. The United States Army was informed on July third, 1918, by the government of General Fedor Orbelesky that vast amounts of that equipment had been sold on the black market and that you had murdered Major Boyd when he discovered that fact. You then disappeared."

Evans's astonishment was total. "Murdered . . . Peter?" He struggled to get himself under control. "That's a damned lie!"

"Are you saying that you did not murder Major Peter Boyd." It was a statement, not a question, as if Ardoyle did not care one way or the other.

Evans closed his eyes, trying to make sense of what he had just heard. What in the name of God was happening? Tatiana had disappeared, and now he was being accused of murder and desertion. He heard Captain Ardoyle's voice as if from a great distance, and for a moment he was caught up in swirling blackness. When he was able to open his eyes again, Ardoyle was standing against the windows, watching while the ward nurse bent over him with an anxious expression.

When the nurse was satisfied that he was all right, Ardoyle resumed his seat and by skillful questioning elicited the story from Evans, who spoke slowly, trying to force his sluggish mind to recall the sequence of confused events that had taken place two years before. He told Ardoyle everything that had led up to Peter Boyd's murder at Sevastopol, and the lawyer made occasional notes.

"Then you are certain that this Colonel Obrechev was the actual murderer? That he arranged to have Major Boyd murdered and then made it appear to you that he had accidentally been killed by a motor truck?"

268

Evans nodded. "Even to the extent of a coroner's inquest."

"But you have no witnesses or proof to that effect?"

"No."

Ardoyle hesitated. "In the report you made at the time you wrote that you saw Major Boyd's body in the morgue at Sevastopol. There was no mention of General Obrechev as the murderer or indeed that Major Boyd had died in any manner but accidentally."

"Yes . . ." The memory of his friend's badly battered body and the facial abrasions sickened him.

"There were signs that he had been killed by a motor truck?"

Confused, Evans looked at him. "I . . . he was my friend, a very close friend. I was distraught. . . ." And drunk, he thought. Very drunk.

"But you did see signs that he had been struck by a motor vehicle?"

Evans struggled to remember. "It seemed so. I think . . . there was gash on the side of his head . . . cuts. They kept his body covered with a sheet . . . I. No, damn it," he rasped, "I only found out later that Peter was murdered. I found his pistol . . ."

Ardoyle nodded. "Major Peter Boyd was shot to death with his own automatic pistol. The army has accused you of being his killer."

Evans stared at him in shock.

"Captain Evans, believe me when I say you are in very serious trouble. The army has constructed a strong case against you based on circumstantial evidence, but one which will be very difficult, if not impossible, to refute. It appears that only you can testify on your behalf. If you are found guilty, you will be given the death penalty. Even if the sentence is commuted, you will still spend the rest of your life in a military prison."

Evans could not believe what Ardoyle was telling him. So much had happened in between; it was all so distant, another world. . . .

"When Major Boyd's body was returned to the United States for burial, a confirming autopsy was performed because of the differences between your report and that of the Provisional Government. The autopsy showed that Major Boyd was killed by a single forty-five caliber bullet to the heart at close range. The bullet was recovered and compared to a bullet fired from a pistol found in your possession. The pistol belonged originally to Major Boyd, who purchased it from Whiteley's, in Westbourne Grove, London, May, 1914."

Suddenly Evans knew exactly why the pistol had held only six cartridges when he found it in Obrechev's valise. Obrechev had shot Pete with his own pistol, and the weapon had automatically cycled another round into the breech. Obrechev had kept the pistol not because of its value, but to plant on him. Evans began to laugh softly at the neatness of the entire concept. Not only could he be used to persuade the Czechs that they had been ordered by the Allies to cooperate with the Crimean National Front, but he remained in reserve as a scapegoat for the murder of Peter Boyd. Obrechev had calculated everything so beautifully—everything but Tatiana's possession of a small pistol, and that tiny miscalculation had killed him.

"It would hardly seem a laughing matter, Captain Evans."

Evans got himself under control again and tried to explain.

"Pete was killed so that he could not report that the Crimean National Front was selling American supplies to anyone who would pay, including the Germans. I got drunk. I was as valuable to Orbelesky drunk and stupid as sober and stupid. They convinced me that I had been ordered by the Allied Commission to persuade a Czech regiment to assist the Crimean National Front as the price of Allied support of their independence after the war.

"Obrechev and I spent weeks on trains chasing the Czechs, and during that time he made damned certain I had plenty to drink. He must have been planning to kill me after I persuaded the Czechs to cooperate and Ekaterinburg was taken. That way there would be no one left who knew the details of his little game. The pistol, which he would have slipped into my belongings, would have proved I murdered Pete. Very neat."

"But he obviously did not."

Evans looked at him, not understanding.

"Kill you, of course. Why?"

"I . . . I left Ekaterinburg without telling him."

"And where did you go after that? There are twenty-two months for which you will have to account."

Evans hesitated. The question that haunted him was whether or not Tatiana was still alive. He had agonized over ways he could find her and whether or not to ask the American Embassy in London for help. Twice he had been on the verge of doing so but both times had concluded that it could place her in even greater danger. He was almost certain she had not been stabbed. He seemed to recall her bending over him, and in the account of the attack listed on his medical record, there was no mention of a woman. If she had been killed or hurt, that fact would certainly have been included.

But what could he do? The civil war still raged, and the Bolsheviks appeared to be gaining the upper hand. The Americans had left at the end of July, and there were strong demands in Parliament that British forces be pulled out as well.

He decided to take another tack. "Look here, the fact that I sent a report to Odessa informing them of Pete's death and telling them in some detail about the German merchant ship I saw in the Balaklava harbor ought to prove that I did not kill him. I admitted to being duped, for God's sake."

Ardoyle studied him for a moment, then shook his head. "I have seen the report you sent to Odessa. It reports that Major Peter Boyd was killed in a motor accident but says nothing about the German merchant ship."

Somehow that news did not really surprise him. If Orbelesky and Obrechev were willing to murder Pete, why should they balk at tampering with telegraphed reports? Obrechev could easily have arranged access to his code books—for Christ's sake, he had done nothing more than lock them in his desk. Once again the crushing weight of his own stupidity came down on him, and Ardoyle had to repeat his question before he heard it.

"Where did you go after you left Ekaterinburg?"

He shook his head wearily. "I can't tell you that. I believed I was acting within the scope of my orders up to the time I left Ekaterinburg in late July. Those orders were transmitted to me from Odessa through General Orbelesky's headquarters. What I did after that is not important to the case."

"I believe I have to be the judge of that." Ardoyle was plainly annoyed. "For instance, each time you have been asked for your rank, you have given it as major. I can assure you that you are still a captain, but may I ask why?"

Evans shrugged without noticeable disappointment. "Obrechev again. He told me that I had been promoted to major."

"Why would he have done that?"

"To ensure my cooperation, I suppose. He was trying to make me think that I was being rewarded."

"When were you told of this promotion?"

"In August 1918—"

"August, was it? Two months after you disappeared from Sevastopol—disappeared as far as the United States Army is concerned. You told me a few moments ago that you left Ekaterinburg in July. Where did you go?"

Evans looked stubborn. "I can't tell you that."

Ardoyle sighed. "Look here. I can't very well defend you if you refuse to take me into your confidence, can I? I must know exactly what happened to you during that time. The Bolsheviks have taken control in the Crimea, and if this Colonel Obrechev is in their custody, it may be possible to obtain his testimony."

"If Obrechev had been alive when the Reds took over, he would not have lasted five minutes. The Bolsheviks shoot high-ranking White officers with a minimum of ceremony."

"You said *if* he had been alive, Captain Evans. Do you know for a certainty that this man Obrechev is dead?"

Evans was suddenly tired. His mind was tending to wander, and for an instant he lay again in the wet grass beside the railroad line as Obrechev hurried toward the fire. Nicholas stepped forward, one hand out, and Obrechev shot him . . . he heard Tatiana's pistol pop twice, and Obrechev lay on the ground with a bullet hole below his left eye. . . .

"Do you?"

He was wringing wet with perspiration, and he drew a shuddering breath. "I . . . I can't tell you, at least not now."

"Damn it, man," Ardoyle snarled, "you don't need someone to defend you. You want a bloody miracle worker!"

The ward nurse intervened then and chased Ardoyle out. The ordeal of the interview had so exhausted Evans that he vomited into the basin she held. His insides felt as if they had been wrenched about with a red-hot crowbar. The nurse arranged his pillows so that he could look out across the sweep of lawn to the Berkshire hills, and after a time he slept.

The following day his bed was screened off from the rest of the ward, and a military policeman took up residence in a chair placed against the windows.

For weeks Tatiana watched the dirty snow recede to reveal brown earth that one day flushed green and exploded with all manner of plants. The air softened, and the days grew intolerably long until the sun barely set at midnight.

Inside, the metal walls of the shed glistened with moisture, and the air was so hot and steamy it was difficult to breathe. Tatiana's back ached, and her hands were raw from the harsh soap and the rough surface of the washboard; but her tub faced a gap in the corrugated metal walls, and she at least had a constricted view of the muddy yard to occupy her mind.

The piles of laundry were endless. The thirty women in the shed worked twelve hours a day. All were paid the same rate—ten rubles a week. A quota was established at the beginning of each day, and those who did not meet it weren't hired the next. So far Tatiana had survived six weeks, but at the cost of near exhaustion.

The afternoon was coming to an end. She dared not straighten for fear her back would give out. The fierce ache had subsided to a numbness that penetrated as far as her thighs. Tatiana plucked the next shirt from the pile, pressed it into the cooling water and began to scrub it against the metal board.

Outside, a flower glowed a brilliant yellow in the strong sunlight. She watched it with an aching heart; there had been thousands of such flowers every spring at Tsarskoye Selo. The water boy tipped the steaming kettle into her tub, and she withdrew her hands for a moment, then plunged them in again, gritting her teeth against the pain.

All the months with Evans seemed like a half-forgotten dream. They had assumed an air of unreality that masked all but the pleasant times. She had never dared return to the American Mission, partly fearful of meeting the sergeant again but also because she knew that whoever had attacked Evans would be watching for her as well.

But it made little difference. Tatiana knew he was dead; there was no other way to account for the fact that he had never tried to find her. Every day for two months she had returned twice a day to the vicinity of the small church on the back street where he had asked her to marry him. It was the only place in all Archangel they had in common. She refused to entertain the thought that he had recovered and abandoned her. Only in those moments between his proposal of marriage and the attack had she understood how much of her depression was self-indulgent, a reaction to the treatment and imprisonment she had endured. She realized then and since how much he must have loved her to have endured the misery she had caused him. She knew finally that he loved her for herself and not as a surrogate for Olga. Then, an instant later, he was gone. As with everyone she had ever loved, as if all had lived only in a dream.

Reality was this job and an insect-infested cot in a warehouse for female refugees run by the French Red Cross. The cot was hers from 6:00 P.M. to 6:00 A.M. at seven rubles per week including one meal a day. When half the refugees in Archangel were starving, she had found work that paid sufficient to enable her to buy food and shelter.

With Evans's death, Tatiana had been forced onto her own resources. During the year and a half they were together, each had learned that in the final analysis one had only oneself to depend on. So she had determined to earn her passage out of Russia. She was the last of the Romanovs, and it was her duty to make the world understand what had happened to her family.

She stopped and wiped her streaming face with the next dirty shirt. Her hands were swollen, and the skin was raw and cracked. Her hair would be coarse, unwashed and uncombed; not even in the worst of her depressions, the absolute worst of her imprisonment, would she have looked as she did now. Tatiana sighed and touched the paper envelope tucked into her camisole. Only yesterday had she finally accumulated enough money to purchase the cheapest steerage ticket to Oslo. It had cost nearly three thousand rubles, every last kopeck of her money, including that from the sale of the horses and the two Mexican gold coins Bill had given her.

The bell rang, ending the twelve-hour shift. It was so hard . . . she stared at the pile, on the verge of tears. The superintendent stirred the dirty shirts with his shoe as if to emphasize that she had barely managed to meet her quota. She stumbled from the shed to gulp the cool evening air and, holding herself upright by sheer will power, trudged toward the refugee center on the river front two miles distant.

Sheremetiev stared at the Mexican gold coin. He had found three others in Archangel, and all had been traced to refugees who had been found to have no connection with the Romanov woman.

He turned the coin over and examined the embossed Mexican eagle: the same coin he had found in Nadezhdinski Zavod and in Ust-Usa, in the possession of the river boat captain.

Beside it lay a freshly drafted report to Dzerzhinsky and a request for additional help. It was the hardest document Sheremetiev had ever prepared. He lit a cigarette, wincing at the harsh taste against his raw mouth. What else could he do? There was no one he could depend on. Dolrov had not arrived, might never arrive. What the devil could possibly have happened to him? Sheremetiev added another paragraph describing how he had bribed an orderly in the American Mission hospital who produced the information that the American officer, William Hughes Evans, had been sent to England with cholera in addition to the knife wounds. The man hadn't any information about the woman, however.

Where in hell could she have gone? Too restless to sit still, Sheremetiev jumped up and went to the window. Gray rain slanted down on the nearly deserted street. Summer in Archangel! He snorted. Either pouring rain or baking sun. He could see nothing but docks and warehouses stretching along the river front. Battered tramp steamers and freighters rusty from long confinement during the war years were anchored all through the roadstead. As he watched, one inched its way against a wharf. He could even see the rain-slickered pilot standing on the bridge wing. The docks were piled with tattered canvas-lashed crates, acres of drums stacked on end and rows of cannon parked wheel to wheel. Millions of rubles' worth of supplies to fight a major war waiting to be taken down a single-line railroad track now rusting away to scrap.

At least he knew she had not escaped from Archangel. The coin had been sold only two days before, and the coin dealer had been persuaded by the breaking of two fingers to provide the name of the party he purchased it from—the manager of the Norwegian All-Cargo Shipping Company. Tonight he would interview the manager. One way or the other he would soon know from whom he had obtained the coin. Then it would be only a matter of waiting at the dock on the day the ship sailed.

Evans stared at the envelope addressed to him in his father's firm handwriting. Ardoyle watched impassively. The letter inside was much as he expected: a diatribe against his total lack of responsibility, his insistence upon throwing away every chance granted and a professed lack of understanding as to why he insisted upon embarrassing the family at every turn. The old man referred to "criminal activities" twice, meaning that he had accepted the army's charges without question. Only in the last paragraph did he briefly mention wounds and illness.

I am given to understand that your wounds, while serious, are healing without complication. Your mother, needless to say, is prostrate. We had accustomed ourselves to thinking of you as dead, and she had only recently begun to recover from that blow. Be that as it may, I strongly advise that you instruct the officer defending you to request a change of venue to the United States, on the grounds that you are severely ill and need constant medical attention. It should be obvious that a better defense of your activities can be managed from here.

Meaning that his father would be in a better position to pull strings and apply pressure. "I suppose he's written you?" Evans asked.

"As a matter of fact, yes. He offered to retain any additional legal representation I felt necessary. However, I fully agree with his proposal to shift the court-martial to the United States. I've already prepared the necessary documents." He removed a sheaf of papers from his portfolio and handed him a pen. "Oh, yes, your father also arranged to have his London bank send this down."

Evans opened the buff envelope. Inside was a sheaf of British bank notes.

"Two hundred pounds. I took the liberty of telling him that you were dependent entirely on your military pay, which had been stopped."

"I didn't know." Evans put the envelope on the table beside the bed. "Thank you. That was very thoughtful."

The day had grown quite warm, and the scent of summer eddied through the open windows. He could hear preparations for morning rounds being made. His guard was half-asleep in his chair.

"Look here, I've made some inquiries at the British Foreign Office and among some of our own people who were stationed in Odessa in 1918. They are all in agreement that this General Orbelesky was an opportunist of the first order."

"Was?"

Ardoyle nodded. "He's dead now. He and Admiral Kolchak had a falling-out. In any event, Kolchak's troops unexpectedly pulled back outside a town called Orenburg, exposing the Crimean National Front army's right flank. The Bolshevik forces took advantage, and Orbelesky was captured, along with his entire staff. They shot him the next day."

Evans laughed softly. "So they got the old bastard after all."

"Certainly no cause for rejoicing. The point is, Captain Evans, he can no longer be called as a witness in your trial."

Evans started to ask about Mathilda but stopped. He didn't give a damn what had happened to her. He was just beginning to comprehend the nature of the charges against him and the shape of the web in which she and her husband had enmeshed him, perhaps starting that night of Rasputin's supper in Petrograd.

"I suggest you sign these documents." Ardoyle offered his gold fountain pen and the change of venue papers.

Evans hesitated. "How soon before I would have to leave England?"

Ardoyle pursed his lips. "A week, perhaps less. Only the approval of the court president is required."

Evans handed back the pen and dropped the papers on the blanket. "I'll think about it."

The lawyer finally lost his temper. "Damn it, man, you are deliberately making this as difficult as possible. You have refused to cooperate with every suggestion I've made. You have withheld information vital to the conduct of any decent defense, and now you are refusing to accept my advice that the trial be moved to the United States. I would appreciate it very much if you would release me as your defense counsel. I will cable your father to that effect immediately."

Evans let his head sink back onto the pillows as exhaustion crept over him again. "All right." He nodded weakly and closed his eyes. He did not hear Ardoyle leave.

The military policeman went off duty at eight in the evening, when all ambulatory patients were required to return to their wards. Evans forced himself to stay awake until the nurse had made her midnight rounds and gone down to the canteen for a cup of tea. He slipped out of bed then and made his way to the wardrobe, where he rummaged through the racks until he found a uniform that fit, dressed quickly and went back to his own bed. He made certain that the screen was angled properly, stuffed his gown and robe under the blankets to simulate a sleeping form and carefully eased the window open.

The ward was on the ground floor, and Evans had no difficulty leaving the hospital. He stayed in the shadows as he made his way across the grounds. The night air was mild, and the moon was nearing full. The envelope of bank notes bulked comfortably inside his shirt, and he had until at least three o'clock, when the nurse made another round, before anyone would discover he was gone. Even then she might not check his bed closely. If so, he would not be missed until six o'clock wake-up.

A week before he had found a 1910 edition of *Baedeker's Handbook for Great Britain* in the library. Thumbing through it idly, he found a description of the nearby village of Uffington and, best of all, a mention of a railroad branch line and halt less than three and a half miles away. That night he had stayed awake to count three trains—at 9:35 P.M., 11:03 P.M. and 3:25 A.M. Each train whistled once as it passed, except for the last, which whistled twice, each sound separated by nearly two minutes. A milk train, he decided, picking up raw milk to take into London for processing and delivery, probably the same day.

Ardoyle's resignation, as well as Britain's Alien Registration Act soon to go into effect, had forced his hand. When his father heard about Ardoyle, he was certain to be moved immediately. The Alien Registration Act would require for the first time that all travelers to and from Great Britain have a passport and obtain a visa. In his present circumstances he hadn't a hope in hell of procuring either. In addition, there were rumors of the impending departure by British forces from northern Russia. All came together to make it imperative that he leave Britain immediately.

Within a mile he had to stop and rest, amazed at how weak he was in spite of all his walks around the hospital grounds. The moon poured a silvery sheen across the countryside as he labored to catch his breath. Ahead the road peaked and started down a long slope to the halt. Far across the valley he could see the bulk of White Horse Hill.

The slope made walking easier, but even though Evans stopped several times to rest, he was still on the verge of collapse when he reached the halt. The last dairyman's wagon had departed, and it was deserted. A dozen cans of milk stood on the platform, elevated to the level of a car door, and he sank down gratefully in the gorse along the track. His arms and legs felt like jelly, and his chest ached badly. The cholera had robbed his body of any reserves of strength, and his chest hurt where the knife had cut deep. He stared at his shaking hands, willing them to stop.

His watch showed just past three o'clock—twenty-five minutes to wait. The moon was full on White Horse Hill now, and he could see a vague outline near the summit. He tried to concentrate on the horse—*Baedeker's* claimed it had been carved by Alfred the Great to celebrate a victory over the Danes on those very slopes a thousand years before.

The train whistle woke him. Something brushed his face, and he stumbled up in panic and burst out of the gorse to see the train drawing away from the halt. Evans bolted for the platform and jumped as the last open car ran by. He landed painfully and lay gasping, his nostrils filled with the choking, oily smell of coal.

The goods train ran into the yards of the Great Western Railway in brilliant morning sunshine. Evans stood on the lowest rung between the cars and gauged his moment, head swimming with fatigue. The train entered a long curve, and a signal lamp slid by; other tracks snaked across the line, and the curve deepened. He swung out and released his hold but misjudged the speed and tripped.

He picked himself up. His uniform trousers were torn at the knees and filthy with coal dust. The day gave every promise of being exceptionally warm and he discarded the jacket, threw away the necktie and rolled up his sleeves. He picked his way through the trainyard, trying to remember the city's layout from his previous visits years before. He had never spent more than a few weeks in London at any one time, and most of his sightseeing had been from a cab window as he made the rounds of night clubs and theaters.

Evans crossed several back streets and trudged east along Waverley Road. He passed a number of men dressed much as he, in bits and pieces of uniform. Even though it was barely seven o'clock, many of them stood about the streets talking. Unemployed demobilized soldiers, he realized. The papers had been full of the unemployment problem and the growing civil unrest as the millions of young men released from military service waited to be reabsorbed by a nation recovering from war and the sudden cessation of wartime production.

Just as he reached Harrow Road, his legs gave out, and he sank down against the rough surface of a building grimy with coal smoke. His head was buzzing so badly that he thought he would be sick. The sun was hot, burning the crown of his head. He was terribly thirsty. An almost-forgotten need for alcohol coursed through him, and he staggered to his feet before he got hold of himself. Waves of darkness alternating with nausea swept through his body, and he closed his eyes, ready to abandon himself to unconsciousness.

The image of a mountain meadow, warm sun, a chuckling stream . . . Tatiana emerging naked and glowing from the icy water, laughing . . .

He opened his eyes. Two solemn children regarded him with curiosity. A boy, dressed in old clothing but neat for all that, held his sister's hand.

"Get . . . get me . . . a drink," he managed, but they ran off.

He leaned back against the building, mustering strength, then staggered into Harrow Road. He passed several shop fronts, all shuttered, before he saw a large house that had been converted to workers' flats. A faded red card in the window advertised rooms. He pushed aside the gate hanging from one hinge and forced himself to walk up the steps without staggering. A haggard young woman with a baby on her hip answered his knock. She barely looked at him, merely accepted the pound note he held out.

"Room's two shillin's a night. No visitors. Clean sheets is a tanner more." She fumbled the change from her dress.

He followed her up the three flights of stairs, half-strangled by the

278

thick odor of must, human bodies and airless rooms. She pushed open a door and left without another word. The room made only the smallest pretense to being clean. The cot was made up, but the blankets were filthy. The walls were water-stained, and names, cartoons and odd graffiti covered the ancient wallpaper. A half-empty pitcher of stale water stood on the window sill, and he gulped it down before collapsing onto the cot.

When Evans woke, twilight was filtering through the room and his head ached abominably. He was still quite weak; but the nausea had gone, and his hands no longer shook. He washed in the shedlike lavatory attached to the back of the house and obtained directions to a small café farther along Harrow Road, where he ate a huge meal of eggs, sausage and fried potatoes washed down with cup after cup of tea.

Afterward he did not return to the boardinghouse but walked along Harrow Road until he found a cheap clothing store, where he bought a leather jacket, two shirts, two pairs of pants, socks and underwear, sturdy workingman's boots and a canvas bag to carry them in. He asked the clerk for directions to a Turkish bath and there bathed away the last of the coal dust.

At the junction of Harrow and Cornwall roads he signaled a motor taxi and told the driver to take him to the Surrey Commercial Docks, a name he had picked out of a newspaper story dealing with reviving trade to the Scandinavian countries. As the taxi made its way through streets jammed with traffic, he counted the packet of bank notes. His resources totaled 196 pounds in notes plus 3 shillings, 5 pence in coins, the equivalent of nearly $1,000, if the old exchange rate of $4.80 to the pound still held. At least enough to get him to Archangel, by God.

The proclamation had been pasted to the wall during the day. Tatiana edged her way through the crowd to read it, made nervous by the angry shouts of disbelief and defiance. The small print was hard to read in the overcast twilight, and the press of people was so great that she was unable to get close. But she heard enough to understand. "The Provisional Government, to prevent the spread of unfounded rumors and demoralization, has forbidden all further emigration by Russian citizens." Stunned, Tatiana wandered the muddy streets, trying to cope with the news. It all had been for nothing! The endless hours in the laundry, her desperate plea to the Norwegian shipping line manager to accept the Mexican coins . . . The passage money, every last ruble she had been able to earn . . . gone. Tatiana groaned aloud.

They would never give back her money. Even so, she turned toward the docks, weeping openly.

The telephone jangled, and Sheremetiev sat bolt upright in bed, disoriented for a moment. The woman beside him muttered sleepily. A voice began to speak as soon as he picked up the receiver.

"We have found her. Dock fourteen, Norwegian All-Cargo Shipping Company."

Sheremetiev shouted with exultation. The woman sat up, her sleep-fogged face gaping at him as he kicked the sheets away and bolted from the bed.

"Wait, don't go! What's the matter?" she whined.

He cursed her while he dressed and hurried out into the white night. He tried to maintain an easy trot; but the rains had turned the roads to mud, and it was hard to see in the half-light.

He had been forced to modify his orders to kill immediately on detection. A woman, mistakenly identified, had been killed so brutally with a club that it had been almost impossible to identify her as the wrong person. Christ in heaven, if they would only send real agents from Moscow and not these dregs scraped up from former tsarist punishment battalions! Fools and killers! They were hardly better than the dockyard scum he had found in Archangel. The Cheka's lower echelons were full of them. Ruthlessness, Dzerzhinsky wanted—as if hatred were ever a measure of loyalty to the revolution or to anything but ignorance and stupidity.

Crowds had gathered along the approaches to the docks, and mounted soldiers patrolled with drawn sabers before the barricaded dock entrance. What in the name of God was going on? There were hundreds of people, and more arriving all the time. Slowly he pieced the story together. The Provisional Government had stupidly forbidden further emigration, and as a result, refugees had poured into the river front area, determined to get passage money or down payments refunded or to force their way onto ships in the river. Their mood was ugly, and he could see troops running into position behind the barricades. A sudden roar went up, and the crowd surged forward. The soldiers unslung their rifles. He didn't wait to see more; he already knew, through long experience, what would happen next. He heard the crack of rifle shots as he ran along the seemingly endless fence, looking for another way in.

For three hours Tatiana had been caught up in a line that snaked through narrow, trash-strewn alleys between weather-beaten warehouses, sick at the loss of her money. Abruptly the line surged clear of the alley where the day's heat was trapped, and Tatiana stumbled into fresher air and leaned against the wall for a moment.

She had never in her entire life given so much as a second thought to money or its importance. Before the revolution there had been no need, and after her father's abdication and arrest he had handled all money matters vis-à-vis the household until Ekaterinburg. The difficulty of earning and saving sufficient for her passage still amazed her. The pitiful amount she earned in the laundry barely sufficed to keep her alive and pay for the bed. Without the money and the gold coins Evans had given her, she would have been lost.

The line flowed into the muddy open area before the offices of the shipping company and instantly transformed itself into a mob. The sun appeared briefly as a flat orange disk sinking toward the horizon and cast a weird light that eliminated all dimensions. Between the buildings Tatiana could see the shipping that filled the Dvina River—so close, yet impossibly distant.

A heavyset man with a reddish beard whom she recognized as the one who had taken her gold coins stepped onto the shipping company porch and stood looking at them, hands on hips. As the crowd became aware of him, their shouts died to a tense silence. Two armed militiamen appeared beside him, and they glanced uneasily at each other. A militia officer in full uniform stepped out of the offices, paused to say something to someone inside, laughed and drew the door shut. He posed himself on the steps and glared at the crowd.

"I'll have no disturbances!" the officer roared. "The managing director of the company, Mr. Neilsen here, has consented to speak to you. Keep your mouths shut and listen!"

Neilsen grasped the railing with both hands. In heavily accented Russian he shouted, "The Norwegian All-Cargo Shipping Company will honor its passage tickets. I have nothing more to say."

Someone shouted from the crowd, "The government has forbidden Russian citizens to leave. Give us our money back!"

Neilsen shrugged. "That has nothing to do with me. All tickets will be honored."

"Give us our money back!" the crowd began to roar. Tatiana found herself screaming as well as she was pushed forward from behind. Sudden rifle shots cracked in the distance, and the mob went dead silent; a piece of broken pavement crashed onto the porch, and the militia officer flinched.

"Shoot!" he screamed, and pointed. "Shoot!" One of the militiamen, frightened out of his wits, reacted instinctively and fired twice into the center of the crowd. A woman near Tatiana clapped a hand to her face and screamed. Even more than the shots, the scream acted as a catalyst, and the crowd surged into motion in all directions. Tatiana saw a man with a revolver take careful aim and shoot a militiaman as he clawed at the door. More shots were fired, and the officer stumbled into Neilsen. They both went down as a rush of bodies poured onto the porch.

Tatiana was knocked to the ground; someone kicked her in the side, and a boot stamped her leg. She fought back, sobbing, kicking and thrusting herself through the mud. Legs swarmed about her. Something struck her face, and blood spurted from her nose. Another boot struck her side, and she collapsed. A pair of hands yanked her up, and a man's body pressed her against a wall.

The face turned, and she had the impression of a hawklike visage with a smear of blood across one cheek. They were buffeted by panic-stricken people; his right hand fumbled toward his pocket, but a fat woman knocked him away. The man cursed and struggled back toward her. As he strained for her, Tatiana saw his face clearly.

Sheremetiev!

She screamed and struck his hand away, and he disappeared into the mob. Shrieking with terror, Tatiana struggled against the flow of the crowd. A man fell, and she darted into his place, found an open space between two buildings and slipped into it. Smoke poured from the shipping company offices, and more shots were fired. She heard boat whistles and the high-pitched whoop of a British gunboat siren. Her torn blouse was soaked with blood from her nose, and the pain was so intense she was certain it was broken. The mob's howls echoed strangely as she slumped, exhausted, into the mud, unable to move any farther.

Sheremetiev!

The name sounded over and over in her mind. She remembered vividly the last time she had seen him, that night in the Perm railyard when, his face twisted with hatred, he had slapped her. . . . Tatiana shuddered. The dreams that had foretold the death of her daughter were suddenly alive, and she buried her face in her hands. The terror refused to leave her, and she felt drawn again to the marble corridor. For an endless time she struggled against herself.

The darkness was intense, and the pall of smoke pouring from burning buildings along the waterfront added to the confusion. Fire trucks raced past with bells and sirens. Columns of militiamen and soldiers were everywhere. No one paid the slightest attention to her, other than to order her to move on when she stopped to rest. The fitful rain kept the fires in check, and Tatiana was soaking wet when she reached the refugee center. She stumbled onto her cot, too exhausted to undress, and fell into a horror-ridden sleep.

Her clothing was still wet when the elderly woman next to her woke Tatiana at 5:00 A.M.

"Time to get up, dearie," she started, then sucked in her breath at the sight of Tatiana's clothing and face.

282

"My child," she whispered, eyes darting about to see if anyone was watching. "What happened to you? You mustn't go . . ."

Tatiana repressed a groan and sat up, holding tightly to her side. "It's all right, Auntie," she managed. "There . . . was a mob. I'm sore, that's all."

She took off her sodden clothing. An ugly yellowish green welt was visible beneath her breast where she had been kicked. Tatiana had only one pair of undergarments and, ignoring the old woman's protests, pulled her only other dress on over the ragged and still damp camisole and limped out to wash in the tub of water that stood in the yard.

When she returned, the old woman had heated their tea—birch tea—and toasted a slice of dark bread that was more sawdust than flour. Tatiana lay back on the cot to rest for a moment. The shivering began to pass, replaced by a sense of warmth and such a wonderful lassitude that she wished never to move again. She wanted only to drift silently in the darkness, warm and safe. She felt Alexandra wriggle at her breast, and beside her, Evans smiled at them both.

Sheremetiev stalked through the bodies, cursing under his breath. All about him others searched for relatives, friends, children, wives, husbands. He sank onto a pile of broken timbers to catch his breath. It was nearly noon, and he had been searching since the militia had dispersed the rioters shortly after it began to rain. He had been over the area twice, and she wasn't among the injured or dead; of that he was certain.

Sheremetiev smashed a fist against his thigh. He'd had her! Actually had his hands on her! He took a deep breath to bring his anger under control. So close, so damnably close. Another minute, less, she would have been dead. If he could have reached his clasp knife in time . . . The dead would number in the hundreds, he thought. One more would not have been noticed.

He saw one of his agents working through the scattered bodies, stopping now and again to lift a blanket or shawl or turn a body over. Sheremetiev gave him instructions to take the other four men from Moscow and search the hospitals. The man glanced uneasily at him.

"Influenza wards as well?"

"Every ward," Sheremetiev snarled. "Surgical theaters, childbirth wards and *influenza* wards. Do you understand?"

The man hesitated, as if about to argue, then nodded and trudged off. Sheremetiev stared after him. Influenza had reached epidemic proportions in Archangel. Thirty and forty people were dying every day. I don't give a damn, he thought. Let them all die for all I bloody well care.

XIII

The Dutch freighter made its way through the tangle of shipping jamming the Dvina River opposite the sprawl of Archangel. The sky was overcast and threatening rain. The smell of burned wood came clearly across the river, and smoke still rose from burned buildings. Evans stood at the railing, studying the scene. The mud flats on either side were gray, lifeless, and in the distance he could hear church bells. Figures appeared on the wharves and docks. Inland he caught an occasional glimpse of the city.

The Dutch steamer hooted, and the engines went astern with a shuddering jar. The ship seemed to hesitate, then began to pivot. Rain began to fall with a sibilant hiss, and Evans stepped back under the shelter of the bridge wing. The anchor let go with a roar of chain, and the engines shut down. The sudden cessation of vibration was unsettling.

The tedious voyage, first across the Channel to Rotterdam, then north to Kristianstad and Trondheim in Norway and finally, two weeks later, Archangel had given Evans time to regain a measure of strength. With little else to do, he had walked for hours each day around the decks and, as they approached the North Cape, even lent a hand to the crew. Sea air, exercise and plentiful food had gone some way to restoring his nerves, if not his health.

Evans had thought long and hard about how he might find one woman in a town that by all reports now contained almost 200,000 refugees, a task complicated by the fact that if Tatiana were still alive—and he refused to entertain any other possibility—she would be doing her best to remain anonymous.

In spite of the murder, desertion and embezzlement charges against him, there was only one place in all Archangel where he dared go for help. He was counting on the fact that with the departure of the American contingent of the Allied occupation force, there would be no army personnel at the American Mission. Then again, the idea that he might return to Archangel would, he hoped, be too ludicrous for serious consideration.

He waited, unattended, in the hallway. Through the glass partition he saw only a single male clerk industriously pounding a typewriter. The present consulate had been officers' quarters before the troops had left, and it still smelled faintly of sweat, gun oil and tobacco. There was only one American official in all Russia, in all the world, in whom he dared confide—DeWitt Clinton Poole. He had known Poole in school and served with him in Moscow in 1917. Their families were close friends as well. Poole was one of those who had "gambled" on him. Gambled and lost, Evans thought ruefully.

Poole stepped out of his office, looking exactly as Evans had last seen him in Moscow: slender, almost spare, with thinning hair and a celluloid collar. The electrical plant was not operating properly, and the light bulbs were reduced to an orange glow. He peered at Evans in the gloom, head cocked to one side, before he recognized him.

"By golly, it *is* Bill Evans!" Poole pumped his hand. "Come in, old man, come in." He led Evans into the sparsely furnished office and bustled around his desk. "Sit down. Sit down. Can I get you anything. Cigar? Drink?"

"I'll take the cigar, Witt, but not the drink." He sank into the chair, childishly grateful for Poole's profuse welcome. Poole selected two cigars, clipped the ends and passed one across to Evans. He lit both and sat back to examine Evans critically.

"You don't look good," he said.

"I feel terrible." Evans grinned. "You heard then?"

"I know the army is looking for you. Murder and desertion?"

Evans nodded. "Let's not forget embezzlement."

Poole chuckled at that. "With your family's money, I found that one the hardest to believe. You always were wild and irresponsible but . . ." He shook his head. "Of course, I don't believe any of it for a moment." He chewed on the cigar. "But I do admit to being rather curious about where you've been for the past two years. We made extensive inquiries at Sevastopol, but all the Orbelesky government would tell us was that you had killed the officer sent to investigate the shortages and disappeared."

Evans closed his eyes for a moment, fighting the exhaustion tugging at his brain. "It's a long story, Witt. I'm not guilty of any of the charges—well, technically guilty of desertion maybe. But there's more at stake than clearing myself with the army. I need your help."

Poole gave him a wry look. "Seems to me I've heard that before. Once from your father, now from you. You made a mess of things in Stockholm, Petrograd and Sevastopol. Your record is a disaster. Bill, you've had more choice plums than anyone I know. But your record—"

Evans interrupted. "Look, Witt, you could spend days bawling me out, and you'd be right every minute. Most of what's happened to me is my own damned fault. But not the crimes the army is charging me with."

Poole examined the end of his cigar. "You know, Bill, if I had any brains, I'd call a guard and place you under arrest."

"At least hear me out first."

Poole remained silent, so Evans began. "You didn't know Peter Boyd, but he was probably the best friend I ever had. He was murdered in Sevastopol, and I was blamed for it. I first met General Orbelesky and his wife, Mathilda, in 1916, in Petrograd at a party for Rasputin. . . ."

He spoke as concisely as possible, trying to eliminate any tinge of emotion, concentrating only on getting the facts across to Poole, a man considered by many to have one of the sharpest minds in the Consular Service. Poole smoked his cigar and watched him closely, asking few questions. The only time he showed any real excitement was when Evans described finding the royal family in the Perm railyard.

"I'll be damned, the tsar himself? Bill, you aren't stretching this a bit, are you?"

He listened with growing amazement as Evans told about the family's execution and his year and a half flight across the north of Russia to Archangel with the tsar's only surviving daughter, Tatiana.

"We hadn't been in Archangel two hours when we were attacked. How they knew we were here I don't know. I don't think they followed us after we left the village because it would have been easier to kill us in the taiga if they were that close behind. I thought at first the Whites were involved since the Archangel Provisional Government has strong ties to both Kolchak and Orbelesky, but I found out just before I left England that Orbelesky had been killed in April, a month before we reached Archangel."

His voice had grown hoarse, and he was so tired he was virtually limp. This was the first time he had told the entire story, and the process of narration had forced him to examine a good many "facts" that he had taken for granted—including much of his own behavior at the beginning. The result hardly made him feel proud. Poole went across to the liquor cabinet, and before Evans could stop him, he poured a tumblerful of clear liquid.

He studied Evans's face for a moment, then grinned. "Here, it's mineral water."

Evans drank gratefully and fell back into the chair, eyes half-closed. It was now raining hard, and the clock on Poole's desk showed five in the evening. He had been talking for nearly two hours.

"Witt, you are the only other person alive who knows about Tatiana. . . ."

"Obviously not," Poole pointed out. "Someone tried to kill you. Why? From the way you described yourselves, you were only two more poor woods runners. We have two possibilities—one they wanted the money you realized from selling the horses or two, those men you killed last spring really *were* Chekists. If so, Moscow knows about the grand duchess's survival."

Evans nodded thoughtfully. "But I can't understand why the Bolsheviks should still want to kill Tatiana. I should think they would prefer to insure her survival and blame the Whites."

Poole watched the rain for a few moments, fingers tapping on the desk. "No, Bill. This is a revolution in all ways. The side that executes the tsar and his family demonstrates a clear and undeniable break with the past—at least that's the way the Bolsheviks would see it. I would agree that General Orbelesky merely preferred a dead martyr to a live tsar because they are so much easier to control. But a surviving daughter is no threat to the Whites since the Bolsheviks have already accepted the blame. Even if General Orbelesky were still alive, I doubt if he, or any of the other White leaders, would care now what happened to her. They would only have to claim that Obrechev was a Bolshevik agent. I am quite certain her only danger is from the Bolsheviks.

"In addition, the Cheka is out of control. It's become a law unto itself—like the tsarist secret police during the 1880s. When Nicholas abdicated, he loosed the demons the autocracy had restrained since the days of Ivan the Terrible. God only knows what game Dzerzhinsky may be playing against his opposition in Moscow.

"But I'm afraid this all has little to do with you or the young lady, my friend. The United States government does not recognize the Soviet system, nor will it in the foreseeable future. At the same time the president has made it quite clear that members of the Russian ruling class will not be welcomed to the United States. You can be certain, daughter of the tsar or not, that the government will not extend itself one iota to assist your Tatiana. You told me yourself that you were never married, and so she cannot claim help on the basis of citizenship. If you find her, I would suggest that—"

Poole stopped. Evans had fallen asleep. My God, he thought, we are the same age, yet he looks twenty years older. He was painfully thin, and his face was lined, the skin thickened and weather-beaten. His hands were scarred, and the knuckles were enlarged from constant hard labor. He was a far cry from the foppish, good-looking dandy he had last seen in Moscow. What was the slang term these days? Sheiks? There wasn't a trace of sheik left in him. His appearance alone would have been enough to convince Poole. Still, he thought, if I had any brains at all, I'd cable Washington.

The room was dark and very crowded. Tatiana could sense bodies on either side and hear their moans of pain. For a long while she was sure she was in the laundry. The darkness puzzled her at first, and the air was so foul and heavy that it hurt her lungs. Waves of nausea assailed her, and twice she retched, rolling onto her side and drawing her knees against her stomach to ease the pain. She could bring up only strands of foul mucus, and there was no water or cloth to wipe her mouth. The worn blanket that covered her was filthy, and she was naked beneath it. Was she in prison?

Tatiana drifted, sometimes awake, sometimes asleep, always enduring. The light came and went without pattern. Always there was pain and fearsome dreams that terrified her. They were endless and full of ghastly images and tortures, hazy one moment, startlingly vivid the next. She woke once as someone fed her broth, which she promptly vomited. Someone wiped her lips, and someone gave her water to rinse her mouth. Another voice demanded her name, angrily, stridently, and frightened, she gave it without opening her eyes. The voice laughed as if at a joke, and she drifted away.

She had no idea how long she had been in the ward. The wall had windows every few feet, but they were so high that she could see only the top of an old building and a section of sky, alternately blue or overcast. Her mind was clear, but everything that had gone before was hidden behind a kind of mist. She was so weak she could barely move. After a while, when an old woman pushing a trolley paused by her cot, Tatiana managed a smile.

"Ah, Daughter, you are recovering!" the old woman exclaimed. "How lucky you are." Tatiana was too weak to answer, and the old woman took a bowl from the trolley, slipped an arm behind her head and spooned lukewarm soup into her mouth. The taste was delicious.

"Drink all you can, my girl. You need your strength. So many have died." She clucked and shook her head. "Oh, so many. It is God's judgment on Mother Russia for our wickedness."

Tatiana slept as much as possible, hoarding her strength and cursing her body. She learned from the old woman, who came twice a day, that she was in Saint Stephen's Infirmary. She also heard from her all kinds of rumors which a nurse occasionally would find time to confirm, correct or supplement. The White Finns were threatening from the west, and the Bolsheviks were pressing hard on the railroad front, pushing ever closer to Archangel.

Nine days after regaining consciousness, Tatiana was able to leave her bed for the first time and walk slowly between the rows of cots. On the tenth day the nurse told her she would have to leave the following day because her bed was urgently needed for new influenza cases that were now being placed in the corridors and even in the courtyard under canvas shelters. Tatiana knew the death rate was appalling.

That night the rumor shot from bed to bed the length of the ward. British soldiers were withdrawing from Archangel in two days. Tatiana drew the evil-smelling blanket over her head and begged to die. For the first time since Ekaterinburg she thought of suicide. As soon as the British soldiers left, the Bolsheviks would appear with their lists and laws, and the arrests and interrogations, imprisonments and beatings and executions would begin. Sheremetiev was already in Archangel— or had she only dreamed that? Reality had become such a fragile concept for her.

She could never endure imprisonment again. Yet it was inescapable. Hadn't *they* murdered her family on the steppe? Hadn't *they* found her in the depths of the northern forests and murdered her daughter? Hadn't *they* followed her to Archangel and murdered Bill? Hadn't Commissar Sheremetiev himself tried to murder her? Her stomach revolted, and for a moment she thought she would vomit at the prospect of his hands on her.

She was alone, sick, without resources, with nowhere to go and with no possibility of escape. She was a condemned prisoner awaiting execution, and it was more than she could endure.

Sheremetiev glared at the tired nurse. "I don't care about your rules. I want to see if my wife is here!"

"I can understand your concern," the nurse told him with professional patience, "but we cannot allow anyone but our own medical staff into the influenza wards. If you will just give me her name, I'll check the list. . . ."

"But she was unconscious when taken away," he raged. "How would you possibly have her name?"

The nurse surreptitiously pressed an electric button beneath the makeshift counter. "Sir, we have only three women in the entire ward without names. If you will tell me her name, I will check the list. If it does not appear, I will check her description. Only then"—she breathed a sigh of relief as two militiamen appeared in the hallway—"would a doctor consider allowing you inside the ward. Surely you are aware that influenza is now killing more than a hundred people every day. . . ."

Sheremetiev knew he was going about this the wrong way, but he could not control himself. He thrust his face into hers. "I do not give a damn—" The two militiamen yanked him back and braced him against the wall.

"Easy, Comrade, easy." One of them smiled pacifically. "This is a hospital. They'll help you here. No need to get upset."

Sheremetiev saw who they were, and the surprise sobered him. "All right." He nodded, then appealed to the militiamen. "My wife was taken away while I was at work. I don't know where she went or what's happened to her."

"Well, Comrade, it doesn't pay to get angry. Now about your wife, you just answer the questions and we'll have a look at the list."

Sheremetiev cursed inwardly. "All right, yes," he mumbled. He had to get out of here. "I'll . . . her name is Maria Antipova Galitina." He used the first name that came to mind and was shocked that the thought of his long-dead lover still had the power to affect him so.

The nurse nodded, anxious now to help, and ran her finger down the closely written list, shaking her head with obvious disappointment. "No, I'm afraid her name is not here. Describe her, please."

Still confused by his reaction to memories of Maria, he stuttered, "She's about twenty-three, quite pretty with dark chestnut hair, blue eyes and pale skin. She weighs . . . about . . . as much as you, Nurse, and is about your height."

The nurse shook her head. "I'm sorry, the three women who haven't been identified are middle-aged." Her long white skirts swished as she turned to the next person, and when Sheremetiev started to object, the militiamen nudged him out of line.

He stumbled once and put a hand against the wall. Just before the door, he turned. Both men were still watching. He held out a hand as if seeking help. "Where . . . I've been looking for two days."

The older, more sympathetic, conscious of his own fears for his family, asked, "Have you tried Saint Stephen's? They made the church into a clinic."

Sheremetiev nodded as if in gratitude and went out into the rain. Dredging up vast reserves of self-control, he viciously suppressed any further thoughts of Maria. Smoldering anger replaced self-pity, and he hurried down to the street.

All those who had been in the mission the day Evans was stabbed had long since departed, and so he had no idea if Tatiana had been killed, kidnapped to be murdered later or managed to disappear on her own. Of the three possibilities, he admitted only the last. The one thing Evans knew for certain was that she had not accompanied the ambulance that night; otherwise, she would have been able to tell them who she was. If that had been the case, Poole, as the ranking American diplomatic official in Russia since the closing of the Moscow embassy and the Vologda mission, would have known.

Evans's first task then was to wade through the visa and other aid applications for any hint of Tatiana. The task was complicated by the fact that he had not the faintest idea what her handwriting looked like or what name she might be using. At the same time Poole initiated requests to the British and French and the few remaining neutral consular missions for any information regarding a young woman of her description, but reduced staffs and overwork made it unlikely that anything would be turned up in the time remaining to them.

Evans haunted every refugee agency in the city, poring over what meager files they could or would make available, questioning staff members and turning aside all suggestions that he enlist the help of the Provisional Government. It had allied itself with the Kolchak regime in Omsk, which had inherited the remains of the Orbelesky government, and he could not bring himself to approach it despite Poole's belief in its disinterest.

In between, he stalked the streets, peering into the face of every young woman he passed. His desperation increased, and the few hours' sleep he allowed himself were haunted by dreams in which he found Tatiana's grave.

Tatiana ran from the infirmary and fled, terrified, into the anonymous safety of the crowds. Within a single block she was ready to collapse, but fear drove her on. When the nurse had come to examine her at noon, she had addressed her by her full and correct name, Tatiana Nikolaevna Romanova, and not the one she had been using all these months.

Crowds of refugees milled aimlessly in the streets, buffeting and jostling. Tatiana struggled through the press, further exhausting herself until she all but collapsed into a doorway, where she fought silently to restrain her sobs.

How could she have been so stupid as to give her real name? Tatiana huddled into herself, crushed by frustration, fear and exhaustion. There was nothing more she could do. Nothing. Nowhere to go. Every avenue was exhausted, and she hadn't the strength to continue. Even the refugee center seemed too far away to offer protection.

"Hey, you." A hand shook her shoulder roughly, and Tatiana woke with a start.

"Not so bad." The speaker was a youngish man with long hair and stylish, if unwashed, clothes. "You hungry?"

Not knowing what to expect, Tatiana nodded hesitantly, and the man squatted down. He exuded a smell of cheap perfume and sweat, and his greasy face was pocked with blackheads.

"Well, I can take care of that. I can make sure you get all you want to eat, anytime. Your own room, nice bed, some decent clothes." He fingered the material of her thin dress, then rested his hand on her knee with easy familiarity. "All you have to do is be nice to me and some of my friends."

"Be nice? How?"

The man laughed, showing very bad teeth. "You must be straight off the farm, darling. When I say 'be nice,' I mean just that. Spread your legs; do whatever makes them happy. The real trick is to groan a lot, make them think—"

Tatiana exclaimed in disgust and started to get up, but the man grabbed her arm. "Hey, now . . ." She slapped him as hard as she could with her free hand, and he lost his balance. She darted away, expecting him to follow, but when she paused at a safe distance to look back, he was sitting in the street, laughing. He waved, and she ran to the next corner.

Tatiana leaned against a wall as her strength ebbed away. At the end of the narrow street she could see the Dvina, gray and choppy now that the sun had disappeared behind heavy clouds. She was near physical and mental collapse, confused, all her will to continue living gone. She had no money, nowhere to go and no one to turn to. A chill wind blew dust along the street, and with no hope, she walked slowly toward the river.

The man from Moscow watched Sheremetiev. He still recalled the sick despair with which he had received the summons to a late-night interview at the Lubyanka. But instead of a beating or summary execution, he had been escorted to the office of the legendary Felix Edmundovich Dzerzhinsky. The director had been cordial enough, even offered him a cup of tea and a chair.

"Comrade Lusenov, I want you to report to me directly concerning the state of health and mind of Comrade Sheremetiev, who will be your superior in Archangel."

Lusenov had nodded, not trusting himself to speak.

"I believe that Comrade Sheremetiev has been working far too hard," Dzerzhinsky mused. "Perhaps it is time he was given easier duties." Even now the phrase shot a current of fear through him. *Easier duties* was often synonymous with *execution for failure.*

But of course, Dzerzhinsky was correct. Sheremetiev had become obsessed with this task of finding this one woman, the last surviving child of bloody Nicholas. Dzerzhinsky had admitted frankly that he was concerned that Sheremetiev might have turned it into a personal vendetta.

"There is no room in the Cheka," the director had pronounced in a cold voice, "for personal feelings and vendettas. We must purge any such bourgeois tendencies, especially on the part of former tsarist officers."

"She was in that hospital, under her real name, and you bastards passed her by!" Sheremetiev raged like a madman. Lusenov sensed that he was barely in control of himself. It would not take much for him to tip over the edge, and Lusenov surreptitiously wrapped his hand around the butt of the pistol in his coat pocket.

"Now, when I check myself, I find she has slipped away again! You goddamned useless fools!"

Sheremetiev struggled to bring himself under control. He was so angry that he was shaking. Three times now he had been within a handbreadth, and three times she had escaped because of the incompetency of this miserable scum with whom he was forced to work.

Lusenov was on the verge of telling Sheremetiev that it was he himself who had first checked that infirmary and missed the woman, but he wisely decided to remain silent.

Sheremetiev stared at the Chekists before him. "Understand this. If you fail once again, I will have all of you shot for dereliction of duty. Now go back to that hospital, and find out where she went. Get out!"

After they had gone, he lit a cigarette with hands that shook so badly the match went out. The smoke helped calm him, and he leaned back in the battered chair, trying to think. He had been over and over it so often. What did a woman, alone and knowing she was being hunted, do to earn a living in a city of refugees? Constant checks through secret party members in banks and coin shops had yielded no hint of further coin sales. Was that really she at the docks that night? Of course, damn it! She didn't seem injured then . . . if only he had been able to reach his knife, it would have been finished then and there. Now if this sneaky bastard Lusenov was correct . . . or . . . Sheremetiev knew that sooner or later Dzerzhinsky would send someone to spy on him. Lusenov, with his weasely manner, seemed a natural candidate. Was the woman in the hospital really *the* Tatiana Nikolaevna Romanova? Tatiana was a common enough name, and there was always a rash of copycat christenings whenever the royal family had a child. Even so, the use of the full name was too great a coincidence. But to give her full name? That was foolish in the extreme.

Sheremetiev took a deep breath, struggling to think clearly. With a pencil he marked the location of the makeshift hospital on the city map, noting its nearness to those shipping company buildings and warehouses burned in the rioting. It was also within a half mile of where the four scum he had first hired had attacked her and the American in May.

Concentrate on the hospital and the docks where she had actually been seen, he told himself. If she wanted to escape, wanted to leave Russia, there was only one way—by ship. To find a ship would have been very difficult, and she would have had to live within walking distance of the docks, specifically the Norwegian shipping company.

Sheremetiev groaned suddenly. Of course! How could he have been so stupid! She had to live near . . . He drew a quick pencil line inland along Troitsky Boulevard, marking the edge of the refugee settlements, then extended the line to the river parallel to both infirmary and shipping company. The area so demarcated formed a rough rectangle of less than two square miles and included mostly run-down buildings and ancient warehouses. It also held the heaviest concentration of refugees. But there was a way to narrow the search even further, he thought. With red ink, he marked the location of every refugee center and hospital or clinic that lay within the rectangle; then he marked with an X every one of the centers that accepted only women.

He stared at the result. Clinics, hospitals and refugee centers for women all grouped into a unequal triangle. Almost in the center of that triangle was Saint Stephen's Infirmary. He shouted with fierce joy. Somewhere inside that triangle he knew he would find her.

It was DeWitt Poole who, when Evans told him he thought Tatiana would be trying desperately to earn sufficient money for passage out of Archangel, suggested he concentrate his efforts in two areas: the docks near the shipping company headquarters and the refugee centers nearby. Evans had wanted to search among the shops and banks, certain that Tatiana would have tried to sell the gold coins, but Poole quickly convinced him that he would be wasting his time.

For two weeks Evans plodded from shipping company to shipping company, questioning anyone who would speak to him. After hours he made the rounds of the refugee centers, begging to see records, personal effects left behind, anything that might provide a clue. By September 27 he was starting on the third round of both. He slept little and ate less. Poole watched him with mounting concern, knowing he was operating on will power alone. But there was nothing he could do to help other than to offer suggestions. His office staff had been reduced to the two marines who served as guards, clerk and general handymen. Tomorrow General William Edmund Ironside, the British commander of the expeditionary force, would order the last ship upriver.

"Bill, the British pull out on September twenty-ninth, that's the day after tomorrow," Poole reminded him. "I've just been notified to close the consulate and leave with them. I've also been instructed to bring all Americans with me. The Bolos will be in the city before the last British ship rounds the first bend in the river. Everyone expects a bloodbath, and I don't doubt it will happen. The Bolsheviks are nothing if not consistent. So you'll have to leave as well."

Evans's laugh was cynical. "Witt, I'm not leaving Archangel without Tania. If I go back, the army will hang me. If I stay, the Bolsheviks may hang me, but before they do, I'll find her, and we'll try to get through to Finland. We survived two winters; we can make it through a third."

Poole knew it was useless to argue; Evans's reasoning was irrefutable. Even with all considerations of Tatiana set aside, there was no way that Evans could ever prove he had not killed Peter Boyd, and the army's case, based solely on circumstantial evidence, seemed strong enough to earn him at least a ninety-nine-year sentence in a military prison. It would be kinder if they executed him.

Evans was thinking that while his position made sense in a twisted way, he was running very low on resources, courage and health. He had left, after two weeks in Archangel, only 20 pounds sterling. Even though each pound was worth a hundred times the official prewar rate of 5.75 rubles on the black market, outrageous inflation had rendered even that nearly valueless. Without Poole's generosity in allowing him to live and eat at the American Mission, he would not have lasted two days. He had no idea what he would do after the consulate closed.

Evans was also conscious that Poole was again jeopardizing his career by helping him, and the knowledge was agonizing. God alone knew how much damage he already had done to the man's career.

That afternoon Evans pushed into still another refugee center for women, his fourth of the day. The place seemed vaguely familiar, and he leaned against the wall to catch his breath and consult his smudged list. Saint Stephen's; he had first visited here two weeks before.

It looked like a Dickensian workhouse: Women of all ages and descriptions were gathered in the dingy reception area, some aged, some very young, some with the helpless air of the newly widowed. Many had children who clung with desperate strength to their skirts. The women were uniformly pale and gaunt, with shadowed, deep-set eyes. They reminded him uncomfortably of the Belgian refugee women he had seen in magazine photographs at the beginning of the war.

The woman at the desk wore a French Red Cross uniform and looked almost as worn-out as her charges. She was not the same woman who had been there on his previous visit. After listening to his story, she shrugged and gestured hopelessly. "Look about you. How am I to remember one specific woman? There are more than four hundred now living here. We have room for only seventy-five."

"But aren't there any records I could see?" he persisted, knowing the probable answer. The aide started to shrug again, but something about Evans's obvious exhaustion and poor health must have touched her.

She led him along the hall to a tiny cubicle. An iron door stood half-open, and inside the dank cell a single barred window admitted a bit of light.

She waved an arm toward the stacks of cardboard cartons. "Until a month ago we attempted to maintain records. Perhaps your wife is listed here. Perhaps not." She shrugged again. "But you must hurry. The records will be burned soon. We do not wish them to fall into the hands of the Bolsheviks, you understand."

Evans did, and he mumbled his thanks. He pulled the first box to the window and began to withdraw files by the handful. They had been kept by weeks, which was a blessing. Three times before, he had been given access to files, and in only one case was there an attempt to put them in order. But here each week was contained in single manila folder. He immediately discarded all files predating their arrival at the end of May, but even as early as that the files were showing signs of disarray. He went through the lists slowly racking his brain to guess at the name Tatiana might be using.

He almost passed right over it. With a shout he grabbed up the folder he had just discarded and dragged out the list. Near the end of the third page one name jumped out at him—Lili Dehn!

The Red Cross aide smiled when he showed her the file. "See here, she occupied bed number forty-three in the first ward." She tapped a bell and sent a young girl hurrying away to check. Evans paced nervously, light-headed with expectation, hands shaking so badly that he had to jam them into his pockets. The girl returned with the wardess, who had refused to help him before. She was a large, rawboned French woman, singularly unattractive, and she stared at Evans with the hostility he recalled from his first visit.

"The client, Lili Dehn, is no longer here."

Evans absorbed the shock. It had been too much to hope for after all. . . . "Please, tell me what you can remember. What did she look like?"

The aide spoke in French, too quickly for Evans to catch, and the wardess nodded reluctantly.

"She had light brownish hair, a chestnut color. She was about my height. Very thin. Very pale." She stopped as if finished, then added, almost reluctantly, "A refined lady, I thought."

"When did she come here? Do you know where she went or what happened to her?" He asked the last question with trepidation, dreading the answer.

"She came in June, I believe. A week ago, perhaps two, she was taken with influenza to the infirmary in Ulitsky Street. It is called Saint Stephen's."

Evans kissed the astonished aide and dashed out. There were no cabs in this district or in all the city, for that matter. Gasoline was unobtainable, and horses were too valuable as food. Ulitsky Street was nearly a mile away, and he half ran, half walked the entire distance.

Lili Dehn! He was certain now. Tatiana and Lili had been very good friends, but Lili had left Russia in 1918, after her release from the Peter and Paul Fortress. Tatiana had once told him she had received letters from her in Tobolsk. And it was Lili who had given her the pistol with which she had killed Obrechev. It began to rain hard, and the streets emptied as people sought shelter.

"There was another gentleman here, not more than two hours ago, inquiring for a young woman," the French Red Cross aide said. This man was much older than the other and not nearly as nice-looking, but he did seem concerned.

Caught by surprise, Sheremetiev snapped, "Describe him," then added, "if you please."

The aide tossed her head resentfully at his tone. "He was quite tall, pale and thin, as if he had been sick. An American, I believe. But he asked after another woman, a different name."

Because she was French, Sheremetiev had taken a chance and asked for Tatiana Nikolaevna Romanova. As expected, the name meant nothing to her. An American? he thought in surprise. Christ in heaven, it couldn't be . . . where could he have come from? According to the orderly at the American Mission hospital, the man had been dying in June, when they put him aboard the hospital ship. Had the bastard lied? Sheremetiev wasted no more time on speculation. If the woman were dead, no one would believe whatever story he chose to tell. Close questioning at the infirmary had yielded no clues other than a name and description. Even so, it was starting point—there were four refugee centers within one mile that admitted only females, and this was the third.

"Ah, my friend Evans." He smiled, thinking furiously. "I wasn't sure he would have gotten this far. You see, we have divided up a list."

"I understand."

Sheremetiev hesitated, but the woman was obviously not going to volunteer information. What name? he screamed silently, then forced himself to remain calm. It did not matter yet. He knew the woman was in Archangel, and now the American had arrived to assist him. He restrained a smile at the thought. He could double his chances of success by finding and following the man while continuing to search for the woman. If that didn't work, they could always come back and force the false name from her.

"Do you know where he went from here?" Sheremetiev asked, switching the subject to allay her suspicions.

The aide gave him a slight smile. "He did not say, but I would suspect he has gone to Saint Stephen's Infirmary on Ulitsky . . ."

Sheremetiev did not wait to hear more.

The thunderstorm burst over the city while he was inside Saint Stephen's Infirmary. Evans stood under the shelter of the portico as pale sheets of lightning flickered and rain fell in torrents. He hugged the thought to himself. It had to be she. If she were as sick with influenza as they said she was, she might well have been delirious when they asked for her name. He could hardly contain himself. There was no Lili Dehn listed in their records, only a Tatiana Nikolaevna Romanova. It was she! Damn it, it had to be! And she was alive. So alive that she had left the infirmary only an hour before!

He huddled against the stone pillar, elated, exhaustion forgotten. Where would she have gone? Back to the refugee center? Of course! She would go there for her things . . . but had he passed her? Unmindful of the rain, he dashed down the steps.

Sheremetiev came to a conclusion only slightly at odds with Evans's as he studied the street in front of the refugee center, empty now in the pelting rain. She had left the infirmary but had not yet returned here. Why? Because she had taken shelter from the rain, that's why. He laughed aloud. They had her now, damn it. He made his decision quickly and gave Lusenov instructions to wait in case he missed her in the streets.

"Do not take the slightest chance," he warned. "As soon as you see her, kill her. There must be no mistakes this time." Sheremetiev did not wait to answer Lusenov's anxious questions but motioned a second man to follow and hurried into the rain, intending to scour every inch of the route between the center and the infirmary.

Ten minutes later Evans scrambled up the steps of the refugee center and burst into the lobby. The Red Cross aide looked up in astonishment as he raced toward her.

"Did she come back?" he demanded between gasps.

The young woman jumped up and helped him to a bench against

the wall. Evans was deathly pale and breathing hard. She pressed a hand against his forehead and found the skin hot and dry.

"Did she?" he demanded, struggling to get to his feet.

She pushed him back. "Who? The woman for whom you are searching? No, at least not since you have—"

"The infirmary said she left no more than an hour ago. They don't know where she went. I thought she might have come—" He broke into a harsh fit of coughing, and the aide stared at him in distress.

"Calm yourself, monsieur. You will become ill yourself with the influenza. You are soaking wet. You must get into dry clothes and drink something warm, or you will surely become sick. And in your condition—"

He brushed her admonition aside. "Look." He grabbed her hands and stared directly into her eyes, appealing for help. "If she comes here, will you give her a message, please?"

"But of course, monsieur . . ."

"Tell her Bill is searching for her. Bill. She'll understand. Tell her to go to the American Mission. Do you know where it is?"

"Yes, of course. Bill, that is your name, and she is to go to the American Mission."

"Yes, at once."

"Are you staying there, monsieur? At the mission?"

"Yes. Tell her, please." He started for the door.

"But wait, Monsieur Evans. There is no need to hurry. Your friend, the Russian gentleman, has caught up to you. He has gone to Saint Stephen's, I am sure—" She stopped at his stricken expression. "What. . . ?"

"A Russian! Did he give his name? Anything?"

"No, monsieur. He said only that he was your friend and that you had divided a list."

"What did he look like?" Evans demanded.

"A big man, older than you . . . perhaps forty, no more. He had a thin face and was—"

"Look," Evans broke in, "there isn't time to explain. Whoever that man is, he wants to harm her. He is a Chekist, a Bolshevik secret policeman. Please, if she comes back, hide her until I return. Will you do that?"

"But, monsieur, there are no Bolsheviks in . . . Yes, monsieur," she agreed, swayed by the look of desperation in his face.

He grabbed a pencil and wrote a quick explanatory note to DeWitt Poole, which he pushed into her hand with a ten-ruble note. "Please find someone to take this note to the American Mission. Please."

The Red Cross aide nodded, frightened but calm. "Yes, Monsieur Evans. I will do it. You may depend on me."

Outside he paused again. It was raining harder than ever. She had to be somewhere between the infirmary and the refugee center. He dashed down the steps and hurried into the road. Certainly in this rain she would take shelter.

Tatiana stood on the edge of the wharf fascinated by the swirling river current. Rain hissed against the water, but she was oblivious of it and the British soldiers huddling near a warehouse, watching her with bored curiosity. A chill wind whipped her sodden skirt, and one of the soldiers hooted.

The gray anonymity of the river was spellbinding, inviting, promising only a moment of pain and then extinction. The urge was irresistible. Her body seemed to move of its own accord toward the splintered, unfenced edge. A shudder racked her, and something tried to draw her back—a voice from her childhood warning against mortal sin. But what else was there for her to do?

She had been taught that to take your own life meant you would burn in hell for all eternity. But how could there be a God? How could a God who professed to love all mankind allow the kind of hell in which she had lived these two past years? What kind of God would allow her family to be brutalized and murdered, her own daughter, Bill . . . ? Still, she hesitated, years of religious training erecting a solid barrier between her and the river.

"Is there anything wrong, madam?"

The voice startled Tatiana. She gasped and nearly toppled from the wharf; but a hand shot out to steady her, and a British soldier drew her back from the edge.

"I was afraid you might fall in," he said tactfully. His Russian was heavily accented and faltering.

"I . . . I was only watching the river."

The soldier nodded sympathetically, understanding. "Of course you were. But you could catch your death in this rain. Haven't you a home to go to?"

Tatiana started to shake her head, then changed her mind and nodded. She gave the soldier a distracted smile and drew away from him. He made no move to restrain her; but an expression of intense sympathy which she could not bear to see passed over his face, and abruptly Tatiana ran toward the street. The moment had passed, and she knew it would not come again.

A doorway provided a measure of shelter from the slackening rain, and she pressed into it, totally astonished at the surge of energy and anticipation that went through her. She remembered then an officer in the *Konvoy,* her father's personal guard, telling a story about his service in the Japanese war. He had once been so close to death that he began his prayers while waiting for the stroke of a Japanese bayonet.

For some reason the enemy soldiers did not see him, and he escaped a few minutes later. Tatiana was struck at the time by the way he described his feelings afterward—how he had been suffused with life, energy and happiness, so grateful to be alive that he had cried unashamedly. She understood those feelings now; she had faced herself in those moments before the soldier took her arm, and she knew that she was strong enough to live on her own. Hadn't she and Bill crossed two thousand miles of Russian wilderness to reach Archangel? Surely, she herself could travel the three hundred or so more miles to the Finnish frontier.

The rain had thinned to a drizzle, and Tatiana retied her scarf. She would, she decided, return to the refugee center. She might still find some of her belongings.

"Sorry, mate." The British sergeant shook his head. "Ain't seen no one like that. But then there's hundreds of women wandering about. Me lads'd only be likely to notice a real dolly, so to speak." He squinted at the tall American.

"But . . ." He shouted to four soldiers inside the guardhouse, and they clumped out, handling their Enfields with the relaxed precision of professional soldiers. The men were wet and sweating under rain slickers and heavy wool kits but good-natured enough for all that —the imminence of their departure for home, Evans thought, and a surge of apprehension ran through him. Tomorrow.

"This 'ere gent's an American. Looking for 'is wife, a Russian lass. Could you describe 'er again, Mr. Evans?"

Evans did so, adding that she had just recovered from influenza and would very likely be quite pale and weak. The tommies exchanged shrugs, and Evans nodded his thanks and turned away. Where in hell was she? he muttered to himself. Where the devil was the Russian—

"Er, Sergeant, ah, Mr. Evans, sir. You say she was slight wi' blondish hair?"

Evans looked at a very young soldier in a uniform that seemed far too big for him. The others jeered, but the sergeant cut them off.

" 'old your bloody tongues, the lot o' you! Go on, MacIntyre."

"Well, it were like this." His Scots brogue was so thick that Evans had to strain to understand him. "There was a wee lassie astanding on the dock for some time awhile ago. She were just standin' there, staring at the river like. I asked her if there was anythin' wrong. She said no and run off."

"What did she look like?" Evans stepped forward, mind racing, praying this was not just another false lead. There had been so damned many of them in the last two weeks.

"Well, sir, she were wearin' a dress, like. Gray it was. I noticed it 'cause me sister has one that color. Give me a start, it did. She were wearin' a jacket too, like you see on those who've come in from the country. A sheepskin—"

"My God!" Evans started. "That could have been her—"

"Did you see which way she went off?" the sergeant intervened.

"Well, I think she must've gone . . ." He hesitated and pivoted, trying to remember. Evans resisted the urge to reach out and shake the boy for his maddening deliberation.

"That way, as best I can recall. I thought, Poor lass, not much for you that way, is there?"

He had pointed to a jumble of commercial buildings that led back toward the city proper. Evans repressed a groan, but the sergeant read his expression.

"How long ago, MacIntyre?"

The boy screwed up his face. "Just on ten minutes ago, Sergeant, not more 'n that. The rain was just endin'."

Evans thanked the soldiers and was about to turn away when the sergeant caught his arm. "MacIntyre 'ere may 'ave seen your lady, sir. If so, 'e knows what the lassie looks like." He turned to the Scots soldier. "You go along with Mr. Evans 'ere an' 'elp him." He glanced at his wrist watch. "But be back at sixteen 'undred 'ours sharp, mind. We goes off then," he explained to Evans, who thanked him profusely. MacIntyre slung his rifle and followed Evans.

The rain stopped, and the clouds began to break up. The atmosphere became steamy and humid as the streets filled again with people. Sheremetiev was grateful for the fact that he had chosen to leave Lusenov at the refugee center and take the Hungarian with him instead.

Poijer was tall and cadaverous and ugly as a frog. He was a former prisoner of war who had somehow fallen into the Cheka. His intelligence was limited, but he was dependable to a fault, provided that his orders were phrased with meticulous precision and that he was required to make no independent assessments.

"Do you have your knife?"

A two-edged trench knife appeared as if by magic in Poijer's hand and as quickly disappeared. Sheremetiev nodded in satisfaction. "Listen to me. You know what the woman looks like. We will probably see her somewhere in the streets. You will walk on that side, and I will walk on this. Look at every face. If you see her, signal me by raising your cap and wiping your brow. I will cross to meet you. If I see her, I will do the same. Once we are certain, we will approach her from either side. If I touch my forehead like this"—he demonstrated—"you will stop her and ask a question."

Poijer screwed up his face as his brain lurched ponderously into action. Sheremetiev saw his features rearranging themselves in a parody of thought and repressed his impatience.

"Ask her," he supplied, "how to get to the cathedral. When she stops to answer, kill her immediately. Stab her once in the throat so that she cannot scream and again in the heart to make certain. Then go back to headquarters, and make certain you aren't followed."

Poijer nodded.

"It's very important that you kill her instantly," he emphasized.

Poijer nodded again and, at Sheremetiev's request, repeated his instructions word for word. Sunlight burst on them as they separated to either side of the road. It was better to have Poijer, he thought. The man liked to kill, and this task would call for little besides simple butchery.

The alley widened into a street that had at one time been paved but was now in such poor repair that the clinging, viscous mud was almost ankle-deep. The street was filled with people of all shapes, colors and descriptions, and Sheremetiev thought fleetingly of the Great Fair at Nizhni-Novgorod to which his father had taken him in 1901. Only then the people's clothing had been brightly colored and new, not drab and patched, and the vendors and hawkers had shouted their wares with zest rather than stand in one place, weak with hunger, silently offering goods which no one wanted.

Poijer plowed along the far side, his bulk and height like the bow of a powerful ship serving to separate the crowd. Sheremetiev could see him glancing his way every few seconds. An urgent, almost sexual tension was growing, and he felt they were coming close. The street emptied a few hundred feet ahead into a large square into which other streets ran like the ill-placed spokes of a wheel. Just entering the intersection was the slight figure of a woman wearing a gray wool skirt and a sodden sheepskin jacket. Her kerchief had come undone, and a sudden burst of sunlight blazed on her chestnut hair. When she ducked gracefully, almost happily, he thought, around a crowd of arguing children and strode toward the benches lining the edge of the park, he had a good look at her face and nearly shouted with joy.

He snatched his hat off and rubbed his forehead with vigor. Poijer caught the signal instantly. He closed in fast, almost running. The park overflowed with the tents and shelters of refugees, and the crowd spilled into the intersection to create a seething maze of people.

"Sheepskin jacket, straight on," he muttered. Poijer hesitated only long enough to spot the woman, then quickened his pace. Sheremetiev veered off to the side, hand inside his coat, gripping the Luger, thumb resting on the safety. With his left hand, he unbuttoned the coat.

Poijer was closing the distance rapidly. He thrust through a swirl of people and strode on. The woman was walking quickly, but Sheremetiev could see that Poijer would reach her well short of the benches. He increased his own pace and eased the Luger free. If anyone tried to interfere with Poijer Sheremetiev intended to shoot at once. The shots would cause enough confusion to enable them to disappear into the crowd. He risked a glance around for the sight of a militiaman, but there was none immediately in sight. Poijer, almost running now, leaned forward and reached for the woman's shoulder. Sheremetiev saw the flash of a knife blade.

A combination of excitement and desperation drove Evans on in spite of the weakness that seemed to have turned his muscles to water. Not even in the worst times on their long, horrible trek across the taiga had he been this near collapse. The sun hammered at his head, and the street wavered before his eyes. His mind was detached from his leaden body, and he saw the muddy road as if from a great height. At times he had to struggle to remember where he was and what he was doing. Once he stopped, gasping for breath, and a hand fell on his arm. He jerked about, startled, and saw the British soldier watching him with concern.

"No, I'm all right. It's . . . just this . . . damned heat." He pushed away from the wall and went on.

The street debouched into a wide intersection, and Evans groaned in frustration. Too many people. He paused to think, oblivious of the jostling crowd pushing against them. A Russian also looking for her would . . . why was everything so fuzzy, just slightly out of focus? Even the noise of the crowd had a curious, hollow sound.

"Look, sir," the soldier said to him, drawing him out of the press. "This lady of yours, do you have any idea where she might go?"

Evans shook his head. "I . . . I didn't . . ."

He was only half aware of the soldier now, and when he spotted a bit of shade and, beyond it, the inviting coolness of a park, he started toward it; the young soldier followed with a quizzical expression. Evans saw a church dome glowing in the afternoon sun, and the street wavered with heat.

"I'll . . . look there, sir, there she is!" The soldier grasped his arm and pointed, then caught at his rifle as it slipped off his shoulder. Evans followed his finger but saw only a whirl of people. A tall man lunging through the crowd caught his attention, and then he saw Tatiana.

"Tania!" he shouted hysterically. The woman heard his shout and turned suddenly.

Sheremetiev gaped in disbelief. The woman had ducked away from Poijer's hand and was running. Poijer stumbled to a halt and shook his head, like a dazed bear in a baiting ring. Sheremetiev shouted, and Poijer located her at the same instant. The big man lunged through the crowd, and Sheremetiev drew his Luger and ran after him. Everything was happening too quickly; a British soldier appeared from nowhere to parry Poijer's killing stroke with his rifle barrel. The butt reversed and flew in a short, blurred arc, and Poijer collapsed as if poleaxed. The boy saw Sheremetiev at the same instant, but there was no time to bring the rifle to his shoulder and fire. Sheremetiev's shot knocked him down. The blast drove the crowd into instant panic. People ran blindly in every direction, and the woman disappeared. Sheremetiev thrust the pistol back into his coat and cursed as it caught on the lining. As he turned to run, he saw Poijer lying like a dead man, arms and legs sprawled. The British soldier was trying to lever himself up again, and beyond, Sheremetiev caught sight of a mounted militiaman urging his horse through the crowd. He didn't wait to see more.

Evans caught Tatiana up in his arms, laughing and crying at the same time just as the soldier shoved them away. As he stumbled back, he saw the Scot smash the butt end of his rifle into a man's face. A shot blasted across the square, and the soldier lurched and sat down. Then they were carried away toward the park as people screamed, cursed and trampled one another in their rush to get away from the gunfire. A horseman charged past, and Evans was jammed against the low iron fence surrounding the park. He lunged, cleared a space and lifted Tatiana over. She clung to his hand so hard he fell over after her. Then they were scrambling away with hundreds of others.

The far side of the park was not fenced, and the crowd swept them back into the road again. A heavyset man was running beside them, head back, lungs laboring, one hand clutching his chest, heedless of anything besides his own terror. He swerved into Tatiana and knocked her down. Evans felt her grip loosen and tried to stop, but the pressure of people behind drove him on.

They were in the middle of the street, and there was nothing to interrupt their flight. Evans roared with frustration. He stopped short, ducked low and pivoted to slam a shoulder into the man directly behind, who caromed into another. Into the space thus opened Evans charged, head down, legs pumping as he had done so many years before as a member of the Harvard eleven. He broke through to find himself alone in the street.

Tatiana lay against the curb. He turned her over gently. There was mud along one side of her face, emphasizing her pallor. She lay still in his arms, her body thin and nearly weightless. An eyelid fluttered then, and she was smiling up at him. He sank weakly against the curb. When she kissed him, her lips were soft and warm and trembled against his.

*   *   *

305

Sheremetiev saw them as he stepped onto the graveled walk. The sound of his boots made the man look up. Sheremetiev stared at him, the Luger hanging loosely in his right hand.

He must be the American, Sheremetiev thought without curiosity. He stood up, pulling the Romanov woman with him, but turning so that his body shielded her. Sheremetiev could tell by the defensive stance that he was not armed. The man was tall, taller than he had imagined, and worn with exhaustion. It showed in his eyes, his face and his slightly stooped posture. The woman was equally haggard, and when she noticed him, her eyes widened with terror.

He sighted the Luger, squinting slightly to center the front blade in the rear notch. It was over. A year and a half's chase finished in spite of Dzerzhinsky, and he knew in that moment that he was doomed as well. He knew too much, his background was wrong and he had outlived his usefulness. A trick of the bright sun through the leaves made her hair dark, and he saw Maria's face, eyes staring, mouth wide with screams. Sheremetiev hesitated, and the muzzle wavered.

Had it begun with her or before? His eyes were filled with tears. What had these two to do with the success or failure of the revolution? What was the difference between their execution and the shooting of workers on the Troitsky Bridge, or the boy officer in Petrograd bayoneted to death by his own sergeant, or the hundreds, if not thousands, of men and women he had sent to the firing squad and the hangman in the Don, or even the two German soldiers that day in 1914 at the beginning of this madness? Sheremetiev lowered the pistol. It simply wasn't worth it anymore.

He heard a shout, and as he turned, a tremendous weight smashed into his chest. His vision cleared for an instant, and he saw the maple leaves above him and thought to himself that it was early in the season for them to turn.

Tatiana watched as Evans knelt beside the body while a young British soldier, half leaning against a tree, stared at the man he had killed, then turned and vomited. Sheremetiev was dead, and her mind refused to credit the fact. Why had he turned away? She swayed and sat down abruptly. Evans was at her side, urging her to lie back. The soldier struggled out of his tunic, and she could see a splotch of red along his ribs. . . . Then gentle hands were placing her on a stretcher, and she started in panic, but Bill was beside her instantly, smoothing her hair with his hard hands. He looked older, she thought, and so thin and tired. A well-dressed man was staring at her, smiling. Bill spoke to him, called him Witt, and he said something to her, but the sky and the trees swung dizzily, and she closed her eyes. An ambulance bell clanged, and she faded happily into sleep, knowing she was safe forever.

AUTHOR'S NOTE

To the best of anyone's knowledge, no member of the immediate Romanov family escaped the Bolshevik executioners the night of July 16–17, 1918, at Ekaterinburg. In the sixty-three years since those outrageous murders, numerous women have appeared, claiming to be one of the four daughters—and not a few men have claimed to be Alexei. But not one has survived the test of identification by relatives or by those who knew the family well. This does not, of course, preclude a survivor.

Serious questions have been raised concerning the validity of "evidence" uncovered by investigators working under the auspices of the White government of Admiral Kolchak. A reexamination of the evidence sixty years later suggests not only that the executions might not have taken place in Ekaterinburg after all but that at least one member of the family might have escaped death at a later time and place. If so, why did the survivor not come forth, prove who he or she was and claim a hero's welcome?

To answer that question, one must look at the conditions that would have confronted such a survivor.

Conditions were chaotic in all Europe in 1918. A dozen armies, foreign and domestic, stormed across Russia and western Siberia. Governments rose and fell with a greater rapidity than at any time before or since. Two of those governments, the Ural Soviet at Ekaterinburg and the All-Russian Congress of Soviets in Moscow, were in desperate straits. People thought to be above such reprisals were shot after drumhead court-martials. The Grand Duke Michael, the tsar's own brother, was shot through the bars of his cell by overworked executioners. The Bolsheviks had convinced themselves not only that Nicholas Romanov was the greatest criminal Russia had ever produced but that all classes of people desired his execution.

Accordingly, it was announced in Moscow that only Nicholas Romanov had been executed. But investigators sent by Admiral Kolchak's government in Siberia to investigate the murders after Ekaterinburg was wrested from the Bolsheviks, produced the rest of the story. The entire family and their servants were shot and bayonetted to death by their guards. Afterward it was alleged that the bodies were hauled deep into a forest, burned and buried in pits filled with quick lime. Their clothing and personal effects, including a family pet dog, were thrown down a nearby mine shaft. Because of the manner in which the bodies were allegedly destroyed, the White investigators were unable to produce any physical evidence beyond an unidentifiable finger recovered, oddly enough, from the mine shaft, some corset buttons, jewel chips and the like. For Admiral Kolchak's government, this was enough to prove the family had been murdered at Ekaterinburg, but it is well to remember that *all sides* participating in the revolution and civil war showed a fine disregard for truth time after time. Truth was anything that served the cause.

The Bolsheviks' explanation that they had no choice but to execute the archcriminal Nicholas because the Whites and the counterrevolutionary Czech Legion were attacking Ekaterinburg with the express purpose of freeing the tsar is, at best, suspect.

At no time after Nicholas II abdicated did any political party, from the mildly socialist Constitutional Democrats to the most rabidly anarchistic, seriously suggest that Nicholas be returned to the throne. In fact, there is evidence to suggest that even within Admiral Kolchak's inner circle of advisers, there were those as opposed to Nicholas as anyone in the Ural Soviet. In spite of Bolshevik claims to the contrary, no political or military grouping on either side made a serious attempt to rescue the royal family. Even Kerensky's pathetic gestures in the spring of 1917 seemed to have lacked conviction.

Then, too, the royal family was almost destitute by the spring of 1918. They retained the clothes on their backs, a few personal effects and a handful of jewels hidden from their captors. After the war the Bank of England conducted a thorough search among the allied nations for bank accounts belonging to the Romanov family and found that all had been closed by Nicholas well before 1917 and the money donated to war-relief efforts in Russia. Any accounts remaining in banks of the Central Powers would have been rendered valueless by the raging inflation that followed the Armistice. A surviving member of the family would have known of this. There was, therefore, no economic inducement to come forth.

In addition, it has been suggested that leadership of the exile community would have attracted a survivor. But the exile community was composed largely of disaffected members of the court or family already abroad, and few of them would have been inclined to recognize Nicholas's offspring. The majority of those who remained loyal had barely escaped with their own lives, and many were forced to live off the charity of relatives, including Nicholas's own mother, the Dowager Empress Marie.

Finally, the Soviet government has never been known to tolerate the slightest challenge to its authority. That, in fact, was probably the real reason for the royal family's execution. The deaths of Nicholas and Alexei removed any possibility of a serious challenge from royalist factions still extant. It is inconceivable that the Cheka or its descendants would have permitted a survivor to go on living, no matter where in the world he or she took refuge. Remember the murder of Leon Trotsky in Mexico in 1940? Twenty years later the Kremlin was still making certain.

There may have been one or more survivors, but if so, the world at large will probably never find out. Any survivor would quickly have realized that there was little hope of ever reoccupying the Imperial Russian throne. The day of the monarchy in Russia was over. Therefore, the survivor would certainly have sought the most remote and secret existence possible. To go public, so to speak, would have been akin to signing a personal death warrant.

I have taken certain liberties with the time frame (the North Russian Expeditionary Force actually left Archangel in September 1919; the Siberian Expeditionary Force left in 1920) and with the personalities of the major characters. All else, I hope, reflects actual conditions in Russia at the end of World War I and the continuation of its terrible suffering through four more years of revolution and civil war.

Joe Poyer
California, 1982

JOE POYER *lives in Southern California where he claims to write to an undeviating daily schedule. In his spare time, he collects Baedekers Handbooks and antique firearms and travels at the slightest excuse. He has had a life-long interest in the events surrounding the Russian Revolution of 1917, and the background for* Devoted Friends *was researched extensively among the few remaining survivors of the original Russian emigré communities in Los Angeles and London. Mr. Poyer is the author of nine previous novels, including* North Cape *and, most recently,* Vengeance 10.